Lloyd Devereux Richard
Maidens. He was born in Ne
in Europe, Africa and Ce
school. He served as a se
of Appeals judge, researc
of published opinions, including the appeal o_
sentenced to death. A father of three, he lives with his wife,
Cameron O'Connor, and their two dogs in Montpelier,
Vermont. *Maidens of the Cave* is his second novel.

Also by Lloyd Devereux Richards

Stone Maidens

Maidens Of The Cave

Lloyd Devereux Richards

ONE PLACE. MANY STORIES

HQ
An imprint of HarperCollins*Publishers* Ltd
1 London Bridge Street
London SE1 9GF

www.harpercollins.co.uk

HarperCollins*Publishers*
Macken House, 39/40 Mayor Street Upper,
Dublin 1, D01 C9W8, Ireland

This edition 2023

1
First published in Great Britain by
HQ, an imprint of HarperCollins*Publishers* Ltd 2023

Copyright © Lloyd Devereux Richards 2023

Lloyd Devereux Richards asserts the moral right to be
identified as the author of this work.
A catalogue record for this book is
available from the British Library.

ISBN: 9780008648343

This book is produced from independently certified FSC™ paper
to ensure responsible forest management.

For more information visit: www.harpercollins.co.uk/green

Printed and Bound in the UK using 100% Renewable Electricity at
CPI Group (UK) Ltd, Croydon, CR0 4YY

To my daughter, Marguerite

PROLOGUE

IN NAOMI WINCHESTER'S heart it didn't feel wrong. It felt right—crazily, spectacularly right. Something inside her had changed and she knew with joyous clarity that anyone who made her feel this way was definitely Right. Maybe even forever.

Her close friends would all say that Naomi didn't live by feelings or flights of fancy. She was a serious student whose feet were firmly planted on the ground and whose eyes were firmly glued to her textbooks. Pursuing a joint major in prelaw and business meant hitting the books seven days a week, which she did religiously. She excelled across the board academically, and her class standing in the topmost tier at Calhoun Seymour University—CSU—was a given. "She has a head on them shoulders," her father would say of her proudly in a deliberately hokey accent, a nod to his humble farming roots.

And yet here she was, skipping an early bird Econ 302 study session, kicking stones in a deserted Applebee's parking lot far from campus, caught up by a strong flood of the sublime that no A on a term paper could ever come close to delivering. She reached into her bag and pulled out the new lip gloss she'd splurged on, then applied it with care.

She glanced at the silver watch that her grandmother had given her for her high school graduation. It was a family heirloom, and it made her think of her gran, who had worn it for as long as

Naomi could remember before giving it to her only granddaughter. Sweet Gran. She'd always encouraged Naomi to shoot for the stars, somehow making her believe that almost anything was possible.

Naomi sighed. Only five minutes until their agreed-upon rendezvous time, and the anticipation was almost too much.

He was so considerate of her, even in choosing their meeting spot. Initially he'd offered to pick her up outside her dorm, but then he must have realized that she might feel self-conscious about being seen with someone older, so he'd suggested the Applebee's parking lot. She'd ridden the local bus from campus, an easy trip. And he was right; she hadn't wanted to draw the attention of classmates or anybody else who may not approve of a female student dating someone older. And besides, they were only going out for a walk in the park, taking in some fresh air among the redbud trees and dogwood that were blossoming all over southern Indiana this month. Applebee's was on the way to the park. It all made perfect sense.

Naomi checked her watch again and took a deep breath.

At the approaching crackle of tires over gravel, she whirled around. He pulled the car's front bumper straight up to her shins as he said he would—8 a.m. sharp.

She hurried to the driver's side.

The tinted window lowered. "Naomi, my dear," he greeted her with a smile and slight nod of his head. "I've a Thermos full of coffee and two mugs. Hop in." His smile widened in the first rays of sunlight over the treetops. "The view from the bluffs should be terrific."

She beamed at him, then quickly circled to the passenger side of the black compact car and climbed aboard.

"It's so good to see you . . ." She wanted to say his first name, but wasn't sure how she should address him in her excitement.

He nodded. "Call me Trip. It's an old nickname."

As if anticipating her next question, he shook his head and said with self-deprecating humor, "Odd name though it may seem, please don't ask where it comes from. Suffice it to say I was a very young lad at the time, a boy really. And somehow it just stuck." He tossed up his hands self-mockingly.

"That's fine with me. This is so exciting. I really think it's cool we're getting out early like this!"

Her outburst of excitement made her suddenly self-conscious. In a more controlled tone, she added, "I mean, we're both nature lovers, how cool is that? Trip."

For the occasion she'd selected her handwoven scarf of blue and green raw silk, very chic, and something she thought his educated eye would take greater pleasure in than the thick-stitched and ubiquitous muffler in red and white panels—the school colors of CSU—worn by so many of the undergraduate women who dated jocks on campus.

"The gear's all loaded in back." Trip nodded over his right shoulder as he pulled out of the parking lot.

Naomi crooked her neck. A black nylon knapsack made with durable stitching rested on the back seat. A handsome coil of blue and gold braided rope was affixed across the top outer flap by a thick purple bungee cord. Beneath the rope, a cluster of metal pieces of different sizes hung on a metal rack attached to the pack.

She giggled, uncharacteristically. "Kind of overkill for a walk in the park, isn't it?"

"It's my little surprise." He smiled. "You'll see."

The smell of honeysuckle wafted in through the air vent, and with it, another zany shot of excitement shivered her shoulders. No one would believe her. No one would believe that bookworm Naomi Winchester was out on a date with such a handsome and brilliant man. She tried not to stare at him, gazing instead out the window.

Southern Indiana forests were dimpled and pocked with steep-sided ravines and high bluffs; the road rolled like a rumpled ribbon up, over, and down the newly budding hillsides. Through breaks in the forest, outcroppings of cream-colored limestone rock gleamed in the morning light. Naomi knew that limestone was porous and under the sunlit landscape were vast underground caverns that tunneled through the hillsides for mile after mile.

The whine of the car's motor rose higher as Trip downshifted. They exited the highway and soon were racing along a smaller paved road bordering a fallow field of brown soil on the driver's side and a line of tall oaks and hemlocks out Naomi's window. Old growth, she thought. Protected woods.

Ten minutes later he turned onto a well-graded dirt road. They passed a weathered wooden sign: *Standish Bluffs National Forest* was carved and painted white in large letters. Beneath it, Naomi read: *The Bluffs Overlook Trail 7.4 Miles Ahead*.

"You aren't afraid of heights, are you?" he asked.

The out-of-the-blueness of the question startled her. Truthfully, she didn't know if she was afraid or not. "Well, I . . . Not really."

"Good then. There's an exposed layer of fossils, Crinoids from the Devonian Period—whole unbroken columns of this ancient life form that are easily visible *in situ* from an overhanging limestone cliff face. It's an undisturbed shelf—which is why I brought you here to see it. The level of detail is quite remarkable, and so is its state of preservation."

"Okay," she said, trying to sound calm. Mature.

He ducked his chin and motioned with his head for her to look over his right shoulder again. "You see that purple and yellow webbing that's resting on the back shelf? That's for you. It's a safety harness."

"Yes. I see it," she said. "But . . ."

"I bought it online for you. You can't find anything close to it in sporting goods shops around here," he added. "After we park the car I'll show you how it works. It's the same kind that linemen wear to climb telephone poles. Completely secure."

The car jounced over a rut in the road and made her bite her lower lip hard enough that she tasted blood.

"But I thought we were just going for a walk? In the park? Are these shoes okay for climbing?"

Trip gently patted her shoulder. "Please don't worry, my dear. They're more than adequate for our purposes. Wearing a harness is purely precautionary. I didn't tell you because I wanted it to be a surprise."

"Well, you certainly surprised me all right!"

She turned her head to look out the passenger window, hesitant to say more and risk losing all of the warm fuzzy feeling of this, their first official date. Her female intuition told her that sharing her fears too much now would risk spoiling his fun. Their fun. Still, the thought of dangling midair over a cliff to view a fossil bed *in situ* made her cringe, and the glowing excitement she'd first felt jumping into his car had taken a definite detour.

"I plan on sharing the find with the Geology Department next week. So, my dear, think of our little outing as the paleontological equivalent of a bouquet of flowers."

He'd called her "my dear" again. She laughed, suddenly feeling almost giddy. "How could a girl refuse a paleontological bouquet!"

He turned into a parking indent by the roadside and stepped out of the car, quickly pulling on his blue climbing harness, adjusting the straps positioned around his waist and upper thighs. He raised the back hatch and placed the purple nylon webbing beneath her passenger door on a bed of cedar needles.

"It's pretty simple," he said pointing down at the climbing harness. "Stand your feet inside each loop and I'll help you shimmy it into the correct position and show you how it attaches."

It annoyed her, his wanting to get down to business so quickly. They'd been driving for nearly half an hour. It wasn't just someplace near campus like he'd said yesterday. She wouldn't be hurried into climbing gear to be roped down a cliff.

"You mind if I stretch my legs a little?" She studied his face for any sign of disapproval and found none.

"Ah! I should have suggested it myself, Naomi," he said, looking a little embarrassed. "Shall we take a walk to the overlook then?"

"Yes, I'd like that very much, if you don't mind."

"Mind? Of course not." He sprung up from a squat with an encouraging nod. "It's a grand idea."

The trail between the trees was narrow going so he led the way and she followed behind.

Naomi relaxed. His always being considerate of her feelings was one of the things she found so appealing about his manner, and the way he listened to her ideas had a way of bridging their age difference; he treated her as an equal, not a child. Not like her parents, who never seemed able to realize that she was much more than just their precious little girl; she was a grown woman with full command of her intellect. When she spoke her mind, they'd frequently eye each other—a parental code she had first noticed in junior high when she challenged them after a school debate that she'd won on the country's slow acceptance of equal rights for women. As if parenthood came imbued with a prerogative of overarching wisdom that trumped whatever insight she may bring to their kitchen table, even as recently as this past winter break when she pressed them on a woman's right to choose.

During the months she and Trip had met in his office after class, he'd never flinched once or rolled his eyes when listening to her perspective. He treated her as an intellectual equal. He'd solicited her opinions on all manner of things, listening quietly as she fleshed out her thoughts, and she came to realize that she had never before expressed her beliefs in such depth or with such clarity. It was exhilarating.

The ground slanted upward as if taking flight. They walked clear of the trees. A breeze freshened across her face and it swayed the long grasses growing in dense pockets between huge broken chunks of the yellowish-white limestone that jutted through the turf.

The small path whitened into a fine gravel of the same limestone color. Ahead, only the sky was visible through the rusted metal pipe railing that guarded viewers from plunging over the high promontory.

She caught up to him at the railing and feasted on the view. The drop-off was an exhilarating several hundred feet and offered a spectacular sweep of the pea-green woodland that stretched for miles around. A meandering creek threaded through the wilderness far below them. Trip cinched his blue nylon waist-belt tighter, and Naomi stepped back from the railing. The idea of being lowered by her waist like a circus acrobat brought her sharply to her senses.

"Look, Trip. I've never used climbing gear before. I never even climbed trees when I was a kid for that matter. I mean, wouldn't it be better if I took an instructional course first, or started somewhere easy, for beginners?"

Trip's eyebrows raised in surprise. "You didn't think I was going to rope you down from this railing?" He shook his head and smiled. "You needn't worry, my dear. I realize now that I *should* have said something to you yesterday. I'm just a nut about safety and insist on using proper gear whenever I venture outdoors."

He faced her now and placed his hands firmly on her shoulders. "There's absolutely no reason for you to be afraid. I'm not suggesting we rappel over anything approaching this high a drop-off. Good Heavens, I wouldn't dare be that foolish!"

Naomi nodded cautiously.

"I'm sorry if I scared you. Where I'm taking you *is* just a beginner's pitch. In fact, we will be descending the trail quite a ways farther down before reaching the ledge where the fossils are."

They retraced their steps back to the car, where he helped her into the harness, adjusting her thigh and waist straps. Then he led the way down a side trail that wound in switchbacks beneath the high bluff.

She lost herself in the beauty of the newly leafing forest. The redbuds and dogwood were in full bloom. Pink and white flower petals dotted the forest floor. Chartreuse shoots of yellowwood, beech, and oaks were unfurling their waxen leaves to the joyous chirps of songbirds.

The trail veered closer to a series of smaller ledges where second-growth spindly trees shivered in the breeze, perhaps stunted by the rocky soil, she thought. The rock outcropping from which they'd taken in the panoramic vista now towered overhead.

Trip disappeared around a sharp bend in the trail beside an eroded ravine where the footing was uneven. Carefully she side-stepped down the crumbling scree. Her sneaker slipped and she grabbed hold of a thin sapling, bending it to the ground.

"Trip?" She waited for him to come lend her a hand. "Trip?" Sighing, she pulled herself to her feet awkwardly and made her way over the broken limestone that had sheered from the cliffs over the eons.

A minute later she rounded a corner and saw him seated on a limestone boulder, an open water bottle raised to his lips. She tugged at her harness where it pinched her thighs too tightly.

"It will feel better when your weight is suspended on the rope," he said, offering her the water bottle. "The trick is to let the rope do all the work."

She sat down next to him and stared up the cliff face, sheltering her eyes with her hand.

"I'm not climbing up *or* down that, whatever you say!" The declaration came out sounding sharper than she would have liked.

He peered at her for a moment longer, then nodded in agreement. "Okay, then we won't," he said. "That settles that."

Naomi raised her face to the warming sun and her heartbeats slowed to their normal rhythm. "Thank you for being so under-standing, Trip. I'm still kind of a big baby in some ways, you know."

She turned her head away from him, embarrassed for giving voice to her cowardice. Gazing farther down the trail, she noticed a dark cleft in a rock wall. Next to it there was a small peg with pink ribbon tied around the end.

"What's that?" She pointed to the ribbon.

Trip sat with his back to her. He was fiddling with the climbing pack at his feet. He turned and announced, "I've another surprise, a special one, Naomi."

He dipped his chin playfully. "Now if you would be so kind as to close your eyes for me."

She leaned back, placing her palms flat against the warming rock. The sun shone orange against her closed eyelids.

"I'm ready," she said softly.

She heard him whisper, "Good," and wondered what he would present to her. She'd seen the gleam of gold in the sunlight before closing her eyes. A ring? No, he couldn't be offering her a ring already, even a friendship ring. Could he?

The touch of his hand against the back of her neck sent shivers down her spine. Goose bumps raced over the backs of her arms. He was lifting her shoulder-length brown hair gently—the first time he'd ever touched her skin. Her heart sped up. He was going to kiss her.

A sharp pinprick sent her springing forward on her Reeboks. Her eyes shot wide open. Then a sudden jolt stiffened her body, as if she'd touched an exposed electric wire and she couldn't let go.

"Hey . . . that . . . hurts . . ."

She slid off the boulder and crumpled to the ground. As if her head was an errantly placed video camera, she now viewed the world cock-eyed with her cheek plastered flat against the grit and dust. Her chest heaved uncontrollably.

"T . . . rip," she gasped between choppy shallow breaths—breaths that she could hardly take in. It was as if there was a great weight pressing down on her chest. Her hands felt leaden, knuckles thudding uselessly at the ends of her stiffening arms. She was losing sensation all over her body.

Suddenly her left hand, on its own, twitched upward into view. She watched its fingers—hers—silently spasm open and shut; she was powerless to control the simplest movements, or even to lower her hand to the ground.

A strange sucking sound grew louder in her ears, and Naomi realized the rasping noise was coming from her own throat, starved for more air. Black dots swirled in her vision, as if she was going to pass out at any moment. Her muscles were contracting and releasing erratically, and the spasms came faster and faster. Her legs and arms lost feeling.

But her hearing was strangely unaffected. She heard birds singing from somewhere close by. Their singing grew louder and louder while she desperately rolled her eyes, searching for some sign of Trip.

Where was he? Why had he disappeared? Maybe he had panicked and was going to get help?

In her periphery she caught movement—his iridescent blue climbing boots came into view, the toes pointing at her face from just a few feet away. They remained together, quiet, at a stand.

She could even hear him breathing over the zany cries of the birds. Why didn't he kneel down closer so she could see his face? Why wasn't he talking to a 9-1-1 operator on his cell phone? Why didn't he comfort her in his arms?

His shoes remained still, together. As if he were a disinterested observer.

Hoarse rasping sounds from her throat were broken by a violent shockwave. The prolonged convulsion stopped her gasping for air, as if a switch were thrown on and then off again one last time. The convulsion went on and on as if it would never end, blurring her vision, and when the shaking finally stopped, all went dark.

CHAPTER
ONE

IT WAS MONDAY, March 26, and Christine was running late as usual. She pulled open the heavy door to the large function room on the mezzanine level of the Chicago Marriott and entered as quietly as she could. The room was dimly lit and filled with agents seated in front of a podium and overhead screen.

The door closed behind Christine with a pronounced thump. Patricia Gaston, the new director of the FBI's Chicago branch, glanced up from the podium, squinting in Christine's direction, then proceeded with her comments. With the aid of a laser pointer, Gaston was reviewing a new reorg chart displayed on the screen.

Christine searched for her name on the labyrinthine roster of names clustered beneath boxes representing each divisional unit of the branch office. There it was—Christine Prusik, Forensics—near the bottom of the screen, directly under the name Ned Miranda. *Who the hell is he?* Based on the screen diagram, the revamped structure pushed her further down the hierarchical chain. Not what she'd imagined after fourteen successful years at the Bureau. Maybe Roger Thorne, the former Chicago branch director who this past winter had taken a higher-up Bureau position in Washington, had alerted the new branch director to Christine's habit of bending—and yes, she admitted, occasionally breaking—the rules. She did have a tendency to go solo without keeping her superiors punctually informed, but it was only because time was of the essence in a criminal investigation. That was a truth that never changed.

Christine caught a sideways glimpse of Gaston's flashy red suit when the new branch director stepped away from the podium. The director's voice found its cadence in a confident monotone as she flashed through a series of PowerPoint slides, illustrating a slew of new administrative forms. The laser pointer zigzagged in accompaniment with each new graphic, underscoring the refrain that all personnel were expected to complete these forms and deliver them in a timely fashion to the various unit heads—including Christine, head of the Forensics Unit—who were required to sign off promptly. Daily, weekly, monthly, quarterly, and annual report forms.

Christine shook her head in consternation. Daily reports? What about police work? But a change in management meant putting her best foot forward, and she would give it her best shot. "First impressions last longest," she could hear her mother telling her on her first day of eighth grade at St. Agnes's in Detroit. Yortza Prusik had ironed the pleated pale blue blouse of Christine's uniform early that same morning so she'd look her best. "Say 'yes ma'am' when spoken to and be sure to always smile. Button your lip unless asked to speak by one of the nuns. Do you hear me, Christine?"

So Christine had learned the drill: say yes, smile, and answer politely when asked a question. Unfortunately, she was never very good at that particular drill.

Christine scrolled through her phone messages and emails as Gaston droned on. Her phone vibrated. It was the incoming call that she'd been expecting from Dr. Ernie Hansen, the Carbondale, Illinois, medical examiner.

Local Illinois police had earlier reported that a missing Lincoln Technical College student's dead body had been found on an embankment of the Little Muddy River in a remote quadrant of the Shawnee National Forest in the wilds of southern Illinois. Hansen's call to Christine had come at the recommendation of Dr. Walter Henegar from Crosshaven, Indiana, who'd said good things about Christine's crime-solving abilities based on his work with her on a particularly brutal series of murders during the preceding year.

Christine exited the meeting hall to take the call in the lounge. She confirmed her arrangements to meet with the medical examiner the next day at his office in Carbondale, a smallish city of 26,000 located near the bottom of the state, not far from the confluence of the Mississippi and Ohio Rivers. She thought it unusual that Hansen would call in the FBI so early; over the phone she discerned obvious distress in the doctor's voice, an uneasy bewilderment. Whatever had caused the young victim's death, this local ME clearly wanted her assistance right now.

Finishing her call with Hansen, Christine reentered the meeting room. The overhead lights were now on and Patricia Gaston was shaking hands and greeting agents up front.

A tall, thin man with closely cropped dark hair approached Christine. He cleared his throat. "You must be Christine Prusik," he said tentatively, as if he'd just double-checked her Bureau profile picture on the computer system.

Christine held out her hand and they shook. "And you must be Ned Miranda," she said, recalling the name directly above hers on the overhead screen.

He nodded and forced a quick smile, glancing back at Patricia Gaston, who was making her way toward them.

Watching the slight, well-tanned woman now in charge of Chicago's Bureau branch shake hands as she walked down the aisle, Christine felt a sudden apprehension. Regardless of how well-intentioned and conscientious Miranda may be in performing his duties, this younger agent was now her new boss and she, Christine, was now twice removed from the branch office's topmost command. Whatever else this meant, it couldn't be good news.

Miranda made the introductions and the forensic anthropologist offered her hand to Gaston, whose thin fingers barely pressed the ends of Christine's. It was an awkward shake that felt, more than anything else, like a queen obliging her subject.

"Ned's told me so much about you, Christine. You've quite a storied history. So many unusual cases that you've worked on."

"Why thank you, Director Gaston," Christine said politely, unable to tell whether she'd just been complimented or mocked.

"I asked Ned to mark out some time for us all, perhaps later this week, when we could discuss the direction of the forensics unit."

Christine nodded in what she hoped was a cheerful manner. Gaston's choice of the word *direction* sounded like ominous code for "It's time to dismantle and retrofit the forensics team."

"Look," Christine said, setting aside departmental worries, "I have an important matter to bring to your attention, Patricia. It really can't wait. I've received two calls from downstate, a Carbondale ME who's got a body, a young college student who'd been missing for a number of days. They found her body today under bizarre circumstances. He's requested our help."

"Ned, I have to run." Gaston pressed her hand on Miranda's

forearm and lifted her shiny leather briefcase from the floor. "It was so nice meeting you, Christine." She left the room.

"Give me a sec, Christine," Ned said, gesturing for her to wait as he followed the branch director out the door.

Christine couldn't believe her eyes and ears. Gaston hadn't shown the least bit of interest in the news of a young woman's death that fell squarely within her lawful jurisdiction. Prusik had a sinking feeling that she and her forensics team were headed for darker days.

Technically speaking, Christine's field of expertise—forensic anthropology—was largely limited to the study of skeletal remains in order to decipher how a particular death may have resulted: naturally, by suicide, or homicide. She was a duly certified member of the American Board of Forensic Anthropology, though she'd never felt it necessary to add the acronym ABFA to her stationery or business cards for purposes of getting her job done. If it was determined that a death had been caused by a third person or persons, it was the forensic anthropologist's job to pick up any clues that could be gleaned from the bone evidence in order to identify the cause of death and the circumstances, if possible.

With any luck—and a thorough examination of the site where remains are found—a good forensic anthropologist might gain some sense of the Who, When, Why, and How. Christine relied heavily upon the technical and scientific colleagues who composed her forensics team, and they, in turn, relied on sophisticated lab testing and software analysis to enhance any clues recovered. On those occasions involving multiple crimes of a similar nature, her team had access to the vast universe of the federal and state interlinked crime databases.

Steady budgetary cutbacks—except in the case of a few departments that were the recipients of colossal fiscal increases for the War on Terror—had put pressure on all regional Bureau laboratory teams to commingle resources and participate with other departments in the handling and examining of major crime scene evidence. Increasingly, therefore, Christine and her forensic team were expected to investigate all major crimes assigned to them, including the examination of dead bodies in various states of decomposition, not just skeletal remains.

Christine had taken several years of post-doctoral training and become quite adept at postmortem exams. She generally welcomed the added responsibility, finding fieldwork and postmortems a challenge and an opportunity to escape the daily drudgery of desk work and the insidious torment of office politics that went with it.

A minute later Miranda came striding back into the meeting room, grooves deepening across his forehead. "What's wrong?" he said. "You look upset."

"Me, upset? That the new branch director has zero interest in a murder case in her jurisdiction?" Christine forced a chuckle, shaking her head in disapproval. "This is a significant matter, Ned, and it will most likely require our resources straightaway."

"Listen, Christine." Miranda stood closer to her so not to be overheard by hotel staff busily at work cleaning the carpet. "If you'd made the meeting on time, you would have understood the reason for the new reorg chart."

Miranda was right. She'd come in at the end of Patricia Gaston's remarks and only glanced at the overhead screen before ducking out to take the call from the Carbondale ME. Clearly, she'd missed something important. "Okay then, what exactly is going on?"

"Patricia has asked all unit heads, including Forensics, to produce detailed technical descriptions for each position under your direct or indirect supervision. As a unit head, you are responsible to see to it that each of your direct reports completes a Professional and Technical Qualifications Profile consistent with the Hayes-Stanley Worksheet in two weeks' time."

"Professional and Technical Qualifications Profile? What the hell is that?"

Miranda gave her a a cut-the-crap look. "The PTQP program is combined with the Hayes-Stanley Worksheet. A software link is in an email that was already sent to you and all other agents. Click on the link, then log on, creating a unique password. The program will load and guide you and each member of your forensic team on how to address and complete the worksheet, using special metrics devised for the purpose."

Christine felt suddenly fatigued.

"Regardless of whether you like what I'm telling you, keep in mind, Christine, that completing it accurately and timely is crucial, as it ties directly to salary and bonus scales." Miranda paused and then added, "Oh, and one other thing. Developing the final document for your unit's reports will require your attendance at a Unit Head meeting to be held twice a week until completion."

Filling out forms was foreign to her DNA. Christine abhorred chain-of-command speak and the accompanying hierarchical administration—who reports to whom—that invariably brings a slowdown in the field, if not a complete stoppage, as now apparently would be the case, she feared. Getting her *real* job done took precedence. It just had to.

"Come on, Ned. The local police depend on us. So now what? I'm supposed to fill out a form telling you of a crime scene needing our investigative assistance? And then you go tell Patricia, and wait for Patricia to tell you that she'll get back to you about it? Then you come tell me to wait until what—a form is stamped?" She hadn't meant to sound so strident. She burned to get going to the Carbondale ME's office.

Miranda's cheeks flushed. "Lose the sarcasm, Christine. It won't work with me. I'm not telling you how to do your job. This initiative is a separate task, in addition to your normal duties. And compulsory, I might add."

An older woman in a maid's uniform was tugging on her cleaning cart; a wheel had gotten stuck on the lip of the carpet. Christine helped the woman lift the machine free. "Gracias," the woman said.

"De nada," Christine replied, stepping over to a large exterior window to get away from the vacuuming noises. Cars were crossing the Chicago River below. Miranda followed her to the side of the meeting hall.

"I apologize for sounding brusque," she said. "If I've learned anything in my years here, it's that cooperation from a skilled working team is of vital importance. We need to be able to function together. It's . . . it's these nonessential aspects, the endless busywork, that tend to muck things up. Do you know what I mean, Ned?"

Miranda briefly closed his eyes, then popped them back open and checked his watch. "Unfortunately, I've got to run now. I'll catch up with you this afternoon and we can discuss it more then." He strode off, leaving her standing in the hall while the cleaning crew bustled around her.

"CHRISTINE!" BRIAN EISEN, her chief forensics technician, caught up with her by the mezzanine elevator, holding his eyeglasses in one hand while rubbing the bridge of his nose with the other. His shirttail was hanging out, as it frequently did, given his habit of cleaning his lenses on the material and then forgetting to tuck it back in.

"What do you have, Brian?"

He handed her a wrinkled sheet of paper. "I found this on my chair. Everyone on the team got one. What's going on?"

Christine scanned the memo.

> *Priority One: During the next two weeks employees in all units are expected to complete a Professional and Technical Qualifications Profile using the Hayes-Stanley Worksheet that your unit head will be distributing to you shortly. Each employee's completed profile must contain measurable metrics as described in the worksheet. Unit heads will be attending weekly meetings to ensure that these metrics conform to your particular responsibilities in order to ensure that your profile is both accurate and complete. Of course, you are all expected to perform your normal duties as well.*
>
> *This is a Priority One task!*
>
> *Patricia Gaston, Branch Director*

Now she understood why Brian had left the office to seek her out.

"Are we being set up for some massive wave of layoffs?" he asked.

She wondered herself whether there was an ulterior motive for this busywork initiative, such as coming up with justification to scale back departments. Miranda had said nothing to explain the need for such a wholesale reorg, although he was right that her being late to the meeting meant she had missed the crux of it. The combination of the reorg and the branch director's complete lack of interest in the Illinois student's death did not bode well for Forensics, or for the Chicago Bureau as a whole, as far as Christine was concerned.

"Don't sweat the small stuff, Brian. Don't quote me, but Gaston strikes me as a meticulous administrative type. It's probably all about her needing to look good in DC somehow. We'll get through this like we always have before. You've got nothing to fear as far as your job goes, but you are quite right to ask the meaning of this."

Christine marveled at her careful choice of words. Brian was the most loyal colleague on her forensics team, someone with whom she could have safely shared her concerns. But why unnecessarily upset the conscientious scientist upon whom she daily depended?

She tabbed open the unread emails on her smartphone. "Has Dr. Hansen, the Carbondale ME, faxed his preliminary notes on his formal identification of the victim found by the creek bank?"

"Yes." Eisen took out a flip pad from his inside Navy windbreaker pocket.

"She's been identified as Ellen McKinley, age twenty. She was reported missing from Lincoln Technical College by the local Starksboro, Illinois, police a week ago. Apparently she wore a Medic Alert ankle bracelet that made the ID easy. She was allergic to penicillin."

The elevator doors opened and they both stepped inside, watching their descent through the floor-to-ceiling glass wall that overlooked a large multistory atrium. Plummeting downward made her stomach queasy, matching the unease she felt meeting her new bosses. Why must it always be such a struggle? Hadn't she ably proved her value over the course of her career at the Bureau?

The elevator decelerated without a bump and its doors opened onto the main hotel plaza. They stepped out in unison.

"Look, Brian, I'll be at the McKinley crime scene in Carbondale tomorrow. Whatever changes are coming in management structure, let's be clear about one thing." She kept her eyes steady on his. "I need you and the others on the team to stay focused on this," she said, nodding at the flip pad he held open. "We'll get through filling out the forms and whatever else is required of us. But we remain a forensics team above all else. Are we clear?"

"Absolutely, Christine. We're clear."

They pressed through the outside doors into the bracing wind that Chicago was famous for and headed back to work.

CHAPTER
TWO

NED MIRANDA SAT in front of the branch director's desk, his ears warmed by her rebuke. "Of course, Patricia, I understand the importance of the new initiative. But what about the other call, the one we got from the Crosshaven, Indiana, sheriff's office? About the dead college girl found in a cave last Sunday? I still haven't told Forensics about the sheriff's incoming report, at your request. I bring it up now because of the fact Christine just received notice of another death from the ME in Carbondale, Illinois. Apparently, another young woman's body was discovered down there, too. Quite possibly the two are related."

Gaston slapped shut her notebook and started neatening her desk. "How many times must I repeat myself, Ned? It's a local law enforcement matter," she said coolly. "Why the local Indiana police chose to notify us is not my concern. Have you any specific proof connecting these deaths?"

Miranda shook his head.

"My advice to you is that you say nothing to Ms. Prusik or the Forensics unit about this dead Indiana girl," she underscored. "The first order of business is completing the profiles. I want rough drafts from Forensics and all the other units on my desk in a week's time. That's not too much to ask, now, is it, Ned?"

Miranda held up both palms. "We're good, Patricia."

She smiled and nodded curtly. "Good. Because the profiles are related to something else entirely. And frankly, I'm not sure I have clearance to apprise you of this." A small smile broke the tension in her face—more conspiratorial than reassuring—and then she said, "But I will because I need your eyes and ears on this one, Ned."

"Of course, Patricia. You can count on it."

"I've received word from Washington that there's a leak. They have reason to suspect it's coming from someone in the Chicago branch." She stood and walked to the window, where she appeared to study the traffic that was almost at a standstill sixteen stories below. "It's not necessary for me to get into particulars. Suffice it to say, I want you to carefully monitor Forensics' activities. Checking in on them regarding their profiles will give you plenty of opportunity to shadow them without their suspecting anything."

"What am I looking for specifically?"

Gaston shrugged. "Anything suspicious or out of the ordinary—if an agent leaves his or her desk and heads for the elevator before the end of the day, I want you to find out where the agent's going and why, and to report back to me ASAP."

"What about the other units? The Accounting department is much larger than Forensics."

"Thank you for telling me how to do my job, Ned," Gaston said stonily. She drew a long, controlled breath. "A specialist and his team of agents from headquarters have joined us on-site. They're housed in an adjacent office down the hallway from us. His name is Meachum. He'll be handling the Accounting and IT units. And will likely be double-checking Forensics' work, too." Gaston stood beside Miranda. "Look," she placed a hand on his shoulder, "keep a low profile, but be conscientious. I need a second set of eyes, eyes on my side, eyes I personally know and trust."

"I'm on board, Patricia."

"I'm sure Meachum knows what he's doing, but I don't know him."

Miranda nodded. "What about Prusik? She's primarily a criminal investigator, so she's frequently in the field. How do you suggest I—"

"Must I remind you that Special Agent Prusik isn't past forging a Branch Directive?" Gaston interrupted, ignoring his question and jabbing her index finger against the open notebook on her desk. Its perfect plum nail polish matched the bruised color of her lips.

"She did it with Roger Thorne," Gaston continued. "She signed an agency directive without his authorization. Way above her pay grade. And how she ever avoided termination for cause is beyond me. She won't get away with flouting authority like that on my watch."

Miranda shifted his weight, uneasy with the unfolding predicament. He refrained from saying that Prusik's procedurally unforgivable act of forging the previous branch director's signature had, in fact, directly led to the capture of Donald Holmquist, a brutal serial killer.

"I know she's good at pursuing cases," Gaston acknowledged impatiently. "But it's important that she and her forensic unit follow my orders like everyone else. You detail her every move. I want daily reports on her movements. I want to know about any misstep ASAP, day or night. Are we clear?"

"Absolutely, Patricia. Meaning no disrespect," he continued, "she's already spoken to me about this new incident, a death that a local medical examiner—"

The branch director raised her eyebrows. "Did I not make myself clear at the podium downtown? The reorg and profile initiative take top priority. Whoever's responsible for leaking classified information from this office must be found ASAP, Ned."

Miranda nodded. "Absolutely, Patricia . . . it's just that I'd be doing you a disservice if I didn't point out that this branch is first and foremost a forensics office. It's what they principally do here."

"Not for the next two weeks it isn't. And what doesn't concern me shouldn't concern you, either. If this mole is in Chicago, he or she will be found out. Even if it means temporarily interfering with Special Agent Prusik's forensic duties. Do you understand me?"

"Fully."

Gaston walked behind her large walnut veneer desk, took a seat in her plush leather high-back chair, and resumed studying her notes. "Then that will be all, Ned. Keep me posted."

"CHRISTINE, WE NEED to talk," Miranda said, entering her overstuffed office. Banker's boxes full of old cases crowded the window ledge. Her desk was covered with precarious heaps and mounds. More files were stacked on the two chairs in front of it. Prusik was stooped over her large forensic case on the floor, shoving things into its open top.

"Listen, Ned," she said glancing up. "I've got thirty minutes to make the afternoon Carbondale flight."

"What?" He stopped short. "We haven't discussed your going anywhere. You have no authority to leave the premises."

"Of course I do." She straightened up and patted his arm. "It's one day down and back, tops, a preliminary exam. Come along if you want, unless rotting flesh isn't your kind of thing."

"What didn't you understand about the reorg chart, Christine?" He gave her a stony stare.

"Oh, you must mean the part about my reporting to you?" She smiled sweetly. "I fully understand that, Ned. You didn't think I was planning to leave you out of this?"

"Christine," he gave a sardonic chuckle, his forefinger in a scolding waggle, "that includes your discussing *in advance* with me the logistics of any incoming inquiries that come to your attention. You can't just pick up and leave."

Christine checked to make sure she had a spare clean blouse in her case in the event that her stay was longer than expected. Then she stood up straight and took a breath.

"These days Congress is throwing an awful lot of money at Homeland Security measures, which we both certainly can understand. Let me ask you, Ned, if the question du jour is how to best keep the public safe, shouldn't our focus be on that task? To put a stop to someone who performs a murderous act upon an innocent life, and consequently, upon that innocent person's family, the community, and friends—they're all struck down to a greater or lesser degree by the terrifying nature of the act, aren't they? You see, an action that deliberately ends one person's life is all that it takes to dismantle many lives. It starts with one dead victim.

"My team and I deal day in, day out with the dark end of the bell curve, bad-news people who make a practice of killing others. I will report back to you by the end of tomorrow whether or not we've got a real live killer on our hands, or just another tragic accident." She clicked shut the forensics kit and slipped it inside her large Bureau-issued case. "As far as the profile exercise goes, that shouldn't take too long. I can study the protocol while I'm in transit. No big deal."

Miranda eyed her for a minute before responding. "Next time clear it with me before you make your plans," he finally said in a voice more neutral than angry, which Prusik took for tacit consent.

She nodded and left her office before he could change his mind.

PATRICIA GASTON INPUT her name and password and the screen lit up with the great seal of the Federal Bureau of Investigation. She then relinquished control of her computer to Evan, the equipment tech, who leaned over her desk awkwardly and clicked through to access the web-based portal.

The course logo spun from a vanishing point filling the screen, one letter at a time: P–T–Q–P. Beneath the acronym appeared in smaller print, *Professional and Technical Qualifications Profile*. A familiar-looking insert box appeared in the middle of the screen, requesting name and password.

Evan Messier stood abruptly and moved away from Gaston's desk. "Type in your name and then select a unique password. It must have a minimum length of ten digits, alphanumeric, with capitals. And don't use your existing password." The technician turned his head away from the monitor, giving her privacy while she typed the necessary information.

Gaston quickly selected a password and jotted it down on her legal pad. "I'm not interested in wading through the actual course material. Could we get on with the demonstration?"

Evan hurriedly plugged his own laptop into a floor jack at the foot of Gaston's desk, placed it on the seat of a guest chair, and kneeled on the floor, rapidly clicking his keyboard. After a time, his fingers fell motionless.

"It takes a half minute or so to load," he said without glancing up.

Then Patricia Gaston appeared on Evan's laptop screen, her face looking downward from behind her desk; a wall certificate of commendation displayed behind her—the date was even readable. "Well that certainly is a sharp picture," she said, her voice crisply projected by the laptop's speaker as she spoke.

Evan ran through some other salient parameters, demonstrating the full range of the surveillance program, which explained to her nontechnical mind why it had taken a half minute or so to fully load.

"Once each agent initially signs in and creates a unique password, the tracking program takes over. It stays on twenty-four/seven. Even after the agent shuts down his or her computer, the functions are fully operational, like a zombie computer."

Evan stood, only halfway meeting Gaston's gaze, clearly uncomfortable. "Anything else you need to know?"

"No," Gaston said, nodding almost imperceptibly. "This should take care of everything."

CHAPTER
THREE

EARLY TUESDAY MORNING, Christine Prusik pulled the surgical mask high over her cheekbones. If she'd had her druthers, she'd have pulled it all the way over her eyes. Ellen McKinley, age twenty, was as pale as candle wax. Lividity showed through along her backside where the blood had settled and saturated the flesh a venous purple.

Cold, too-young-to-be-dead flesh was never easy viewing for the first time. *Just get through the gates* she told herself, referring to the blunt trauma experienced upon first viewing a victim. Then she could get on with the measurements, recording every puzzling bruise, anything that might later provide a dispositive insight into the killer's identity.

In a very real sense, it was a horse race against time. Win, or face losing and having to go through the gates all over again, examining another dead body.

Dr. Ernie Hansen, Carbondale, Illinois's presiding medical examiner, glanced up at Christine from his position by the postmortem table. He was a tall man with well-tanned skin, which contrasted starkly against the cadaverous flesh stretched before them. Judging from his uniform hair color—still mostly brown—she guessed Hansen was in his forties.

"Cause of death, Doctor?" Christine said.

"She didn't drown. Her lungs are clean." Hansen blew out a held breath through his mask.

"So what are we thinking killed her?"

"Best guess, hypothermia led to her cardiac arrest. The Little Muddy River is damn cold this time of year. She must have swum out of that cave under her own steam, though. That or she floated with her head up. Either way, she'd have been mighty cold. Best I can figure, she's been dead seventy-two hours or more," Hansen said. Almost as an afterthought, the medical examiner observed, "You know she was on the college swim team?"

Hearing that pricked Prusik's ears. "Really?" she said. "A twenty-year-old on the college swim team dies of a heart attack swimming clear of a cave?"

Dr. Hansen nodded. "My first thought too, Agent Prusik. It doesn't add up. But there's no evidence of her being attacked or molested to explain it. No contusions to the body or head beyond a few nicks and scrapes. There's no sign of strangulation either. And she hasn't been sexually assaulted."

Clearly something was bothering the doctor.

"So what have we got?" she said, folding the backs of her wrists against the protective gown. "A fully clothed young woman dead on a creek bank who'd likely swum free from the cave, then crawled a few feet up the bank and expired unmolested in the quiet of deep woods?"

"I know. It's a damn puzzle. It's why I wanted to get another opinion on this. The parents are coming in this afternoon to make the formal identification. According to her father, whom I spoke with on the phone yesterday, neither side of their family has a history of heart disease. So go figure," Dr. Hansen added, rubbing his forehead with the back of one gloved hand.

"I'd like to speak with them after the formal identification, if that's okay with you, Doctor."

"Sure," the medical examiner said. "I assumed you would be."

Her parents should know whether McKinley had any boyfriends, or was dating someone on campus, Christine figured. She would ask them for their daughter's roommate's name and any other girlfriends she may have had.

"You said she must have swum out of the cave. How do you know that, Doctor?"

"As reported, she was found on the embankment not far from the stream's outflow from the cave." Hansen lifted the victim's right hand. "And see here, under the fingernails?"

Christine observed a dark rim of dirt jammed under each nail.

"The mud is the same kind as that found in the creek bank. Crime scene photos showed finger marks in the mud. They were hers. She managed to drag herself out of the creek. No footprints appeared near her body, which means she died there alone, best I can figure.

"There are no signs of a struggle that would indicate she ended up on the creek bank after running through the woods first," the doctor said. "Only her finger marks in the mud that led up from the water, which suggests just the opposite. That she'd definitely swum from the creek side."

Christine imagined the desperation of the young woman, clawing her fingers in the mud, struggling to save herself. Instantly, inevitably, she flashed on her own riverbank nightmare of some sixteen years earlier, when she'd been attacked in a New Guinea rainforest and come terrifyingly close to death. The memory of the assault often took her by surprise, sending her heart rate into the rafters.

Without speaking, Christine quickly looked left-right, left-right, zigzagging her eyes from side to side. Eye Movement Desensitization Response Therapy was a surprisingly effective therapy that she'd learned from her friend and colleague Dr. Emil Katz. She was enormously grateful that performing the EMDR exercise could often nip in the bud the Mobius strip of her brain's PTSD reaction as it cycled through the memory of her assailant's brutal attack. Lucky for her it worked this time and her heart rate returned to its normal seventy beats per minute.

"Everything okay, Special Agent Prusik?"

"Fine. And it's Christine, Doctor." She took a breath. "So there's no evidence of an assault? Then the question becomes how she found herself in the stream in the first place."

The doctor nodded. "I want to show you something peculiar, Christine. If you could help me roll her over."

Christine donned a new pair of latex gloves and together they turned the victim onto her stomach.

Dr. Hansen lifted the victim's short blonde hair to reveal the nape of her neck.

"That mark, it's a bruise or indentation of some kind. Almost looks like an emblem. At first I thought it may have been a poorly done tattoo removal. You know, I've seen a lot of high school and college age women sporting tattoos these days, and I'm beginning to see removal scars in my general practice."

Christine peered more closely. The mark had the intricate definition of an insignia, maybe a symbol of an animal of some kind. The impression was the size and shape of a large signet ring.

She screwed a special filter over the close-up lens of her digital Canon camera to enhance the faint indentation mark. Back in the lab, Eisen would enlarge it with the aid of a high-resolution software program. Near the midpoint appeared a distinct impression. Under Christine's 20X hand magnifier, she discerned a tiny pinprick of dried blood.

"What do you make of it?" Dr. Hansen asked. "I thought of excising it for tissue analysis."

"It looks like she may have been struck from behind, Doctor. I'm glad you didn't remove the tissue," she said, "until I had a chance to observe it firsthand."

"Frankly, I wanted your opinion first before taking any tissue samples for microscopic and chemical toxicity testing, other than the blood tests and vaginal swabs that I've already taken, of course. From a cursory examination of the victim's overall physical appearance, it doesn't seem to me that alcohol or drugs were operative causes at work here. However, I'll have to wait for the toxicology results to be sure. And as I said, there's no evidence of sexual activity."

"Let's get that tissue sample of the neck mark on a rush back to my forensics lab. I'm assuming you're okay with that?"

"Not a problem, Christine. I'm grateful for the help."

The phone rang on the wall in the corner. Dr. Hansen answered it, nodding amid a sprinkle of uh-huhs. After a minute or so he said, "Okay then," and hung up the phone.

The sag lines on the ME's face told her it wasn't good news.

"You asked about evidence of an assault. Police divers just found a likely scene inside the cave, not far upstream from where this girl's body was recovered. Signs of a possible struggle, and they recovered a torn shirt too, possibly the victim's."

"How soon can the police escort me to the crime scene?"

"Two deputies are waiting outside," Dr. Hansen replied.

Christine made sure Hansen removed the tissue sample,

gouging out a large enough plug of the victim's flesh on the back of her neck to include the distinctive impression. Centermost and discernable under magnification was the pinprick of blood, which looked to have been made by a needle puncture—an injection of some kind to shut her up for good, Christine thought.

She removed her gloves and headed for the door.

"Hold up, Special Agent." Hansen retrieved a brown evidence bag from the counter. "I almost forgot to give you these."

Christine opened the top and peeked inside at purple and yellow heavy-duty nylon webbing attached to a metal plate.

"She was wearing this nylon harness when they found her and brought her in," he said. "Obviously it's some kind of climbing gear. Perhaps you can locate where it was purchased."

"Thank you, Doctor." A climbing harness reinforced the idea that McKinley had been inside the cave. The metal coupler on the front of the harness had a serial number stamped into it, from which the manufacturer could tell her where it'd been purchased. With any luck, the torn clothing the deputies had earlier retrieved might contain a drop of blood, saliva, or sweat—precious DNA that might reveal the identity of her killer to her geneticist Leeds Hughes. At least then her death wouldn't have been completely pointless.

"I'm sure glad that you got down here so quickly, Christine. It's much appreciated."

They shook hands again and she exited the building into the parking lot, where an Illinois State Police van was idling. She placed the bagged harness inside her rental car and introduced herself to the waiting deputies. One of the men rummaged in the back of the van and handed her a pair of jeans and a spare rain jacket. Christine held up the jeans against her waist—by cinching her belt and rolling up the cuffs, they'd be serviceable enough to wear into the cave. The same went for the rain jacket.

CHRISTINE SHIVERED IN the dim overcast, chilled to the bone even though they'd exited the numbing cavern airs nearly a half hour earlier. Amid budding yellowwood and oak, two state policemen squatted near their van, packing up the climbing rope and equipment used to reach the crime scene on a cave floor surrounded by immense limestone stalactites and stalagmites, the large crystalline structures that looked like nature's version of giant teeth.

Standing in the dark, sucking in the cool vaporous air, she'd aimed her LED headlamp's narrow blaze, searching for clues, her mind pulsing on potentially relevant images illuminated by her camera's strobe. Caught in one of its pulsing flashes was a scatter of men's size elevens across the sandy rock floor. Without a clear impression of the brand design from the sole impressions, they'd retrieved an emulsified Quick-ready casting of one good shoe print. There was little else of forensics value, other than the torn shirt the officers had earlier recovered and bagged.

Inside the high-vaulted underground dome, Christine was drawn by the trickling sounds of water. Several nearby formations glistened wet, the moisture spilling from a source beyond her view—an underground creek, perhaps. The whole time below the surface she'd had to push back the suffocating feeling of being closed in. Even so, she'd marveled at nature's work, which Pernell Wyckoff, her in-house chemist and fiber expert, had explained was merely the result, over eons of time, of rainwater percolating through the surface, dissolving the soluble limestone bedrock, itself composed of tiny crushed skeletons of corals that once had lived and died in an ancient, long gone sea. Still, it was remarkable to Christine how this simple action of minute quantities of carbon dioxide acidifying the rainwater could explain what her eyes had beheld.

Earlier they'd combed the banks of the Little Muddy where Ellen McKinley's body was found. Inside the flagged area, Christine photographed the fingernail grooves in the mud that Dr. Hansen mentioned, although the previous night's rains had smoothed the grooves into narrower indentations that failed to enhance Christine's understanding of the state of the victim in her last breathing moments.

How was it that she'd had the strength to pull herself free of the chilly creek waters, only to expire with hardly a fight so soon afterward? Surely she hadn't died from the cold alone? Christine was certain that the needle mark inside the bruise on the young woman's neck held the answer.

She followed the state police van in her rental vehicle along the forest road back to the blacktop that led to Starksboro, Illinois, home of Lincoln Technical College, or LTC, where Ellen McKinley had been a junior.

After four hours of clambering inside and around the damp underground cavern, she was famished. It was already 3:30, well past her lunch hour. She spotted a Subway restaurant in a strip mall on the main drag and quickly signaled to turn. The state police van braked, did a U-turn, and joined her at Subway. She paid for her order and left the troopers waiting for theirs, wanting to make calls from the privacy of her rental car. As she finished wolfing down the turkey sandwich, her phone rang. She blushed when she saw Joe McFaron's name displayed on its touch screen.

"Sheriff McFaron, what a pleasant surprise!"

"Wish it were under better circumstances, Christine. I apologize for my not calling you sooner."

"Funny thing, your calling me right now. As we speak, I'm practically in your backyard."

"I know it," he said in the same serious voice. "That's kind of why I'm calling actually. Doc Henegar mentioned that you were helping Dr. Hansen downstate in Illinois there."

McFaron was a thorough, well-grounded law officer who respected jurisdictional turf and had shown better acumen for politics than she when they'd worked together on the Holmquist case nearly a year ago. She was glad to hear his voice. It had been her fault that they'd fallen out of touch.

"Yes, I arrived last night and I've spent most of today examining the victim and the crime scenes. I . . . Wait," she interrupted herself. "So you have a business matter to address?"

"Well, yes. I thought you'd know by now. I'm following up about the female student who'd been reported missing from Calhoun Seymour University for nearly a week. She was found inside a cave this past Sunday. Her body, that is. I reported it first thing to your office," McFaron said.

"Is that right," she said slowly, processing the news. Christine was head of Forensics, yet neither Gaston nor Miranda had mentioned this Indiana death to her. So far as she knew, no one on her team had an inkling of it either. She'd alerted both Gaston and Miranda to the Illinois student's death yesterday morning after Gaston's podium speech and yet neither of them had blinked or said a word.

"Three amateur spelunkers from a caving club at CSU down in Benson, Indiana, were mapping an unexplored sinkhole in the Clear Creek Formation, which is actually in Crosshaven County, when they discovered the body. The victim's name is Naomi Winchester."

"I certainly appreciate the heads-up, Joe." She got out of the rental car and slammed the door hard enough for one of the officers inside Subway to glance her way.

"They entered through a chimney using climbing rope and gear. Quite frankly, it's a difficult crime scene to reach. The CSU campus is just south of here, only about a forty-five minute drive from Crosshaven. The victim's a student there." McFaron paused. "You still there, Special Agent?"

"You've got my full attention, Sheriff."

"As I said, Doc Henegar mentioned that Dr. Hansen in Carbondale had spoken with you, so I figured your office was already working on the Indiana case, which is why I'm giving you a holler."

"So you're handling this case even though you say she is a student in Benson County?"

"As it turns out, the location of the body was technically over the Crosshaven County line, which is why I'm the one calling you, rather than Sheriff Rodney Boynton, my counterpart from Benson County. Sheriff Boynton, of course, has an active interest. We'll definitely be cooperating on all matters, as I suspect any investigation may well involve witnesses and persons of interest from the university there."

The degree of Gaston and Miranda's undermining of her forensics office was becoming painfully clear, and Prusik fought to contain her frustration. "What'd you find, Joe?" she asked in as even a voice as she could manage.

"For starters, we recovered a woman's pink windbreaker. It has a spot of blood on it. The cavers knew enough not to handle it. It's been tentatively ID'd as belonging to Winchester by her roommate. Also according to the roommate, to her knowledge Winchester has never shown an interest in caves or even been in one. My nose tells me someone used one of nature's own holes to get rid of the body."

"For your ears only, Joe, it looks likely that this Illinois student who was found on a creek bank may have met a similar fate. While I was examining her body, police cavers discovered what must have begun as an assault inside a cave, too." She told McFaron how they'd guided her inside to the cave floor and she'd confirmed as much. "The creek where her body lay was a downstream outflow from the cave."

Christine was anxious to get a jump on this new case in Indiana. Both victims being young college-age women and found within the same week of each other in or near a cave meant one thing to her: their deaths were very likely connected, and more were likely in the offing unless the killer was stopped. Gaston's PTQP profile assignment would have to wait because a homegrown evil had come knocking on Christine's door.

"Listen, Joe, I have to meet with the Illinois victim's parents and interview her roommate. Still . . ." She hesitated, realizing the lateness of the hour and the fact she hadn't yet made a return plane reservation to Chicago. "Tell you what. I'll drive over to Crosshaven tomorrow morning early."

"I'll look forward to seeing you then."

"As far as my being notified," Christine said, "let me say that things have changed. There's been an influx of new personnel at the Chicago office. That, and a few communication wrinkles, which can hold until I get there."

McFaron advised her on the best route to travel from

Starksboro, Illinois, via the back roads, cautioning her about the coal truckers that drove too fast, hepped up on pills. "They're bigger than you are and they don't slow down, Christine. Watch yourself."

When the call ended, Christine closed her eyes and took a few long, deep breaths. She wasn't going to fly back to Chicago after all. She thanked the troopers in Subway and said she no longer needed their assistance, as she had interviews on the LTC campus to attend to alone. She headed back to her car, contemplating the distressing truth that two young women abducted and assaulted inside caves within proximity of their college campuses and found within a week of each other was no mere coincidence—no more than those two passenger planes that struck the World Trade Center towers within an hour of each other were.

CHAPTER
FOUR

PAUL HIGGINS SAT in front of the three-monitor array and opened the software link. The left monitor, which was next to his phone, blipped to life. The letters PTQP spiraled forward individually, filling the screen. A moment later a user name and password box appeared with a blinking cursor. He quickly typed in the information and waited for the program to load.

At roughly the twenty-second count, the thought occurred that the server must be overloaded with others' logging on at the same time. Or maybe it was because of the overnight backup reports running on the mainframe? But that wouldn't explain it. He'd come in a full hour early because the server was always noticeably faster then, and he could think more clearly in the peace and quiet of an empty office. And he hadn't seen a soul wandering in the hallway or shuffling around in the other offices either.

He tapped instructions in machine language, opening his Operational Program Index, and then ran a subroutine that pulled up a black screen with lines of white-lettered code indicating RAM and hard drive usage requirements on programs he regularly used. The new PTQP web program still displayed as actively loading. A web-based portal wouldn't necessitate that much of a download.

He quickly exited the desktop and closed down the computer, then nervously tugged a few locks of long dark hair behind his ears while listening intently in the dead quiet of his office. There it was—the faint internal audible, a flickering transistor sound emanating from deep in his machine, similar to the sleep mode sound when his terminal wasn't really shut down. The accelerated ticks told him that a program was still running live. And it wasn't one of his. This was way beyond educational programming. He'd seen it demonstrated at a training seminar last year—Constant Running Programs, they were called—allowing managers to check up on employee productivity by watching how much time workers actually spent working versus hanging out on social media, personal messaging, or perusing online websites. In other words, wasting company time.

Which meant his computer was now an invaded piece of crap hardware reporting back whatever he was doing online. He ripped off a Post-it note to cover the optical lens on the upper edge of the monitor, but then hesitated. They'd know then that he knew it was a surveillance program. He innocently rubbed the adhesive edge of the blank Post-it note against the monitor's frame, like he would before marking up passages of printouts that he wanted to show Eisen or Prusik.

He left the office and took the elevator down to the street level. Leaving the building he nearly ran into Ned Miranda.

"Hey, how's it going? Paul Higgins, right?"

"Yes, right." They shook hands. "I was just going to get a bagel."

"Any issues loading the PTQP program?"

Higgins glanced up at the second-in-command, who was a couple of inches taller than him. The slight IT specialist on Prusik's forensic team shook his head.

Sunlight blazed off the outer glass door as Miranda opened it. "Good to hear. See you upstairs."

ON THE DRIVE to Crosshaven, Indiana, early Wednesday morning, Christine braked hard in the road hollows where thick patches of fog blotted out her view of the pavement. Within an hour the rising sun dissipated the vapors. She passed through desolate downtown centers with old redbrick fronts. Faded mannequin displays in abandoned and rundown stores looked hardly changed since the Great Depression, she figured, because the inhabitants no doubt shopped at malls or big-box stores now, leaving the downstate county seats to the courthouses, police, and fire stations.

Her phone had already vibrated on mute several times; each time Miranda's name flashed across the screen. She fumed seeing his name the first time and wisely left it unanswered.

On the previous afternoon she'd met with Ellen McKinley's parents and then Stacy Kittredge, the dead girl's roommate at LTC. Afterward, Christine had checked herself into a Motel 6, bone-tired and frustrated, having learned nothing much useful from either of the interviews. Aside from the postmortem evidence, she hadn't a clue to go on, unless McKinley's not having a boyfriend and her being a solid-A student on a full athletic scholarship was significant. One interesting detail—on the day McKinley went missing, her class schedule was open, meaning her friends wouldn't have noticed her missing until much later. The killer may have known of her open schedule, too, and planned on it to his advantage: an obsessed student, perhaps, or one of her teachers, someone who'd taken a special appreciation of her although not yet a boyfriend?

She ruminated over the pertinent forensics evidence: first and foremost, the unusual bruising on the back of McKinley's neck, perhaps a point of entry for some knockout drug, keeping her quiet and easier to handle? Aside from that mark, McKinley's body showed remarkably few outward signs of a struggle with her assailant—her fingernails were jammed full of riverbank mud, not the perp's flesh. The scant evidence of shoe prints on the cave floor, including one of McKinley's, hadn't yielded much: the torn shirt with minor bloodstains the state police had bagged for forensics testing was a size ten and likely the victim's; if they got lucky, hair and fiber analysis might turn up something. And the puzzling fact that McKinley was on the collegiate swim team and had managed to save herself from drowning only to suddenly expire on the creek bank shortly thereafter without so much as a struggle was mystifying.

Christine's phone was vibrating again and she pulled off the road. She waited for Miranda's message to complete before ringing up her voicemail.

A battered, shadowy hulk whipped past her rental car. The ground shook as it passed, jostling her from side to side in the Chevy Impala sedan. *Shit!* She hadn't even seen it coming. McFaron was right about the coal truckers. And she'd thought city drivers were dangerous. Driving on the undulating broken pavement with no shoulders was like playing Russian roulette. Coal trucks didn't hesitate to barrel right up behind her bumper, like the two that already had in the last hour. Hepped up on pills, Joe'd said.

Christine took a moment to compose herself and then left the message: "Listen, Ned, I've been busy down here. It's a developing situation. I've examined the Illinois victim and attended the crime scene. I'm headed to Crosshaven, Indiana, on an urgent

call there, which I'm sure you must know about. You'll appreciate my surprise when I learned from the local authorities there
that a missing student's body had been found inside a cave, and
that it had been reported to our Chicago office this past Sunday."
She bit her lower lip and finished the message: "It's too early to
say for sure, but the apparent similarities of the two crime scenes
both involving female students and attacks inside caves are especially concerning, as it likely means this is the work of a serial
killer. I shall investigate and report my preliminary findings of
the Crosshaven victim ASAP."

Within moments of hitting the send button, her phone began
vibrating on the passenger seat: Miranda. The phone beeped, indicating Miranda's message, which also flashed across the touch
screen: "You have no clearance to investigate Indiana death. Return to office. Call me ASAP. Ned."

All the while the three cardinal rules of forensics protocol
buzzed in Christine's head: Investigate. Investigate. Investigate.

TRIP DRESSED CASUALLY in jeans and a sweatshirt, not
wanting to draw the attention of anyone in the humble farming
community. The meeting place was the basement of a Baptist
church on Quarry Road in the township of Oolitic, far enough
from Benson, he hoped, that no other attendee would recognize
him from the campus.

He pulled into the gravel parking lot and cut the engine. It was
a noontime meeting. A small group of people stood outside the
doorway finishing their smokes before filing inside. He waited
until the last one had disappeared inside the church door before
getting out.

Trip took a seat in the rear of the narrow basement room. The space was set up with folding chairs all facing a table in front where two placards were propped up. *I was living in the pollution instead of the solution* was written on one, and *Hatred destroys the hater* on the other. He couldn't argue with that.

A coworker had suggested he try a meeting, telling Trip that it had relieved him after losing his wife to share his feelings with a roomful of strangers, as strange as that might sound.

Trip thought it even stranger yet that he had actually come. Speaking in a group about personal issues didn't appeal to him. It never had. But he feared the worsening bouts of rage that now were coming out sideways at work without his realizing it.

Had this guy at work seen him act inappropriately, he wondered. He knew his anger had caused him to be short with Eileen Plante, a secretary, the other day. Over a simple misunderstanding, even though in his mind her failing to copy the pages he'd asked for an hour earlier was anything but a simple mistake. He'd taken it as a grave insult, which it damn well was! Deliberate on her part, she'd done it to piss him off, the same way his childhood mistakes would piss off his grandmother and her German man-servant Karl. His parents had been good people. He could almost remember what it had felt like to be loved by them and to love them in return. Almost. But when they'd died and he was sent to live with his father's mother, everything changed.

Still, it was troublesome that he couldn't remember what he may have said to Eileen, or how he may have behaved in front of her. It wasn't part of the grand plan and he feared that his forgetting things would spoil everything. The rage was interfering with his sleep, too. More and more he was tired during the day, and fatigue caused people to make mistakes. That wouldn't do.

A man seated behind the table up front called the church base-ment meeting to order. Someone else read "The Steps" and right afterward, people went around the room saying their first names. On his turn, he identified himself as "a visitor," just as the co-worker had said for him to do.

A woman two rows up raised her hand and addressed the group about a struggle she was having with her husband's drinking and abusively swearing at her and their children. Her voice trembled. Then she began sobbing. A woman next to her hugged her close.

The woman's sudden meltdown made Trip uneasy. When she spoke again—something about having to lock herself with the children in the basement for protection—Trip stood up so fast he knocked over his chair.

He caught a few heads turning, which sent him back up the basement steps two at a time, pulling hard on the handrail.

Outside in the parking lot, Trip wrestled with himself. He couldn't stay there, not with all that crying and talk of danger and abuse. It was as if Karl was still after him, even today.

Trip fumbled the keys in the car's ignition. He dropped the clutch and the engine stalled. He could practically feel his breathing constrict, as it had when Karl would grab him by his twelve-thirteen-fourteen-fifteen-sixteen-year-old skinny adoles-cent neck for not measuring up to the German's impossibly high standards.

"Trip, you tink you're so smart I can't tell you didn't clean up your room?" Karl's bark was sufficient to flush Trip's face every time, guilty or not. "Dirty socks are still under your bed. No more games."

And of course his grandmother would watch the choking or

the hitting, nodding her approval, and adding her own refrain of disappointment:

Oh, Trip, how could you. Not again. You know better than to fool around, really. Go to your room immediately! Clean it right.

Sweat lines creased down Trip's cheeks in the church parking lot—tinctures of boyhood shame and panic adding to the yawing emptiness, the chasm inside him that grew with each passing day, threatening to engulf him forever if he couldn't contain it first.

He blinked out the windshield. There was no salvation here, no easy way out, just as there had been none when he was a child. What had he, Trip, done to make his mother and father die? Or what had he done to deserve this punishment from their dying? Because that's what it felt like at his grandmother's big, unforgiving house: he was being punished for their deaths.

But maybe he deserved punishment. Maybe being throttled was a perfectly reasonable outcome for not hanging up his shirts neatly enough in their prescribed color-organized sections. He didn't think so, but it was so hard to know. Sometimes he really did feel that everything was all his fault.

The car engine coughed back to life. He goosed the gas pedal a few times, then spun the wheels leaving the church parking lot. It had been a bad decision to come. The meeting had only made matters worse. He drove west along the state road to sort himself out. Screamed so loud inside the small car it made his ears ring. Old resentments clouded his mind the way a sudden storm trough could snuff out a clear blue sky.

A gust of wind buffeted the car. The tops of the trees swayed. To the west, the sky was darkening as far as the eye could see.

The weather was changing again, another front was approaching. And this time the storm would be terrible.

CHRISTINE CRUISED UNDER the grove of dark hemlock boughs. Piney air wafted in through the air ducts of the Chevy Impala. It had been nearly six months since she'd last passed through the tight wreath of forest hemming Crosshaven's outskirts. After yesterday's call, she toggled down to Sheriff Joe Mc-Faron's contact information and called his number.

"Hello, Joe." She heard muffled background talk on his end. "Joe?"

"Hey, Christine, by any chance do you work with a guy named Veranda?"

"It's Miranda. Yes I do. Don't tell me he's phoned you?" She pulled over to the roadside and stopped the car.

"He's called more than once, according to Mary." Mary Carter was Sheriff McFaron's dispatcher and designated commander of all things related to the office, including the twice-daily walk to Libby's Crullers for sustenance, Christine recalled.

"Mary wouldn't give out my cell number, which probably means you should give him a holler," McFaron said, "before he sends in the SWAT team after you."

"Oh, should I now," she snapped, scrubbing fingers through her short chestnut hair.

Joe laughed. "Well, don't bite my head off, Christine. I'm not the one harassing you."

Christine sighed. "You're right, Joe—as usual, mea culpa." A smile crept over her face as she gazed farther down the road.

"Amazing, I can see that greasy diner of yours up ahead through the trees. But I haven't smelled it yet. Did Shermie Dutcher convert to vegan cooking?"

"That's a good one. Not yet, but he might have taken your advice and let up on the Crisco some, because of the chimney fires." Someone interrupted the sheriff, a man's voice.

They'd broken the ice with small talk, nothing too personal, Christine mused. Nothing broaching the topic of their prolonged silence—a silence that might, perhaps, be called a breakup. She shrugged at the thought. In reality, it was their relentless work schedules and the very real fact that they lived and worked six solid interstate hours of driving apart. That's what had gotten in the way, Christine repeated to herself. Just as undeniable, hearing his voice again had sparked something. She had missed Joe—his decency and rock-solid presence, his soft-spoken way—missed him too much maybe. Was it deliberate that she had stopped making the extra call to check in and see how he was doing? That she had stopped making a conscious effort to keep their relationship—even the word made her cringe—moving forward?

She had pulled away from him ever since that last time they'd shared a bed in his Crosshaven home. His childhood home, with walls of photographs, remembrances on shelves, and an old kitchen with high cupboards that looked tended to, had beckoned her to add her female chemistry to the mix. That's what had chased her out the door. Maybe. She wasn't sure. But now was not the time to be analyzing her feelings.

"So what's going on? Are you at the crime scene, Joe?"

"Kind of." Over the phone she could hear his footfalls and the others' voices receding. "We're holding court at Doc Henegar's place. There's an Indiana State Crime Lab courier here, too, for transporting evidence."

"I'd like to see whatever you've got before he leaves," Christine said. "If I may, that is."

"I expected that you would. It's why I called you as soon as I could yesterday," he said. "Do you want me to come show you the way or do you remember how to get to Doc's place?"

She shuddered at his mentioning the doctor because of what it undeniably meant: that she'd have to brace herself to pass through the gates again. "I remember, Joe. Stay where you are. I should be there in five, ten minutes at the most."

"Well good, then. See you soon."

For all of the heaviness of the moment, his voice had a welcoming warmth to it, and Christine couldn't help but smile. "Good. See you soon."

CHAPTER
FIVE

SHE MADE THE call from the idling car, watching a shabby truck pull up in front of Shermie Dutcher's Diner. An old farmer in bib overalls climbed out of the pickup and walked stiffly to the diner's door and disappeared inside the greasy spoon, probably for an early lunch. It was half past eleven.

"I understand from Sheriff McFaron's office that you've called there trying to reach me. I'm returning your call, Ned," she said in the best business-as-usual voice that she could muster.

"Christine, just what the hell do you think you're doing?"

She put Miranda on speaker and rested the device on the dashboard. "Tell me, Ned, just when were you planning to let me and my team in on the call made to our branch office from Indiana? You know, Naomi Winchester, the missing—read deceased—college student from CSU in Benson? The one whose dead body was discovered inside a cave by some student spelunkers last Sunday?"

She continued without giving him a chance to respond. "Or had you forgotten my job description *is* forensics? You deliberately held that information from me, even after I reported to you in real time the call from the Carbondale ME's office regarding the Illinois student's dead body. Yet you said nothing, even as I prepared to leave my office for the airport. How is that, Ned?"

She cut it there. After all, he was her boss.

"You heard Patricia after the podium address downtown on Monday, Christine. And you heard it again from me back at your office. That's strictly a local matter. It doesn't involve us, which means it doesn't involve the Forensics team. Which means it doesn't involve you."

She waved a hand to cool her hot cheeks. "But listen, Ned . . ." He cut her off.

"No, you listen. You've blown me off once already by missing our scheduled get-together in Patricia's office yesterday. Tuesday at three, or didn't you remember? If you'd picked up my calls yesterday morning, you'd have heard the reminder, Christine. You would have had plenty of time to fly back to Chicago. But you wouldn't have remembered because you didn't answer your phone or return any of my calls or messages."

This time she let him fume without interruption. He was right, of course.

"I want you to know that I defended you, Christine, with Patricia," he said. "She was ready to put you on a leave of absence until I told her that I'd agreed to your going to Carbondale to make your preliminary assessment and evaluation."

Miranda's words produced a smile across Christine's lips. "Why thank you, Ned," popped out of her mouth.

"Yeah, well 'thanks' doesn't cut it, Christine. Whatever it is you're doing now, you're way out of line, and you damn well know it. Your primary duty is to report to me. In fact, as I recall, you said that you would do a quick down and back to Carbondale for only a prelim. And you *will* be back for Patricia's staff meeting on Thursday morning, which, I needn't remind you, is tomorrow."

She heard him take a breath.

"Christ, how do you think it goes over when a unit head expected for a scheduled meeting with the Branch director blows it off? The message it sends is not a good one. Not to Patricia, it isn't. Not to me either."

"I'm sorry, Ned. I screwed up. Mea culpa."

This time there was silence on the other end. He'd played himself out. She felt a sudden urge to rally him, to own some of his diatribe for his having gone out on a limb on her behalf with Patricia.

"I do have a history. We both know it. You've said as much. So has Patricia," Christine said. "And history, in large part, is also why I am still in charge of the Forensics unit. We produce results. And I *have* been taking down a few worksheet notes, outlining an overview of my unit's profiles, as you requested of me.

"You may find it hard to believe, Ned, but I genuinely believe what you and Patricia are bringing to the table is important, necessary, and of vital importance to the Bureau's proper functioning." *Whoa, Christine*, she counseled herself. *Let's not go too far.* She took in a breath. "And yes, I recognize that it's the primary goal of Patricia's in the next week or so to get these profile descriptions done. *And* that I am expected to do my regular job too. Patricia's follow-up email said as much."

"That's certainly good to hear. Could you fax me those notes some time today, Christine?" His voice sounded considerably calmer.

"Absolutely I will. Just as soon as I reach Sheriff McFaron's office," she said, wiping her brow with the back of her hand. Her cheeks still glowed. Christine stepped out of the car for fresh air and to stretch her legs.

"One other thing, Ned. Right now I'm headed to the second crime scene in Indiana, apparently inside a cave in Crosshaven County. Things are moving fast. They've requested my assistance . . ."

She hesitated, waiting for another unpleasant knee-jerk reaction. But none was forthcoming.

"Just send me your notes, Christine. We'll talk later." He ended the call.

WITH SHERMIE'S DINER to orient her, Christine remembered the route that she had taken the first time she'd visited Doc Henegar's country-fried pathology lab slash private general practice slash fly fisherman establishment.

On this occasion a train of police vehicles was parked in front of Dr. Henegar's place. Christine took her place five car-lengths back from the rustic establishment. It was almost noon.

Inside, the commotion was centered in the kitchen.

"Hello, Dr. Henegar?" Christine called from the front hallway. "Joe?"

The rapid-fire slap of claws against linoleum announced the doctor's two yellow Labrador retrievers, Billy and Josie. The dogs whined and nuzzled her. She kneeled and yielded to their licks. They'd remembered her.

Sheriff McFaron appeared behind the dogs.

Christine quickly stood. "Hey there, Joe. Long time no see."

She offered her cheek for a kiss and was surprised when he kissed her warmly on the lips instead. Smiling, she looked up at him.

"What a nice way to start the day." She nodded in the direction of the kitchen, where loud voices were escalating. "So what's all the fuss?"

She separated from his embrace and stooped to pick up her forensics case. His apparent fondness for her was bewilderingly intact and quite surprised her.

"It's just breaking up. Bunch of jurisdictional brouhaha. Indiana State Police, Benson City Police, Head of CSU security police, myself, and now you, Special Agent of the FBI. Sheriff Boynton of Benson County already ducked out of here awhile ago on business."

"I take it the vic is situated in Dr. Henegar's posh morgue facility back there behind the kitchen?" Keeping it to the impersonal *vic* couldn't stave the gnawing apprehension already building in her gut. Soon enough the cold dead flesh of another young woman would confront her, challenging her to piece together its clues in time to prevent the next young woman from dying.

"You'd be right," McFaron said. "She's been there since Sunday night, since the cavers discovered her body and the Staties removed her."

"Just for the record, can you confirm for me that a call did go out to our Chicago field office Sunday when her body was found?"

"I sure can. I've got a faxed copy back at the office, in conjunction with the Indiana State Police crime report, which I faxed your way as well." He shoved back the brim of his cowboy hat, revealing some gray flecks of hair at his temples that she hadn't remembered seeing last fall.

"Great." She shook her head. "Just great."

"That doesn't sound so great. Is everything okay?"

"Dirty politics. Nothing I can't handle," she said gruffly.

"You know why they say not to wrestle with a pig, don't you?" the sheriff said with a grin.

She shook her head. "Why don't you edify me?"

"You'll both get muddy, but the pig will like it."

She sighed. "I suppose."

"Some people like to fight dirty, Christine. There's not much you can do about it but be aware."

"Yeah, well . . ." She shook her head, not agreeing there wasn't anything she could do about it. But it wasn't worth tussling over now, pig or not.

They headed into the kitchen. McFaron made the introductions all around. Dr. Henegar approached her, dressed ready for hunting camp, not a hint of doctor in the torn lumber shirt and soiled dungarees. His full beard and thinning hair were a little whiter than she remembered from her last visit nearly a year ago.

"I hear Ernie Hansen got a hold of you," Doc Henegar said with a ready smile and an extra-warm handshake. "Hope I wasn't overstepping protocol or anything giving Ernie your name, Special Agent Prusik. He's a fine ME."

"Not at all, Doctor. I'm honored that you recommended me," Christine said, returning his smile with genuine amiability. "Apparently it was timely, too, given the developments you've got here."

Dr. Henegar nodded his head over his left shoulder. "Would you like to examine the body?"

She flicked two fingers back and forth between herself and Henegar. "Just the two of us would be a good idea."

She had no jurisdictional authority granted to her, only a friendly invite from Sheriff McFaron. But that didn't mean she had to show her hand to the local police who had no clue that she was "way out of line," as Ned Miranda had so aptly phrased it. At least he hadn't ordered her to come back *now*.

It was abundantly clear that this contingent of local law enforcement assumed the FBI would be cooperating with local police, which only underscored in Christine's mind how absurd her predicament truly was.

Christine followed Dr. Henegar down a corridor off the kitchen. "This might come as a pleasant surprise, Agent Prusik," Dr. Henegar spoke as he led the way. "Not the victim's body, of course. You'll see what I mean."

She prodded his shoulder gently. "Christine, please."

"That's right. I remember," Henegar said. "I go pretty much by Doc, but you can call me Walter if you'd prefer."

He flicked on the light switch and illuminated a new metal-lined double door, plenty wide enough to fit an emergency rescue gurney through. Inside, the brightly lit room had grown by several-fold from what she recalled.

"Wow, nice work, Doc!" she said, taking in the bright, stainless-steel countertops awash under new banks of drop-ceiling fluorescent lighting.

"And the pièce de résistance," Henegar said, opening a floor-to-ceiling vault door, revealing a cavernous four-tray compartment morgue. The topmost tray was the only one occupied.

"Tell me, Doc, you didn't do all this," Christine held out her arms, "because of what I said the last time I was here? Really, I do apologize. I wasn't very tactful."

"Oh no, we were long overdue for an update. If anything, that case of yours helped accelerate the renovation. This is a fully functioning pathology lab, state and federally certified." He pointed at the two framed plaques hanging on the wall. "Not that I wasn't before, you understand."

"Of course not, Doc."

"I've even been slated to receive a young government-paid intern soon. In a way though, it's a damn sorry statement of the times we live in. You know, having to increase the space and all. I wish we needed *less* room for dead bodies, not more." He gazed down at the floor.

Christine patted his shoulder. "I hear you, Doc. Me too."

Dr. Henegar handed her a one-piece Tyvek disposable gown and donned his own. Capped, gloved, and gowned, she assisted him in positioning Naomi Winchester's body on the stainless examination table.

Winchester's young face gave Christine a start. The dead girl's sightless eyes were wide open. Even though no life lighted them from the inside anymore, Christine felt a connection to the young woman. When queasiness started to overtake her, she had to remind herself that although Naomi hadn't escaped her pursuer, she, Christine, had. She flicked her eyes left to right, left to right.

"You okay, Christine?" The doctor's voice brought her back to the present.

"I'm fine, thanks. Just caught a little chill." Christine got out her digital recorder and notepad, the spreading and sliding calipers, and her camera with a close-up attachment.

"Any notables to direct my attention to, Doc?"

"Yes, I'm glad that you asked. There are three things particularly worth mentioning. State police divers removed her from the cave, so I can't be certain that her head may not have been accidentally bumped in the process of retrieving the body."

"Bruising while evacuating her body wouldn't have shown postmortem, right?" she said.

"No, but take a look here."

Henegar rolled the body to one side and pointed out a distinct mark on the back of the victim's neck.

"You see what I mean?" Henegar leaned close, aiming his gloved finger at the small bruised indentation. "The impression's slightly raised the flesh even."

Christine stooped, paying closer attention. The mark was clearer than on McKinley, but otherwise identical in dimension to the Illinois victim. "Quite extraordinary," she said.

"I thought so, too." Dr. Henegar nodded. "Not a likely place for inadvertent bruising that you'd expect to find."

"You said three things?" She slipped on her portable head-mounted magnifier.

With his gloved fingertips Dr. Henegar carefully separated a row of hairs on the right side of the dead girl's temple.

"The dark bruising here, it's a bit diffuse but perimortem for sure."

"She may have fallen and struck her head there," Christine said, venturing a guess. Tripping inside a cave was easy enough to do. She'd caught herself a couple of times yesterday, falling forward on spread fingertips inside the damp Illinois cave.

"My thought, too," he said, "but not a hard enough force to do any permanent damage. Certainly it may have been sufficient to knock her senseless, though."

Christine asked his help in turning the body completely over, revealing the backside of the neck under better light. She picked up her camera with the filtered close-up lens and snapped several pictures at different angles.

"I take it you've already taken fluid and tissue samples?"

"Swabbed her, there's no sign of rape. Her underclothing was intact. Blood and saliva samples are already up at the State Police

Lab in Indianapolis. The windbreaker with a smudge of blood on it I also sent to the crime lab for DNA testing and typing. Her lungs are clear.

"One more thing is odd," Doc Henegar said. He pursed his lips. "She may have suffered a myocardial infarction. It's only a hunch. I haven't much to go on yet. From all outward appearance her coronary arteries certainly appear healthy on X-ray plates. No anomalies jump out there. She's fit looking; the right weight for her age.

"Nothing in the faxed medical reports from her primary physician would lead me to expect tachycardia, either. Perhaps extreme stress, a sudden fear induced by being inside the cave, I just can't be sure. Like I say, it's just a hunch. But there was definitely some kind of heart failure involved in her death."

"So what other than tachycardia could make a healthy heart suddenly give out?" Christine said. "What's the takeaway here, Doc?"

"The State Path boys phoned me early this morning. Her electrolytes were off the charts. Don't quote me on it, but one of them looked it up on the U.S. Army Toxicology website that he happened to be familiar with because of weekend guard duty. Lo and behold, nerve gas poisoning shows similar skewed electrolyte results."

"What?" Christine wrinkled her brow. "That can't be right. Surely, there'd be a more definitive test than a comparison of electrolyte imbalances?"

"I'm glad you're here, Special Agent Christine. The guy was only best guessing anyhow. Otherwise," Henegar raised his eyebrows—the same color as his puffy salt-and-pepper beard—and said, "I have nothing else to report." He let out a sigh.

Christine removed an optical instrument from her forensics case to inspect more closely the indentation mark on the surface of the skin near Naomi Winchester's C-3 cervical vertebrae.

At 30X power the pale landscape of the bloodless pebbled flesh zoomed up at her as if she were making a lunar landing. Under the increased magnification, the faint oval impression the width of a signet ring face was knurled along the edges. Within its diameter there appeared a partial curvature, a line folded upon itself, as if depicting the leg of a creature in a squatting position. Centermost was a bluish speck, a pinprick of dried blood. It was an injection site of such extreme uniqueness that the likelihood that Christine was dealing with the same killer was near one hundred percent.

"I'd like a deep excision of the tissue surrounding this mark, Doctor."

Christine wrote down the name and address of the Chicago lab that her forensics unit often sent samples to whenever they needed more sophisticated readings than her lab could perform.

"I'll be putting in a call to Brian Eisen, my chief technician, with instructions. I'd also like a copy of your medical examination report sent with the tissue sample, if that's okay with you."

"That's fine," Dr. Henegar said. "I'm assuming that Sheriff McFaron and you are both working together on this matter."

She nodded. To say anything more might only get Dr. Henegar in hot water. She knew that Miranda's tacit approval allowing her to stay on in the field, investigating this second death, did not amount to an outright consent. But it was far better than his insisting she return to Chicago immediately.

"One other thing I noticed," Dr. Henegar said, pointing along the sides of her rib cage. "These mild skin abrasions would suggest her body may have been lowered by a rope to the cave floor."

Christine nodded. From the abrasions it struck her that Winchester was likely dead already when her body was lowered inside the cave. "I'd like to see the crime scene now if we could."

In truth, Christine didn't want to see the crime scene. She didn't like caves, and the previous visit inside the cavern where Ellen McKinley had apparently been attacked triggered a strong claustrophobic reaction, which, though she'd managed to control it, had surfaced her other darkest fear, one that she could never really escape in spite of the fact that she knew it was near impossible: that the attacker in her past who she'd managed to evade once was still very much out there, alive and kicking and desperately wanting to finish the job that he'd started.

CHAPTER
SIX

THEY STOOD IN a semicircle on a slope surrounded by scraggily second-growth oak, yellowwood, and beech. The three state troopers were already geared up. Joe and Christine were cinching on their climbing harnesses. The rope was secured around the base of a large beech tree fifteen feet from the entrance into the cavern. As she prepared to enter another tomb of a crime scene for the second day in a row, her anxiety skyrocketed and her breathing grew shallower.

Two of the troopers went first, followed by McFaron, and then it was her turn. She ducked her head inside the rock cleft, listening to the muffled voice of one of the troopers already on the cave floor instructing McFaron on the best foot placements.

The sheriff called out when he reached bottom. "Christine, take it nice and slow."

"Oh, Lord," she muttered. Then in a louder voice, "Here I come."

She put her full weight onto the rope, gripping hold of the metal clamp device the way Sergeant Belker, who stood directly above, had shown her to do. While Belker played out the rope, the sleeve of light from the great world above shrank away, and as she worked her way down, the temperature dropped markedly. Her helmet lamp offered paltry illumination on a narrow band of cave wall that she clumsily smacked her legs against, completely dependent upon Belker's secure belay.

The damp air of the cave fell heavy on her lungs. Lower down, Christine proceeded slowly over the tumble of rockfall that eons ago had pulled away from the roof of the cave. She released the metal hand lever in incremental jerks, afraid of slipping and falling despite the coaxing voice of Sheriff McFaron standing some fifty feet below her.

The scatter of headlamp beams from Joe and the troopers below drew nearer. Rather unexpectedly, her feet touched the rock floor and she eased her weight off the rope.

She looked up the nearly vertical wall she'd descended and had half a moment to be impressed with herself before wrestling with a panicky impulse to climb right back out as quickly as she could.

McFaron grinned at her in the dim light of their collective headlamps. "Nice job, Special Agent." His voice sounded echoey in the cavernous space.

Sergeant Belker rappelled with surprising speed down to the cave floor and joined them. Two troopers quickly knelt and placed chemical light sticks on the rock floor every few feet, marking the way. Instinctively, Christine knew not to stray from the plotted course. A step off the marked path could mean serious injury.

The sergeant walked ahead to the crime scene. His headlamp shone weakly against a far rock wall of the cave, casting a weak yellowish hue. *Perhaps his batteries needed to be replaced*, Christine thought.

"Let's not lose them, Joe." She shoved him gently. "Hanging out here is not my idea of fun."

"I'm with you on that. Be sure to watch your step."

The troopers stood grouped, their headlamps brightening one

spot beneath an impressive limestone formation that reached nearly to the domed ceiling, its circumference and length the natural equivalent of an ancient Greek column. Rows of lesser spiny stalagmites—the upright concretions formed by the action of water dissolving limestone and dripping from the ceiling onto one spot for tens of thousands of years—lined the surrounding surfaces. Across the chilled air the scatter of their headlamps cast elongated shadows of the formations in a disorienting manner.

She recognized the hefty column from the crime photographs taken by the state police of Naomi Winchester's body *in situ*. In the photographs, the victim's head was seen to have been placed at the foot of the large formation in a manner suggesting that the pillar functioned as a gravestone. Could the killer have been showing respect for the body, Christine wondered.

The troopers wore elasticized over-slippers on their boots and were careful not to step close to the area demarcated with tape where the victim had been found. In Christine's estimation, their care was almost pointless; the caving club members who had found her body were untrained in forensics and no doubt had smudged any trace outlines of footprints before adding their own to the crime scene. Even so, she and Joe pulled on over-slippers, too.

She kept her eyes trained on the illuminated area looking for anything out of the ordinary. It was remarkable to her that there were no clear signs of a skirmish. No blood, no disturbed rocks or sand that she could see. A fine spray of grit overlay the solid bedrock, which would have been enough to show evidence of a struggle, but there was none. Those who found her would have surely left shoe prints. Perhaps the caving group had been careful not to tread too close after all.

Christine made a quick sweep of her headlamp around the

cirque of the cavern, judging that it was as large as a basketball court. Deeper down the main passageway her lamp's beam faded into the darkness. She wondered if the killer could have retreated out of the cave by a different route. If he was familiar enough to bring Winchester here, he likely knew the layout of the cave.

"Does this lead out by another exit?" she asked Sergeant Belker, shining the headlamp at the passage beyond. Sergeant Belker was a big man with a big gut. He loomed a bit taller than Joe McFaron, whom she knew to be six foot two. Sweat bled down both sides of Belker's face even in the cool cave air.

He shook his head. "I have no idea, Agent Prusik. Best I can determine . . . the main access point is . . . the way we just came down."

"Private and cozy," she assessed. She closed her eyes for a moment and took in several deep breaths to relax herself, trying to visualize the scene as it may have unfolded.

"Very definitely a man with considerable strength in order to lower her body by rope," she said, "since signs of any bruising to the victim were minimal."

"Lowering someone with the sophisticated gear available nowadays wouldn't require superhuman strength, ma'am," Belker said.

Christine nodded. "Good to know. And where was the victim's jacket recovered?"

Belker pointed in the direction they'd down-climbed. "According to the caving group, it had fallen behind a rock near the cave floor we just roped down. Best I can figure, it may have slipped from her waist or got caught up somehow."

She scanned the cave floor with her headlamp, searching for a fiber, torn clothing, anything that her team could test. With it, if she was lucky enough, they might be able to identify fragmentary DNA. Remarkable advances in the last decade had enabled forensics scientists to assemble a killer's identity from the minutest bit of evidentiary material.

"I would like you . . ." she addressed Sergeant Belker then pointed to Belker's two deputies. "I'm sorry, I didn't get your names?"

"Bruce. Deputy Bruce Williams, ma'am," one deputy said. "This is Deputy Joseph Bishko." Bishko dipped his head politely.

"Yes, I would like you, Sergeant, and Deputies Williams and Bishko," Christine said, "to search the perimeter in a widening circle from where the body was found. Snap pictures of every footprint you find in here. Anything you come across, photograph and/or bag it."

Christine knelt near the base of the spectacular stalagmite against which Winchester's head had been positioned. Its massive circumference gleamed ghostly white under her LED headlamp. She angled her head upward, tracing her beam up the smooth-sided pillar of crystalline calcium carbonate that rose into the vapory heights of the cavern, perhaps some forty feet or more. Its similarity to a Greek temple column was an apt comparison; in this case a temple column used as a headstone.

The damp cave air was itself a significant aspect, too. It struck Christine that the killer may have grown up in the general vicinity and been familiar with caves from an early age. Dark places may have formed an integral part of his psyche and imaginings. From very early in his life it was all about the dark, the cold, and being achingly alone.

Christine wrapped her arms tightly around her chest, chilled to the bone; a rising discomfort from the confining space suddenly overtook her patience.

She turned to McFaron and said in a lowered voice, "I've seen all I need to see. Let's get the hell out of here before I lose it."

"I'm with you on that. This place gives me the creeps."

McFaron spoke briefly to the troopers, who then helped the sheriff and Christine feed the fixed climbing rope through their ascenders. The sergeant anchored the rope from below this time, while another trooper stationed himself at the entrance above, checking the slack as the sheriff and Christine ascended. Christine was first this time.

She climbed the steep chimney wall slowly, her hands trembling as she reached the midway point, feeling uneasy putting her full weight on gear she had no prior experience using.

Joe was right behind her. Ten minutes later, welcome sunshine warmed her face. She watched McFaron decouple himself from the gear.

"I know it's been a while since we really talked," she started right in, forcing to the surface the relationship issue that had been troubling her ever since she first heard his voice on the phone yesterday. "But can we focus for a minute on the crime scene?"

The transition felt as awkward as it sounded to her. They weren't alone; there was the trooper stationed at the entrance, now belaying Sergeant Belker.

"I'm all ears, Special Agent." Joe's voice remained composed. He always carried himself well. She liked that about him; very little ruffled the man.

She nodded, rubbed her chilly palms together, then cupped and blew air into them to warm her fingers.

"Good then, what do we know?" she said rhetorically. "Naomi Winchester's life ended with a man she completely trusted. As dark and creepy as I felt descending into that hole, the killer felt right at home. He chose that spot because it was comforting, quiet. The dark is soothing, less confusing to him. Calming even, and it allows him time."

"It's certainly a well-hid enough place," Joe said. "I'll give you that much. Who'd have thought a bunch of spelunkers would happen across her body this fast? He sure as hell didn't."

"You're right about that, Joe. He didn't count on their finding her, which means he may not have had much time to cover his tracks, get his story straight." She shook her head, deep in thought. "The victim may have willingly joined him to this spot. Judging from the marked abrasions along her rib cage, I believe the killer finished her off before lowering her body into the cave. It's further supported by the fact that there is little evidence of a struggle down there."

"Uh-huh. Although, Doc said that the knock to her head wasn't sufficient to cause her death. Which means the killer may have lowered Winchester unconscious to the cave floor, and then finished her off down there."

Christine nodded. "True. I don't expect these officers have recovered anything of forensics value. The absence of any evidence of a struggle, other than the blood on the victim's jacket, tells me she was definitely dead by the time the killer laid her body out by that formation."

"I tell you what, a cave is a damn good location if you're intent on killing somebody," McFaron said. He then added, "And her jacket being torn and bloodied, her not wearing it, that's sign enough of a struggle in my book."

"And he may not have seen her jacket fall in the darkness," Christine said. "Judging from his placement of the victim's body, with her head next to that impressive stalagmite formation, it shows a certain degree of respect for her in death. It's very much like an altar, the way he carefully oriented her body directly away from the dripping and seeping waters that were nearby. It's a protected spot he chose, a sanctuary amidst natural crystalline formations. Maybe it's his own sick version of a shrine."

McFaron shrugged. "He could have been showing respect for her dead body by leaving her in the cavern, but it's just as likely he was trying to cover his tracks."

"Well, there were none to speak of, really." Christine had the sudden thought that perhaps the killer wore coverlets over his own boots. Perhaps he was in law enforcement and knew all the tricks of the trade?

Christine couldn't afford to wait for the test results of the tissue sample from Ellen McKinley. She needed something to point her in the right direction. Or any direction. She'd phone Brian Eisen as soon as they reached the cars, where she'd have cell reception again.

McFaron was just getting out the keys when the sound of a car's sudden acceleration blasted through the quiet of the afternoon. Ahead, flickering in and out of view from behind a stand of oaks and pines, a dark-colored car sped down the access road. They heard the sound of spitting tires greasing the shoulder as the car took a curve a little wide.

They raced to the trailhead to catch a plate number, but instead found themselves staring down the road at a funneling cloud of dust. Too late. The car's motor boomed loudly from perhaps a half mile away, still accelerating hard, still spitting gravel.

"Well, will you look-y here." McFaron pointed at his Explorer and the two state-owned vans. The air had been bled from all three vehicles' tires. "Whoever it was hightailing it out of here apparently didn't want us to follow."

"Didn't want us to follow and didn't appreciate the fact that we were here in the first place," Christine said. She took a breath. "Listen, would you like to get a bite to eat someplace? I'm famished."

"That sounds like an excellent idea," McFaron said. "I think I know just the place. The right amount of ambience mixed with the perfect amount of grease."

Christine laughed, her spirits suddenly lifted. "I can't think of a better place than Shermie Dutcher's Diner, either. I'm good for the homemade meatloaf sliding in gravy and overcooked vegetables. What about you?"

In response, Joe nodded. "It's like you read my mind, Special Agent."

LEEDS HUGHES'S WHITE lab coat pulled tightly across his broad back as the scientist tapped his toe to the driving bass riff of the Black Keys' "Everlasting Light." The white strands from his earbuds protruded down the sides of his neck into the MP3 player in his breast pocket, as the scientist inserted samples that Christine had overnighted into the high-resolution DNA fragment analyzer. Hughes was in his mid-thirties and bore more than a passing resemblance to Joe Cocker in his Woodstock days, with his coppery brown curls pouring over his temples and merging into his distinctive muttonchops. He had a bit of a paunch and a penchant for listening to blues rock and fusion rock while working.

Hughes jumped at the tap to his shoulder. He hadn't heard Ned Miranda approach. "What are you working on?" Miranda said.

"The overnighted Illinois samples," he responded blankly. The earbuds now dangled loosely over Hughes's lab coat. The technician eyed Miranda with a subdued expression, not unfriendly but not particularly inviting either.

Miranda cast his eyes over Hughes's lab counter: an open notebook with a grid containing handwritten numerical values, a rack of labeled vials, and spectrographic printouts tacked to a cork board. Nothing he wouldn't have expected to find in a forensics laboratory. Nothing to report to Gaston on, other than the fact that Hughes—like Brian Eisen and Paul Higgins and the others on Christine's team—seemed wary of his presence and wasn't very forthcoming.

"I won't have results to report for a while," Hughes offered, which sounded to Miranda more like *if you haven't anything else to ask, I'd like to get back to my work.*

Miranda nodded. "By the way, how's your profile coming along?"

Hughes shrugged his shoulders. "It's coming."

"Good, then." Miranda hesitated, feeling the need to break through the awkward reception. Hughes was probably five or six years his senior but ranked below Miranda, which didn't help the awkwardness. "Look, I realize this all may seem like work for work's sake, having to complete this rather lengthy profile using the associated metrics. But I want you to know that I'm here to help. Any questions you may have, if Christine's too busy, please feel free to come and see me. Okay?"

Hughes nodded and then pressed the earbuds back in place.

Miranda turned and exited the lab. Before closing the door he said, "I'll be coming back through from time to time to check . . ." Miranda cut short his words. Hughes's back was to him, facing his equipment, and the man's head was bobbing to a rhythm that only he could hear.

EISEN WALKED INTO Hughes's office soon after Miranda left.

"Pernell's found something interesting," he said, referring to Pernell Wyckoff, who, at sixty-two, was the oldest member of the forensics team and served as its chief chemist and fiber expert. "A minute fragment of what appears to be solid gold was lodged in the tissue sample taken from the victim's neck."

Hughes lifted his eyebrows in surprise. "More than I've got. No DNA is resident on the sample shirt other than the victim's own. Gold you say?"

"My best guess is whatever was used to jab the back of the victim's neck struck a vertebra and broke off."

"How small?"

"Pernell says one-hundredth of a millimeter, admittedly hardly more than a fleck."

"Sure it didn't rub off the ME's tools during the postmortem?"

"Contamination is ruled out according to Pernell. The fleck was embedded deep in the tissue," Eisen confirmed. "We'll need Christine to request a bone scan on the victim's corresponding site of vertebral impact."

"By the way, Miranda was just here poking around, asking if I had any questions about the profile we're supposed to be completing."

"Do you?"

"I haven't actually started it yet."

Eisen grinned. "Yeah, me neither." He shrugged.

"Look, should Christine call and I don't pick up for some reason, be sure to underscore that we need a bone scan of the cervical vertebrae section. Better still, have her get a bone or disc sample from directly beneath the puncture site for you to analyze for foreign fragmentary substances."

"Sure thing." Hughes nodded.

"Say listen, any nibbles yet on your grandfather's fishing camp?" Eisen asked. Hughes was unmarried, and like Eisen, a quiet man who was wed to his job.

"Nope."

"I know it's been in your family for quite some time. I'm sorry that you have to sell."

Hughes rolled his shoulders, then cleared his throat, and said, "Yeah well, you got to do what you got to do. Sis wasn't counting on being divorced and left high and dry with two kids to provide for either."

"It's good that you're there to help her, Leeds."

Eisen left the lab. Hughes didn't reinsert the earbuds this time, his mind on other things. He went to his desk and opened the side drawer, picking up the cheap burner phone he'd purchased from a street vendor downtown, leaving the glossy Bureau-issued smartphone undisturbed on his desk.

CHAPTER
SEVEN

DR. RANDALL CREIGHTON III slumped back in the driver's seat, pleasurably spent. The big V-8 motor purred softly in the parking lot, piping small white puffs out the twin oval exhaust pipes. Tinted glass camouflaged the condensation from their heated breathing. Her goodbye kiss had turned them both on so much they'd had sex again on the passenger side, its luxurious leather captain's chair in the full recline position. Through the smoky-colored windows the twilit sky looked dark as night already.

Afterward they made themselves decent and she gave him a transition face. Was it happiness, hope, expectation, or something else entirely?

He hadn't a clue whether she really didn't want to leave, or just wanted him to think that she didn't. Delving beneath the surface with women was not his forte. On the surface he could skate just fine. He could call the shots, pick up on the green lights, smile his smile, and then make his move.

He answered her transition face by saying that he'd get in touch soon. She gave him a big smile—her upper teeth pearly round like sweet corn—then stepped out of the large SUV. The door closed with a thick German *plunckt*! It was another Porsche quality he liked.

Randy wheeled the Porsche Cayenne out of Lot C—designated parking for upper class students only, and their visitors—realizing as he waved one last time to his Energizer bunny date that he could have been her father dropping his daughter off at college. His own daughter was a high school senior in the custody of her mother, who lived a thousand miles away in the outskirts of the Big Apple, his ex's home turf.

Randy spooled up the engine revs of the metallic black Porsche, enjoying the sonorous lift from its glassy smooth acceleration all the way to redline; he upshifted into third gear and breezed through the last downtown traffic light in Benson, Indiana.

A pang of loneliness suddenly surfaced. Call it the just-dumped-off-Betsy-Higginbotham effect. He flashed on the endearing affection she'd shown him. Her hesitation at the open car door before he reassured her that he'd call seemed genuine; her passion sure was.

Threatening what should be a pleasant after-sex buzz, the void panicked him. He fumbled open the center console bin and grabbed the pewter flask nearly full of scotch. He took a long draught, wiping the back of his hand across his mouth afterward.

The warm glow of the single malt helped dampen the sharper sting of anxious feelings with which he never coped well. Mostly, it was fear. The same fear that chased him from his marriage into the younger flesh of a string of female techies that he obsessed over for months before actually initiating any close contact. Mostly, his efforts to cop a feel got him a slap in the face. Too soon, he figured, too whatever. At least he had the balls to take a chance.

He couldn't see the forest for the trees, was that it? Or maybe, he thought, it was just the reverse? That he could see the forest all right, the big picture, but got so damn lost dealing with any single female tree. One thing he knew, he was out of his depth when it came to a woman's demands. He detested complications, which usually didn't start until some time after the third or fourth date, if it got that far.

Randy took another swig of the scotch on the long straight-away heading north of Benson and switched on the vanity light beside the spacious rearview mirror. Swaddled in the comfort of German engineering and luxury, with fifteen-year-old Lagavulin single malt scotch whisky coursing through his veins, he gazed into the mirror and toasted himself. Randy still retained the boy-ish good looks at fifty that had served him so well with the ladies, in spite of his laboring through a dozen or so crazy, marital black-out years, medicating himself with maybe just a tad too much to drink. But who was counting? His ex-wife would have pushed anyone over the edge with all her demands.

Randy, the third in a direct line of illustrious scientists, was a highly regarded pharmacologist based in Indianapolis, Indiana, where he headed up the hugely successful Macalister Pharmaceuticals research laboratory. Randy loved his work, and he loved the attention, money, and respect it brought him, too.

Randy's grandfather, a renowned physicist in his own right, had done pioneering research on the effect of radium atoms on cell mutation. His only son, Randall Jr.—Randy's father—worked for DuPont in the 1960s on the lead team developing high-impact plastics and their derivatives for the military. When Randy was only a young teen, his family had abruptly pulled up stakes from their posh New Jersey residence and moved to the Midwest, where his father landed a job as a chemistry teacher at an all-boys private academy outside of Indianapolis.

Not exactly chasing the big bucks, nor was it a prestigious advance for someone in his late fifties who'd been a top researcher at one of the best labs in the country. Neither of Randy's parents had ever explained the reason for their sudden move, although he overheard his mother once say in a heated exchange with his father that it would all catch up with him one day and land him in hot water. Much later, when Randy went off to college, he learned from an aunt how the Creighton men always had their fingers in too many pies. Creighton the First, as his aunt had called his grandfather, had strayed from his marriage almost from the start, and done so openly, without seeming to care about the consequences or how much it hurt his wife or family.

Randy had accepted the position to head up Macalister Pharmaceuticals' advanced research division nearly ten years ago, overseeing a large team of technicians and scientists studying biological compounds that might lead to the eventual production of new lifesaving pharmaceutical compounds. The financial risks were high, but attaining lucrative new patents could mean a multibillion-dollar bonanza for the company, not to mention his getting a crazy-big slice of the bonus pie along with cementing his role as a major player in the next generation of world-renowned pharmacologists.

In simplified terms, Randy's particular specialty involved experimentation with potassium and sodium ions and the delicate chemistry that mediates the electrical transmission of nerve signals through a mechanism that operates at extremely fast speeds when all systems are functioning smoothly—speeds that allowed human beings every day to make instantaneous decisions that mean the difference between life or death, such as braking hard before running into a pedestrian, or outstretching a hand to cushion a fall. It was Randy's belief that these ion gates linking nerve cells held the key to treating nerve and muscular disorders and more. It was an important area of basic research at Macalister, one that could certainly lead to the development of better treatments for cardiac arrhythmias, multiple sclerosis, diabetes, and cancer, too. The research Randy headed up could also be applied to the mapping of the nerve pathways of chronic pain sufferers, which might lead to the development of new pain relief alternatives without the addictive side effects of opiates and their progeny.

Recently, Macalister had received a sizable chunk of NIH grant money to study the potential pharmacological benefits of a highly toxic poison called Batrachotoxin. Batrachotoxin, whose name derived from *batrachos*, the ancient Greek word for frog, was a highly lethal and naturally occurring secretion produced by the skin glands of a small tropical species, *Phyllobates terribilis*, more commonly known as the Golden Poison Dart Frog. An infinitesimally small dose of one part per million of the toxic substance could irreversibly prevent rodent nerve cells from activating properly. Injected into a lab mouse, the microdose would cause, at the nerve cell level, a total disruption of the ion gates, permanently locking them open. Without a working ion gate, autonomic nerve pulses would accelerate without check, leading to irreversible cardiac failure and death within moments. There was no known antidote to Batrachotoxin poisoning.

Indigenous to the South American rainforest, the brightly colored *Phyllobates terribilis* was guaranteed safe passage wherever it went. All creatures steered clear—except man. Through their ingenuity, the Emberá tribe of western Colombia's rugged rainforests long ago had learned to harvest the frog's secretion to coat the tips of their blowgun darts. A glancing skin prick from one poison dart is all it took to drop a twenty-pound howler monkey from fifty feet up in a tree. Within seconds of being nicked, the monkey would be in freefall, and its lifeless body would soon land with a thud on the forest floor.

Collecting enough golden frog skins for his laboratory's research needs presented Randy with a bit of a problem, though. Conservationists had become alarmed by the sudden decline of the frogs and successfully influenced the world's lawmakers to restrict all further trade in the wild-caught poison frogs. By international agreement, lawful trade in these protected poison frogs was a listed transaction, meaning no dice to his being able to openly harvest the little devils from the Colombian rainforest anymore. They were now a protected species, and the penalties for being caught were stiff. Worse would be the hit to his reputation, which in practical terms meant no more cash from Uncle Sam. No more attention, no more prestige, no more high flying.

Randy knew that the Pembroke Research Center at Calhoun Seymour University held a storehouse of legally harvested golden frog skins, kept frozen in liquid nitrogen storage. The frogs had been collected from the South American rainforest well before the restrictions in trade. Professor Shamus Ferguson, whom Randy had known since grad school biochemistry days at Northwestern University, headed up CSU's Pembroke Research Center. He and Ferguson routinely vied for funding and grants from many of the same private sources and government agencies.

Ferguson, the paranoid prick, wouldn't sell Randy any of the precious skins that contained the Batrachotoxin needed for Creighton's basic pharmacological research. Ferguson was an ass. An insecure, competitive ass.

Randy headed north on the highway back to Indianapolis, thrumming his fingers along the top of the steering wheel, feeling momentarily refreshed by the scotch and his outing with Miss Higginbotham. Out-of-office dating was a pleasant change of pace. Why hadn't he thought of it sooner?

His buddies in the squash court locker room were always shaking their heads at him, repeating their mantra: "Randy, you don't shit where you eat, man." But Randy's proclivities for too long had directed him otherwise, and as smart as he was, it took learning the hard way—suffering four HR complaints, two of which had been formally filed with state labor boards and had required $24,500 in legal fees, on top of steep fines and heady settlement dollars, to sweep under the rug. Even his lawyers had given him a hard time following his last misadventure.

Randy took another swig of the scotch just as his cell phone buzzed. The caller's name flashed across the A/V screen on the center dash.

"Speak to me, Harold." Randy's hands remained on the steering wheel at the ten and two o'clock positions. Bluetooth took care of the phone connection.

"Don't mean to bother you, Boss." Harold Bullock oversaw things whenever Randy was out of town at a conference podium. He'd been a tech at Macalister forever. "There's a guy from a Chicago FBI office that wants to speak with you—said it was urgent."

"FBI?"

Randy's foot suddenly came off the gas, a knee-jerk reaction, his mind whirling then catching on the fling that had turned into a near disaster with what's-her-name, he couldn't think.

He wiped his brow with the back of his sleeve. It was a blind date, and he'd driven her over the state line to that honky-tonk bar in Illinois a couple of weeks ago. She'd seemed willing enough. He'd just gotten a little rough while they were hot and heavy, in the thick of it, after maybe a little too much to drink and maybe a few too many lines of coke. It was all a little out of control, but fun. Maybe the green light had shifted to yellow though, before flashing red.

"I know. That was my reaction too." Harold's phone voice mirrored the same bewilderment as Randy's. "Said something about requiring your expertise, to quote the guy, but he wouldn't say any more than that over the phone."

"Oh. Good. Well . . . that sounds like it can wait till morning, then."

Creighton relaxed in his seat, the rush of paranoia fizzling out of him like a spent party balloon. He was off the hook. Here he was thinking that his number was finally up, when all the time it had only been the FBI seeking his expertise.

Hardly without noticing, he'd drifted into the breakdown lane and stopped the car. He finished off the whisky flask, sticking out his tongue for the last few drops, then tossed the flask back in the console bin.

"Leave the particulars on my desk, Harold. I'll ring him in the morning." He disconnected the call.

He was dating himself saying "ring him." What did it matter? They were calling him because they needed to speak with *him* because he ran the best pharmaceutical private research operation in the country. To hell with Linus Pauling and all the other Has-Been-Hero-Nameplate labs of the late twentieth century that populated the coasts east and west. He had more gene patents, more ongoing advanced research, and more NIH grant dollars overflowing the coffers than all of them combined, based right here in the amber waves of the grain heartland of America. And fuck that little Miss What's-Her-Name, making him worry that she'd ratted him out. He should have known better, should have seen it coming, that she was just another bitch out to set her hooks in him.

In the now dimmer twilight, a cloudbank to the west encroached then snuffed out the last shreds of sunlight. Rain was forecast. Randy upped his speed to outrace the storm, heading due north all the way home, doing his best to distract himself with thoughts of the lovely and lithesome Miss Betsy Higginbotham, a trace of whose perfume still hung in the Porsche's cabin air. But her perfume was fading fast, and he could feel the disturbance rising.

THE WINDSHIELD WIPERS could hardly keep up. Clyde's Outdoor Gear Shop stayed open till 10 p.m. on Wednesdays. He was nearer it than home and needed to pick up his special order of one hundred and fifty feet of 9mm braided Perlon rope. Carabiner clips and a couple of Quickdraw connectors that he used to hitch a rope to an anchor bolt were also on his list of things to purchase.

Trip pulled in front of the store. The dirt parking lot was deeply grooved by runoff from the steady torrent. He shook the soaking rain from the top of his jacket and stepped inside the store; smells of metallic filings and wood dust filled his nostrils. An exceptionally loud female voice turned his head toward the clerk's counter, where a short, muscular young woman was gesticulating with her arms while mouthing off about some exposed rock exploit of hers to the bearded clerk standing behind the counter and nodding politely.

Trip went to the rope aisle, listening to the woman go on and on about an extreme solo effort on a downstate limestone outcropping as if she were the only person to have ever climbed it. He studied different thicknesses, grades, and lengths of the silky rope. Just as he thought they weren't as good as what he'd special-ordered, a red 30% off tag hung next to a rack of Petzl headlamps. He picked one off the rack and placed it in his handbasket.

The woman wouldn't stop boasting. Her incessant chatter was grating on his nerves. She kept name-dropping difficult local climbing pitches that she'd already bagged, as if each of her exploits was a Hollywood actor she'd personally hung out with and fucked. Why didn't she get whatever it was that she came to the store for and get the hell out? Increasing agitation triggered a sudden buying compulsion and he treated himself to an assortment of rigging devices, including a spring-loaded cam that could be squeezed inside a tight crack in the rock to secure a hold.

Filled shopping basket in hand, he approached the counter. The young woman's strident voice hiked louder as she corrected the store clerk, who Trip knew to be an accomplished rock climber and guide himself. But Trip knew her real game. It wasn't the clerk she was toying with. It was *him*. All along that bitch knew Trip was overhearing every word she said, and there was nothing he could do to stop her pestering him.

The clerk looked at Trip, then held his hand up to the woman and said, "Excuse me a moment, ma'am."

He went back into a supply room and returned with the special order of braided rope and placed it down on the counter in front of Trip, then returned to the woman to finish tallying her purchases. The woman fell silent and turned Trip's way. Through clenched teeth he managed a serviceable smile—a rather poor attempt at public courtesy—as she quickly picked up her bag of purchases and left the store. Trip paid the clerk, slipped the rope coil over his shoulder, and headed out to the car with the bag of gear. The rain had abated and fog rose from the ground like shreds of steam.

"Hey, you wouldn't be a caver by any chance?" She stepped toward him, her legs scattering wisps of fog.

He stood at the back of his car, the rear hatch open. The sound of her voice stung his ears. He'd thought she'd already left.

"I noticed the sticker on your front bumper. I'm a caver too," she said in a friendly voice.

He didn't budge to greet her, gently hefting the rock hammer that he kept in the back. Some never learn, his grandmother would always say to him. They needed to be shown. He had been that way. He had learned his lessons the hard way. Karl had shown him only too well.

"Do you cave around here?" She stopped between her car and his, tucking her fingers in the back pockets of her jeans.

Trip squeezed the rock hammer's ribbed grip. He refused to look up; he wouldn't give her the pleasure of his acknowledgment. Quickly he slammed the hatch shut and got in his car. Through the spray of rain droplets across the windshield he watched her, shaking her head, walking back to her own car—a slant-roofed hybrid type—talking to herself. *Dismissing him!* He should have shown her the hammer. He should have told her to get the fuck off his damn back!

He started the engine, then sat back from the steering wheel waiting for her to leave the lot first. Dense ground fog from the soaking rains made for slow going. The headlights cast weak fuzzy beams only a few feet in front of his car. The hybrid's taillights twinkled dimly in the saturated air. Trip knew they were nearing the state road intersection. The faint red glow of the traffic light suddenly loomed above them. The hybrid's taillights gleamed brighter and the loud-mouth bitch started backing up her hybrid, making him do the same. She'd overshot the stopping line.

Trip heard a rumble over his left shoulder. The low beams of a large truck came lumbering at highway speed, approaching the crossroads. The truck had the green light. Trip switched off his car's own headlights. With only his parking lights on, he gently rode up close to the hybrid's rear bumper, then revved his motor, dropped the clutch, and floored it, billiard-balling the hybrid car directly into the path of the oncoming truck. Trip jammed on his brakes as the high corrugated sides of the tractor trailer flashed in front of him; it was a coal carrier with a full load, as it turned out.

But the woman had reacted quickly and turned her steering wheel hard to the right. The truck clipped her left side panel, sending the car into a vicious spin onto the berm of the road. Simultaneously, the truck driver had veered in the opposite direction in an attempt to avoid the collision, crossing the highway at a sharp angle, causing the truck's double-rowed tires to skid sideways, its airbrakes screeching, causing the full load first to careen and then tip over. The ground shook as the coal truck rolled down the steep embankment, dumping its heavy cargo in great thumping heaves. The sound of metal ripping and twisting could have raised the dead—mayhem wrapped into invisibility by the thick fog.

Trip weaved his car slowly around the trail of broken bits in the road and tucked in behind the smashed hybrid car. He got out with a flashlight. The hybrid had been crushed in two at the driver's-side door, like an empty beer can. The woman's body hung limply out of the busted passenger-side window. He shone the flashlight into her eyes. There was no pupil dilation. Her neck was clearly broken. He walked back to his car.

Still, her endless boasting bothered him. He felt certain that she'd gone to her maker thinking that she was a better caver than he was, more knowledgeable about down-climbing into a cavern under the press of a dead weight in tow. She could not possibly fathom how far out of his league she was.

Cautiously he drove across the highway with his window open, listening for sounds of oncoming traffic. But there were none, probably because of the late hour and poor driving conditions, he thought. Trip followed the coal truck's skid marks and then stopped. The ground was torn up where it'd left the highway and disappeared into the ravine that he knew was heavily ledged. He could barely discern the undercarriage of the overturned coal carrier through the misty air. Briefly, he listened for signs of life. He thought he may have heard a man groaning.

But that wasn't what was nagging him. He sat for a moment longer in the darkness, thinking. He'd been wrestling with it ever since leaving the climbing shop—even before ramming the boastful bitch's hybrid into the path of the oncoming coal truck. *He'd been seen. He could be identified.*

He couldn't return home yet.

Emergency vehicle sirens began to blare in the distance. He circled the car back the way he had come. Ten minutes later he stopped short of the lumpy dirt parking area that was covered in standing rain puddles. The lot in front of the shop was empty except for a lone Ford Ranger pickup. A decal adhered to its rear bumper advertised the shop and told him that the truck's owner was the clerk from whom he'd made his purchases earlier.

He got out and opened the back of the hatch, quickly cinching down the snazzy nylon loop of the rock hammer over his wrist. No need to waste a precious ring prick on him. Quietly, Trip clicked the hatch shut.

His watch read quarter to ten—fifteen minutes before closing time.

CHAPTER
EIGHT

THURSDAY MORNING, SHE rose at 6:30 sharp. After their late lunch at Shermie Dutcher's the day before, Christine had made a number of work calls from her room at the new Red Roof Inn. She and McFaron had agreed to meet at 8 a.m. for coffee at the inn. She showered and tucked a towel around herself amid spare no-nonsense décor, which included two wall paintings of Florida beach scenes that were bizarrely out of place; Red Roof's décor shipments must have gotten mixed. The thin layer of carpeting was depressingly cheap, but the room was clean and spacious, allowing her to spread out her papers. It suited her just fine.

Her phone rang before seven. "Good morning, Brian. I'd hoped you might call last night."

"Higgins went home early, if you must know. Said he wasn't feeling well."

"Sorry for sounding impatient. Nothing serious I hope?"

"No. He worked on it from home. In fact, we split up regional and nationwide retail store databases and worked until midnight."

Christine smiled. "Thanks, Brian. So what can you tell me?"

"The Tuff-Nuff brand climbing harness is sold extensively throughout the country at all the major outdoor chains and big-box stores."

Christine felt sure the climbing gear was purchased locally—

somewhere in the vicinity of the Starksboro, Illinois, and Benson, Indiana, university campuses. She instructed Eisen to contact stores from those locales first.

"There's one more thing, Christine. Pernell found something embedded in the tissue sample—fleck-sized, metallic. The consulting lab he uses for foreign material identification came back 24 karat gold."

It made sense that the injection source was from a metal tip. *But gold?*

"Pernell doesn't think it was postmortem contamination because the fleck was in the center of the sample. It may have broken off, striking the vertebrae." Eisen added, "Pure conjecture on our part, but—"

"Certainly plausible," Christine said. She flashed on the distinctive mark left on the back of Naomi Winchester's neck. It had been a penetrating blow. "After my examination of this second victim, consider it highly likely. And yes I will be sure Ernie Hansen, the Carbondale ME, performs a cervical scan. Was Pernell able to identify any lethal substances in the surrounding tissue?"

"No, but we've sent the sample to a lab in Indianapolis. Pernell knows a PhD in pharmacology there. It's called Macalister Pharmaceuticals. They specialize in identifying steroidal compounds and unknown alkaloids. Poisons can get pretty esoteric."

"Good. Stay on it, Brian." The call ended.

She tucked in the clean white blouse she'd packed in her forensic case before leaving Chicago three days earlier. Her navy polyester pants suit looked good as new after a rinse in the sink and drying on a hanger overnight. The miracle of synthetics never ceased to amaze her.

Christine pondered her next steps. Making a personal appearance at the Friday morning staff meeting less than three hours from now was out of the question. She'd definitely call Ned Miranda, but would wait until she was underway. Gaston might be angry with her for missing the meeting—correction, definitely would be angry—but Christine hoped that the branch director would soon realize she was saving her ass, too. The murders *were* linked. Should another female student come to be murdered because of their office's failure to investigate—as much as she hated indulging consideration of that eventuality—it would not bode well for Gaston's career aspirations.

Still, she'd wait until she was on the road to call Miranda.

Christine and McFaron shared a quick bite of crullers and coffee in the Red Roof's self-serve dining alcove. He informed her that a bad accident had occurred late last night on the highway leading toward Benson. A coal truck had collided with a car inside the Crosshaven County line. Sheriff Boynton had attended the scene with him since it involved a fatality, another CSU student.

"You're kind of quiet, Special Agent. That's not your usual . . ."

"Opinionated self?" she said sounding a bit morose, and then shrugged. "It's difficult enough just trying to do your job."

"Always is."

"So why can't people just leave well enough alone?"

"Let me guess, you're referring to your new handlers?"

She smiled. "Oddly enough, your choice of phrasing is an apt one. It actually does feel like I'm being handled."

"So when has that ever stopped you?"

She checked her watch. "You're right. It's high time I hit the road."

McFaron helped her load her bags in the back seat. "Remember what I said about the truckers."

"Right, they're hepped up on pills." She hesitated getting in the car. "Thanks for your moral support, Joe. And for going inside that cave with me yesterday, too."

Christine watched him get in his truck and tip his cowboy hat before backing out. On the road she passed shoots of newly sprouting corn. The air smelled sweet after the heavy rains, but it did nothing to improve her mood. After driving for half an hour, she passed a road sign indicating that Irasburg was just ahead, meaning she'd missed the turn for Benson. She made a U-turn and pulled over to the side of the road, inputting the destination into the GPS, which she'd neglected to do at the outset.

She flicked open her briefcase and took out a favored road trip CD—Bach's *Goldberg Variations*—and slipped the disc into the dash slot, then closed her eyes and let the piano recording elevate her mood. Music, much like the limbering rhythm of her backstroke down a lane of smooth water, relaxed Christine, framed life as a meditation, a mantra, not a series of detached and uncomfortable moments dealing with other people and their demands. If only she could pass the time listening to music or swimming laps, she'd do just fine.

She checked her wristwatch: 8:30 wasn't too early to place a call to Ned Miranda. He picked up on the first ring.

"It's Christine."

"The meeting's not until ten, you know. Couldn't it wait?" She'd obviously caught him at a bad time.

"Look, Ned, things got busy yesterday. I know I promised to make the staff meeting. However, I've missed my flight." There was silence on the other end. Maybe her catching him off guard was a good thing.

"What do you expect me to say to that, Christine?"

"These murders are definitely connected. No question. He's leaving his mark on them. Literally. This shouldn't come as a complete surprise. You consented to my examining the Indiana dead girl's body. And I did just that. As part of completing my preliminary assessment—"

"The deal was, Christine," he interrupted her, "you promised to be back in Chicago for today's staff meeting. End of story. As long as you are mentioning preliminary, I never did receive those preliminary notes you promised me? Of your unit's PTQP overview profile you had promised to fax yesterday? Or did you forget that too?"

Christine turned down the volume of the music. "What can I say? You're right. I'm sorry." She stared out her window into dense woodland that fell steeply away from the roadside. "The fact is I never did get to the fax machine at the sheriff's office."

"Now isn't that a surprise," he said, followed by silence.

"I'll call in on my laptop, in time for the meeting at ten," she said.

"You're pushing your luck, Special Agent."

"I actually believe I'm acting in the Bureau's best interest, sir." He didn't respond so she continued. "The deaths are definitely connected. If another young woman is murdered, how would that reflect on the Chicago Bureau? I would think *that* prospect should concern Director Gaston. Believe me, she won't want to deal with the kind of parental outcry that will surely follow should another young female student turn up murdered in her backyard, jurisdictionally speaking."

"Christine, you could have phoned me yesterday to discuss all this before missing your flight. But you didn't." Miranda's disgust still didn't have an edge to it. She took that as a good sign.

"I'll try to catch Patricia before the staff meeting," he said. "Tell her that you're wrapping up a preliminary assessment of the Indiana victim and that the local sheriff's department needs our forensic expertise. Stay close to your phone, please. I'll send you a pass code to teleconference in on your laptop." He clicked off.

That didn't go so badly. He hadn't read her the riot act. In fact, Miranda sounded rather reasonable considering that she'd be missing the staff meeting. Once she arrived on the CSU campus, Christine vowed to herself to draft an outline overview of her forensics staff's particular responsibilities. That much she owed Miranda.

"THANK YOU, BRIAN. I understand." Christine tossed the phone on the passenger seat and lowered her window. She'd hoped for traction, but still was getting nowhere. Eisen had called as soon as he'd heard the results of the lab tests run on Ellen McKinley's tissue sample. Inconclusive. Nothing positive detected for foreign substances. In actuality, "Inconclusive, unable to obtain valid results" could mean several things: that the sample was too small; or that the active causative agent, assuming one had been injected, was too diffuse to measure because it had probably already been fully absorbed by her system; or that the body had been contaminated from having lain *in situ* too long to recover anything useful from the dermis.

Ten minutes later Christine reached a large parking area. Two aluminum flagpoles as tall as the treetops—one flying the Stars and Stripes, the other the Indiana state seal—were flapping in front of the CSU Administration Building, an imposing edifice whose façade was quarried from local limestone that she knew was prized at home and nationwide for its dense uniform grain, perfect for monuments and the exterior facing for government buildings.

She asked the lot security guard for directions to the campus coffee shop, then parked and took the paved path he'd indicated, following a cluster of students. Caffeine and donut addicts, she imagined, needing their before-class fix.

She entered the small on-campus cafe, stood in the queue, and ordered a large latte with a raisin scone. She found a seat in the corner and took a sip of her latte.

A mellifluous classical composition played over the loud-speaker system—a Bach sonata, one of her favorites, featuring a violin solo that could always put her thoughts on pause. Christine leaned her head back and closed her eyes, actively listening. The string of rising and falling notes never failed to extinguish whatever worldly worry of the moment may be threatening. The music was better than any pill could ever be.

Christine opened her eyes as the recording finished. A student with wire-rim glasses was smiling at her from the next table, channeling her nirvana moment, no doubt.

"The *Sonata da chiesa*," she said to him.

He nodded. "Great stuff. You're a Bach fan?"

Christine smiled. "That would be an understatement."

"There's a concert on campus tomorrow night. Bach is featured."

"Really? Where?"

"Winkler Auditorium at 8 p.m. They hold student performances there every Friday night. The acoustics are great." He grinned and walked over, shouldering his book bag. "My girl-friend plays the cello."

"Thanks for the heads-up," Christine said. She checked her watch: 9:30 a.m. "Say, listen, would you happen to know a good place on campus with wifi to link in for a conference call?"

"Sure." He pulled out a campus map from his book bag and folded it open. "Here's where we are. There is where you want to go," he said, indicating a larger square centrally located on the map. "You can take this with you. I don't need it anymore."

"One more thing," Christine said. "Do you have a recommendation for a nearby accommodation, perhaps a place with a quieter atmosphere?"

"Sure do," he said with a friendly nod. "Le Maquis Auberge. My girlfriend's parents stayed there last fall and liked it a lot. It even offers a touch of country French cuisine, Indiana style, if you're into that sort of thing."

Christine smiled. "Perfect. Thanks for the suggestion. I'll give them a call."

Outside, the student turned and pointed her in the direction of the Student Union Building. Christine smiled and waved. The young man hurried off to class. She marveled at how helpful a perfect stranger could be. Perhaps it was the magic of life on a lovely wooded campus, pursuing your dreams. But things weren't all idyllic, and life could be downright deceiving, she reminded herself—which was why she was here in the first place.

AT 9:45 A.M., Miranda texted Christine the call-in number and pass code. She closed the door to the small study space on the second floor of the Student Union Building just as her phone screen lit up with an incoming call from Brian Eisen.

"Make it quick," she said without further explanation as she set up her laptop to connect online to the staff meeting.

"Higgins has done some research on the college caving club that found Naomi Winchester's body," her chief technician said. "There's a professor at CSU, a Shamus Ferguson, who is an avid caver himself and a founding member of the club."

Christine jotted down the professor's name on her flip pad. "I'm assuming you have something more interesting than just a name?"

"Possibly, yes. Naomi Winchester took an introductory cell biology course that Ferguson taught last semester."

"Was she a teacher's pet? Did she do any extra work for him? Also, look for any evidence that Ferguson may have socialized with her at school societies, meetings, or better still, privately. For instance, does he ever take female students caving alone? Does he have a history of dipping into the student body for personal pleasures, if you get my drift? Also, have Higgins do a deep background search on him."

"I'll get right on it."

It wasn't really that unusual, Christine reflected, a professor engaging in an inappropriate relationship with a student, as her own professor had with her when she was in grad school. It was pretty commonplace. But mere sexual impropriety, of course, was not what she was concerned about.

"Ferguson heads up a big-deal science center at CSU," Eisen continued, "called the Pembroke Research Center. It gets a truckload of federal grant dollars according to the CSU annual financial report filed last year with the Indiana state legislature. Land grant institutions of higher learning like CSU are taxpayer funded, so they've got to disclose every penny spent and received."

"Interesting." Christine pondered the thought. "Keep on him, Brian. Follow the money trail." Perhaps there was a larger context to the intrigue, and the murders represented just the tip of the iceberg. "In my experience not everything is recorded on the books. Not if there's something to hide."

"I'll keep you updated."

"Catch you later," she said. "And don't forget you're covering the staff meeting in my absence, right? You need to be there in less than five minutes."

"On my way now, boss."

Christine typed in the pass code to join the meeting online. She had volunteered Brian Eisen to stand in for her as a further showing of good faith. Miranda deserves that, Christine thought.

Waiting to be announced as joining the call, Christine jotted down some quick notes, listing each person on her team, underscoring their names. She began itemizing their expertise, the equipment operation, their scientific background and training, keeping at the forefront their oddball personalities, which to her were as much a part of them as their investigative skills. She drummed her fingertips on the desk, thinking how lost she'd be without each one of them, how none of the fullness they each brought to the table could ever be catalogued in a job description done in accordance with the Hayes-Stanley metrics, which she hadn't the stomach to wade through. It was hopeless, an absurd task. Managing her specialists and their particular needs and idiosyncrasies in accordance with the form's metrics would be like trying to herd kittens.

And of course she hadn't begun her own profile, either. Hadn't even looked at it, much less selected a password or uploaded the software onto her laptop.

The automated voice on the computer link interrupted her train of thought, announcing her name as now joining the call.

Her laptop displayed a jerky, out-of-focus image of seven men seated around a table and one woman at the far end. The red of Gaston's suit glowed brightly on the laptop's monitor, creating a strange halo effect around the branch director.

"Good morning, Christine. It's nice of you to join us via telephone since you were unable to work us into your busy schedule otherwise." Gaston's voice lagged fractionally behind the movements of her mouth.

"Good morning to you, Patricia. I've asked Brian Eisen to sit in for me. With his help and the others on my unit's team, we've been fashioning a rough draft effort which I hope to share with you soon."

Christine spoke while scanning her forensics remarks from the two postmortems, as if the notes represented her unit's particular profiles.

"Well, I am certainly glad to hear that you're making progress while away from the office, Christine. Of course, I should tell you that we've sent Mr. Eisen back downstairs to continue the work he is paid to do. I've asked only unit heads for updates on their reports, not subordinates. You are the unit head, not Mr. Eisen. I see you are looking at your papers. Perhaps you'd like to share a brief overview of your thoughts thus far. How are your direct reports coming along with their profiles? How are you coming along with yours?"

"On such short notice, Patricia, really I can't say very much in the form of an actual progress report." Christine's briefcase hit the floor and she muttered an expletive. "By next week I will have a more formal write-up pulled together to share. But in general, we are coming along fine."

"Perhaps I'll ask Francis Haskins of Statistical to speak first then. That will give you some more time to gather your thoughts."

Christine's cheeks glowed. The branch director wasn't going to let her off the hook so easily.

Christine spread the contents of her briefcase across the carrel desktop like so many puzzle pieces, searching for the piece of paper she'd used to write down directions to Dr. Ernie Hansen's morgue across the back of one of Patricia Gaston's podium handouts. She picked up the underlined names she'd written down and studied them as if they held answers of some sort.

"Christine?" Gaston's voice startled her back to the moment. "I think it would be helpful for the other unit heads to hear from you, given that you've found a way to manage this profile completion initiative long distance."

"Look, Patricia, truth be told, I'm having a hard time with the initiative in any practical sense, given the two deaths down here. All I can say is that my unit is working as hard and diligently as they always have."

"The point is, Christine, I haven't approved you for telecommuting on the job. You were quite clearly told that your first order . . ."

The laptop screen suddenly froze in a craze of small colored squares—mostly reds and browns—the blurred head and top half of Patricia Gaston fractured into the digital equivalent of an Impressionist dot painting.

Disconnected appeared across the top line bar of her laptop. Disconnected pretty much summed up Christine's feelings too.

She shrugged, then punched in Ned Miranda's cell number.

"Ned? The wifi's spotty here. I got disconnected. I'll put you on speaker."

Christine could hear Patricia Gaston's voice in the background, mid-command, instructing Miranda that she—meaning Prusik—must hand in her unit's draft job descriptions by next Friday. In person. On time. No exceptions.

"Did you get all that, Christine?" Miranda said brusquely.

"I heard. Next Friday. In Chicago. In person. On time. Draft plan in hand. No exceptions."

"No. I want you in the office tomorrow," he said. "There'll be a plane ticket issued and waiting for you at the Benson Airport terminal. See that you're on the plane later today."

Christine stared out a small window onto a campus pond where two male drakes were harassing a female duck who was flapping across the water in a zigzag pattern, trying to evade her pursuers. She let out a breath she hadn't realized she was holding.

"Okay, Ned. Listen, I have to get ready for an interview, a bigwig professor who heads up something called the Pembroke Research Center down here. He's tied to the caving club that discovered Naomi Winchester's body."

"Hold on, Christine. You've got no clearance to run a full-scale investigation. I thought I made myself clear." She heard a door close on Miranda's end. He must have stepped out of the conference room.

"You did, perfectly clear. I have to speak with him as a potential witness at the crime scene. He heads the caving club here. That's all. Hopefully it leads to getting a better fix on this killer's MO. Maybe I'll even get lucky with a clue from Winchester's roommate or one of her classmates."

"Whoa! Slow it down, Christine. I acquiesced to your doing a preliminary assessment of the dead body and crime scene only. You can't be doing a full-fledged investigation on the school campus like this. You just can't."

"Let me ask you, Ned, if it was your daughter or your sister working hard at college, preparing for a happy, productive life and she turned up on a cold hard slab—"

"This isn't a discussion we're going to have right now, Christine. Do you hear me? No school officials. No investigative interviews. She'll have both our heads." Clearly he hadn't shared any details of her whereabouts with Gaston.

"I know you know how to do your forensics job, Christine." Miranda dropped the edge to his voice. "But you and I both know Patricia's top priority at this moment is completion of the PTQPs. It doesn't matter whether or not you think they're important. Patricia does. Therefore, they are important. How is your team doing with them?"

She held her impatience in check and tried again. "Let me ask you something, Ned. The crime scenes show no obvious signs of a struggle. No witness reports, no suggestions even from the first victim's roommate that Ellen McKinley was even dating someone. They both seemed to have vanished into thin air. What do you make of that?"

She could hear Miranda breathing lightly into the receiver, considering her words. "Look, doing your forensics job doesn't excuse you from delivering your unit's report, Christine. Are we clear?"

"Yes. Abundantly. Now may I speak for a moment? These two women were both conscientious—their orientation to success links them somehow. What if highly motivated headstrong women of superior intellect are his trigger? What pushes the killer over the edge?"

"I'm sorry. We're not having this conversation, Christine. I'm advising you to pass your forensics notes and hunches to the local authorities and get busy supervising your direct reports. Be on that plane this afternoon. Report to me first thing Friday morning. With your own profile in hand. Don't disappoint me, Christine. I expect to see you tomorrow."

Miranda ended the phone call. He'd heard what she'd said but apparently didn't give a damn. Fortunately, Eisen had reached her before the conference call. He'd discovered a significant lead, or rather Paul Higgins had. Professor Shamus Ferguson liked caving and also ran a major scientific laboratory on campus called the Pembroke Research Center. And Naomi Winchester had been his student.

CHAPTER
NINE

TRIP STEERED THE car into the old barn that was set back several hundred yards from the road and well protected from view by a stand of hemlocks that grew behind the house. He closed both barn doors before turning on the spotlights that hung from the high joist beams.

Inside the car trunk, gear was grouped into neat piles. He took stock of items that were depleted. The clattering of a diesel motor sent him peering through the crack in the barn doors. A UPS delivery truck was parked at idle alongside the drive. He watched the deliveryman jog to the front door with the package—the new biopic field dissection kit from Fulton Scientific that he'd ordered for his upcoming trip, no doubt—and then return to his truck. No signature necessary, just as he'd requested.

Trip returned to the opened trunk and studied its contents. Hard-core discipline and thorough planning had gotten him this far. Not losing focus, no slipups—his grandmother's manservant Karl had taught him the consequences of slipups all too well.

When Trip was an adolescent, he'd thought that once he'd gotten older he would be able to defend himself against Karl. In the year between his sixteenth and seventeenth birthdays he'd grown five inches and put on muscle and he was sure the tide would turn. What he discovered instead was that he was still no match for the German manservant's brute strength. Trip realized then there would be no doorway in, only the daily struggle and Karl making good on his threats. It was as if he and Karl were immutably caught like the star in some as yet unnamed constellation, stuck in their respective, unheavenly positions: Karl, the explosively bright mass of swirling gas hovering in permanent place over the barely discernible cluster of the cosmos that was Trip.

Could stars ever break out of their constellations? Ever find a new patch of cosmos to inhabit? His adolescent self had often pondered the question as he gazed up at the shimmering night sky. It was as if two people lived inside Trip: one that couldn't seem to straighten up, and one that wouldn't—that needed to suffer, that enjoyed suffering. Those first five years he lived in his grandmother's house, Trip was stuck on this juxtaposition of selves. He blamed Karl's and his grandmother's negative reinforcement for his stalemate. Her constant harping and Karl's meting out corporal punishment as if on cue had discouraged him from ever trying harder. How could he make peace with the taciturn German whose predilection for neatness was exceeded only by his uncontrollable temper?

The answer came after a particularly hot July night that Trip had spent tossing restlessly on top of his sheets, unable to sleep, when dawn broke dim-lit out his bedroom window and gauzy humid vapors enveloped the bottoms of tree trunks in the deep woods behind his grandmother's house, as if woven in place by huge nocturnal spiders. Patches of low-lying mist hugged the banks of the Ohio River farther out, guaranteeing that it would be a nasty sweat of a day.

The hum of an insect had drawn his attention. A paper wasp

had landed on the window screen. Moments later, another alighted beside it.

Trip leaned his forehead against the window frame and gazed at the thick ivy that grew in a gnarly maze up the three-story mansion's limestone façade, making a welcome highway for the carpenter ants and everything else with six or eight legs that would come crawling into his bedroom whenever he wedged open the screen to let out the fetid air on extra hot nights.

There, affixed to the rain guttering beside his window was a paper wasp nest, a near perfect globe-shaped home to the stinging insects. He marveled at their workmanship and imagined that it would even appeal to Karl's rigid sense of perfection. While Trip stared at the wasp nest, he didn't know then that the stars were already realigning themselves.

Downstairs, Trip got out a plate from the cupboard for break-fast. A sunbeam pierced the acrid tobacco smoke hanging in a head-high layer in the kitchen. Karl's Chesterfield cigarette lay smoldering in a thick glass ashtray while Karl held open his daily rag with its scare headlines: HE SHOT AND STABBED HER TWENTY-SEVEN TIMES. Had the murdered woman for-gotten to neatly fold the bedsheets or keep her room spanking clean, Trip wondered?

"Good morning," Trip said, shoving two slices of bread in the toaster, drawing the German's attention. Karl didn't respond with more than a measured glance, then picked up a fresh pack of cigarettes, removing its plastic seal and tamping the pack lightly against the butt of his palm without so much as a word.

Trip cleared his throat. "There's a red squirrel nesting in the guttering beside my window on the driveway side."

"So vhat?" Karl hunched his shoulders, annoyed by the

interruption. It wasn't a good moment Trip had picked, with Karl preparing a fresh cigarette to smoke.

"No problem. I'm just letting you know," Trip said. "I heard it gnawing all night."

"Listen, squirrels can't eat true metal," Karl said with great Germanic irritation.

"Okay," Trip said, banking on the fact that Karl's was a physical universe ruled by action, not logic or words.

The toast popped up. Trip spread raspberry jam on both slices then headed for the dining room past Karl, whose face was hidden behind the newspaper again, a fresh Chesterfield wedged between his two fingers.

Trip heard the newspaper pages slap together and he froze, still facing the dining room door, holding his plate of toast.

"Dis squirrel, Trip, you say it is on dee driveway side?"

Standing absolutely still and without turning his head, Trip said, "Yes, the window facing the driveway."

Trip's bedroom was on a third floor corner of the large house, meaning the ceiling in his room sloped severely on one side following the roofline. One window faced the backyard, the other overlooked the driveway and garage bays.

The wasps' nest hung on the backyard side under the eaves, partially enveloped by the ivy along the guttering edge, in a place where Karl wouldn't be able to see it climbing the ladder from the driveway side.

After breakfast, Trip went upstairs and unlatched the hook on the window screen that opened out on the backyard side. A wasp landed on the screen. A shiver traveled up his spine.

The sound of the extension ladder banging against the side of the house dropped Trip into a soldier crouch against his bedroom wall. Karl's heavy footsteps began ascending the sectionals of the aluminum ladder. The manservant's straw hat appeared, his gloved hand tamping along the guttering, checking for damage.

Trip hunched himself as low as he could, acutely aware of the man's every movement. Karl's muttering in German grew louder—it meant he wasn't finding any sign of squirrel damage.

Quick as he could, Trip pushed open the screen on the far window that overlooked the woods. Wearing a heavy, long-sleeved flannel shirt and leather gloves, Trip fed his grandmother's old hook-handle cane out the window, took measure, and with his free hand pressed against the inside bedroom wall for added purchase, he gave it all he had, smashing the cane handle dead center, feeling its solid wood penetrate all the way through the basketball-size home to several hundred stinging insects that would search out and destroy the nearest evidence of who was to blame: Karl.

He dropped the cane and heard it bounce on the garden path three stories below before slamming shut his window.

One wasp clung to his heavy flannel shirt, uselessly stinging a thick fold of his sleeve. He mashed it between leather-gloved fingers before sinking back against the wall next to the driveway side.

"Trip . . ." Karl's gargled voice bore little resemblance to his normal authoritative one. Insects bounced against the driveway-side windowpane, strafing. Trip didn't dare look up. He stayed in a squat, leaning against the wall, listening hard.

Suddenly, the shadow of Karl's flailing arms projected onto the far wall above Trip's bed. At the same time, Trip heard a strangled cry and the metallic screeching of the aluminum ladder sliding sideways against the guttering.

A momentary silence stretched into what seemed an eon while the ladder and Karl were airborne. At last there was the unmistakable thud of six-foot-two Karl hitting the paved drive below, and the sectional ladder clattering afterward.

Trip thought he heard moaning. His chest heaving rapidly, he watched the second hand on his watch go fully round the dial twice more before getting to his knees and peering over the windowsill edge.

Karl's body lay sprawled, quite still, on the driveway, the back of his head haloed by a dark puddle of blood leaking from his cracked skull. Trip's nemesis of five long years was barely recognizable, his face was so ballooned with welts.

When Trip unhooked the breezeway door latch that led to the garage area, he was chased back inside, ducking and swatting; the wasps wouldn't let him anywhere near the body they weren't finishing punishing. Twenty minutes later the angry insects had to be fumigated by the EMT crew in order to load Karl into the ambulance. Trip had stood beside his grandmother on the back porch, watching the vehicle leave. Much later, after dark, he retrieved the cane, wiped it down, and returned it to its place in the downstairs hall closet.

His daily siege with the German finally over, when he went to bed that night he felt as if he were celebrating his own private VE Day.

CHAPTER
TEN

MCFARON RODE THE brakes. The Ford Explorer was engulfed in a whiteout. Houses and trees visible on the roadside only moments before suddenly vanished, as did all traces of the road in front of him. Slowly, carefully, McFaron pulled off the road. Travelers in this part of the state often met their maker at crossroads shrouded in dense fog patches like these.

He watched mist collect on the Explorer's windshield for a moment, and then called the office. Mary Carter rattled off a series of messages. An argument at Shermie's, but nothing urgent, which was good. He was having a hard time focusing this morning. Another young woman had been killed in his county, an apparent accident at a dangerous highway crossing on a fogbound night.

Sun spires suddenly penetrated the fog, and then lifted it. Crosshaven's desolate downtown—a hodgepodge of small stores—slowly appeared in the distance as if out of an apparition. He could see dark smoke belching madly from the spindly chimney of Shermie Dutcher's place. Shermie's was familiar, it was reliable, and the very sight of it brought the sheriff back to his senses.

Five minutes later McFaron opened the diner door as Dutcher, the cook and owner, shouted, "You'll answer to McFaron now!"

Dutcher eyed Pikey Arthur, an irritable gnome of a man who

was seated on a stool at the far end of the counter. The cook slouched over to the sheriff with hands on his hips and a dishrag over one shoulder.

"What seems to be the problem, Shermie?" McFaron said, placing his trooper hat on the counter.

"Mary didn't tell you? Motor Mouth here can't keep his cool. He threw a full cup of coffee at Barnesy and missed, hitting a perfect stranger. Now I'm short ten bucks for the cleaner's bill and the price of the meal, and probably short a customer, too. Good thing the coffee didn't burn the man, or old lamebrain here'd be in real trouble."

Shermie leaned raw knuckles on the counter and whispered, "Barnesy pushed the Piker, I'll admit. Got him stirred about something. Like he always does. Still no excuse for him to go losing his temper like that. Not in my place." He did a few circle wipes with the dishrag on McFaron's patch of counter.

Without asking, Shermie poured the sheriff a cup of coffee. Bags under the cook's eyes sagged heavily from years of drink. His face was an unreadable crisscross of lines and cracks.

"Thank you, Shermie." McFaron took a sip.

There was the sound of a toilet flushing, then Delbert Barnes appeared, zipping up his trousers.

McFaron cleared his throat. "Listen up, y'all. There's a young woman's body down at Doc Henegar's that by all rights shouldn't be."

The diner got quiet.

"Her body was found by some CSU students deep in a cave last Sunday. Some sick monster's idea of fun. Let me tell you it's *not* fun to have to talk to her parents or think about how she died. So I don't need to be coming in here to settle a beef between two damn fools. You with me, Barnesy? You too, Pikey? It's time for you to grow up."

McFaron put on his hat and left the diner without another word. At his truck door, McFaron heard the sound of quick steps coming up behind him.

"I didn't want to say nothing inside there, Sheriff, but I saw something last week, before them students found the girl's body." Arthur spoke rapidly, checking over his shoulder to be sure that no one else was coming.

McFaron rested one hand on his gun holster. "What's that you saw then?"

"I was walking old Duke, you know. It was the Tuesday before last, I'm sure of it, 'cause Shermie has his dinner specials on Tuesdays. Well, Duke's ears pricked up first. Then I heard it coming, too. This car came barreling down the access road along them state woods fast as lightning. You know the place where the trails start in?"

McFaron nodded. "I do."

"I jumped into the bushes before he could see me. Then, it went rushing right past me and Duke."

Arthur hunched lower on his haunches, as if reenacting the moment.

"Old Duke was whining awful fierce. It went zooming by the both of us, skipping up stones and dust and all."

"Did you catch the make of the vehicle?"

"It was black, with dark tinted windows, so I couldn't see his face. But it was a man all right. He was driving a foreign car, a hatchback type. I'd swear to it."

"That's good, Pikey. Real good," McFaron said, jotting notes in his flip pad. "Did you happen to catch the license tag?"

Pikey shook his head. "The dust kicked up pretty good. I only caught the first two numbers: a 5 and a 2." Arthur raised his fingers one hand at a time, saying each number.

If it was a 52, that was confirmation that the vehicle was registered in Benson County, where CSU was located, McFaron thought. The first two digits on Indiana plate registrations always indicated the county of the plate owner.

"Old Duke growled pretty loud when we started back down the road. And then I knew why, Sheriff."

Arthur stepped closer to the sheriff's Explorer truck.

"I'm listening," McFaron said.

"Old Duke cocked his head and looked at the sky. Made me look up, too. Over the treetops they were coming." Pikey played out his arms. "There were six, seven, eight turkey vultures spreading their black wings, hovering in tight circles over the woods, over that gully." He eyed the sheriff. "The same woods them students went caving in and found that girl's dead body. I knew it meant something bad."

"How would you know that, Pikey?"

"Because I ain't seen turkey vultures gliding like they meant it, over them woods this spring, not till then. They only show their faces like that, Sheriff, when something's dead."

"SPECIAL AGENT CHRISTINE Prusik here to see Professor Shamus Ferguson." She spoke into the speaker box mounted inside a glass vestibule that faced the Pembroke Research Center, waiting to be buzzed in.

She gazed through the reinforced plate glass entry. The research laboratory was impressive indeed, taking up all three floors of the modern facility. It was many times larger than her

Chicago branch's forensics lab. Glass-paneled walls on all three levels faced an interior lobby that gave it more the appearance of a luxury hotel than a scientific research complex. Christine could see technicians in hospital green gowns operating sophisticated instrumentation with lighted panels. Other techs wore elbow-high rubber gloves and worked under protective stainless-steel fume hoods. Machines and instrumentation like that took deep pockets. It was obvious that nothing had been spared in the facility's construction and layout.

Christine buzzed again, impatient for some forward motion. She'd just concluded an initial interview with Cindy Lawson, Naomi Winchester's roommate, at her newly reassigned dorm room. The room she'd shared with Winchester was sealed off with police tape, pending further investigation by the state crime lab and local sheriff's office. It aggravated Christine that she and her team hadn't already preemptively been granted priority access to the room under the FBI's jurisdictional authority. Instead she was left to monkey around the campus on her own, while running the risk of having Sheriff Rodney Boynton catch word of her presence. She had not sought out his official approval—which wouldn't likely be forthcoming anyway, considering McFaron's description of the man—for the same reason she hadn't invited McFaron along with her in the first place. The lighter presence of one law enforcement officer sometimes opened more doors than the more obvious presence of two.

She'd confirmed with Lawson that Winchester had indeed taken an introductory cell biology course from Professor Shamus Ferguson during the last term. Lawson couldn't say whether Ferguson had hit on her or ever asked her out on a date. If he had, Winchester had kept it to herself. Maybe the age difference would explain Winchester wanting to keep it a secret? There was no way to know for certain unless someone had seen them together.

One thing Lawson was certain about—if there had been any get-togethers between Winchester and Ferguson in late February or early March, it would *not* have included a cave outing. Lawson was quite emphatic saying that Naomi disliked caves. In fact, they'd spoken on the subject when Lawson had earlier shared a story about her brother and his best friend getting caught by a flash flood inside a nearby cavern. The waters had risen so swiftly all they could do was wedge themselves into a pocket in the cave's ceiling. It had been touch and go for more than an hour before the high water slowly receded. The story had made Naomi so nervous that she'd had to leave the room.

Lawson was quite sure that Winchester had left their dorm room close to 7:30 on the morning that she went missing, now more than a week ago. Lawson had heard the door lock click shut from her bed; shortly afterward, her own alarm clock sounded at 7:45 a.m. Lawson assumed her roommate was headed to the library before classes like she often did. If Winchester was planning to meet up with someone, she'd kept mum about it. A few other random bits of information emerged from the interview, but nothing of an obvious import.

Christine's phone vibrated. It was an incoming email message from Patricia Gaston. She clicked open the attachment:

To All Agents: Please remember to incorporate *SPARK!* Metrics on your *PTQP* profile reports. In preparing your draft profiles, **S**pecific **P**rompt **A**ccurate **R**ealistic and **K**een are the metrics as defined on the **Hayes-Stanley Worksheet** that will

get us over the finish line all winners! Thank you again for your
commitment to excellence!

Patricia.

Christine erased the email, then regretted doing so as soon as
she had. It would have been wiser to say something proactive in
response, to keep Gaston off her back, maybe even woo her to
Christine's camp.

She shrugged. *Y-uh, as if that's ever going to happen.*

A short stocky man with a crew cut and a scraggly red beard
opened the glass security door. He was wearing a green Tyvek lab
coat, unbuttoned, that revealed a T-shirt displaying a cartoon of
a bulbous-eyed winking frog with the caption: *Dendrobates croak
for a living.*

"Ms. Prusik?" he said rather dully.

She smiled and displayed her identity badge. He studied it
carefully then handed it back to her. His face was heavily freckled, as were the tops of his hands.

"My name is Jacob Graham. I'm Professor Ferguson's research
assistant. I'll take you to his office." His tone was decidedly neutral.

They rode the elevator to the third floor in silence and walked
down a long corridor along a bank of glass windows that overlooked a campus quadrangle filled with students milling on their
way to class.

Graham knocked on an oak door with a brass nameplate that
read *Shamus Aloysius Ferguson III.* Hearing no response, the research assistant poked his head inside the door. The office was
clearly vacant, papers strewn across a large oaken desk. Shamus

Aloysius Ferguson III had scrammed awfully fast was Christine's first thought. No wonder it had taken so long for someone to show her in.

"Wasn't he here earlier?" she asked. "You said?"

Graham nodded. "Yeah, he was. He told me to go fetch you a couple of minutes ago, ma'am."

Christine shrugged. *Fetch* sounded like a revealing choice of words to her. The kind of word used by a man who views women as inferior, or objects of scorn.

"Well, where would he have gone, Mr. Graham? This is a large complex and I haven't got all day."

"Are you looking for Shamus?" A young man in blue jeans torn at both knees wheeled out on his chair from behind a nearby cubicle. His T-shirt featured a graphic of a rainforest and the words *Columbia, S.A. Golden Frog Count 2015.*

Christine approached the sandy-haired student and displayed her badge. "And you are?"

"Tim Millard, a doctoral candidate here." He gave Christine an appraising look. "I'm guessing that you're not researching frog alkaloids, am I right?"

"Nothing's been ruled out yet, Mr. Millard. Did the professor happen to mention to you where he was going?"

Millard grinned, pointing at himself. "Mention his plans to moi? Wow, that'd be a first, wouldn't it Jacob? No. He left in a hurry with his coat and bag."

Christine looked at Graham, then back at Millard. "Do either of you have his cell number by any chance?"

Millard shook his head. "Heavens no. I'm about the last person in the world he'd share that with."

"Now why is that, Mr. Millard?" she said, none too pleased

with the grad student's easygoing manner, which seemed too jocular under the circumstances.

"Don't you know, Agent Prusik? He is an esteemed member of the CSU faculty, and we are but slovenly peons paid a mere pittance to do his bidding. We don't count except when Shamus is looking for the frog count, right Jacob?"

Graham shrugged and shot Millard a look that said, *Cool it*. "He's referring to the frog count results we're in the process of amassing for Shamus, ma'am."

"Is this about Naomi Winchester by any chance?" Millard inquired.

"Well, now that's a very good question," Christine said, putting down her briefcase. "Have you anything to share in that regard, Mr. Millard?"

"She was found in a cave, right?" Millard ventured.

Christine nodded. "Go on. I'm listening."

"Did you know Shamus was a founding member of the on-campus Hole Earth Club? In fact, I think it was someone in the club who discovered her body first. Shamus himself is a fairly serious weekend spelunker."

"You wouldn't be trying to implicate your boss, would you, Mr. Millard?" Christine said, surprised by his bald intimations.

Millard raised his palms. "Hey, I'm not accusing the man of anything, Special Agent Prusik. I try my best to limit myself to the frogs, ever since Peter Franklin's death. Though it's pretty common knowledge around the lab here that Ferguson has more than a fond eye for the ladies."

"Peter Franklin?" Christine paused. Millard was full of interesting information, but clearly he had something against Ferguson. "Who's Peter Franklin?"

"He was a grad student here a couple of years ago," Graham interjected. "He worked with us on poison frog research. He was found dead in his car in the parking lot right outside this building. The coroner's determination of the cause of his death was," he cleared his throat, "unsatisfactory to some of us."

Millard cut in. "The university will go to any length, spare no cost, I'm sure, in determining what caused Naomi Winchester's death. And yet it thought nothing of short-changing Peter."

"Why do you say Peter was short-changed, Mr. Millard?" Christine asked.

"Because he was in great physical shape, that's why. We'd run a 10K road race together the weekend before he was found slumped in his car seat. The coroner's report listed myocardial infarction as the most likely cause of his death." Millard shook his head, frowning. "I don't buy it. Not for one minute, not then, and not now."

"Why is that?"

"Because it was murder, plain and simple. Ferguson didn't want him staying on in his research job after Ferguson single-handedly denied him a spot for a doctoral candidacy at CSU." Millard threw a pencil down at his desk.

Graham stood by quietly.

"You seem pretty sure of yourself," Christine remarked. "I'm assuming the state police crime lab was involved?"

Millard rolled the chair back into his cubicle, then reappeared, standing this time. "Do you know what mimics a myocardial infarction almost as well as a myocardial infarction, Agent Prusik?"

"Sorry?"

"Poison dart frogs have a remarkable defense mechanism. They manufacture toxins ingested from an insectivorous diet in the South American rainforest, feasting on certain ant and arthropod species. These same toxins are then secreted through glands in their epidermis, coating their skins with a lethal sheen.

"Two micrograms' worth of this toxin rubbed across, say, a simple paper cut on your finger would result in the catastrophic failure of your central nervous system's ability to regulate your heart rate," Millard said. "It would make your heart speed up until the muscle itself could no longer beat, but only vibrate uselessly."

"You'd be dead in the space of less than a minute," Graham added rather matter-of-factly.

"Batrachotoxin is the active ingredient," Millard continued. "The most potent biological toxin known on Earth, and thankfully it is in rather short supply. No one's managed to synthesize it cost effectively yet, though not for lack of trying."

Graham disappeared inside Ferguson's office and returned with a scientific article. "You may find this interesting background reading." The reprint was authored by Shamus Ferguson.

"And this is what you think happened to Peter Franklin?" she said, waving the article at Millard. "That someone deliberately poisoned him with this toxin?"

Millard shrugged. "Easy enough stuff to obtain around here," he said, "if you're inclined to murder someone, that is." He expelled a long breath. "Peter was working in the lab that afternoon. He was fine, in good spirits. I was here. His family has no history of heart problems. I know. I asked around afterward. It doesn't add up. I ran with the guy most every week. We were close. Good friends . . ."

Tears welled in Millard's eyes. Christine softened toward him. "You tell me how a twenty-six-year-old who works out and runs regularly," Millard continued, "who has no history of heart trouble and none in his family, is suddenly found dead of a heart attack in his car? Oh, and if you're thinking drugs, none were ever found in his system. Peter didn't drink alcohol either."

"Tim, you didn't mention the lab break-in." Graham turned to Christine. "Three complete Dendrobatidae skins were taken from the liquid nitrogen canister room. Nobody really put two and two together at the time, Special Agent."

"Except you two, that is?" Prusik gave them a troubled expression.

"That's enough Batrachotoxin to kill a hundred people," Millard said. "Maybe more."

"The scuttlebutt at the time was that Peter may have—"

"That's bullshit and you know it!" Millard took a step toward Graham.

"It's only what I heard, Tim. Besides, we didn't actually learn about the missing frog skins till weeks later," Graham said. "It never came up. The police never really asked questions."

"May have what, Mr. Graham? You were about to say Peter Franklin 'may have'?" Christine prompted.

"Before coming to Pembroke, he had been a summer intern at this private lab up in Indianapolis, Macalister Pharmaceuticals. After not being admitted to the graduate program here, the talk around here was that he may have sabotaged the storeroom supply. Maybe to sell skins to Macalister. But no one really followed up on . . ."

"That's bullshit!" Millard interrupted. "I suggest you ask Ferguson just what became of those skins. And of Peter Franklin."

"That's not fair, Tim," Graham said, his face flushing. "Shamus was out of town at a fundraiser when Peter died. You know that."

"You mentioned earlier that Peter Franklin was denied admission to the PhD program by Ferguson personally?" Christine directed her question at Millard. "Aren't applications reviewed impartially by the university's admissions office?"

"Jacob, I'll let you respond to that." Millard shrugged and grabbed his book bag. "I'm a teaching assistant and have to earn my keep overseeing a bio lab class. Nice meeting you, Special Agent."

"Thank you for your candor, Mr. Millard." Christine gave him her business card. "Please feel free to call me if you have anything else you'd like to share. I'd appreciate it."

Millard nodded and left.

"Generally speaking," Graham said, clearing his throat, "you're right about the application process being impartially reviewed by committee vote. However, Peter's application for admission had already been declined. He was petitioning for reconsideration by the Academic Oversight Committee at the time of his death."

"Your friend there sounds pretty adamant about Ferguson controlling the outcome. Would you happen to know who else is on that committee?"

"Wait here a sec." Graham went into Ferguson's office. A minute later he handed her a handwritten list of names. "I could get in trouble for giving you this."

"I won't disclose how I obtained the information, Jacob," she said, "but I'd appreciate your identifying each of these names for me."

"Joel Abrams, he's a prof at the business school. Alice Catrall is from the sociology department. Steve Belknap's the history department chair, and then there's Shamus, of course, who heads the Pembroke Research Center and represents the biology department. The last name is Corbin Malinowski, who's a professor at the CSU law school."

"You wouldn't happen to know if the vote was unanimous, or a split decision? Were there any holdouts?"

Graham shook his head. "I only know these people were to convene because I had checked Shamus's calendar and he was planning to be out of town on a speaking engagement. His schedule conflicted with the committee's meeting time, which is why they rescheduled."

"This is very helpful, Jacob," she said. "One last thing. Could you get me the campus phone numbers for these professors?"

Christine smiled when he'd obliged. "Thank you again for your cooperation, Jacob." She picked up her briefcase, ready to leave, then hesitated and turned to him and said, "I don't suppose you happen to know an undergraduate on campus named Cindy Lawson? She was Naomi Winchester's roommate?"

Graham blinked. "No, I don't think so." His voice barely croaked out the words, his face flushing at the mention of the young women's names.

"Anyway," Christine said, "I spoke with her just before coming over here. She had the wild idea that someone may have broken into their taped-off dorm room and stolen some of her dead roommate's private items. It appears the police tape had been tampered with."

In fact, the police tape had appeared to her untouched; she'd found, however, that pitching lies at interviewees could sometimes uncover truths.

"I don't know anything about that, ma'am." His freckled face flushed an even deeper shade of crimson.

"Yeah, well it's probably just a case of nerves. Having a roommate die on you is pretty scary stuff. I just thought I'd ask. Again, thank you for your time"—she waved the reprint article—"and for providing me a copy of your boss's poison frog article, too. I'm sure I'll find it interesting reading."

The research assistant buried his hands deeper inside his lab coat pockets, studying the floor intently, his ears glowing like embers. Graham was a hard man to read. One moment he was taciturn, the next he was reminding Millard about the frog skin theft from the lab. Why even bring it up unless he was trying to deflect attention away from something else—but what? And his display of shameful embarrassment when she'd mentioned Lawson's name, was it shyness or guilt? Did he know more?

Graham glanced up at Christine's face, making brief eye contact. "It's been pretty upsetting having two women on campus die in the same week."

"*Excuse me?*" she said.

Graham vanished again into Ferguson's office and returned with a copy of the day's local paper, the *Benson Gazetteer*. An article on the front page described a horrifying highway accident at an intersection involving a CSU student named Jane Pirrung, whose hybrid car had been struck broadside by a fully loaded coal carrier late the previous night. Christine then recalled McFaron saying he had to visit the scene of a deadly car accident that involved a CSU student.

Christine asked Graham a few questions about Pirrung, whom he hadn't personally known beyond overhearing his boss mention that she was a member of the same on-campus caving group that had found Naomi Winchester's body. Graham said she could keep the newspaper.

After leaving the research center, Christine sat down on a

bench to collect her thoughts. She would pursue interviewing the members of this Academic Oversight Committee, and the first person she would seek out was the last name listed: the law professor. Lawyers were always cautioning people, giving advice that could be influential in the process or at least carefully considered by others on a committee. As for Jane Pirrung, the college student's death was added to the list of things she needed more information about.

CHAPTER
ELEVEN

THREE DAYS AFTER they had carted Karl's body to the city morgue—his face ruthlessly swollen from the countless wasp stings—a Sergeant Simrell stood at the back door and flashed his badge at Trip.

"Your name's Trip, right?" the cop said, motioning for Trip to follow him back outside into the driveway.

Trip obeyed the cop. The sky was an electrifying blue. High pressure had lifted the humid dank air; even the Ohio River had a silvery gleam far below them. A puffy cloud reflected perfectly in a placid bend of its vast reaches.

"Your grandmother says that you and Karl didn't exactly see eye to eye." The cop started right in with his root-out-the-bad-guy routine.

Trip nodded. "He was strict, I guess."

"Show me exactly where your room is?" the cop said leaning his head back, gazing upward at the ivy-encrusted window of the three-story mansion. The prick already knew where his god-damn room was, Trip thought.

Trip pointed to the small third-floor window choked by the ivy that clung to the limestone façade and grew especially thick on the driveway side, where the sun rose every morning.

"So he was cleaning out the guttering, you say?" Simrell said, jotting down a note in his flip pad. "Your grandmother said you'd told her that Karl climbed up there on a ladder because you told him the leaves were clogging it up, right?"

"Yeah . . . I suppose," Trip stammered.

"Then you did see him lying on the drive afterward, right?"

The unrestrained eagerness in Simrell's voice annoyed Trip. It was as if the cop had some kind of upper-hand move underway that Trip couldn't see coming. *But what?*

"Ever open the window in your bedroom that looks down on the drive, Trip?" Simrell looked back up at the ivy-encrusted double-hung.

Trip shrugged. "Yeah sure, when it gets hot in the summer-time."

"Like now, for instance, this July heat wave we're having. You open it now, don't you?"

"At night mostly, yes. I open it. The third floor gets pretty stuffy under the eaves."

"I bet it does."

The cop leaned closer, eyeing him with a grin. "You ever get so mad," the cop said in a sneaky little voice, with his eyebrows raised for effect, "that you want to give the prick a shove off his fucking ladder?" Simrell flicked Trip's shoulder with his index finger.

"I didn't do anything. So what if I didn't like him?" Trip answered defensively.

Sergeant Simrell grinned. "Yeah, I bet. I know the type. Always checking the soles of your shoes for dog poop before you go tracking it all through the house, am I right?"

Before Trip could respond, Simrell leaned in. "In fact, it's no secret at all that you hated the man's goddamn guts."

The accusation caught Trip off guard. His eyes rested on a darker smudge on the driveway, a bloodstain from Karl's cracked head that the previous night's rains hadn't completely washed away.

Sergeant Simrell put an arm around Trip's shoulder in a gesture that Trip took to mean anything but empathetic concern, and walked him farther out into the driveway.

"Now show me again the route you took for a walk in the woods while Karl lay bleeding to death here?"

Trip pointed toward the garden fence. "There's a path that leads from the garden on the other side of the gate. By the patio door, it goes straight down into the woods from there."

The cop shoved back the brim of his hat, flipped back a few pages of notes, checking something.

"Thing is, Trip, that doesn't jive with your grandmother's statement at all. She was gardening at the time and said you never showed your face on the patio. So you couldn't have come through that gate, could you? She would have seen you for one." The cop flipped out one finger.

"And, for two, we both know that's a load of bullshit." He flipped out a second finger for effect.

Trip kept his head down wishing there was another nest of wasp pals nearby that he could smash over Simrell's fucking know-it-all face.

"Your story's crap, Trip, just say it," the cop continued. "You had to have gone out by the back door; seen Karl all busted up and stung right in front of you. Yet you did nothing. You didn't tell your granny. You just took off into the woods?"

Trip took a step back. "It's not crap."

The cop flapped the notepad against his thigh, obviously

dissatisfied. "You're going to stick with that line then? What's it going be? Huh, Trip?"

The cop started walking back and forth now in front of him, recycling through Trip's statement, pointing out the holes in Trip's version of events, but really all the while trying his darnedest to get Trip to slip up, to admit to the fact that he'd caused Karl's death. That he'd brought it about. But really, it hadn't started with him. It had started with Karl. Karl had brought everything on himself.

The cop's hand suddenly flopping on his shoulder took him for a start. "Hey Trip, thought I lost you there for a minute."

"I don't know. You might be right. I guess I did go out the back door then," Trip relented, not caring anymore what this cop was driving at. Nothing this cop was fishing for mattered anymore to him. Karl wasn't ever going to thump his way back up the stairs for another room inspection, he was never going to mete out another punishment. Not in this lifetime. Not ever.

"Then you did see him lying on the drive, right?" The unrestrained eagerness in Simrell's voice was pathetic.

Inside, things had already shifted. With Karl out of the picture for good, Trip was in control, not this loser cop.

"I might have seen the end of the ladder by the hedgerow," Trip said without hesitation. "But that's all."

It hadn't made Trip flinch one damn bit seeing the dead German sprawled and bitten on the driveway. Raised yellowish-white welts had covered Karl's exposed flesh where the wasps had repeatedly stung, puffing up so fast that his features were unrecognizable and his skin no longer resembled human skin. He knew then there'd be no Karl coming back for him, no more strangleholds, no more face slams into the linoleum floor at scuffmarks he'd left on Karl's fresh wax job. No more Karl twisting his gut in knots.

It was a done deal, no matter the antics of this keystone fucking cop.

JACOB GRAHAM GAZED down at the quadrangle from Shamus Ferguson's office, watching the FBI agent get up from the bench outside the Pembroke Research Center. His eyes followed her movement down the paved walkway until she disappeared into the wooded campus in the direction of the main liberal arts buildings. He figured she was off to interview one of the teachers on the committee list he'd given her.

Graham hurried down the hallway and slid his access card through the elevator's electronic reader, repeatedly pressing the *Down* button even though the display panel lit on the first press. After a minute, the doors of the large freight elevator eased open. Protective quilts covered its sides to safeguard bulky machinery and other lab equipment traveling from floor to floor.

The elevator bumped to a halt upon reaching the basement. Graham slid his access card through the electronic reader again, activating the doors, which slowly yawned open. He stepped into the dark hallway, triggering the motion sensors, and a bank of overhead fluorescent tubes flickered to life.

He stopped in front of a door marked B-6, slid his access card through the slot, and entered a storage room stacked high with boxes marked with black arrows: THIS SIDE UP. Against one wall was metal shelving piled with scientific journals and papers.

There were no windows to furnish natural light in the storage room as the basement was below grade. Graham's shoulder grazed a stack of cartons stamped *FRAGILE!* in red ink. Test tubes jostled inside. He steadied the boxes, then advanced to the far corner, watching his feet under the increasingly bright glow of a desk lamp.

The imposing figure of Shamus Ferguson sat hunched over a desk, proofreading an article he'd coauthored on the synthesis of Batrachotoxin and other complex analogs. The professor swiveled his chair around and faced his lab assistant. "So, is she gone?"

"Yes. I just watched her leave." He rubbed his sweaty palms across the fronts of his pant legs.

"Good, good," Ferguson said quietly, studying his research assistant. "Anything I should know?"

Graham cleared his throat. "She was pretty pissed that you weren't there."

The chair creaked under the professor's weight. Ferguson sawed an index finger across his bristly moustache, thoughtfully eyeing the nervous grad student. "Is this going to be a problem, Jacob?"

Graham dug his hands into his lab coat. "I don't think so."

"Oh, phew, all's taken care of then." Ferguson's words were heavily inflected with sarcasm. "You don't *think so*? What did you say to her?"

Graham leaned a hand against a wall shelf, as there wasn't another chair. "Honestly, she's grasping at straws. I can take care of this if she comes back. Trust me."

Ferguson flicked the back of his hand dismissively. "I very much doubt that." He squinted at Graham. "What do you mean, take care of this?" Ferguson rocked forward in his chair. "What exactly did you say to her?"

Graham's crotch tightened uncomfortably. "It was Millard. He overheard us speaking—the FBI woman and me. Millard butted in, I couldn't stop him. He gave a rather impassioned defense of Peter Franklin."

Ferguson slammed his fist hard on the desk, rocking the lamp. "What is it with you people? Since when do I hire assistants to spew vagaries at snooping cops!"

Graham nodded. "I know, I know, but Tim got pretty choked up. Made it all personal sounding, said there was a cover-up—the way Peter's death was handled. You know, by the university, the police."

Ferguson clutched the sides of the desk in frustration. The professor was a large man subject to frequent volatile outbursts. With this FBI woman poking around, asking questions, Graham feared that an explosive tirade was imminent.

"What else, Jacob? I haven't got time for this. Spill it all out now!"

"She asked about the Academic Oversight Committee. She wanted to know who was on it and what I knew about Peter's getting denied."

"Jesus H. Christ, Jacob! How in God's name did she even know to ask about the committee in the first place?"

"I told you. Millard raised it, telling her that Peter was denied a doctoral spot. It sounded like he had a vendetta against the university, the way he went on." Graham wiped his forearm across his beaded brow in the cool basement air. "So I felt obliged to get her the list. I thought cooperating was the best thing, you know, for damage control. I, I didn't know what else to do since . . ."

Ferguson nodded. "Yes, yes, I get it." The professor gave a wave of his hand. "I left you there holding the bag."

"She'll be back," Graham said. "No question."

"Well, obviously," Ferguson said gruffly. "What else? What else do I need to know?"

"I told her about the other girl, the one in today's paper. I gave the FBI woman the newspaper that was on your desk."

"Now why on earth would you volunteer that?" Ferguson leaned forward threateningly.

"To get her off any more questions about Peter and the Winchester girl, that's why. I think it may have worked too."

The professor's left knee began to jiggle violently. He cocked his head to one side, weighing things. "Well, it *is* public knowledge, the car accident. I can't see why telling her about something that's already reported in the paper would matter one way or the other."

Graham nodded. "That was my thinking, too. She did seem very interested in the accident when I mentioned that Pirrung was an avid caver. I directed her to Sheriff Boynton if she had any further questions."

Ferguson grabbed Graham's shirtfront tightly, pulling himself to a stand and, in the process, ripping off one of Graham's shirt buttons. The research assistant rocked awkwardly into his boss. "What did I tell you about volunteering information? It's not the first time we've had words about this, either!"

"No, sir. I'm sorry. I was only trying—"

"Do you hear me? No volunteering information! I don't pay you to feed the goddamn FBI. Now get the hell out of my sight."

A few minutes later the grad student headed to his car in the parking lot. Given Ferguson's foul mood, Graham hadn't told his boss about the FBI agent's suggestive comments asking him whether he'd entered Naomi Winchester's room. He was sure that the policewoman had only been fishing. Even so, it bothered him—her pushing him like that, all because Shamus Ferguson had dodged her. And then afterward, Ferguson's holding his feet to the fire for mostly his own goddamn shit put Graham into a blacker space.

He checked the car trunk to make sure his gear was there. He didn't want to drive all the way out to Nick's Indoor Climbing Wall only to find that he'd left his kit bag behind at his apartment. The nylon duffel was there next to the new pair of pro climbing shoes that he'd purchased off the internet and hadn't yet tried out. After a solid hour-long workout on the chalk bag, scaling the artificial foot- and hand-holds, contorting and stretching his muscles to the limit, he would lose himself. Then he'd do it all over again until no one—not the FBI woman nor Shamus Ferguson—could touch him.

CHAPTER
TWELVE

RAUL GAVE A friendly wave to his neighbor, the elderly Senora
Sanchez, who returned his good manners with a distrustful hawkish stare. The man kept his cool, smiling and bowing politely to
her without explaining the long roll of foam rubber tucked under
his arm. Once inside the wooden gate of his fenced property, he
went directly to the back shed, hidden from view behind several
Mexican fan palms and a chicken coop.

Raul keyed open the padlock. Inside, cozy fluorescence bathed
him from the opposite wall, where two banks of large terrariums were stacked five high on a makeshift framework that Julio,
a steelworker, had welded together for him last year. The foam
rubber was material for the two brand-new terrariums. He was
running out of space. Farming the creatures, Raul had discovered, was second nature to him.

His internet business had skyrocketed in the last year with the
passage of the trade law banning the import and export of many
different species, jacking up the prices on his specimens. It was
all good news for him; he could hardly keep up with the orders.
Already he had his eye on a remote piece of land on the edge of
town that was for sale, a site that would offer privacy, where he
wouldn't suffer from Senora Sanchez's suspicions. But who could
blame her? It was no real secret that just three years ago he'd been

a mid-level smuggler transporting illegal drugs packed in coffee tins, taking all the risk without reaping any of the reward.

Then he'd met Jose, who'd started him in the live specimen trade, a lucrative business given the large number of Norteamericano aficionados of rare tropical rainforest amphibia of the order Anura. Family sickness had forced Jose back to Costa Rica, and Raul had just finished making the final payment to him, buying out the man who had introduced him to a better way of life. It was less hassle, too, and it went without saying that the clientele did not present the same danger as his drug clientele had.

He unrolled the foam rubber on his workbench. The ten existing glass tanks were already overflowing with multiplying specimens. Cleaning them weekly was critical in order to avoid premature deaths from disease and overcrowding. But it was very dangerous. "Muy peligroso," as Jose had repeatedly cautioned him.

The two new terrariums would relieve the overcrowding and improve sanitation, not to mention help foster his rapidly growing business. He took his shears and proceeded to cut the foam, already knowing the precise measurements. He fitted a drain hole with a metal grate covering in each tank to ensure the correct humidity; maintaining the proper moisture level was critical.

Raul placed the cut foam in the bottoms of the glass terrariums and soaked them with distilled water. Fully one third of each tank he partitioned off for a small water trough for the tads and young froglets. The rest he covered with humus and living mosses, tree bark and leaves, simulating a rainforest in miniature. He finished off the décor with sphagnum moss and a tree branch under which the shy creatures could hide.

Across the room Raul kept several brightly lit vertical tanks in which he reproduced fruit flies and crickets, the principal food stock. He filled a long plastic collecting tube with a hundred or so mature fruit flies, drawing them up the tube's length with a swab of honey dabbed at the far end. Carefully he emptied the live flies into his ten active tanks.

The leaves of small bromeliad plants inside the tanks stirred to life as his growing colony crept toward the food source.

"Muy bueno, niños." He took a moment to watch his eager chargers devour the delicate flies, then refilled the collecting tube twice more and completed the afternoon feeding. One terrarium contained four adult breeding pairs that he fed a handful of live crickets.

He affixed the temperature and humidity gauges and then fitted the new fluorescent lighting inside the hood covers that would rest over the terrariums. A few more botanical details and he'd finished out the new tanks for the now twentieth—or was it the twenty-first?—generation. The froglets' tails had shrunk to mere stumps now; in another year they would reach adult maturity and he could use them for breeding purposes.

Raul pulled on a fresh pair of elbow-high rubber gloves and carefully scooped up the froglets one at a time, then transferred them to their new tank. In the wild, the adult frogs often would piggyback their young, one at a time, to a new water source, he'd read online. Now he watched them settle in, like a conscientious father gazing at his offspring nestling in the cradle.

Raul could see that his young brood wasn't stressed by the move. He smiled. With all the equipment he'd invested in to date, including the laptop and his payoff to Jose for the business, it had taken Raul only two years to recover three times over in earnings. In the last month alone he'd filled seven orders: two through

PayPal accounts and the rest in cash. He preferred cash. But he'd needed to open a local bank account with his newfound gains. PayPal was a part of doing a growing international business, and he was building credit for the loan he'd need in order to buy the property he wanted for expansion and greater privacy. *Gracias a Dios* for the café by the plaza with the strong wifi signal that made doing business easy.

The gringo from Benson, Indiana, had already deposited two thousand pesos in the PayPal account to hold his order for three live adult-phase specimens. He had emailed Raul to say that he would be traveling to Oaxaca in a few days and would pick up his order in person. Raul had responded with instructions on where to find Pablo, his runner, who would direct the man to the meet.

Raul was plenty savvy at bargaining with gringos, but he did not seek the attention of the Federales either. As a rule he chose not to do a repeat business. There were plenty of new customers. He didn't want to draw unnecessary attention. No need to bring more Senora Sanchezes to his doorstep, snooping.

Raul knew that raising rana dorada, or the golden frog, required extreme care, and he had religiously followed Jose's sternly repeated warning: "sin contacto fisico"—no physical contact. Disturbing the golden frog in transport or when cleaning its habitat could cause it to release its powerful toxins and kill him if he got careless. He went through three pair of kitchen gloves every week, as they could develop fine cracks and allow the frog's highly toxic skin mucosa to seep through and come in contact with his own skin. He chose to wear the elbow-high gloves. His hands sweated more inside them, but in two and a half years of raising and breeding many broods he'd been safe and had never come in physical contact.

Raul enjoyed the danger. But mostly he was proud of his precious brood. Some gardeners had green thumbs. Raul's was golden.

TWO MASSIVE SYCAMORES guarded the imposing edifice; their gnarled root caps bulged above grade and appeared to clutch the ground like the talons of a monstrous bird of prey. Christine approached the broad limestone steps of the Herman B. Miller School of Law, its name carved in the stonework above the entry.

Students armed with briefcases and laptops moved quickly up and down the hallways and stairwells. She joined the throng and took the staircase to the second floor, easily locating room 213.

She knocked and at the same time poked her head inside the door. A distinguished-looking gentleman was seated behind a large walnut-veneered desk. "Professor Corbin Malinowski?"

"Yes, I am he." The man rose and greeted her with a pleasant smile. He walked around to the front of his desk, favoring his right leg. "And who do I have the pleasure of addressing?"

Christine closed the door behind her and held out her hand, which he firmly shook.

"Special Agent Christine Prusik with the FBI."

"Please, won't you have a seat, Agent Prusik?" The professor looked fit, of medium height—five nine or ten, she guessed—and he had a full head of silvery hair and a matching pencil-thin Van Dyke goatee. His brown herringbone suit fit him nicely.

"I appreciate your seeing me unannounced like this. I should have phoned you first, I realize." She glanced at the manila folders piled on his desk. "I hope I didn't interrupt anything important?"

"No, no, it's quite all right," he said. "I'm not urgently needed at present. Please do sit."

Christine placed her briefcase on the floor and sat in the leather chair he indicated. He pulled his own chair around to sit closer to her, and then hoisted with both hands the same leg he'd favored over his knee.

Upon sitting, she immediately became aware of a familiar concerto playing softly on a small stereo system on the professor's credenza. "How nice. Brandenburg's Second."

"Yes." Malinowski held up a finger. "There, hear the trumpet?" He danced his hand to the tempo. "A finely structured composition with such a divine integrity, yet so accessible," he added. "Very listenable, do you not agree?"

"Absolutely I do. It's a particularly strong fugue," she said, "and one of my favorites, too. I understand that the music school here is holding a performance tomorrow night with some Bach on the program."

Malinowski nodded. "Yes indeed it is, and I shall be there. I've a season's pass." He rolled his eyes playfully. "It's one of the main compensations for being a university professor here, especially given the high cost of attending concerts in the big cities nowadays." He leaned his head closer toward her. "We're really quite spoiled here. The music program is world-renowned, you know."

"So I've heard. It must be nice working on such a beautiful campus and having access to top-notch classical music concerts." As the score's tempo slowed in transition, readying for the final heralding of the horns, Christine found it difficult to keep her smile in check.

"I see that you are as much of a fan as I am. You should consider attending. If you are planning to stay on with us, that is," he said.

There was an abrupt noise at the door. A student barged into the office without knocking. "Sir, Professor Malinowski, I need to see you about this grade on my seminar paper. I have an interview in Indianapolis early tomorrow for a summer internship. Sorry, I didn't call first."

Malinowski gazed icily at the student. "Mr. Edwards, can't you see that I'm busy here?"

The law student looked imploringly at Christine. "I'm sorry, ma'am, for the intrusion, but—"

"There are no appointments without prior arrangements, Mr. Edwards, as you well know. Leave us *now*."

The student scrolled the paper tightly and left without another word, shutting the professor's door quietly behind him.

Malinowski turned toward Christine. "My apologies, Agent Prusik, for the interruption. All of my students know the rules." He smiled pleasantly. "So where were we? What would the FBI like to know from me today?"

Christine took out her notepad, appraising Malinowski as a stickler for detail and someone who did not like to be pressed. "I'm here principally concerning the recent death of a CSU student, Naomi Winchester, who was found dead in a cave not far from here, Professor."

"Ah, yes." Malinowski's face grew somber. "I saw the local news broadcast a few nights ago, a recap of the sad affair. I don't imagine," he spoke in a softer tone of voice although his door was closed, "that any other topic has so gripped the campus here than that poor student's demise has."

"Did you know her?"

"No, not personally," he said. "She would have been an undergraduate, not a law student. Let me revise that statement. I have taught an undergraduate course or two from time to time, when asked. Civics, mostly, and I did teach a course on challenging legal issues presented by modern scientific advances last year as well."

Christine nodded thoughtfully. "Okay, good. Does the name Jane Pirrung ring a bell, Professor?"

He paused for a thoughtful moment. "No, I'm afraid that I've never heard her name before. Should I have?"

"You'll have to excuse my tendency to pop out with questions like that. Apparently, another CSU student was killed in a serious road accident last night." Like second nature, she studied his face for any reaction. But there was none.

He shook his head slowly. "I'm afraid I can't help your inquiries there either, Special Agent Prusik." He leaned forward, lacing his fingers and resting his hands on one knee in a relaxed pose.

"No worries. Actually, there is something you are familiar with and that you can help me on. I understand the Academic Oversight Committee meets regularly here at the university?"

"Yes, it does," he said with a quizzical expression.

"And you are a member of the committee?"

Malinowski smiled. "It appears that you already know that I am, Special Agent. I should warn you that I am not at liberty to discuss any questions you may have regarding a specific student or students for reasons of confidentiality and school privacy policy."

"Understood," she said. "However, in this case the student is dead."

Malinowski's brow wrinkled in puzzlement.

"Peter Franklin? Do you recall his name?"

Malinowski looked puzzled. "I thought you said you were investigating Naomi Winchester's death?"

"Principally, yes, but if you wouldn't mind bearing with me for a moment, Professor, I think it will become clear."

He nodded in assent. "You may call me Corbin if you like. Any help that I may be to you, I am more than happy to oblige."

"Why thank you, Corbin. Please call me Christine." She flicked her short hair behind one ear. "I understand that Peter Franklin was applying to be reconsidered for the doctoral program in biology at the time of his death?"

"Yes, that is true," Malinowski said, folding his hands on his lap. "He had applied to our committee for reconsideration."

"And I also understand that you are the only lawyer serving as a member of the Academic Oversight Committee?"

"Yes, true, again," he said, nodding. "But I must remind you that committee members are not permitted to speak about student applications for reconsideration." The professor rested his elbows on the armrests, bridging his fingers. "You see, politically speaking, I play a rather important role as the only lawyer on the committee. As I teach here at the law school, the university expects me especially to hold its rules and procedures inviolate."

"Absolutely, I understand. Let me speak more plainly. I am not investigating whether your committee followed correct procedures in Peter Franklin's case. Are you aware that Peter Franklin's death occurred within a week of a break-in and the theft of dangerous biological materials from the Pembroke Research Center's lab, where he'd been working as a technician?"

"A break-in you say?" Malinowski appeared to be genuinely amazed. "I did not know that. I certainly do recall the young man's untimely death. It was known all over campus. It's very tragic whenever a young person dies like that."

"Dies like that?" Christine said. "What do you mean?"

"If I remember correctly, he was found dead in his car on campus. The cause of his death I don't recall ever being reported. I would assume the family may have asked that the school not publish it."

"The connotation being drugs or alcohol, you're thinking?"

Malinowski tossed up his hands. "Well, certainly, yes, that would be a possibility whenever you are dealing with a young person who suddenly dies without any better explanation."

Christine nodded. "Yes, it would. By any chance did you know Peter Franklin personally? Did he ever come by your office, for instance, like Mr. Edwards just did? Before his petition was reviewed by the committee?"

"No, I told you I did not know the young man personally. I needn't tell you that it would have been highly improper, Christine, if he had approached me or any other committee person in advance of our decision."

Christine nodded and stood. "I appreciate your making time for me unscheduled like this, Professor." She smiled. "I mean Corbin."

"If there is anything else you wish to ask me," he reached inside his desk drawer and retrieved a business card, "here is my phone number. Feel free to call any time, even if it's only to jabber about baroque music. Better yet, perhaps, I'll see you at tomorrow evening's music recital?"

"I'm not sure I'll still be in the area."

"Ah. Well, in that case . . ." He smiled and returned his attention to the papers on his desk.

It was 2:30 in the afternoon. Christine stood by one of the massive sycamore trees that fronted the law school, pondering her next steps. She was famished and itched to go for a swim.

After so much sitting and intense inquiry she craved a physical release. She inquired from a passing student where the campus pool was located, then headed back to the Student Union Building to purchase a swimsuit at the school store. Along the way she phoned Eisen.

"Listen, Brian. This is *extremely* important. Ferguson deliberately dodged me. I need you or Higgins to find me his address ASAP."

It burned her that Ferguson had blown her off. What had he to hide? Five minutes later Eisen phoned back with the address: a townhouse apartment just off campus. After the call she sat on a bench beside the walkway to think things through. It was a gamble, with potentially unpleasant consequences either way. Miranda would be extremely upset if she failed to return to the office tomorrow. But murder investigation was her *real* job. Too much was at stake. She'd stay another night and spend tomorrow checking with the other academic committee members, and hopefully catch Ferguson unaware at home. With any luck she'd have something concrete to show Miranda for her efforts.

Was there a possible connection between the deaths of Franklin and Winchester? she wondered. Both deaths were sudden and, so far, unsatisfactorily explained in her mind. And now the recent death of Jane Pirrung, which she may have otherwise discounted as purely accidental but for the fact Jacob Graham said that she was an avid caver. Christine would pursue the matter further with Sheriff Boynton in order to rule out any foul play. Besides, she needed to introduce herself to Boynton, as Joe had advised.

Christine purchased a one-piece navy swimsuit and grabbed a premade turkey wrap at the Student Union Building, then left for the university pool, which the cashier confirmed was open to the public until five, when the varsity swim team began its practice. She showed her FBI badge to the student checker at the pool entrance, who pointed her in the direction of the women's locker room. She paid the extra dollar for a padlock with a key on a bungee wrist strap so she could secure her briefcase, and two more dollars for a white bathing cap, which was required to be worn in the pool at all times. She sat on the bench in the changing room and quickly ate half the sandwich; it would give her better strength for a good workout.

The pool was Olympic-size and had seven lanes. Three lanes were in use. She chose an open lane beside a young woman, probably a college student, who had a pretty decent crawl stroke. Standing at one end, she took some deep breaths, shaking her arms to limber them up like she had done at high school meets before taking her mark. A shot of adrenaline coursed through her veins as the bite of chlorine that hung in the humid air hit her nostrils.

No diving was allowed, so she dropped feetfirst into the cool waters—an ideal temperature for competitive swimming, she noted. She adjusted her swim cap, tucking in loose ends of hair, and started out easy with a breaststroke. Reaching the other end of the pool, she rolled onto her back and launched herself in earnest, carving the water, reaching her arms overhead in sequence with her signature stroke—the backstroke. The lead of the woman in the next lane was fading slightly. Christine upped her stroke count, rotating each arm overhead and sweeping it down smoothly, scooping one hand then the other through the glassy water.

She nailed her flip turn coming off the pool wall on the third lap and found her groove. Resurfacing, she scooped with her left then her right hand, arms milling from side to side while maintaining a steady flutter kick. At the far end, Christine did another flip turn and push-off. When she resurfaced, the student in the next lane had stopped and was treading water, breathing heavily through her open mouth. Christine smiled to herself, in racing mode, imagining she'd winded the other woman, out-swimming her, which it appeared that she may well have done.

As a young competitor she'd often challenge others in the pool to a contest to see who could swim underwater the farthest on a single breath. Some other swimmers would reach the far wall of the twenty-five meter pool before she did, but hardly anyone could touch and return to the other end without breaking the surface for air, swimming both lengths underwater. She could.

For the next half hour she tried to maintain a steady pace, checking her waterproof wristwatch at each turn. Her lap times slowed a tick and she redoubled her effort, the way her father had always demanded of her. It was all about showing up and doing the work. Endurance required it, and building endurance took hours of practice. The same discipline that she demonstrated in her workouts all those years readying for swim meets, Christine applied to her criminal cases. She wouldn't slow the pace until the race was finished, or, in this case, the killer was apprehended.

LE MAQUIS AUBERGE was a modern Tudor-style inn set on a lovely tree-lined property. Christine's room on the second floor overlooked a well-tended garden, where pink camellia blossoms were just budding out. It was a quarter to seven. She'd grabbed two slices of pepperoni pizza for dinner on the way over and wolfed them down sitting in the car. Inside the inn, she ordered a glass of pinot noir from the barkeep and took it upstairs to her room.

She called Brian Eisen and reported the fatal car accident involving Pirrung, telling him the CSU student was a member of the same caving club that had discovered Winchester's body. Eisen had nothing to report on the McKinley victim's tissue samples; she'd been hoping by now the additional gas-chromatograph readings that she'd requested would have borne fruit.

After her call with Eisen, she tabbed the classical music app on her iPhone and scrolled down to a Bach orchestral suite that was especially soothing after a good pool workout. As the chords of baroque music took flight, she lay her head on the pillow and closed her eyes in the hunt for peace.

Sometime later her cell phone's vibrations on the bedside table awakened her. It was Joe McFaron.

"Hey, Sheriff," she said, feeling a little groggy.

"So what's going on in Benson?" he said. His voice sounded tinny, like he was passing through a tunnel.

"Quite a lot really. I've interviewed a few students, including Winchester's roommate, been dodged by one professor, and then graciously treated by another. All in all I'd say a good start for my first day here. How about you?"

"Well, that does . . . sound good."

"You're ranging in and out, Joe," she said. "Are you in your truck?"

"I'm heading back from the state police barracks in Millersville. They impounded the highway accident victim's car at their wreckage yard last night."

"Jane Pirrung?"

"Yeah. The accident occurred just north of Crosshaven at a lighted intersection. Blasted things aren't worth a damn once the fog's set in after a hard rain."

"I assume your ME has the body?"

"You assume right. Millersville's within Crosshaven County. No doubt what killed her though. Her neck was broke and internal hemorrhaging throughout her body. Doc Henegar asked that you give him a call though."

"Anything particular to report about the accident scene?"

"Other than the coal truck that collided with her car and overturned, sending its driver to the hospital with multiple fractures, not much. Oh, I should tell you that Rodney Boynton showed up today, too. Being that Pirrung was a student at CSU, he needed to investigate. I was a little surprised that he didn't mention having talked to you."

"Yeah, well I haven't had time to make his acquaintance, but I assure you I will."

There was a pause. "Okay. One more thing of interest. We recovered a paper sack from inside Pirrung's vehicle. Some climbing aids with a receipt dated yesterday from a Clyde's Outdoor Gear Shop, a specialty store here in Millersville."

"Could I ask you to fax a copy of that receipt to Brian Eisen?"

"I'd be happy to," McFaron said. "Do you recall that dark car that hightailed it from the gravel access road after we left the Winchester crime scene?"

"Yeah, I only wish we'd been a little faster to catch the make and license plate."

"I had a conversation with a possible eyewitness. The man was walking his hound along that access road the same Tuesday Winchester went missing. He caught the first two letters of the tag number on a dark car that drove by him pretty fast. He said it was a foreign make, with tinted glass."

"Joe, that's terrific news!"

"The plate's first two numbers were 5 and 2, which indicates the car was registered in Benson County, home of CSU," he said. "My witness also said he glimpsed the driver's profile. It was a man for sure."

"That would be a lot of cars for the whole county, especially when you include the university," Christine said, "which I understand has more than thirty-five thousand students."

"That's true. But we can pretty much eliminate most of the students, who largely come from out of town or out of state, or they are foreigners on student visas. I've already got the Indiana State Police running a list of dark foreign cars registered in Benson County."

"When you get that list, share it with me, Joe. I'll have Eisen and Higgins get right on it to help narrow down the possible vehicles."

"You sure that's okay?" he said, his voice a little less business-like now. "I don't want you taking any heat from your bosses over this, Christine. Weren't you telling me the new head of your branch office considers this case to be purely a local matter?"

"Let me worry about the politics on the home front. Any fallout that may come is not on you." Christine, suddenly animated, said, "Look, Joe, I have a few more people to interview here. As you might imagine, the university isn't exactly rolling out the red carpet for me."

"Nobody likes talking to the law, Christine, especially on a college campus. Don't forget what I said about keeping Sheriff Boynton in the loop. You really should have spoken to him already. Rodney's a good man, so long as you don't cross him. He was a big help to me when I first got started on the job. I've always respected him for that."

"I know. I know. Anyway, that's great news about the car, Joe, really." The progress felt as good as the current of rain-sweetened air blowing through the crack of her window.

"I'll ask Mary to make an extra copy of the car registrations as soon as the list comes in. It'll be waiting for you when you return." His voice sounded wistful. "Listen, I've got an incoming work call to catch," he said. "Talk to you soon."

Christine went into the bathroom. She leaned her elbows on the sink and placed a hot washcloth over her face. She got cozy under the comforter, feeling exhausted in a good way. She clicked off the bedside lamp and pressed Play on her iPhone, resuming the Bach keyboard suite for harpsichord that always found her sweet spot.

CHAPTER
THIRTEEN

FRIDAY MORNING CHRISTINE rubbed her stiff neck. She'd slept fitfully, reviewing case notes in her head. Other than the uncomfortable pillow, her room was overflowing with country charm, right down to the framed needlepoint on the wall of a barefoot woman in a flowing blue gown walking along a forest path lit by a shining star. The stitched inscription below read, "Your word is a lamp to my feet, and a light to my path."

She'd found the religious image and inscription soothing despite the fact she infrequently attended church, and then mostly only for funerals. Growing up in her Detroit suburb, she'd experienced the drudge of compulsory daily services at her parochial high school—all that forced prayer was enough to last her a lifetime.

She gazed down at the garden beneath her window. A pair of cardinals swooped down to the rim of a stone clamshell birdbath, bobbing their heads in unison. A pair bond.

What Joe had reported last night was very good news. Could the dark car with the 52 license plate have been the same dark car that she and Joe glimpsed speeding away from the crime scene? It was no mere coincidence, not with the air bled from their vehicle tires to prevent a quick chase.

Christine tried reaching McFaron on his cell and was sent to voicemail. She left a message wondering whether he'd gone to Clyde's Outdoor Gear Shop yet and interviewed whoever was on duty Wednesday night when Pirrung made her purchases.

Out her inn window bad weather looked imminent. She cinched the belt of her tan trench coat—a stylish enough cut that improved the wear-and-tear look of her pants suit—and headed out the door. A half hour later Christine jogged up the steps of Hinckley Hall. She'd arranged to meet with Alice Catrall, a sociology professor and member of the Academic Oversight Committee, who fortunately was at her desk on the first floor of Hinckley, grading papers.

Prior to meeting with Catrall, she'd left another voice message for Shamus Ferguson, who obviously was avoiding her. Christine had also phoned the two other committee members. Joel Abrams, the business school professor, she learned, was out of town at a convention in Chicago; Steve Belknap, the history department chair, declined to meet with her and wouldn't divulge any specific information unless compelled by a court subpoena or written authorization from the CSU Administration. Belknap sounded royally uptight, and his words seemed parroted, too—perhaps with more than a hint of coaching from Corbin Malinowski? In any event, she concluded that Belknap was just obeying school rules and didn't take from his curt responses over the phone that he was hiding anything in particular, which made it all the more intriguing that Alice Catrall had agreed to meet with her.

Christine found Catrall's office and knocked.

"Come in. I've been expecting you." Professor Catrall was rail thin and had fine wavy auburn hair, cut short like Christine's. The teacher came around her desk with her hand outstretched and they shook.

"Christine Prusik, I'm with the Chicago office of the FBI, as I told you over the phone. It's nice to meet you, Professor Catrall."

"You as well, Special Agent," the professor said with a welcoming smile. "Please call me Alice."

"You may call me Christine," the forensic scientist said, returning the bonhomie. "I appreciate your seeing me on short notice."

"No problem at all. These are my normal office hours, and with spring break beginning at the end of the day, I doubt I'll be having many visitors. The students are already clearing out."

Christine placed her briefcase on the floor and sat down in the chair facing Catrall's desk. "That explains it. Campus seems so much quieter today than yesterday." She leaned forward and started in. "Look, I'm not here to reopen Peter Franklin's case file, but I understand that his death occurred shortly after the academic committee had met?"

A distinct fracture line appeared on Alice Catrall's smooth alabaster forehead. "It was a terrible thing, Peter's death." The woman shook her head in genuine sorrow. "But I don't think it had anything to do with the Academic Oversight Committee. Officially, we hadn't yet taken a vote on his petition."

"Is that right?" Her statement contradicted Tim Millard's comment that Shamus Ferguson had single-handedly denied Franklin's application for reconsideration.

"Absolutely, we hadn't. It was taken under advisement, yes. We were each given a copy of his application to review, of course."

"So you saw no connection at all?" Christine said, hesitating before adding, "Between his application for reconsideration and his death?"

"Other than that it was shocking to hear, no." Catrall shook her head. "I wish I could tell you something useful, Christine. But the vote to reconsider him never came up, officially."

"To be clear, you are sure that the committee never met formally and discussed his petition?" Christine reiterated. "You couldn't have been out sick or missed an impromptu meeting?"

"I didn't miss any meetings, and after his death there was no need for any formal discussion of his appeal." The slender professor sat quite erect behind her desk, very attentive, giving Christine the distinct impression that the line of questioning wasn't what the teacher was expecting.

"What about the coroner, the police?" Christine asked. "Didn't anyone investigating Franklin's death question you or other members on the committee afterward?"

"At the time, you know, I thought that they might," Alice said, "since Peter Franklin had died so soon after submitting his application." She glanced away from Christine—was it from the weight of a particular memory, or something else, Christine wondered, her own frustration mounting.

The facts weren't bearing out. Was her gut instinct wrong that there was a connection between Franklin's death and Winchester's? Certainly there was a connecting thread—Shamus Ferguson. Christine perceived Alice Catrall knew something more. A different approach was needed. So far this sociologist was the only committee person other than Corbin Malinowski who was willing to speak with her directly about the matter.

"I understand Peter Franklin did his undergraduate degree here at CSU. Does the committee have a policy or quota, written or otherwise, discouraging CSU undergraduate students from applying to its graduate programs?"

"Not to my knowledge. If they do, it's beyond the scope of the oversight committee. We only reconsider appeals from denied applicants based upon pertinent academic information that may not have been known at the time of the original application, or that may have been overlooked." Catrall bit her lower lip. That wrinkle reappeared across the dome of her forehead. No question the woman was hedging.

"You knew he was an undergraduate here?" Christine pressed. "Was he ever a student in one of your classes, Professor?"

"Look, every other term I teach one of the main survey courses that all undergraduates are required to take. They must choose sociology or sign up for one of three other survey courses in the social sciences: those being anthropology, psychology, or the urban studies program. Peter may well have taken my survey course." She gesticulated spreading her fingers. "It's taught in Weinberger, the largest amphitheater classroom on campus. I get as many as two hundred students at once in the survey course. If he had been one of mine, it would have likely been several years ago anyway."

Christine nodded agreeably so as not to give the impression she sensed anything was deliberately off. "Look, I know you need to make headway on that stack." Christine glanced down at the pile of papers on the sociologist's desk, then handed her a business card. "Should anything about the committee's discussion come back to you, something that may have struck you as odd at the time, I urge you to call me, day or night. It might shed crucial light on Peter's death and other more recent matters. Anything that you wish to share with me, Alice, I assure you, is strictly confidential. It won't get back."

"Are you here on campus because of the young woman recently found dead?" Alice said, looking up from Christine's business card. "Is that part of the FBI's investigation?"

"I can't discuss anything ongoing, Alice," Christine answered, "but yes, the FBI is cooperating with local authorities who are investigating the circumstances surrounding Naomi Winchester's death."

"So you think Peter Franklin's death was suspicious, too?" the professor ventured. "May somehow be tied to hers?"

Christine smiled appreciatively. "Look, I've been at CSU for only a couple of days. It's a huge campus, with so many departments and thousands of students. Most of the time, information gathering is all about ruling out dead ends. And believe me there always are a lot of dead ends. Anything you can remember will likely only close off a few more." Christine shrugged. "Police work is frustratingly slow going."

"Yes, I would imagine that it is," Alice said sympathetically. "It sounds a lot like my own work, trying to make heads or tails from unwieldy data-gathering surveys. Gaining a bit of solid evidence, something cogent, is difficult at best, and often requires making an educated guess based on your gut."

"Exactly my point," Christine said, then stood and collected her briefcase. "I'm grateful for your time, Alice."

Professor Catrall shook Christine's hand and then lowered her eyes to the papers on her desk.

Christine retraced her steps back toward her rental car under a steady patter of rain. Less than ten minutes later her cell phone rang inside her trench coat pocket. It was Alice Catrall, sooner than she'd expected. She ducked under the eaves of a nearby dormitory and took the call.

"After you left my office, you got me thinking. So I checked my course files. Lo and behold you were right to ask me whether Peter Franklin ever took one of my survey courses. He hadn't taken the survey course but was enrolled in my Modern Urban Studies seminar two years ago, as an undergraduate."

"I see. And is there some important connection you can think of?"

"Well, yes, that's why I'm calling you back, Christine. Reviewing my course notes jogged my memory of it. He'd handed in a term paper late, it was a team project. Each team had three students. Anyway, when I cross-checked his team's paper with a software program I use to make sure a student's work product isn't plagiarized from the internet, it came back nearly verbatim, a canned document downloaded from a website. It wasn't even cleverly word-doctored to prevent my detection; it was outright plagiarism."

"Well, that certainly is significant," Christine said, walking to the rental car. The rain had abated. "What did you do?" She got in the car and turned on the motor, feeling chilled.

"Normally, I would have reported them to the dean's office straightaway," Catrall said. "But I decided to confront them individually. I called each student to my office and questioned them separately. Peter said that his part of the project was limited to researching the underlying issues. He denied having cheated. He claimed the other two students were tasked with actually writing the paper. He was pretty convincing. I even penciled in my notes beside his name 'research only.' The other two looked sheepish but wouldn't fess up to having cheated either."

"Did you report them?" Christine could hear Catrall sigh.

"I lost my will to get them in trouble with the dean." Catrall sounded ashamed to admit it. "Instead, I gave all three students incompletes on their academic records, with the option of retaking my course or another one that would fulfill their undergraduate social science requirement."

"That was pretty decent of you."

"I apologize for not speaking of this matter earlier. Truthfully, it made me uncomfortable."

"I understand. Calling me back was the right thing to do, Alice. You needn't apologize."

"Honestly, it's dismaying how prevalent plagiarism is these days, especially at the undergraduate level. I don't know whether it's because students are required to take courses in areas of study in which they have no true interest, or just a sign of our times."

"So I take it," Christine said, "you didn't raise this incident at the Academic Oversight Committee meeting, or with anyone else when reconsidering Franklin's petition?"

"No, it never actually came up." Christine thought she heard Catrall sigh again.

"Thank you, Alice. Like I said, this stays between you and me. If you think of anything else, please call me, day or night."

So Peter Franklin himself hadn't such clean hands after all, Christine concluded. And something was very definitely still agitating the quiet-voiced sociology professor, too.

"THIS ISN'T ABOUT our winning the coveted five-year grant awarded by NIH, is it?" Shamus Ferguson could hardly contain himself in the idling Land Rover parked beside his large A-frame cottage with a wraparound deck that overlooked Morgan Reservoir. A pontoon boat was moving slowly across the middle of the large manmade lake. Its aluminum skin glinted in the sunlight. "We won it fair and square, Randall."

"I imagine that you did, Shamus. I imagine that you did," Randy Creighton answered in an unnervingly calm voice. "I'm not distressed about it. We get plenty of funding elsewhere. But that's no call for your accusing me because the FBI's landed on your doorstep."

"Let's examine that for a moment, shall we?" Ferguson said. Creighton was the first person Shamus had thought of when Jacob Graham told him that an FBI lady had come knocking on his office door.

The other end of the line remained silent for too long and impatience got the better of Ferguson. "Come on, Randall! Do I need to spell it out? Didn't we go through enough scrutiny the last time? The FBI is now asking about Peter Franklin. Let me remind you that it took a lot of maneuvering on my part to keep the lid on the Franklin debacle. Here at CSU, and with NIH. Nobody likes reading about young people turning up dead on school campuses, you know. It's our shared research that's at stake, for Christ's sake!"

The distraught professor ran his hand through a full head of curly brown hair streaked with gray.

A tyrannical schizophrenia ruled Ferguson's relationship with Creighton, as both men were vying for limited research dollars and were in direct competition—like Watson and Crick and other geneticists before their time had been as they frantically fought to be the first to map the structure of DNA. In Ferguson and Creighton's case, the race was to be the first to unravel the Batrachotoxin equivalent of the double helix. It was widely believed that the toxin's medicinal value would lead to breakthroughs in the development of a whole new family of drugs to treat cardiovascular diseases, strokes, multiple sclerosis, and even cancer, and there were already hopeful signs that it would be useful in pain management advances. That meant scoring big chests of money. Money that would pour in for years to come.

But all those riches could dry up overnight if either one of them were foolish enough to kill the Money Train—the NIH grant funding that was key above everything else in pressing forward the vital basic research. Doubly, because NIH carried with it name recognition as the most prestigious and largest biomedical research agency in the world. Both men knew that huge amounts of money were essential if the molecular breakthrough of the century were to be forged. And whose name would top the list as the principal discoverer of the toxin's life-giving properties was still to be determined.

Ferguson's keeping a lid on the Peter Franklin death two years before had taken a personal toll. In the end, he knew perfectly well that maintaining his prestige was a matter of handling other people's perceptions. Sloppiness wasn't rewarded, and any hint of there being a suspicious death connected to Batrachotoxin research at his research center would destroy his credibility and everything that he'd worked so hard for. Even he didn't have enough political capital should the lid come off Peter Franklin's death.

"I appreciate what you did, Shamus. I have no vendetta here, no bone to pick with you or the FBI." Creighton's steady confidence only worsened Ferguson's anxiety.

"It's pretty basic stuff, Randy," Ferguson said, his voice rising. "You scratch my back and I scratch yours. But I don't go sending the feds breathing down your neck over a few measly million that you probably can make up in six months of speaking engagements from your savvy business investors."

"The door's always open, Shamus. The private sector has its benefits."

"Does that include breaking and entering? That was a pretty sloppy job you pulled if it does."

"Back to that old accusation, are you? Come on, Shamus. That was a long time ago. It's water under the bridge. I had nothing to do with the disappearance of your frog skins, or Peter Franklin's death."

"It's perfectly logical for me to suspect that your lab was behind the theft, and maybe even Franklin's death. The last I checked, all Dendrobates are listed species now. CITES has put a full stop to all international commerce."

CITES, or the Convention on International Trade in Endangered Species of Wild Flora and Fauna, regulated the trade in endangered species, including the New World's equatorial poison frogs.

"Where are you going with this, Shamus? Are you accusing me of murder?" Creighton said, irritation finally audible in his voice. "And don't go playing the noble savage with me. We get all the skins we need from Kazakhstan, for Christ's sake. What's this really about? You're not feeling loved enough?"

"You read the papers still, don't you?" Ferguson retorted. "Two college women found murdered in two weeks in neighboring states—one is from CSU for God's sake! Then out of the blue this FBI lady comes knocking on my door. What the hell do you think it's about?

"Are you forgetting Peter Franklin worked for you as a summer intern at Macalister Pharmaceuticals, Randall? And Franklin returned as a technician to our research center right afterward. Rather convenient, isn't it, that the break-in to our storage room happened that same fall? Three whole frog skins were stolen. And then Franklin dies here on our campus! So you'd better start putting yourself in my shoes for a change, Randall. Get my drift?"

"Is that a threat?" Creighton raised his voice. "Stop already with the paranoia. Get it through your head—I don't need to hire former interns to steal skins from you. I didn't speak to the FBI. NIH's funding, hey, it could have gone either way. Congratulations, you got the five-year grant, Shamus. As you already said, in the big picture, it doesn't really matter. I've got other money from NIH. And there are plenty of opportunists out there looking to make an investment betting that Macalister Pharmaceuticals will find the silver bullet. So get off your fucking high horse."

Ferguson clenched the phone in his fist. "Hear this, Randall. If that FBI bitch connects these women's deaths to our research facility, it's going to be bad news for both of us."

"And just why would they, Shamus?" Creighton asked pointedly. "I've got somewhere else to be right now. Appreciate the heads-up. If the FBI calls, I'll let you know. As usual it was great hearing from you, Shamus." Creighton ended the call.

In fact, Randall Creighton III hadn't called the FBI guy back as he'd promised he would, disbelieving their inquiry was to get his professional opinion on some unrelated police matter, worried that the real reason was tied to the Illinois date that had gone so desperately wrong. He hadn't even phoned his lawyer yet, hoping beyond hope that it wouldn't come down to that.

ABOVE HIM HUNG rack after rack of wall-mounted shelving displaying his grandmother's vast collection of oddities and obscure artifacts. One side of the room was devoted entirely to Pre-Colombian Mesoamerican stone idols and clay figurines. Another wall showcased precious silver and gold necklaces, bracelets, earrings, and rings, which his grandmother once told him she'd paid black market dealers plenty for in the '50s and '60s, before the

Central American governments were able to slow the spigot of illegal trade of their treasures and antiquities.

Trip reached high up to a corner shelf above the small writing desk—the same one at which his grandmother had frequently paid her bills and penned her responses to social obligations so many years ago. The same one at which she'd sat and laughed at him shortly after he'd moved into her house. It was on that afternoon, at age twelve, that he'd fully understood what his new life was to be like.

Trip had wandered into his grandmother's study and spotted a leathery stuffed thing perched on the corner of a high bookshelf. He'd never noticed it before, squatting like a gargoyle, its mouth stitched shut with thick black thread.

The crooked-fingered hand of the matriarch fell silently upon his thin shoulder from behind, startling Trip.

"Go ahead," she said with a throaty Midwestern lilt to her voice. "Fetch down old Toady here."

Trip obediently climbed on a chair and clutched the bulbous brown stuffed creature with both hands. Its wizened hawk-bill snout pointed directly at him.

"Toady there was once a real live toad, you know, Trip." His grandmother chuckled, her dark eyes glinting with a fierce stare he never quite knew how to interpret. "He's the real deal."

Trip had never seen a frog or toad that large. It was the size of a squashed football and it had the same golden leathery hue. Arched sockets on either side of the stuffed creature's head housed glossy dark marble beads in place of eyes. On either side of its head, below where the eyes would be, were coarse skin patches with tiny perforations.

"Hand him over," his grandmother commanded. Blue veins

squiggled over the stretched tendons in her aged arms. "Never seen one before, have you, Trip? It's a Cane Toad from Central America."

She pointed out the dimpled patches below the eye sockets. "See these patches?"

He nodded, his curiosity sparked.

Her face drew nearer his. "Stick out your tongue, boy." Her voice was stern; it was an order. "Lick the bumpy place and tell me what you feel."

She held the leathery creature toward him and Trip licked where she said to.

"Good. Now quick as you can, lick the patch on the other side, too," she instructed, grinning after he'd done as she said.

As if on cue, his mouth went dry and his tongue swelled. He gagged. Panic-stricken, Trip dropped off the chair and sprawled on the old Persian rug, rubbing his throat with both hands.

He caught a sideways glimpse of his grandmother slapping her knees from her seat behind the desk and heaving with laughter.

Trip's hands went suddenly numb. The rapid beating of his heart pounded in his ears. He couldn't seem to catch his breath.

His grandmother's next words came in a whisper down low beside his temple. "Toady's still got punch, don't he boy?" she said between fits of laughter that turned into a hacking cough.

"Powerful stuff. He's been watching you . . . from up there . . . ever since you got here." A sputter of railing coughs erupted out of the ancient folds of her throat. "His poison's still got . . . pop . . ."

Trip's tongue started to prickle, and so did his hands. Feeling was returning. But his grandmother's hacking cough worsened, and her complexion flushed beet red. Her crooked fingers grabbed at her own throat now.

Trip had read fear in the old woman's eyes, the same panic she'd taken so much joy in seeing on his face only moments before. Tit for tat, he thought, remaining on the library floor as his heartbeats gradually slowed and his breathing began to return to normal. Tit for tat.

Trip banished the memory from his mind and removed from the corner shelf a small silk-covered box kept shut with a narrow bone spline through a delicate loop fastener. Carefully he lifted out the large gold signet ring on which the silhouette of a gold frog was displayed as a cameo. He placed it on the desk blotter. From a lower side drawer he retrieved the liquid nitrogen canister and unscrewed its lid. Frosty vapor seeped out and condensed in a fine layer, chilling the outer lip of the canister to a frightfully low temperature that would instantly freeze his skin if his bare hand were to accidentally touch there.

He slipped on a double layer of sterile latex gloves for safety. With a pair of insulated tongs he lifted out the parchment-like skin. He angled the tongs under the desk lamp, inspecting the shiny patch like a caught quarry, pleased with its shimmering golden hue.

It was time to arm the ring's needle again. He activated the small spring-loaded lever on the side of the ring's face. Out of the small frog's mouth sprung a sharp tip. He swabbed the tip clean with a cotton ball soaked in alcohol, then carefully rubbed the thawing skin over the needle's tip until it was sufficiently gummed with the deadly poison.

He needed more supplies. The university lab was off-limits

now that the FBI was creeping around asking questions. He'd had to place his new order over the internet. The timing of it was too perfect, as CSU's spring break trip was set to go to Mexico soon, precisely when his order would be ready for pickup.

MIDMORNING FRIDAY, CHRISTINE'S phone trilled—an incoming text. Higgins had found the Big Man on Campus's off-campus address. She'd earlier checked Ferguson's townhouse apartment near campus, finding it vacant, and chided herself for not confronting him yesterday afternoon instead of going for a swim. Higgins had found a newspaper exposé featuring Ferguson and his Pembroke Research Center, which included a photo of the professor hosting a party at his lakeside cottage on the Morgan Reservoir, a large manmade lake a few miles south of the CSU campus.

She punched in the coordinates for the cottage on the rental car's GPS. Miranda hadn't phoned in yet, which was a good thing, too. She didn't believe for a second that it meant anything more than possibly his giving her some slack for a slow start to her day after a more than busy Thursday. She'd make the Monday morning staff meeting for certain. With any luck, she'd have something of substance to report. Substance she needed—substance that Ferguson reeked of in spades: his avid passion for caving and his being a womanizer, according to grad student Tim Millard. Most significantly, Ferguson was in charge of a research facility studying a deadly frog toxin. The scientific journal extract authored by Ferguson, which Graham had given her, described in great detail the deadliness of Batrachotoxin, and that the toxin secreted through the skins of poison dart frogs was found in highest concentrations on the skins of the Golden Poison Dart Frog.

Lab analysis of the tissue sample excised from Ellen McKinley's neck had detected the presence of an unknown toxin, the minutest quantity of which was sufficient to kill a laboratory mouse in a matter of seconds. Add the mysterious death of former Pembroke Research Center technician Peter Franklin, who'd died shortly following a break-in at Pembroke's storage facility where several deadly poisonous frog skins had been taken from their liquid nitrogen canisters. Which suggested to her an inside job—someone who knew what he was doing. Still, she couldn't afford to leap to conclusions. But neither could she just drop everything and head back to the office when she was just beginning to get somewhere. The dead girls and their families were owed that much.

Twenty minutes later the road wound around high bluffs. Soon she glimpsed the sparkle of water between trees. The sun overhead intensified on the reflecting waters of the huge reservoir. It was a relief to finally catch a glimpse of blue sky after the slew of rainy days. Christine spotted the mailbox with the numerals 1980—Ferguson's place—and parked along the roadside. She walked down the sandy driveway. Near the A-frame cottage, a dark green SUV was parked with its back door hinged wide open. A large duffel bag lay stuffed inside. Its plate number: 52-AF69. McFaron had said the car's plate the witness had seen began with 52, which indicated the vehicle's registration was Benson County.

Hearty laughter drew her attention to an outside wraparound deck that faced toward the lake. A heavyset man with a full beard and curly hair appeared and stepped down from the deck onto the drive; he was speaking on his cell phone. He walked toward the rear of the parked SUV and un-shouldered a carry-on bag, laying it beside the duffel. *Packing bags. Was he running?* she wondered.

"Professor Ferguson?" she said loud enough to interrupt him. "Heading out of town, sir?"

The professor wrenched his neck around, startled by her voice. He squinted in her direction, frozen in his tracks, the phone now clutched at his side as if she'd just caught him in some nefarious act.

Christine approached him slowly, holding out her identity badge. "FBI Special Agent Christine Prusik. It's good to finally catch up with you, sir." Walking closer, she held her smile as long as she could to bolster her confidence.

"Who the hell told you I was here?"

"I have a few questions in regards to Naomi Winchester, Professor."

Ferguson shook his head, turned his back on her, and furiously punched a number on his cell phone.

Christine heard the words "Rodney" and "fuck" phrased in a question that she alertly surmised meant Sheriff Rodney Boynton of Benson County would soon be headed this way. She hadn't yet paid Boynton a courtesy call, as Joe had advised her to do.

Ferguson turned on her, red-faced. "Whoever the hell you think you are, get off my property right now or I'll have you arrested. In fact, you're probably under arrest anyway."

Christine figured she only had a couple of minutes at the most. "I understand that Naomi Winchester took a course from you last term?" She advanced toward him as she spoke. "When was the last time you saw Ms. Winchester, sir?"

Ferguson grimaced. He had the look of a man in a great deal of pain.

"Look, I know you've called Sheriff Boynton," she volunteered, closing the gap to ten feet and then stopping. "You can answer my questions here or down at his office if you'd like. The sooner I get answers, the quicker I'll be gone."

"What is it with you people? You think being a cop gives you some kind of special privilege? Get off my property *now* I said!" His eyes widened, his neck muscles bulging. It's not that he looked cornered exactly, but he definitely looked like someone with something to hide.

"I'm not trying to make your life difficult, Professor. I'd just like a few answers to a few very simple . . ."

"Get off my property now or *you* will be the one answering questions! I said now! Leave now!"

Christine started back down the drive to her rental car. From behind her came the loud boom of the Range Rover's rear door slamming shut. She'd struck a nerve. Ferguson obviously wasn't happy to be on the FBI's radar. Where was he going, and why?

A flock of red-winged blackbirds flashed overhead and filled a nearby tree. She did a 180-degree turn and headed back to town. Five minutes later, a tan-and-cream sedan with its blue strobo-scopic lights flashing brightly in the front grille passed her at a high rate of speed. She glimpsed Sheriff Rodney Boynton wearing his Stetson hat through the windshield as the police cruiser flashed by. So eager to come to the aid of the troubled professor, the same law enforcement official who, according to Sheriff Joe McFaron, was cooperating on the Naomi Winchester investigation. McFaron had warned her to check in with Boynton. She was on his patch. Not doing so from the outset was a risk she had weighed and decided against, figuring she'd stand to learn more coming unannounced to the campus, at the same time realizing that eventually word would get back to Boynton. And now it had.

CHRISTINE STAMPED HER feet. Her oxfords were soaked through; the rain had returned with a vengeance and darkened them a soggy brown. She shook her trench coat by its collar inside the high-ceilinged entry of Winkler Auditorium. People milled around her, closing their umbrellas, complaining about the stretch of inclement weather. It was nearly 8 p.m. The lights briefly dimmed, signaling that the performance was about to begin. She checked her trench coat.

The crowd was dressed decently enough, men in cheery spring sport jackets and slacks, and women comfortably attired in off-the-rack pants suits or mid-calf skirts. She was presentable in the spare beige blouse that she'd rinsed overnight in her guest room sink and the navy blue pants suit that she'd had pressed by one of the inn's housekeepers. No necklace, only a pair of drop pearl earrings with old-fashioned pressure screw mounts that her grandmother had given her on her twelfth birthday.

She took an aisle seat toward the back of the amphitheater. Her ticket was a late purchase—good for any open seat in the rear-most tier. The acoustics in the music hall would still be close to optimum. More importantly, as a crime investigator poking her nose around campus, sitting toward the rear was an advantage; she didn't want to draw unnecessary attention to herself.

The performance opened with the Brandenburg Concerto no. 1, arranged for four instruments: an oboe, two violins, and a cello. It was the companion piece to the composition she'd heard in the law professor's office the day before. It opened slowly, each instrument complementing the other in an aural fusion, increasing tempo in the second movement before transitioning to a slower melodic section, and then rising again in a flourish to the finish.

The breathtaking play realigned Christine's mind. It was a salvation of sorts, the effect Bach always had on her temperament. The mellifluous complexity of the chords touched a deep wellspring inside her—like a clearing in the forest, with the sun warming Christine's shoulders. She often wondered whether her strong spiritual connection with Bach had some greater meaning. The orderliness and symmetry of the instruments joining seamlessly together had the power to smooth out whatever wrinkles the day could throw at her, including all considerations from her brusque rebuff by Shamus Ferguson.

The next piece was Bach's Concerto no. 3, adding the sharper keyboard notes of a harpsichord to several more violins and cellos. On stage, the men wore black suits, white shirts, and dark ties, and the women, long black dresses—the usual garb of professional classical musicians. Although only college students, they were obviously the cream of the crop, their musicianship well disciplined and lively at the same time. Christine spotted the cellist girlfriend of the young man whom she'd met in the campus coffee shop on Thursday morning. He was probably somewhere in the audience, too. The snap of the female cellist's head matched her bow speed—delicate yet firm across the strings, producing its magnificent sighing voice, as if delivered through a yawning crack in the earth itself.

Her spirits lifted, Christine moved into the foyer where a crowd was congregating at a cash bar during intermission.

"You look very nice tonight, Christine," Corbin Malinowski

said, addressing her from behind. He half-bowed courteously, smartly dressed for the occasion with a dark three-piece suit and black tie. The high ceiling spotlights shadowed his eyes beneath his brow. She figured he was perhaps in his late forties, but he had the playful air of someone younger, and at the same time, the fatherly wisdom of someone much older.

Her cheeks warmed to the compliment and she smiled. "I wondered if I might see you here."

"Does being on assignment mean alcohol is off-limits?" he said.

"Heavens no! I was just headed to the bar myself," she said. "Would you like to join me for a drink?"

"I'd be delighted," he said. They walked together to the counter, where they each ordered a glass of Chablis, the only choice of wine. They carried their drinks to the side of the lobby, away from the excited chatter of others, and sat in two chairs. Again, she noticed his limp.

"Did you fall recently, Corbin? I noticed you favoring your left leg," she said.

"You know, it's a lesson to me not to go walking out of a room while reading something and running smack into the dining table, which I did. I gave myself a rather nasty charley horse," he said with a half-hearted laugh. "So tell me, how was your day?"

"I'd say it went better than expected. How about yours?" She hedged, not wanting to come off heavy by saying she couldn't divulge anything pertinent to her investigation.

"I'm writing a paper on civil disobedience in the modern era—post–nineteen sixties."

"First Amendment constitutional law issues then?" she said, genuinely interested.

He nodded. "Yes, indeed. After all, where would disobedience be without storming the gates of free speech once in a while?"

"How true." She chuckled. "And yet it's knowing when and where to express my views that I've often found difficult."

Outspokenness was Christine's natural tendency and fundamental to her pursuit of criminal investigation. A good argument and disagreement with others, including Sheriff Joe McFaron, often produced her best insights, even if it risked someone else's displeasure, including Joe's. She realized, however, that not everyone else saw the same advantages to arguing as she did, which was unfortunate.

"While the First Amendment does come into the analysis," Malinowski said, "I am most interested in how the minority's interests are accommodated in the context of the majority's, especially in the arena of sensitive topics such as abortion rights and the bioethics of experimentation on human stem cell tissue.

"Recent advances in the biological sciences have presented society with so many dilemmas that our forefathers could not have possibly foreseen at the time of writing the Constitution—a noble document though it is, the writers' stark appreciation of Lockean notions on the social contract and the solemnity of an individual's rights do not shed much ambient light on how to best proceed in today's technically advanced world."

Christine contemplated his point. She was counting on Eisen's coming through with useful tissue findings on McKinley and Winchester that would help point the way to their killer. Without the information produced by sophisticated laboratory testing, where would she and her team be? "Yes, modern science certainly has achieved remarkable advances. I'll grant you that."

"Here, here, listen to me going on like I'm at a lecture." He raised his wineglass. "When all I really wanted to say is what a pleasure it is to share a glass of wine on this occasion of great music with a like-minded soul."

"Yes, of course." She raised hers and they touched glasses. "To Johann Sebastian Bach."

Christine sampled her wine, then put down the glass and cleared her throat. "Listen, Corbin, I'm actually having a bit of a problem understanding the sequence of things on this academic committee business."

Professor Malinowski rested his wineglass on his knee, surprise registering on his face. "Oh yes? Is this in regard to Peter Franklin again?" he said.

"Correct." She held up her palm. "And I fully respect your confidentiality concerns. You and others on the committee have been more than gracious enough to talk with me."

"Really, others are talking?" Malinowski's eyebrows rose.

She ignored the question. "You said you didn't have any outside contact with Franklin?"

"That's right, none. As I told you earlier, as a committee we meet twice a year following the admission decisions, when disappointed applicants are most likely to seek reconsideration."

"Excuse me for repeating myself, but if I may," she said, "did it ever come to your attention there was a lab break-in and theft of biological material from the Pembroke Research Center during the week prior to your committee meeting?"

Malinowski shook his head, maintaining eye contact with Christine. "You mentioned that yesterday. I wouldn't be divulging any confidences in assuring you that the matter never came to my attention. It was never discussed in committee either, because it simply was not known at the time, nor does it particularly seem related to the matters we typically consider."

His suggesting that it wasn't related to any pertinent matters suggested just the opposite to Christine. "Look, Peter Franklin's dead." Christine lowered her voice. "Whose confidence are you really protecting at this point, Professor?"

Malinowski waggled his forefinger playfully at her. "I can see you've been around lawyers for too long."

Christine laughed. "Point taken. Mea culpa. Really, Professor, what's the big secret at this point?" She finished her wine and placed the glass on the window ledge, folding one leg over her knee.

He leaned forward with an amused expression. "Please call me Corbin so I don't feel so much like an expert being grilled on the stand."

"Grilled? I'm sorry." Christine sat back. "Yeah, I sometimes get accused of coming on too strong. Sorry about that, Corbin. I'm a bit frustrated that everyone on this campus is so nice and yet at the same time so tight-lipped, too. Know what I mean?"

"Peter Franklin was a bit of a campus radical, as I recall," Malinowski said after a slight pause.

Christine sat forward, listening. Tim Millard had said the same thing. "How so?"

Malinowski danced his head left and right. "He got several write-ups in the campus newspaper, something about advocating eco-terrorism as a legitimate means for protecting endangered species and the environment at large."

"Student advocacy is pretty par for the course on a university campus, don't you think? You, yourself, express an avid interest in the civil rights of the minority in your writings after all."

"Touché." He smiled. "But keep in mind that protesting and raising a fuss may have gained him the ire of the university administration, not to mention professors and research scientists who have ongoing dealings with the government and private industry," he said.

Which would include a bigwig like Professor Ferguson for certain, Christine thought. Corbin Malinowski sure had the party line down smoothly. He knew who buttered his bread, and it was just as clear to her that the Pembroke Research Center stood as a bastion to be protected by the university—and possibly by Corbin himself, as a lawyer who both taught at the university and represented its interests on the Academic Oversight Committee.

"From the gist of what you're saying then, am I to take it Peter Franklin's application would have gone nowhere because of his outspoken campus politics?"

"Are you sure you don't have a law degree?" he said, massaging his whiskered chin between a thumb and forefinger. "I know many in the FBI do."

Christine laughed at his charm, noting how ably evasive Corbin was, too.

The lights dimmed twice, alerting the audience to return to their seats for the second half of the performance. Christine thanked the professor for chatting and took her seat. From the rear of the amphitheater she watched him return to his own reserved seat, closer to the stage, in the center of the row—in the prime Orchestra seats. No doubt about it, there was something intriguing about the man. She'd have Brian Eisen and Paul Higgins do background checks on all the academic committee members, not just Shamus Ferguson.

The music resumed and Christine relaxed her neck against

the backrest, allowing the rising and falling pulsations to calm her and clear her mind of work. Her thoughts drifted to Corbin Malinowski and his trimmed silver beard. His graciousness reminded her of her graduate school mentor and the head of the Anthropology Department, Dr. Bob Mathers, whose doting ways she'd found so disarming that one summer long ago. Their affair began soon after commencing a field study in Brazil's vast Amazon basin, where they were conducting a survey under a government grant on intermarriages among closely related kin in the small villages of Brazil's northeastern townships, to determine whether such marrying practices had led to greater prevalence of certain birth defects. Mathers was a married man, nearly twice her age, but Christine had been vulnerable to his charms. His soft touch and easy manner were, in fact, irresistible.

But then came August and the end to their research work. When they'd arrived at the airport in Chicago, Mathers's wife had been waiting at the gate. Mathers and his wife hugged and soon after went to baggage claim without so much as an acknowledgment of Christine's presence. Despite his passionate promises to Christine, Mathers had had no intention of leaving his wife. Christine had been floored, positively devastated by the kindly man's sudden and unexpected turnabout. How she'd managed to complete her doctoral thesis during the long fall and winter terms that followed was still a mystery to her.

A burst of applause brought her back to the present, and she realized she'd hardly heard the chamber orchestra's rendition of Bach's Sonata in B minor for violin and harpsichord. *Pay attention, Christine*, she reminded herself. *Pay attention or you'll miss something crucial.*

CHAPTER

FOURTEEN

"BRIAN, WHAT'S THE holdup?"

It was Saturday morning. Christine was in the Benson County sheriff's outer office, waiting for Rodney Boynton to get off his phone. Boynton had sounded eager to speak with her and suggested that she drive over to his office right after she finished breakfast. She hoped Eisen could give her something solid in order to gain Boynton's support regarding questioning Shamus Ferguson. When she'd finally reached his assistant, Jacob Graham, she'd been told that the professor was off premises for spring break and would be back in his office in ten days. Which possibly was true, she'd seen his car packed. Or, possibly, he was just avoiding her.

"The Indianapolis lab extracted an unknown steroidal alkaloid, possibly a mixture of compounds, from the Illinois victim's neck tissue," Eisen said. She could hear him flipping through pages. "The mouse withered and died within seconds after injection. In other words, lethality was off the charts. We're dealing with a remarkably stable compound, even after several days and tissue necrosis. What it is exactly, though, remains unclear."

"Good work, Brian." So, Ellen McKinley *was* deliberately poisoned, as Christine suspected. "I recommend that you contact Professor Herbert Brill at the University of Chicago's biological research lab. He routinely tests for active biological agents, as you no doubt remember."

"Electron microscopy of the third cervical vertebrae revealed a needle-size depression consistent with the puncture wound on the back of McKinley's neck," he added.

"It doesn't explain Pernell's finding gold there. Gold is too soft for hypodermic delivery . . ." Christine thought back to her forensics notes on how the bruise marks had brought to mind a hieroglyphic design.

"Perhaps the alkaloid was stored in a gold-tipped dart, Brian. South American Indigenous peoples have long used highly toxic secretions from poison frogs to dart their prey, as I understand from reading an article written by the elusive Professor Ferguson."

It was enough to prove that McKinley's death was not an accident from hypothermia, but the information was too tangential to haul Ferguson in for questioning, in spite of the research he and his lab were doing on potential pharmacological compounds found in nature's deadliest frogs. Just as undeniable, the millions in grant money and private investments from Big Pharma, in Christine's view, tipped the scales toward Ferguson as a person of significant interest.

"Listen, Brian, one more thing." She read him the list of names on the Academic Oversight Committee. "I want full financials on all of them. Go back five years if you can. Also, check to see whether anyone else may have been replaced on the committee in the last three years. I want their names and financials, too. Let me know what you find ASAP."

In perusing Ferguson's treatise on the lethality of several South American frog species last night, she'd found particularly interesting the section comparing frogs with deadly skin to other vibrantly colored species whose glands contained little or no harmful toxin—so-called frog mimics that foiled would-be predators from eating them. Evidently, merely looking deadly had its advantages.

Sheriff Boynton's office door rattled open.

"Special Agent Prusik, please come on in," Boynton said pleasantly. "Joe McFaron said you'd be headed down this way concerning Naomi Winchester, am I right?"

He motioned for her to take a seat in the chair in front of his desk. A man in his mid-fifties and balding, Sheriff Boynton was her same height but quite overweight. His chest heaved as he sat back down in his chair, breathing noisily through the back of his throat. He brushed a finger across a tidy dark moustache.

"Seen a few people on campus already, have you then?" Boynton asked.

"Yes, I have, as a matter of fact." Christine sensed a hint of the territorial imperative in his voice. "I wanted to get an early start. I realize that I should have let you know I was here on the campus." She'd bypassed proper protocol, even though Joe had reminded her—twice—to apprise Boynton of her dealings.

He swatted his heavy hand nonchalantly. "Not a problem. Joe and I are working together on this. Well, on Naomi Winchester at least." He pondered an open folder on his desk, his fleshy forehead beading with fine droplets of sweat.

"That's good to hear." Christine leaned forward in her chair, trying to see what Boynton was studying. "By the way, has Cindy Lawson contacted you in the last couple of days?"

Boynton leaned forward in his chair and planted his elbows on his desk. "Let's get one thing straight, Special Agent. I'm sheriff of Benson County. If there's anybody else that you'd like to speak to, you best clear it with me first. Understood?"

Christine canted her palm. "I can well understand your position." Though the man was clearly irritated, she couldn't let it go just yet. "Then you are aware that Lawson claims some things of Winchester's are missing. I suggested to her that the state crime lab authorities may have collected possible evidence since she volunteered that you hadn't."

"I heard you the first time, Agent Prusik. Now, is there anything else you'd like to bring to my attention?" His cheeks lifted and she could see the edges of his upper teeth—the kind of forced smile someone who doesn't want their picture taken makes for the camera. Christine got the message.

"Yes, there is, Sheriff. I read in your local paper about the terrible car accident this past Thursday night," Christine said. "Involving another CSU coed?"

Boynton pursed his lips. "Funny you should ask about that." He picked up what looked like an accident report. "I don't suppose it would hurt to get your opinion on this since, technically, it happened on Joe McFaron's turf."

He withdrew several photos from the folder and arranged them on the desk, facing her. They were a related grouping of black and whites: one overhead and two from different side angles of dark, tire-size skid marks across the road surface.

"I took these flash photos on Wednesday night. Joe was there, too. As you can see, both front and rear tires left their marks." The sheriff pointed to each tire's impression on the asphalt. "See, they're off angle—the rear tires skidded laterally to the front wheels. Best I can figure, she was riding her brakes the whole time she was being shoved from directly behind into that coal truck's path."

Christine concentrated on the pictures grouped on Boynton's desk. "I'm no tire expert, but you're suggesting that her car was deliberately pushed?"

Boynton produced another picture. "Here's a close-up of a broken piece of plastic lens. I matched it to her hybrid car, the rear right taillight. It was laying on the pavement before the intersection, meaning another vehicle had to have pushed hard enough against the lens to crack it. In my estimation, that, together with the tire marks, suggest her car may have been deliberately pushed into the intersection right as the coal truck was coming through at maximum highway speed. The truck had the green light, after all."

"Couldn't it have been accidental? Someone could have been driving too fast and not seen her car soon enough to brake? The news article mentioned the fog was particularly dense Thursday night, after all the rains."

Boynton grunted. "Sure, you could argue that, Agent Prusik. We've considered different options, too—me and the state police boys, and Joe. But we're talking a level grade at that particular intersection, there's no hill before it. And if the car behind didn't see her because of the dense fog as you say, it would have struck with far greater force. There'd have been a lot more than a small piece off her right rear tail lens. We found nothing from the other car, no paint scrapes left either." He held up the transparent evidence bag containing the lens shard. "Wouldn't you agree?"

Sheriff Boynton's logic did make sense. "It seems plausible. Look, you've obviously got your hands full, Sheriff. And in the interest of joint cooperation, I'd like to discuss—"

The sheriff held up his hand, cutting her off. "I think you

know that Shamus Ferguson has already phoned me." Boynton's grin didn't mesh with the deep wrinkle in his brow. "Before you ask me your next question, Agent Prusik, we need to revisit the way things run in my county, on and off campus. You know— what goes and what don't."

"Yes, but I have reason to believe there's a clear connection—"

"Hold your horses, Agent Prusik." His disingenuous grin broadened. "Your boss already phoned here earlier this morning. We had a nice little chat, too. I got the lay of the land, shall we say."

At Boynton's dismissive wink, Christine felt the rush of blood up her throat and across her cheeks, as if she had just been caught red-handed with her hand in the proverbial cookie jar.

"I'm assuming he confirmed that we're down here assisting with a preliminary assessment?"

"You know, you were right when you said I have my hands full, Agent," he said, ignoring her point, no longer bothering with her name. "I certainly don't want any more trouble than I got already. Sounds to me like you've more than done your preliminary inquiries on Naomi Winchester, seen her roommate and some other people, too. But Shamus?" Boynton shot her a dead serious look. "Just who the hell do you think you're fooling with?" He jabbed the open folder on his desk with a stout index finger.

She'd hit a nerve. So it was "Shamus." Boynton was on a first-name basis with Ferguson.

"We've got toxicology results that point to him, his lab," Christine asserted, knowing she was now near the end of a very skinny limb.

Boynton scrubbed his chin vigorously. "What is that supposed to mean?"

"Look, I can't share that information with you at this time.

We're still working on the analysis." Christine leaned forward in her chair. "It would be a big help to the investigation—"

"Investigation? Get it through your head, Agent Prusik. You've concluded your investigation on this campus. Next time you wish to make an inquiry in my county, you best come to my office with a warrant or court order." He rocked back in his chair, eyeing her steadily.

Ferguson obviously carried plenty of political clout on and off campus, meaning she'd need definitive evidence that pointed to him before she could formally bring him in for questioning. She stood with her briefcase. "So I guess this means we'll not be working together any further?"

It wasn't a real question. There was no point in her arguing science and steroidal compounds with Sheriff Rodney Boynton, whose face had morphed into a wary clump of mistrustful flesh. Someone had obviously read him the riot act. He'd made himself plenty clear. She'd need nothing short of solid evidence to bring Shamus Ferguson in for questioning.

"One thing before you go, Agent Prusik. I promised your Mr. Miranda that I'd give you the directions." He pointed to a large Benson County map pinned on the wall.

"Benson-Parker Twin City Airport is the first exit north of town. Your ticket will be waiting on the counter, I think Mr. Miranda said." He looked at his watch. "If you hurry, you might even catch the 11:15 flight."

Boynton leaned back in his chair, twirling a pencil between his fingers. He made no move to rise.

Prusik grabbed her case and left his office feeling stung by the FBI and boxed in by the small-mindedness of this sheriff, who ironically was expert enough to read the subtleties of a traffic accident scene, and yet showed no interest in delving any further when it came to confronting the uglier truths of the powers that be. Whether management at the FBI or at Calhoun Seymour University, in the end it was always about who wields the power, who has political capital to burn. And Christine realized on both counts she had little to none.

With her former boss, Roger Thorne, she'd had a spate of successful outcomes before the Donald Holmquist case the previous year that had nearly ended her career. Under Patricia Gaston's command, she had no personal successes to rest laurels upon, no case victories in the win column—only a bad start and her mother's warning from long ago about first impressions lasting. If adversity had taught her anything it was that she could not dig her way out alone. She needed to trust; she needed the help of others—of her team, and of Joe McFaron, too.

Her phone buzzed, and a Louisville, Kentucky, area code flashed across its touch screen.

THE CALLER WAS a nurse from the assisted living facility in Louisville, Kentucky, where Christine's mother, Yortza Prusik, had retired. Evidently her mother had tripped on a throw rug in the recreation room and struck her head, briefly losing consciousness.

Christine checked out of the Le Maquis Auberge and carried her bags to the car, considering how she would frame it with Ned Miranda—that a family emergency precluded her from making it back to Chicago as she'd promised him she would yesterday. And now it was her mother's health that trumped her leaving on Saturday.

She quickly texted Miranda that a family health emergency

had come up that forced her to delay her return. If nothing was seriously wrong with her mother, there was still the possibility of her making it back on Sunday, at least in theory.

She punched in the coordinates on the rental's GPS, turned the ignition key, and slipped her road trip Bach CD into the disc player. Airing her mind out while on the road would be a welcome relief.

Two hours later, she crossed the Ohio River under a cloudless sky. From the bridge span, Christine glimpsed a flatbed barge plowing up a muddy trough of water, its decks loaded to the gills with rolled steel. On the Kentucky side, she wended her way through light traffic in downtown Louisville, following the instructions issued by the GPS display. The fact that it was not yet Kentucky Derby time meant there were few out-of-state drivers. She passed a diner with a marquee listing the luncheon special of the day: *White Bread and Gravy—99 Cents.* How could her mother have decided to move here with such awful food! Christine could still smell the homemade sausage and pierogies Yortza had cooked in the small kitchen of their two-story home in Detroit.

Yortza Prusik, originally an émigré from Poland, had raised Christine and her older brother, Hans, in Hamtramck—a neighborhood of Detroit heavily populated with Eastern Europeans. Why the older Prusik had retired to an assisted-living community in the heartland of horse country Christine still couldn't fathom. The fact that two other Hamtramck women decided after their own husbands' deaths to move there still didn't explain her mother's decision to Christine's satisfaction.

Christine entered the circular drive of the Randolph Arms Assisted Living Center and stopped under a portico beside wide front steps and a wheelchair ramp. Inside the place, the smell of aged humans and artificial pine-scented cleanser laced overly warm air, leaving little doubt in Christine's mind that it mainly assisted the aged with dying. Stooped and gnarled candidates slouched over aluminum walkers, dressed in clothes and robes that hung limply on bones shed of defining muscle.

A female attendant with dark hair tightly pinned back spotted her from down the hall and approached Christine in her squishy-sounding white nurse's shoes. "I'm so glad you could come," the attendant said. "Christine, am I right?"

Christine nodded.

"Your mother often speaks of you," the attendant said with a broad smile. Christine detected a sweet odor of cinnamon bun on the woman's breath.

"What exactly happened to my mother, Francesca?" she said, reading from the plastic name tag on the woman's polyester smock. "Can I please see her now?" Christine glanced over the attendant's shoulder down the hallway in the direction of her mother's room and ran her fingers through hair that needed to be shampooed.

Francesca patted Christine on the arm. "It's not to worry. She was only a little bit confused. She's good today."

The attendant's non-medical explanation only tightened the knot of anticipation in Christine's stomach.

Christine proceeded to Room 14, on the first floor, and hesitated at the open doorway. She gazed at her mother—still in her bathrobe—sitting on the edge of her bed, staring out the window. Yortza's wet hair made Christine wonder if Yortza had just showered.

Hearing Christine put down her case, the older Prusik looked up. It was a relief to Christine to see her mother's hawkish eyes already tracking on hers.

"Christine?" Her tone was one of stern surprise. Her short gray hair was cut in an easy-to-care-for boyish style, her querulous brow almost identical to Christine's own.

"I was just in the neighborhood, Mother," Christine said, trying not to sound defensive. "So I thought I'd pop by and see how you're doing."

Yortza's brow creased, a questioning look—the face of a mother who isn't easily fooled by a daughter who has tried so many times before.

"If it's a bad time, I could—"

Yortza waved her off. "You might have at least phoned me first." Her voice was inflected with its trademark gruffness. She patted the back of her damp hair with a towel that Christine hadn't noticed her mother was holding.

"Well, Mother, it is a concern when I receive a phone call that you were found unconscious on the floor," she explained, now sounding defensive.

The older Prusik let out a bemused grunt. "Yes, how nice. Your children come running when you fall down. God forbid that you should get back up."

Christine squeezed her mother's thin forearm, no longer toned from forever scrubbing a boar-bristle brush across their Detroit kitchen floor while Christine was growing up.

"Mother, I promise to do better. As soon as things settle down, let's take a drive, maybe to the Mammoth Caves? I hear they're spectacular."

Christine grimaced at the thought after her recent caving efforts. Her mother raised her eyebrows and said, "Man trouble, is it?" Yortza shook her head. "You have too soft a heart, Christine. Easily wounded by the affections of someone you've placed in too high a regard. You put them up on pedestals. I know this already. You don't have to say a word. Just look at you."

"Mother, please. That was more than fifteen years ago."

Christine castigated herself for perhaps the millionth time that she should have never gone back home after the affair with her grad school professor and mentor had ended so disastrously. Her devastation and grief from it had been all too plain for her mother to see.

"Why I'm here has nothing whatsoever to do with putting men in high regard or on pedestals. I'm working a case. A couple of cases, actually."

Yortza searched her daughter's face, then reached out and held both her hands.

"Just look at you—in the prime of life and not married yet. You know what I am saying, Christine? It is a mother's duty to worry for her only daughter about such things."

"I'm here because of *you*, Mother. It's not grief over some man who dumped me eons ago, for crying out loud."

"Had you phoned first, you would have found out that it was nothing." Yortza patted the small bandage plastered across her right temple. "I had a little spill, that's all. I tripped on a rug. It's nothing to be bothered about."

Christine withdrew her hands from her mother's. The older woman's penetrating stare made her uneasy. She suddenly felt hungry.

As if her mother could tell, the older Prusik beamed. "You

know, Christine, it is a specialty dinner tonight. The kitchen is preparing one of your favorites," she said as if no confrontation had taken place.

Christine relaxed, sat down again on the bed beside her mother, and they hugged. "Pierogies?" she asked, surprised.

Her mother grinned. "What else? With three of us from Detroit living down here, we've been able to influence the menu selection."

Christine gazed out her mother's window. New buds on a crab apple were about to blossom. She thought of the young coed victims who would never experience the tender beauty of a tree blooming again.

"Why do you sulk so much, Christine? Those bags under your eyes are unbecoming. You're not sleeping enough."

Christine released a held breath. "It's my bosses. They're trying to handcuff me to a desk instead of letting me take the lead on catching a killer."

"You know how I feel about your doing such dangerous work. You press yourself so hard, Christine. It is unbecoming for such a lovely girl. Life is more than solving crimes, you know. It's more than a race against the clock."

Christine glanced at her wristwatch out of habit. "Come on, Mother. I'm a forensic scientist, trained to investigate the awful things people do. I know my business. It's what I do. What I do is *not* attending useless unit head meetings and supervising busywork."

"Well, meetings and paperwork certainly sound important to me," Yortza Prusik protested. "Since when do you decide everything?" The line bisecting her mother's mottled forehead made

Christine shudder: it looked just like hers would in another thirty years.

Christine sighed. Would her mother ever be proud of what her only daughter did for a living? She studied two elderly residents as they marched around a small courtyard with the aid of their aluminum walkers. Was the point of working hard in life simply to make it to this, a walker brigade?

She felt an urge to call McFaron and tell him that Sheriff Boynton had shut her investigation down, then thought better of it.

Yortza tugged Christine's sleeve. "So, what is it now, Christine? You've such a long face."

"I'm sorry, Mother. I'm working this Indiana case and the local sheriff there isn't cooperating."

"Not that nice sheriff who helped you before? Who saved your life? The one you were so sure about, Christine?"

"No, it's a new case. And yes, Joe's fine, Mother. We're still good." She made it sound all tidy, wrapped with a bow, when her feelings were all a-tangle, her life at odds as much as it ever was. Her mother *was* right about one thing: flying solo for so long was catching up with her. Her youthful grad student years were long gone. Increasingly, in the predawn shadows, she found a decidedly tired face gazing back at her from dim-lit motel mirrors.

"It's your blind spot, Christine," the older Prusik admonished. "It always has been. When it comes to men, you don't see well. Not well at all."

The older Prusik clutched her daughter's cheeks in both her wizened hands. "I blame myself for it, you know? I wasn't there for you and your brother so much of the time when you were young, as I should have been."

Her mother slumped, looking suddenly exhausted. "You see, at some point, I couldn't take it anymore. I just gave up." She turned her head away in shame. "I didn't know how to handle it all, the cooking, housecleaning, working all the time. But worst of all, I didn't know how to handle you and Hans. And I couldn't be there for you."

"It's okay, Mother. Don't—"

"I spent a lot of time in my bedroom, fretting," the older woman continued, as if she hadn't heard Christine. "I was so anxious. I could hear you and Hans downstairs, and, of course, your father, too. But I just couldn't . . ." Yortza looked up at Christine, her eyes brimming with tears. "I never gave you or Hans the kind of affection that a mother should. I know it.

"And your father . . ." She paused, then shook her head in sorrow. "He was always going on about you—your laziness, your not training hard enough, on and on. He wasn't nearly as hard on Hans as he was on you, Christine. I don't know why . . ." Yortza shook her head.

"But you were not lazy at all, Christine. You worked so hard with your swimming, your schooling. I was so proud of you! If only he could see now what all his criticism has done. He has made you not trust yourself with men."

Christine patted her mother's shoulder. "That's not true, Mother." But maybe it was true. Her mother had been absent a lot, and her father *had* been critical of her so much of the time. Longing for his love had produced a great void in Christine's adult life long after Herman Prusik died—the same summer she was assaulted in New Guinea. Had she only come home from field work a month sooner, she would have had a chance to see her father one last time. Maybe they could have talked.

"It sounds like you were anxious, Mother. And a little depressed?"

"Mostly anxious, I think."

"Why? Was it because of Dad?"

"No, Christine. It had nothing to do with your father. I was just so . . . fraught." She wrung her hands, shaking her head. "When a mother is most needed, I wasn't able to do even the simplest things."

Christine took a deep breath. Her mother's sense of guilt and sorrow were palpable. She felt badly for her mother, who'd had to battle her anxiety without meds or therapy—or Bach. Her mother, who thought she was supposed to be able to tough it out, had blamed herself for not always succeeding in doing so.

Seeing her distraught was distressing, and at that moment, Christine felt keenly aware of the lack of love she had felt as a child, with a never-satisfied father and an anxious, absent mother. Had this longing for attention somehow stunted her growth?

Or was it something more? Christine was still fighting panic attacks on a weekly basis, sixteen long years after she'd been attacked in the jungles of Papua New Guinea. Doing doctoral graduate fieldwork on her own, she'd ventured too far into the remote homeland of a people who still practiced a bloodthirsty ritual: vivisection and the consumption of the victim's vital organs. The attack itself was not so much a memory as a never-gone cerebral crush that ambushed her, seemingly at will. Subconsciously, Christine's mind still couldn't accept that she'd escaped, and the eyes of her riverbank attacker continued to haunt her at night and in daydreams.

The panic attacks—her Achilles' heel—seemed as much a part of her nature as solving crimes. She wondered if it would always be that way, or whether she'd ever break free of the disabling scramble of emotions and find true inner peace in life, a serenity and happiness that had evaded her so far.

Christine stepped out into the hallway that reeked of pungent ammonia cleanser. She dialed Joe McFaron's cell number. It had been a couple of days since they'd last spoken, and she needed to hear the voice of someone who was on her side. She got put through to his voicemail.

"Hi, Joe, it's Christine. I'm down visiting my mother in Louisville today. I'll be catching a flight back to Chicago from here. I'd like to catch up with you, compare notes and see where we are before I leave."

She hoped he'd have more to report and could find a way to defuse the situation with Sheriff Boynton. Probably Boynton had already phoned and read him the riot act. Leaving her message made her feel better even if it hadn't accomplished much.

Visiting her mother had been more than she bargained for. But then it usually was. Yortza never failed to say what was on her mind, and that afternoon had been no exception. She'd gone right to the nub of it—Christine's unresolved issues with her father and her star-crossed love affairs or ones that never quite got off the ground in the first place. Maybe her mother was right. She sighed. Forging a real relationship, whatever the hell that meant, would require a leap into the unknown; call it a leap of faith. The thought terrified her.

Growing up had always been about chasing for the next breath. Every high school workout had ended with Christine, heaved over her knees, listening to her father prodding her to do better. She might have told herself that she was backstroking against the clock, but in reality she'd been in a race for her father's approval the whole time. She'd been waiting for praises that never came from the man who held the stopwatch, cramming the proof of her shortcomings right in her face at the end of each practice before she'd even had time to catch her breath.

When she'd finished in first place her senior year with a record-breaking performance at a seven-school invitational meet, he'd said, "Good job," and then immediately added, "Your second turn was a little sloppy though. Next time, you must spring off the wall harder, Christine."

That was how she remembered him. No matter how hard she tried to please him, he'd always be the first to let her know her efforts weren't quite good enough. And yet, ironically, his relentless pushing had produced a miracle for which Christine would always be grateful. Had he not driven her, mercilessly, it seemed at times, to become the swimmer she was, her death in the jungle would have been inevitable, for it was only her strength in the rushing river that had saved her.

CHAPTER
FIFTEEN

SPRING BREAK HERALDED the annual migration of thousands of Norteamericano students to all points south of the border. Throngs of young sun worshippers headed to the Yucatán and Cancun's white crystal sands, while archaeology buffs and the more studious college crowd headed to the central highlands, where scores of ancient ruins lay hidden beneath overgrown jungles south and east of Mexico City.

On the first official day of the break, a hot and sticky Saturday, a group of fifty CSU students and their two chaperones landed in Mexico at the Aeropuerto Internacional de la Ciudad. After clearing customs and settling in to their rooms at the Fiesta Inn, a not-so-trendy, moderately priced establishment, the students were to reconvene for an evening program of slides featuring the ancient culture and monuments of the pre-Colombian Americas in preparation for Sunday's visit to the Teotihuacan pyramids and Monday's trip to the Museo Nacional de Antropología in Mexico City's central district. Tuesday the group would be changing locations, heading south to Oaxaca and the famous Monte Albán ruins.

In the meantime, Phyllis Overton, a romance language professor with an exceedingly pale complexion who was one of the two faculty chaperones, reviewed the itinerary yet one more time and reconfirmed each day's arrangements with the tour operator. The other chaperone, who had volunteered his services several months earlier, couldn't believe his good fortune when he was selected to join the trip. Being a rainmaker does have its unexpected privileges, Shamus Ferguson mused as he sat in the hotel bar late Saturday afternoon nursing a glass of Gran Patron Platinum tequila.

SUNDAY AFTERNOON, CHRISTINE followed Miranda into Patricia Gaston's office with the dread of a schoolgirl being shown to the principal's office. The branch director asked them both to sit while she got up from her desk and closed the door behind them.

Christine felt compelled to say something. "I'm sorry, Patricia, for missing the unit head meeting on Thursday. I—"

"If you don't mind, Christine, I'd like to speak first. Obviously this is important or we wouldn't be here on a Sunday." The branch director planted her palms on the desk and regarded Christine evenly. "I had a call late last night from Calhoun Seymour University's provost. He wanted to know why there was an FBI agent on campus interviewing professors and students without the knowledge of the local sheriff responsible for the investigation of Naomi Winchester's death. I think we both know that you had no authority to interrogate teachers and students on the campus at this juncture."

"Okay, yes, I was there. But as a follow-up to examining Winchester's body, having determined that the two deaths—"

"You're missing the point, Agent Prusik," Gaston interrupted her again. "You didn't have clearance from Agent Miranda or from me to conduct a full-scale investigation. In fact, you had no authority at all. This office hasn't federally preempted state jurisdiction in the Illinois or the Benson, Indiana, case either.

"I might add that the provost was particularly unhappy that you had disturbed a Professor Shamus Ferguson who, I understand, runs . . ." She held her reading glasses to her eyes and read from notes, "the Pembroke Research Center, an internationally known facility that brings the university millions in government research grants each year."

"If I may explain," Christine said, "there is a strong connection linking—"

Gaston raised her palm. "I'm sure you had your reasons. But there's a thing called protocol that we follow here. Unless you are given specific authorization through the proper channels there shall be no further unannounced visits to the CSU campus. That includes me, Miranda, members of your forensic team, and most especially you. Are we clear on that point, Agent Prusik?"

Christine's cheeks glowed. She bit her lip, reminded that Gaston hadn't informed her of Winchester's death when she'd first learned of it. What good was following protocol if they were operating at cross purposes?

Miranda remained silent. It was as if he wasn't even in the room.

Gaston eased back in her chair. "Now then, we've another matter to discuss. The PTQPs are to be completed within another week's time. This assignment originated in the home office. See to it that you stay on task. Do you understand?"

Christine nodded.

"That'll be all then."

Christine stood and left the office. Miranda remained seated.

MIRANDA WAITED A few extra moments after Christine had closed the door behind her before speaking. "He's using an unauthorized burner. I found it inside his side drawer," he said to Gaston.

"That's certainly bold of him," Gaston said. "Have you run a check on calls he's made from it?"

Miranda shook his head. "It's new, unused. My guess is that Hughes purchased a multipack at a discount house and tosses them after each contact. They're cheap and it's safer that way. He's clever."

"Not that clever," Gaston said. "It's a violation of Bureau protocol to use auxiliary electronic equipment without specific authorization."

"Maybe Prusik knows about it," Miranda said. "I haven't inquired as I didn't want to alert her for obvious reasons."

Gaston nodded. "Right, I understand. Has he left the office or done anything else suspicious?"

"He's never very forthcoming whenever I speak with him. Unless I ask a specific question, he has nothing to volunteer."

"I appreciate the heads-up, Ned. Keep up the monitoring."

After Miranda left her office, Gaston placed a phone call to Ed Meachum, the special agent sent from Washington headquarters. If Hughes had logged in to his PTQP program, Meachum and his team would be able to monitor his behavior in the office. If he hadn't, Prusik or Miranda would have to find a way to make him do it. In the meantime, at least she'd report what Miranda had said to her, flagging Leeds Hughes as a person of interest.

HE WALKED TOWARD the window, glancing over his shoulder although no one else was in the office. "Look, I've already told you," he spoke into the cell phone with considerable gravity. "I'll have it to you by Friday."

The agent leaned his left wrist against the fax machine. His diaphragm constricted tightly as he listened to the litany of threats, the caller saving the worst for last: his being found out, reported to his agency superiors for his misdeeds, the times, the dates, everything. They had him where they wanted him—between the proverbial rock and a hard place. And with each anguishing phone call they repeated the same threats, grating his nerves, to make damn sure that he knew just how far they were willing to go to extract it from him. What he owed them. What he could never get out from under. It was hopeless.

"Please . . . I promised you I would. You'll have it. Please don't . . ."

The caller clicked off the line. But it wasn't over. It wasn't even a reprieve. It was like pulling off a fresh scab, a one-way ticket, and there was no getting out, no getting away. It wouldn't have mattered so much if he didn't care so much. But what good was it telling himself that? It was too late. Much too late.

Eisen walked into the office, saw the agent hunched over the fax machine, and said, "Everything okay?"

IT WAS LATE afternoon, and the concourse was humming with activity: parents tugging kids by their hands, men and women in suits, briskly wheeling their flight luggage down the hallways toward their connecting flights. O'Hare International Airport was bustling, which was good.

To avoid the overhead closed circuit cameras, he trailed closely behind a tall businessman towing a large legal case while talking on his cell phone through a Bluetooth earpiece. An easy hundred that he'd paid a janitor pushing a hamper had gained him access through a passageway used by airport employees, which led him straight to Concourse B, without TSA or Homeland Security to deal with.

Just ahead, gate numbers hung above alcoves where passengers were seated, waiting to board their flights. It seemed funny to him, seeing the Air Canada flight between gates leaving for Brussels and London. Toronto was at most an hour by plane and even doable by car in less than a day's drive. The drone of the PA system announced arrival of Fl 314 from Toronto, Canada. He checked his watch. It had arrived on time.

He drifted in front of a sunglass kiosk, keeping an eye on the ramp agent in charge of the doorway to the jet bridge for the deplaning passengers from Fl 314. The doorway opened and the first-class passengers began trooping into the waiting area. He edged away from the kiosk in the direction of the men's restroom, still within sight of the gate. Exiting passengers were now coming in force as the economy seats emptied.

He appreciated the convenience of airport bathrooms. Entering and exiting them didn't require the use of your hands needed for pulling carry-on cases and clutching briefcases. Meaning leaving no fingerprints, either. He entered the bright-lit bathroom and crossed to the far sink next to a bank of gleaming stainless hand dryers mounted on the white tile wall.

He placed the manila envelope on the sink ledge between his sink and the next one, then passed his hand in front of the automated soap dispenser that squirted a glob of foam onto his palm. Scrubbing his hands together in front of the touchless faucet activated a jet of water. He gazed into the mirror while washing. Sag lines were etched under his eyes. He'd been losing sleep—the cost of a troubled mind.

Things had escalated way beyond the original deal. He hadn't seen it coming. He'd only wanted to help his father get out of hock. The old man was up to his ears in debt and had made the mistake of borrowing money from the wrong sort of people, because no right-thinking moneylender would have anything to do with granting his father a loan given his circumstances, his outstanding liabilities. So he'd stepped up, as a good son does. He'd intervened on his father's behalf with the moneylender, or rather the lender's boss, who said he'd make it easy for him. Instead of handing over a large chunk of his salary every two weeks for the next few years, he could clear his father's debt a much easier way.

He splashed water on his face. He was here, again, at the airport meet and drop because he hadn't a choice. He was in deeper than even his father was. Initially, he'd found some peace of mind rationalizing that the decision to pass the information wasn't so bad because it was relatively low-level material—to his way of thinking, it hardly qualified as being of a classified nature. But enlisting him for the easy stuff had only been to get their foot in the door. And now they owned him like they owned his father.

A man wearing a three-quarter-length tan overcoat with wide lapels entered the restroom and stood at the next sink over. Their eyes briefly met: a millisecond acknowledgment that conveyed clearly enough that he was theirs and that he was still cooperating, having delivered the manila envelope as he'd been instructed to.

This was the fourth meet at the airport venue in the last four weeks. After the last time, he was still telling himself it wasn't so bad on the scale of bad things bad people do. It wasn't like selling the Iranians fissionable bomb-making material or passing tactical military secrets to Al Qaeda. It concerned only the home front, and it was nothing like that, he kept repeating to himself.

The ugly truth was much simpler than that: there was absolutely nothing he could do about it until they said so.

He placed his wet hands under the automatic dryer. He winced at the roar of its turbulent air blast, and when he turned around, the man in the tan overcoat was gone, and so was the manila envelope.

SUNDAY EVENING CHRISTINE'S phone beeped on the kitchen counter in her Chicago apartment. She'd just picked up a favorite Szechwan to-go order for dinner from the Chinese restaurant down her block.

The touch screen registered an unknown caller number. "Hello?"

"It's so nice to hear your voice again, Christine."

A smile spread across her face. She put the phone on speaker and poured herself a glass of Cabernet. "Well, what a pleasant surprise to hear yours, too, Corbin."

"I'm at my desk grading term papers during spring break and I thought I would take a moment to say that it was lovely to see you at the concert. Perhaps, when you return to Benson, we could have dinner?"

"Why thank you, Corbin. I'd like that very much. Truthfully, I'm not exactly sure when I'll be back." She hesitated, feeling the sting of her own words and the sting of Gaston's earlier rebuke. Banned from the CSU campus and chained to a desk were thoughts too dark to contemplate; she forced them from her mind.

"Ah-ha, I see," he said, still sounding cheerful. "But a man can always hope, can he not?"

"Well, don't give up on me just yet. By the way, could I ask you a question?"

"Of course you may."

"How long have you been a member of the Academic Oversight Committee?"

"I believe it will be ten years come this May," he said.

"So, I would imagine, then, that you've seen any number of committee members come and go during that time period, right?"

"True, there have been a few. But I really can't discuss the composition of the committee, Christine. It's not such a good idea. Not without the express permission of the university provost, you understand."

"I know, I know. But tell me this much, were the members currently serving on the committee present at the time of Peter Franklin's untimely death?"

"I believe so. But I really can't discuss details of that nature further. On the other hand, there are plenty of subjects I look forward to discussing with you, and I do hope you will call me when you are next in town. I so enjoyed your company."

"And I as well," she said echoing his sentiment.

The spontaneity of his call both surprised and warmed her. She'd made at least one friend on the CSU campus, even if she'd alienated Ferguson and Benson's sheriff Boynton in the process.

CHAPTER
SIXTEEN

MONDAY MORNING CHRISTINE'S staff was gathered in the large conference room, where she hastily collected hard copies of their profiles and put them aside. Standing at the front of the room she nodded at Eisen. "Start us off, Brian. Where do we stand thus far with the evidence?"

"The Indiana Crime Bureau delivered the tissue sample taken from Naomi Winchester to the Macalister Pharmaceutical lab in Indianapolis, where they analyzed it using a gas chromatography–mass spectrometry instrument, or GC-MS," Eisen said. "Which we don't have. We could use one, you know."

Pernell Wyckoff muttered his assent.

"I'll be sure to put it on our Christmas list," Christine said. "So what was the finding?" Brian had a nerve-racking way of dillydallying before delivering important news to her.

"Remember those trace unknown steroidal compounds from before, from the Illinois victim?"

"You know that I do. Spill it, Brian." Christine needed something big to march into Gaston's office with, something that would put her solidly in positive territory.

"Trace amounts of a highly unusual alkaloid, a deadly biological toxin, as a matter of fact, were present big time in the Winchester sample. It's called Batrachotoxin. Dr. Randall Creighton heads up the Macalister laboratory's research division. It turns out Creighton himself happens to be one of the foremost experts on Batrachotoxin research in the country."

"Macalister did you say?" Sheriff McFaron had mentioned that lab. Suddenly she realized the connection. Graham, Ferguson's research assistant, had written down the names of the members of the Academic Oversight Committee on a piece of paper taken from Ferguson's desk—and *Macalister Pharmaceuticals'* name and logo had been stamped at the top. What was Macalister Pharmaceuticals stationery doing in Shamus Ferguson's office? Tim Millard had also mentioned that Peter Franklin had interned at Macalister, and then only a few months later was unexpectedly found dead in his car in the Pembroke parking lot.

"Macalister Pharmaceuticals and the Pembroke Research Center at CSU both have aggressive programs studying poison dart frog toxins," Christine said, "which is more than an interesting coincidence under the circumstances. In your conversation with Dr. Creighton, did he happen to mention a technician named Peter Franklin who once worked there?"

Eisen shook his head. "Dr. Creighton wouldn't offer any particulars over the phone, other than to confirm his ongoing research with Batrachotoxin. One thing he did volunteer that you'll find interesting," Eisen continued, reading from his notes. "He was particularly emphatic stating that his laboratory has nothing whatsoever to do with the activities of the Pembroke Research Center. He repeated the point."

"It sounds like Randall Creighton has something to hide," she said.

"I certainly would have expected greater openness from the

man given he'd assisted the Indiana State Police with Winchester's tissue analysis," Eisen said.

"I would imagine Creighton and Ferguson are very familiar with each other's work in light of its highly esoteric nature. It's also likely they fight for the same research dollars, too," Christine said, itching to catch the next plane to Indianapolis. If Creighton freely volunteered such denials, what else was he covering up? she wondered.

"Paul, what financials have you uncovered so far?"

Paul Higgins, a thin man in his mid-twenties who was the youngest member on her forensics team, was her internet ace. He was bent over his lap, studying notes. "Ferguson's Pembroke Center recently received a fifteen million dollar federal grant, outbidding Macalister, whose own proposal was rejected by NIH."

"Private labs can receive public money?" Christine interjected.

"In this case, yes. NIH made the multiyear grant money available to all research facilities working on innovative compounds in the treatment of multiple sclerosis, certain cancers, and chronic pain disorders. Pembroke won the bid."

"By the way," Eisen interrupted. "That True Catch belay device attached to Ellen McKinley's body?"

"Yes?"

"We've confirmed—rather, Paul did—that it was most likely sold by a Clyde's Outdoor Gear Shop, which is located a few miles from the CSU campus in Benson, Indiana. The same place where Jane Pirrung made a credit card purchase on the night of her fatal car accident."

"Well, well . . ."

Higgins looked up from his notes. "I got in touch with the

climb shop's bookkeeper, who identified thirteen sales transacted that day: eleven were by credit card, including the victim's, and two were cash sales."

"Anything significant about the goods purchased?" Christine asked.

"Pirrung bought several climbing aids called Friends, which were posted on her Visa card account at 9 p.m. on Thursday," Higgins said. "Her credit transaction happened to be the second to last sale—there was a cash purchase made one minute after Pirrung's sale.

"What was it for?" Christine stepped closer to Higgins.

He glanced down, and then said, "For one hundred and fifty feet of Perlon 9mm climbing rope."

Christine flashed on the rope wrapped around the large beech tree above the cave entrance in Crosshaven. She'd fed the rope out as she descended using the mechanical devices the way the trooper had instructed her, down-climbing into utter darkness, only broken by thin threads of the headlamps affixed to her, McFaron, and the other troopers' safety helmets.

"Describe the rope brand?"

"Premtex, it's a high-end manufacturer of premium quality climbing rope. A blue with gold thread outer braid surrounds an internal multi-core nylon dynamic weave with a tensile breaking strength of 6,600 pounds, which is guaranteed by the manufacturer to take five falls without failure. The shop had to special order it." Higgins looked up from his notes. "According to the bookkeeper, the customer paid the full one hundred and sixty-five dollars at the counter. In cash."

Too large an amount of cash to casually carry unless the customer had been planning to make the purchase in advance, she surmised. "Excellent, that's very thorough, Paul. Did you contact the store clerk for a description of the purchaser?"

"I'm afraid that's a dead end, Christine," Eisen cut in. "The Indiana State Police reported earlier today that the clerk's body was discovered in a ditch five miles from the shop, the back of his head bashed in with some kind of tool, a rock hammer perhaps. Unfortunately, the climb store had no security camera."

Christine let out a breath. The store clerk was likely murdered because he could no doubt identify the killer, which means the killer had frequented the store.

"Brian, I want you and Paul to check the names of all customers who made purchases that day. And check for repeat customers going three months back, no, make that six months. Anyone's name pops up that is connected to CSU, you call me immediately. Also," Christine said, "check to see if a name and contact phone number was left by the person who special ordered that Premtex rope," although she felt sure they would find none, or an alias at best. The purchaser was the killer, that was the obvious explanation, and he was covering his tracks well.

Christine looked up, about to ask Leeds Hughes whether he'd found any unknown sources of DNA on the victim's clothing. Hughes's chair was empty. The heavyset scientist was slowly walking toward the door with a cell phone cradled close to his ear.

"IT'S A GOOD offer, Mr. Hughes, close to your ask. And the buyer has no problem with financing. They're prepared to buy it for cash. Shall I fax you the paperwork?"

The Realtor was just doing her job, but her sunny disposition annoyed him.

"Okay then."

Hughes gave her the fax number and clicked off the phone, cutting the saleswoman off mid-sentence, some question about when the well water was last tested. He couldn't answer her now. The reality of it was too bitter a pill to swallow, and for a split-second even his obligations to his sister and her children seemed unfair, unjust. Until he reminded himself of her desperation when she'd cried over the phone to him last fall, telling him that "Doug the thug"—how he now referred to her deadbeat husband who'd run off with some young nameless nobody—had left her and their two children high and dry.

A minute later the fax machine beeped and the purchase and sale agreement documents began pumping out of the laser printer, ten pages of fine print.

He gazed at the pages without reading them, the memories flooding back. Every summer he'd spend several weeks with his grandfather fishing and living on the small lake in northern Wisconsin, building campfires and skinning trout and bass and grilling them on a coal black iron skillet with fresh-cut potatoes. His granddad had deeded him alone the camp. Even though finding time to get away nowadays had become difficult, Hughes was contented knowing that it was always there—the loons' haunting call, the full moon rising and glittering its path of silvery light in the calm lake waters, spending quiet days in the rowboat, waiting for the tug on the fishing line.

His sister and two nephews were living on half his paycheck, and the remainder barely covered what he owed for rent, food, and his increasing outstanding debts, which didn't allow him much margin for entertainment. Selling the fishing camp would

translate into his nephews' college fund or some other unfore-
seen cost that needed to be taken care of.

Hughes knew he was bumping against the upper reaches of a
senior technical scientist's pay grade no matter how he described
himself on the PTQP paperwork. So he would continue to do
whatever it took, even if it left him miserable.

IT WAS 6:15 and the sky was ablaze with the setting sun when
her apartment buzzer rang. Christine had spent the whole of
Monday inside Bureau offices. She'd even made Gaston's unit
head meeting on time and delivered her team's first pass PTQPs.

She opened the hall door and couldn't believe her eyes. "What
in God's name . . . ?" A flush warmed her throat.

"It's been a while since I last was standing here." Roger Thorne
smiled as he inspected the threshold, perhaps caught in the memory. He looked as distinguished as ever. "I'm not disturbing you I
hope?" He gave her a sheepish grin.

Christine ushered him in. "No, of course not. Please come in,
Roger."

They hadn't been in the same room together since last fall
when he'd left his post as director of the Chicago branch to take a
position at headquarters in Washington. They'd worked together
for many years when he was branch director, and their brief affair
nearly ten years earlier hadn't proved too troublesome an impedi-
ment, at least not to her thinking. Of course there was the whole
issue of forging his signature on an agency directive last year
when he still was in charge of the Chicago office, but thankfully
they'd seemed to have gotten past that, too.

"Please, sit down." Christine offered him a cushioned chair

in her living room, snatching up a blouse that was draped over its armrest. She plowed a space on the couch for herself, shoving the contents of the overnight bag that she'd meant to take to the cleaners onto the floor.

Thorne put down his briefcase and took off his overcoat, carefully folding it over the back of the chair. He was snappily dressed in a pin-striped navy blue suit, a white shirt with a button-down collar, and a red tie with sharply drawn horses in various poses. He looked ready for a funeral or a heads of state dinner.

"Earlier today I met with Patricia." There was some hesitancy in his voice.

"And you thought that maybe I could use some extra scolding for blowing off two meetings with her? I actually *did* make today's meeting. Did she mention that?"

Thorne turned red-faced. The outline of arteries appeared on either side of his neck. "You think this is all a joke? The high alerts, the electronic chatter?" His eyes took on that stony look they got when he was angry. "They're constantly moving, circulating in panel trucks and vans, flinging prepaid burner phones out the window hour after hour. Private meets offline at all hours. The country is a sieve, Christine. Our borders are too porous and too vast to protect . . ."

Christine was silent for a moment. "Just what exactly are we talking about, Roger?"

Thorne pinched his brow. "Did you ever once stop and think what else this PTQP initiative might be useful for?"

"Downsizing smaller field offices?"

He shook his head. "My job as deputy director of Homeland Planning Strategies is to monitor movements, both inside and outside of the Bureau. Everything, everybody, day and night, we're operationally active."

"That sounds very stressful, Roger. Forgive me for asking, but why exactly are you here?"

"Because I told Patricia, your boss, that you were damn good at your job." His arteries bulged above his collar. "And worth keeping on board, in spite of the fact you don't listen well and you certainly have a poor attendance record at staff meetings."

"Surely a phone call would have sufficed?"

"I seriously doubt that. As much as you may hate to hear this, it's no longer good enough to *just* chase killers. It's about multi-tasking, Christine. Like it or not, call it a sign of the times if you must. I well remember you saying to your team, 'We must stay one step ahead,' and that is precisely why you must trust your superiors' orders. You *will* follow orders on this PTQP business. Think of it this way: Gaston's orders are mine. It's the chain of command way. Same as it always was."

"So what's next on the agenda? I stick to my office and wait for the higher-ups to tell me when to jump?" She shook her head in disgust. "After the next college woman is found dead? Ignore the forensic chatter of two, possibly three, no, make that really four murders if you add in a techie named Peter Franklin, who mysteriously turned up dead in his car in the Pembroke Research Center parking lot two years ago. Back burner the murders for now all because Christine's getting her priorities straight. Is that the takeaway of the day?"

Something obviously was still troubling Thorne. A sardonic chuckle slipped from Thorne's lips. "You haven't lost your edge one damn bit." His expression sobered. "You seem to have forgotten that I could have had your badge. Had you permanently dismissed from the Bureau for forging my name to that directive in the Holmquist investigation. What if Holmquist had killed someone else instead of you capturing him? What then?" he said, referring to the bizarre Donald Holmquist case that she'd successfully concluded only a year ago.

"So why didn't you? You needn't have come to my doorstep to remind me of that, assuming it really is your and Patricia's prerogative that I stay put on the murder investigation?"

"Well, don't think I hadn't given it serious thought. You're not a one-woman army the last time I checked your job description. Go easy, will you. I shouldn't have to remind you that ignoring a superior's order is dangerous business, especially with a new branch director, and especially in these times of . . . great uncertainty."

"Kind of sounds like you just did."

"Stop jumping to conclusions and just listen a minute, will you?" Thorne opened his briefcase and handed her a manila file folder. "Like I said, supervising your forensics unit's progress on the PTQPs is only the half of it."

She studied the file on a Chrissie Blakemore.

"You weren't involved in this CSU investigation because I turned it over to our St. Louis office to handle," Thorne said. "Greg Morrison was the branch director of St. Louis at the time. He had a daughter attending Calhoun Seymour University in Benson. Morrison had personally phoned me, requesting permission to handle the case back then."

"I vaguely recall something about that," she said. "A missing college student, right? About five years ago?"

Thorne nodded. "That's right. Morrison called me two days ago, after hearing the news about the two college women whose deaths you're investigating. He's retired now." Thorne looked unwaveringly into her eyes. "That call and this file are the reason I am here. That and since Gaston was already at wit's end . . ."

"Yes, yes, you've made your point." Christine perused a few pages of the file as Thorne continued to address her with a few case particulars.

"Chrissie Blakemore was an undergraduate sophomore. No declared major yet," he said. "Her body was found in a shallow cave not far from the CSU campus, and I would imagine not all that far from where your second victim was found."

"I'm puzzled, Roger. This all is rather far afield from your present duties. Why the sudden interest in investigative cases? You could have passed this file on to Patricia Gaston or faxed it directly to me for that matter."

"Because my daughter Kelly is a senior at CSU, and I'm very concerned for her safety."

"Oh, wow, I had no idea your daughter was enrolled there, Roger."

"I was born in Indianapolis. I attended CSU for my undergraduate degree. Some consider it the Ivy League of the Midwest, you know. Lavinia, my wife, wasn't in favor of Kelly going there, but I thought my daughter should experience her family's roots, at least on her father's side." He shook his head. "But these killings . . ."

"Why don't you just transfer your daughter to another school? Wouldn't that have been simpler?"

"Don't think I haven't tried. However, she's midway through her senior year and plans on going to grad school in Chicago next year. She needs to finish out the school year." He sighed. "Besides, she's stubborn as hell, Christine. Not unlike you. She flatly refuses to leave no matter what I say. I was just down there, trying my best to reason with her."

Christine flipped to the postmortem report. There was an asterisk by cause of death, citing a biochemical assay report that concluded that toxin ingestion was a likely cause. "You do realize the two victims that I've examined both sustained wounds to the backs of their necks—an injected substance of a highly toxic nature? From my quick read-through, the exam photos and pathologist's report on Blakemore, she doesn't fit."

"No, perhaps not precisely, but Blakemore was a similarly aged female student whose body was found in a cave or some kind of depression. That biochemical assay report of Blakemore's esophagus and stomach contents is consistent with ingestion of something caustic enough to peel the lining right off her stomach, for God's sake." Christine was impressed that Thorne had actually read the grim details. Thorne had never enjoyed discussing ugly morgue particulars.

Christine perused the chemical and attendant pathology findings in the assay report. Blakemore had suffered violent convulsions triggered by an abnormally high concentration of Scopolamine, a powerful alkaloid, and several other related compounds that likely had caused her death. The actual causative agent was unknown. The word *alkaloid* echoed—Eisen's own use of the word in describing McKinley's tissue findings.

The investigative notes to the Blakemore file were frustratingly few. "The agent who investigated the case, did he keep a personal notebook? There's not much of a write-up here, not even a list of persons of interest?"

"You'll need to check that with Greg Morrison."

"Who's retired?"

"Correct."

"It says here a Samuel Heidegger was the agent handling the case."

"Unfortunately, Sam died three years ago after suffering a massive heart attack."

She expelled a long breath.

"You need to return to CSU."

"And I need to oversee my unit's profiles using weird metrics that sound like I'm manning a shop full of robots. Have you *seen* the Hayes-Stanley protocol?"

"Yes, you do and yes, I have." Thorne's face was drained of humor. "You need to catch this killer, Christine. I'm counting on you."

She shrugged. "Gaston won't let me anywhere near that campus without her personal authorization."

"You'll have authorization."

Christine studied Thorne's face.

"There's one more thing," Thorne said, pressing the tabs shut on his briefcase. "We're watching your team's movements—everyone's movements—because there's a mole in your agency." He held up his hand. "I'm not at liberty to say anything more. It's squarely in Patricia's court. She has our full support."

"Meaning there's an outside team already in place here?"

Thorne ignored the question. "I'm depending on your expertise and unfettered loyalty to task, Christine." He stood. "Pack your bags right now. Take care of business. You've an excellent team. You have the professional determination to see this through. I'm confident of it."

"Where is this all leading, Roger? I mean, besides my dismissal after all hell breaks loose?"

"Believe me when I say that Patricia *is* on your side, ultimately. Work with her. Give her what she wants. And give me what I want, too."

Christine sat at her kitchen table and opened the Blakemore file while forking lukewarm Szechwan chicken into her mouth. It was reasonable to conclude that Blakemore's death was related to the current ones. She'd been a female CSU student, poisoned to death, and her body had been left in a shallow depression. Whoever was responsible five years ago for Chrissie Blakemore's death—if it was tied to the recent women's deaths—it suggested that the killer had evolved his technique, changed his brand to something truly unique, and was now more indelibly leaving his mark. Could something that had been uncovered—or missed—in the Blakemore investigation help her with her own?

And now another dark spot loomed, this one much closer to home: there was an apparent mole in her branch's midst. Surely not someone from her unit, whose scope of responsibilities was scientific in nature and couldn't conceivably benefit anyone interested in harming the country at large?

CHAPTER
SEVENTEEN

THE SULFUROUS HAZE that hung over Mexico City eventually dissipated as the dilapidated tour bus carrying the CSU group made its way out of the urban sprawl and into the countryside on Tuesday morning.

The six-hour drive over twisting potholed highways left the beleaguered students dead on their feet, so Wednesday was declared a rest day. Shamus Ferguson, for one, was delighted. It would give him plenty of time to explore the culturally rich city—and to run his errand.

CHRISTINE STOPPED AT the nurse's station of the Randolph Arms Assisted Living Center in Louisville, Kentucky, for the second time in four days. The call from her mother had awakened her before sunup on Tuesday. Christine had thoughtfully taped her cell number to Yortza's bedside table with instructions for her mother to call her for any emergencies or any reason at all, 24/7, and Yortza had taken Christine at her word.

Evidently, a strange package had been delivered in a puffy envelope addressed to Christine but sent to the Randolph Arms. Mistakenly believing the package was from Christine, Yortza had opened it. When she realized her mistake she'd put it aside and forgotten about it—until early the next morning, when she'd woken up thinking about the odd contents. Christine had gotten on the first flight she could.

It was 11 a.m. sharp when she arrived. "I'm here to see Yortza Prusik," she said to the duty nurse while signing the register. She turned back a few pages, scanning the visitor log, and stopped once she spotted her own signature from the previous Sunday morning. No other visitors were listed to see her mother.

"Are you personally aware of anyone else who may have visited my mother since Sunday morning?"

"They would have to sign the register first if they had, ma'am."

The nurse's perfunctory reply didn't give Christine much confidence. There were too many doors accessing the retirement center, which was a sprawling, renovated maze of wings built in a different era, possibly once a hospital or sanatorium. She imagined that it would be easy to snoop and check out residents without signing in.

"So, it's never the case that someone visits a parent or relative and doesn't sign in?"

The nurse looked sheepishly at her. "Of course, they can. Sometimes a whole family will come for a visit, even grandkids. We don't ask every member to sign in. But we always ask that someone representing the family sign the register for the resident they are here to see."

Slipshod security, just as Christine suspected. She'd hoped for something more—a name, even a false signature on the register would do.

"You needn't get up," Christine said to the desk nurse. "I know the way." In one fluid motion she lifted her briefcase, shouldered her forensic case, and headed toward the hallway wing that led to her mother's first-floor room.

"Mother?" She spoke into an empty room. The door to the bathroom was ajar and unoccupied inside.

Christine's eyes caught immediately on the bedside table. Without waiting, she placed her cases down and sat on Yortza's bed, switching on the reading lamp on the table. Christine's cell phone number was where she'd Scotch Taped it. Inside the drawer lay the puffy envelope that her mother had torn open in a hurry thinking that the package was from Christine.

She flipped open the top of her forensic case and snapped on a fresh pair of latex gloves just as Yortza appeared in the doorway, wearing a cheery day gown and her favorite corduroy slippers, which were wearing through at the big toes. Christine made a mental note to order her a new pair for her birthday this summer.

"Hello, Mother. I thought I'd get started."

"You could have at least called first." Her mother scowled harmlessly, pulling a chair up to her bedside.

Using forceps, Prusik carefully removed the sealed plastic pouch from inside the envelope, and said without looking up, "I told you when you phoned me at the crack of dawn that I'd be here this morning on the first flight. You never opened this pouch, right?"

"No, I did not. Didn't you listen to what I said on the phone?"

"Okay, okay, Mother." Christine concentrated her efforts on the contents of the pouch, which hardly looked more sinister than a broken twig. Nothing definitive registered in her mind. Turning the clear bag in her gloved fingers, she noticed that the stick was thicker at the top. Christine discerned from the faint feathering at its distal end that it appeared to be the rudiments of a creature's withered toes.

She changed her grip and held the bag from its sealed top and a small tag slipped into view. It had lain practically invisible along the bottom seam of the bag, its thin white thread looped around what looked to her now—if she had to venture a guess—like a small reptile's appendage. No guessing was necessary, however. In neat, hand-printed black India ink was the identifier, *P. terribilis*, the Latin binomial abbreviation for *Phyllobates terribilis*, the most deadly of the poison dart frogs: the Golden Poison Dart Frog, whose glandular skin secretions yielded the highest concentration of the alkaloid Batrachotoxin, the most potent natural toxin known to man.

"Jesus!" She placed the unopened pouch back inside the puffy envelope securely, and then looked up at her mother, struggling to keep her anger and fear under control.

"To your knowledge, did anyone here open or touch the contents?" She removed her protective gloves slowly and placed them inside out into the open bay of her forensic case.

"Of course not! I did think at first that you may have found that favorite barrette of my mother's. The one I let you borrow when you went off to college? Or have you forgotten about such small things with all your important tasks chasing after killers?" she fretted, patting the side of her hair and then letting out a sigh. "I so wish I could wear it now with my hair cut short as a boy's. It was one of the few things I brought from Warsaw, if you remember my telling you."

It was pure genius the way her mother could reverse a simple question into an accusation at Christine.

"I'm sorry, Mother. I know you loved that barrette." Christine tried to smile empathetically, but her mind was racing. The killer now knew her mother's address—and was letting Christine know that she was getting too close too fast.

Access to her FBI file was highly restricted. Who else even knew she had a mother still living or that she had moved to a Louisville, Kentucky, assisted-living home? Eisen had once said that the internet was faster-growing than cancer. There were innumerable ways for a clever person to discover and access someone else's personal and family information. Nothing was off-limits or truly unobtainable when it came to the infernal digital universe.

But the withered appendage of a Golden Poison Dart Frog cut the universe down to only one—the killer, whoever that was.

Forewarned is forearmed, Christine thought, silently thanking Shamus Ferguson's research assistant who'd given her the scientific journal publication on the toxicity of the poison frog genus, authored by Ferguson himself.

But her next move was less clear. The fact was she had very little hard evidence to go on in order to mount the kind of full-bore investigation that she'd like to run. It anguished Christine that somehow she had brought this investigation to her mother's doorstep—or rather that the killer had.

"As soon as I saw what it . . ." Yortza Prusik hesitated. "Of course, I checked the mailing envelope afterward and saw that it wasn't sent from you to me at all. So I put the envelope in my drawer and phoned you right away." Yortza leaned forward and whispered loudly, "As you had requested I do when you taped your number beside my bed table. And for your information, the staff suspects nothing, Christine. When Francesca asked me what I received in the mail, I told her it was nothing but a silly keychain from some investment group trying to rob my nest egg." She grinned.

Christine smiled; her mother was no dummy. But she couldn't just leave her mother unprotected. She thought of calling Roger

Thorne to see if he could rig having a local Bureau agent stake out the retirement home for a week or so while she pressed forward with the investigation. Involving Thorne and the Bureau would entail new moving parts. She feared the logistics would bog her down and take too much time when time was of the essence. She considered bringing her mother back with her on the plane to Chicago, but then realized that would mean dragging her mother to Benson first, to the Miller residence, where Chrissie Blakemore had lived before being murdered. It still might be the best option under the circumstances.

"Look, Mother, unfortunately *this* isn't 'nothing.' What would you say to flying back to Chicago with me later tonight? I have to interview someone in Benson and could return to collect you, hopefully before dinner . . ." Christine accessed Midwest Air's flight times, then added, "It would only be for a few days. It would be good for you to take a break from this place. Feel the hustle and bustle of a real live city again. All those years in Detroit, you loved the marketplaces, I remember."

Yortza's eyes widened. "And what am I to find in your refrigerator while you go running off after killers?" She shook her head.

"I'll be right nearby, at my office. We'll pick out all your favorite foods. Chicago's got some great delis. I bet they rival Poletown's and Hamtramck's in Detroit."

From Yortza's drooping face, Christine could clearly see that her offer was a no-go.

"Listen, Christine, stop worrying so much about me. Whoever mailed this package sent it to you. I couldn't care less." Yortza swiped her hand dismissively. "Don't you understand? I phoned you hoping that you'd come straightaway because I'm afraid *for you!* It's *you* who should be worried. It's *you* this person is after.

Not me, for God's sake." Yortza shook a scolding finger at her daughter. "That head of yours—always thinking so much, when it is as obvious as sunshine what is wrong."

Christine blinked at her mother. She could never fathom the older woman's cryptic comments. "And what would that be?"

"You are too old for all this running around. Yes, yes, I understand and am more proud of you for your advancements and many achievements than you ever give me credit for. But this . . . this chasing after killers like you are the only person on earth who can arrest injustice . . . don't you see? You cannot go on endlessly this way. Like it or not, someday you will be old like me, and you will be too old to keep doing it. But by then it will be too late for you to realize I am speaking the truth. Your peace and happiness are important, Christine. At least they are to me. And they should be to you, too."

Christine decided not to argue the logic of the notion that she should stop what she was doing now because someday she would be too old to continue it. For only a second, Christine fantasized leaving her mother with her ankle holster and gun for protection, and then sighed. "Look, Mother, what you say may well be true, but that," she nodded at the mailing envelope containing the plastic pouch, "happens very definitely to be my responsibility, and you are my responsibility, too."

"So *now* you're concerned about me! All last year I hardly heard a peep from you." She gave a dark chuckle, scratching her neck. "Maybe I like the idea of having some creep lurking around here if it means you might come see me more often. So, I tell you what, if I see him, I'll let you know. I've got your number. Okay?"

It was hopeless. The longer she sat half-listening to her mother's distorted appreciation of the danger, the more Christine realized the killer was accomplishing just what he'd wanted—to distract Christine and to slow her down.

"I'm glad you came," Yortza said, startling Christine with a radiant smile, patting the top of her daughter's hand. "It's what I wished for, don't you know? To see your lovely face again; you are so lovely, Christine. You needn't worry about me. I'm not afraid of this ridiculous package or whatever it means." Yortza nodded. "It's so good that you've come back so soon after your short visit last time." Her mother's soft warm hands squeezed Christine's.

Later that afternoon Christine left the Randolph Arms with the deadly evidence in tow. She placed her bags into the back seat of the green Chevy Cruze rental and punched the address where Chrissie Blakemore had resided into the GPS. From the road, Christine called Miranda and left him a brief message that she'd be in the office the following morning.

THE FRONT STEPS to the house were flanked by an old wheel-chair ramp, whose timbers were splitting from age and disuse, and curls of tar paper had separated from the wooden ramp. The Millers' 1950s-style ranch house was situated in a small subdivision of similar-looking houses—with the exception of the wheelchair ramp—located approximately five miles from the CSU campus in Benson. Surrounding the stark neighborhood on all sides was a loamy ocean of up-heaved soil. Dark furrow lines raced right up to the backyard fences and looked ominously threatening, as if the housing development had no business taking up precious farmland space.

Christine stepped out of the rental car and was greeted by the strong odor of freshly spread manure—yet another reminder that farming took precedence over everything else in the Midwest countryside.

She knocked on the front door. Mrs. Miller's kind face appeared, framed by a short perm of tight, graying curls. Christine followed the middle-aged woman into the living room, the woman apologizing for the decrepit state of the ramp that had been built for her husband. Mr. Miller, his wife told Christine, had been crippled by a granary accident at the local railroad storage facility fifteen years before, and had died the preceding fall.

The living room smelled of stale cigarette smoke—perhaps Mr. Miller's—that the dowdy stuffed furniture had absorbed. Christine took a seat on the end of the couch whose armrest was worn shiny. Mrs. Miller sat in the recliner, its doily headrest tarnished from use. A tray of vanilla wafers, a pot of coffee, and two cups and saucers sat on a table between them.

Christine displayed her credentials. "As I said on the phone, I've read Chrissie Blakemore's file as part of an investigation that I'm conducting into the recent death of another CSU student."

"It was such a shame, Agent Prusik. Chrissie was so good to us." She noticed Mrs. Miller clasping one hand in the other, lightly turning her wedding band.

"I understand that Chrissie lived in your house as an aide, and she helped with caring for Mr. Miller?"

"Yes, that's right. In exchange for room and board, she cared for my husband's needs in the afternoon, when her classes were over. Most of the time that meant being in the home in case he needed something."

"Your home is quite far from the campus. It's not on a public bus route, I would imagine. That couldn't have been very convenient for an undergraduate student? Did you or someone else in the neighborhood routinely drive her to classes?"

"No. Chrissie loved her bicycle. In bad weather, I would offer to take her. But she'd insist on getting her exercise. She'd put on her raincoat and off she'd go. Only in the worst winter weather would she let me drive her." Mrs. Miller's smile lingered briefly on the memory, and then faded. The woman poured two cups of coffee and handed one to Christine.

"Thank you." There was no mention in the file of a bicycle being recovered. "I don't imagine you still have her bicycle stored in the garage?"

The older woman shook her head slowly. "Never saw it again after she rode off that last day."

"So, on the day Chrissie disappeared, she had ridden her bicycle from here headed to campus?" Why hadn't the file included that information?

"That's right. I believe your investigator phoned us. But it was Sheriff Boynton who finally came out. After they'd found her body."

It was understandable that Mrs. Miller's memory would be sketchy after five years. "I understand she was a sophomore, in her spring semester, and that she had lived with you since the preceding September?"

"Yes, that's right. She came to us in the beginning of the school year. We'd put a notice up on the CSU student union bulletin, seeking a live-in student for a part-time caregiver."

"How often would you drive her to campus, Mrs. Miller?"

"Well, I don't really recall. It would have only been a few times, perhaps in December and January. By early spring, she always rode her bicycle."

On the drive to the Millers, Christine had passed the turn to the lake road that led to Shamus Ferguson's cottage. Certainly, Blakemore could have been seen by him or other traffic passing her on their way to the campus. Anyone might have offered her a lift if a tire had gone flat, say. A bike would easily enough fit inside an SUV's trunk, too.

"Did she have a boyfriend or a classmate who may have picked her up ever?"

"No one came out here except Chrissie on her bike. She kept to herself mostly. I rather doubt she had a boyfriend. No, wait. There was this time that she took a class trip to Indianapolis, I think."

"Do you recall where she went in Indianapolis?"

The woman shook her head. "I think it had something to do with a school paper she was working on for biology class. On poisonous plants, I think it was. Things you might find in the woods that are dangerous to eat. She spoke of seeing some plants up there on the school trip."

"Can I see the room Chrissie stayed in?"

Mrs. Miller led her down the hallway and opened a bedroom door. The room was spare: a desk, chair, and single bed. "Her parents took most of her personal things, of course."

Christine's eyes caught on a sheet of paper taped to the wall above the desk. She walked closer and studied it: a pencil sketch of a broad-leaved, heavy-stemmed plant covered with large, bell-shaped flowers, a species she'd never seen. It looked tropical in origin.

Mrs. Miller pointed at the sketch and said, "That's a picture she drew after the trip she took to Indianapolis, of a very poisonous plant she said. I can't recall its name. She told me at the time, but I've forgotten now."

Nothing in the Blakemore file approached the gold mine of information that Christine had gleaned in fifteen minutes with this woman. "Would you mind if I borrowed this drawing? And by any chance would you have a photo of Chrissie?"

"You may take it if it can help with your investigation. And I do have one picture of Chrissie." Mrs. Miller's face brightened briefly.

Christine followed the woman back into the living room, where she took down a framed picture from the fireplace mantel. "I asked Chrissie if I could keep this picture."

"When was it taken?" Christine studied the framed picture.

"That would have been the first week in April." Mrs. Miller frowned. "I remember the date because it was less than a month afterward that we never saw Chrissie again."

There was little resemblance to the postmortem close-up. The camera flash on the photograph had washed out much of the young woman's facial features. The background, though out of focus, sent a chill down the forensic anthropologist's spine. She immediately recognized the ribbed outline of stalactite formations.

"Did she like caving?"

"She went the one time, so far as I know," Mrs. Miller said. "She made a point of saying everyone should face their fears. I don't think she really liked it much though."

Even with the overexposed flash, Blakemore's expression looked strained, more like a grimace than a smile. "Would you mind if I borrowed this picture, too?" Christine said.

"Take it if it will help you. Please."

"Thank you very much, ma'am. I'll make sure to get these back to you." Christine slipped them inside her forensic case. "You wouldn't recall who Chrissie went to the cave with?"

"She said it was some group from the campus. That's all I know for sure."

The woman hesitated at the front door and gave Christine an inquiring look. "You think this college girl that I read about in the local paper was killed by the same person who killed Chrissie?"

"It's certainly a possibility, Mrs. Miller." She handed the woman her business card. "I know it's been five years since her death, but if you can think of anything else at all, please call me, day or night."

CHAPTER
EIGHTEEN

THEY'D AGREED TO meet on Wednesday for an early lunch at Gallagher's, a downtown Chicago delicatessen famous for its corned beef sandwiches. Christine had stayed at Le Maquis Auberge the previous night after interviewing Mrs. Miller, then caught the first morning flight from Benson Airport to Chicago. She picked a cozy booth in the recesses of the prized old lunch spot, away from prying eyes.

She spotted the gray slope of the aging doctor's back as he appeared at the take-orders counter and waved him over.

"Christine, how wonderful it is of you to ask me to lunch."

She embraced Dr. Emil Katz, who seemed to have shrunk since she'd last seen him. As he sidled in next to her in the booth, she noticed that the Bureau psychiatrist's dowdy suit was frayed at the collar.

"I should be the one thanking you, really," she said, then leaned over and whispered into his ear, "In case anyone asks, you didn't have lunch with me. In fact, you haven't seen me." Just as she'd spoken, an incoming text buzzed her phone—a message from Gaston to meet her in her office ASAP.

"What is it with that woman—" She caught herself mid-sentence.

"Beg your pardon?" Katz said.

"Nothing, it's nothing." She couldn't afford to get bogged down now. She and Leeds Hughes had met earlier at the office, where she'd given him the envelope containing the double-sealed plastic pouch and contents to be DNA tested and dusted for prints, although she didn't expect that anything helpful would be found. Eisen had scheduled her in for tomorrow morning to meet with Randall Creighton, who headed the research division of Macalister Pharmaceutical labs in Indianapolis.

Katz smiled and shook a benevolent finger at her. "Christine, Christine."

"I mean it, Dr. Katz."

"I'm sure that you do. Why is it, Christine, in the last few years you increasingly place such complications on our relationship?"

He smiled again, his right lazy eye slotting wide out. Katz's easygoing manner under her present predicament was comforting.

"Not what the doctor ordered, eh?" she said.

With an intense scrutiny, he waggled his forefinger again. "You doubt yourself so much of the time, Christine. It's unappealing coming from such an accomplished scientist. You've heard me say it before that you need to take better care of yourself. Your troubles, in my opinion, stem largely from that."

He studied her face more closely with his left eye, then nodded. "It seems to form a substratum of your personhood, and may even explain why you have these difficulties with management and interpersonal relationships."

"Wow! Enough with the compliments already, Doctor."

He was treading dangerously close to her mother's well-worn territory. She would never allow anyone else—except Yortza Prusik—to make such candid observations without defensively overreacting. But Dr. Katz had been there for her time and again.

She'd confided in him for years about the protracted fears that ruined her sleep and had sabotaged her at embarrassing moments on the job.

Dr. Katz leaned closer to her side. "Have you ever known me to say things to be deliberately hurtful?" He gently pressed his hand over hers. "Don't you know that you are the daughter I never had? I would never do anything to hurt you."

"Thank you, Dr. Katz," she said, her eyes welling for a moment before she blinked them clear. "You are very kind to me."

He patted the top of her wrist. "So what have you got for me then?"

Christine took a breath and shifted gears. "First and foremost, we're talking about a serial poisoner, Doctor—and a man who kills without so much as leaving a scratch, other than the point of entry of the swift-acting poison, which he injects into the back of his victims' necks.

"There are no indications he disrobes them either before or after death," she continued. "Nor any definitive signs of physical violence either peri- or postmortem; and there is no apparent sexualizing based on body placement and the state of the bodies at the crime scenes or on the surrounding surfaces. We've struck out recovering any bodily fluids or other identifying DNA evidence at the scenes."

"Poison, you say?" Katz scrubbed his chin. "What kind, do you know?"

"A steroidal compound that I believe is extracted from a rainforest amphibian of the Dendrobatidae family: in particular, the Golden Poison Dart Frog. Its skin secretes Batrachotoxin, which is considered to be the deadliest known toxin on earth."

"I see," Katz said, puffing out his cheeks. "A very intriguing choice of toxin and not an easy potion to obtain, I would imagine."

"Normally, that would be true," Christine said. "But it points to a couple of research laboratories in Indiana that are known repositories for this poison. As a matter of fact, one of these labs had a break-in a couple of years ago and several of these deadly frog skins were stolen, enough to kill perhaps one hundred people, from what I understand."

"Well then, you've quite a good lead."

"We have, but like everything else," she rolled her eyes, "it's complicated. Our new branch director isn't a fan of staffing agents to assist with local crime solving. Gaston's order of the day is that all departments split their efforts, focusing time on her pet project—"

"Yes, yes." Katz nodded, interrupting Christine. "I am well aware of Director Gaston's profile initiative." Katz blew air from his cheeks again. "And that you won't do what you're told because your *real* job is to track this killer of young women, who may soon kill again, if he hasn't done so already. Am I correct?"

Katz had a remarkable ability to read her mind. "On all counts, Doctor," Christine said. "We've struck out on recovering any fragmentary DNA evidence. There is one additional bizarre fact: both crime scenes occurred in caves. The locations are very private and remote. It gives him ample time to stage their deaths, and any silent ritual that I believe he is conducting."

"Ritual? How so?" Katz dipped his head closer to her as the restaurant chatter picked up.

"The second victim's body was positioned on a protected

shelf—her head next to a large stalagmite formation, the body supine, with her hands folded over each other and resting on her chest."

Christine placed several photographs on the table in front of the psychiatrist, showing the inside of the cave floor and the stalagmite formation in relation to the victim's body before the state police removed it. Other photos displayed the taped outline of where the victim's body had lain.

Katz studied the pictures while chewing the end off a mangled ballpoint pen. The waitress brought their corned beef sandwiches. The rich smells of the thick red meat distracted Christine's train of thought. She took a bite of her sandwich, then a sip of the iced tea.

Katz held a napkin to his lips and spit out a morsel of blue plastic pen, still studying the pictures.

"So what of this kind of killer, Doctor? Someone who doesn't perpetrate violence on the bodies and yet who goes to such great lengths to hide them, leaving few forensic clues behind, other than a few shoe prints."

"Asexual killers' motivations are all over the map." He gave the bridge of his nose a vigorous rubbing. "He may very well be impotent. But it would be a grave misunderstanding to dismiss a sexual motivation; an underlying latent sexuality may still be present, as you have described his predilection to fix the position of the dead body."

Christine had difficulty imagining her killer's dark mind at work, although his bringing his victims inside caves and the method of poison delivery said something about his nature. "A man who cannot complete the sexual act and instead poisons his victims, is that what you're saying?"

"It could very well be. It is not beyond the realm of possibility here." Katz clasped his hands around the thick sandwich.

"Impotent asexual killers," Katz said, "often suffer from a deep-seated rage. A rage in its origin that was first directed against them in childhood, which is then transferred in adulthood to an unlucky someone, a young woman—or women, in your case."

"This transference that you speak of, is it similar to the process of a therapeutic relationship?"

"Yes, except, of course, it is unbeknownst to the untrained victim here, who quite suddenly and unfortunately receives the man's rage all at once."

Christine followed his train of thought, deconstructing the possibilities, the motivations of her killer, puzzling how such a rage-filled man had managed to hold it together long enough to attract them in the first place.

Dr. Katz launched into his sandwich while she nibbled hers, her mind still on the conversation. The corned beef was succulent and the sauerkraut as good as her mother's.

"Before the moment of actual transference," Katz continued, "this killer may experience a slow build-up of animus toward his victims, which allows him ample time to get to know them first, and for them to get to know him. At first, all can seem quite fine, you see."

"Please explain, Doctor."

"People who suffer from a persecution complex believe that others are always out to get them. These fears, of course, are not founded in reality. It is paranoid thinking at work." He tapped his temple.

"The antecedents of this kind of disorder always have

precursors in childhood. Your killer likely had caregivers who were not so kind to him, and who helped, unwitting though it may have been, to develop this predisposition of your killer's. Of course, we are speculating when we talk of such things."

"Explain to me how his placing the victims out of sight in a cave indicates a man who may suffer from feelings of persecution?"

"The cave is his comfort zone, a safe place where his rage no longer needs to be contained. In the normal course of his life, he undoubtedly spends a great deal of energy suppressing his rage, disguising it. This must be exhausting for him."

Christine nodded slowly.

"If the man feels threatened in the young woman's presence by something she does or says, or, upon sensing his own inability to perform as a normal man can sexually, his distress could become extremely difficult, sudden, uncontrollable. It would reach a moment when he no longer could suppress his conflicted feelings. His mind goes off track, willy-nilly, exaggerating the meaning of the victim's actions or words until reaching a point when he can no longer rationally interpret them. At that point his brain signals are misshapen until he becomes overwrought by a heightened state of paranoia.

"Symptoms of persecution complex can manifest in normal everyday interactions that, because of the sufferer's imagined beliefs, cause him to overreact to a perceived wrong. Even the littlest thing can be a trigger."

Dr. Katz gesticulated with such animation that a piece of corned beef went flying from the sandwich onto the floor without his noticing it.

"But for him, you see," the doctor went on, "it would not be little at all. It would be a monstrosity to his distorted mind's way of perceiving it. This type of thinking reflects a belief that everyone has it in for him, or that a particular person or persons—your victims here—certainly do. Once this woman is on your killer's radar"—Katz's cheeks ballooned—"it is kaput."

Christine nodded slowly. "What's puzzling is that he hasn't shown up on anyone's radar until it's too late. He's certainly doing a good job of containing his rage."

Katz's head seesawed from side to side. "As you've indicated, the victims appear to go willingly. Which means that your killer is able to harbor these paranoid feelings long enough to engage in a successful initial meeting with these women, possibly even develop a relationship of sorts with them in order to gain their trust."

Christine followed his point. "In both cases, there are no accounts of witnesses reporting a struggle or seeing anyone strange hanging around the victim beforehand. I've spoken with their college roommates—normally you would expect roommates to share everything and know the ins and outs."

"Yes, yes, of course, unless they specifically don't share for whatever reason that may be." Dr. Katz laced his fingers together. "You must remember that the way this type of individual sees the world is all cockeyed. For example, when you see someone parking in a handicap space, you or I wouldn't question it. To someone who feels persecuted, that person who pulled into the handicap space did so deliberately, just to annoy him so that he would have to park somewhere else farther away. It's always personal—a war is being waged against *him*; people are always doing things just to aggravate *him*."

"So how does that affect the way they function?" she said. "Are there any outward signs I should be looking for?"

"Like I said, he may have learned strategies to contain these exaggerated inclinations. Your killer's disciplined. He has learned how to temper the most severe feelings, concealing his rage from his victims, especially to secure the company of a woman he targets. And his expression of rage directed at successful college women—smart high achievers—tells me that you must watch your step, Christine."

Christine checked her watch. She had some errands to run before her meeting with Gaston. She'd purchased a ticket on the first flight Thursday morning to Indianapolis.

Dr. Katz reached out and held her forearm firmly. "Delusional impulses can manifest quite suddenly." He snapped his fingers. "Just like that. A paranoid's personality has a hair trigger, Christine. This killer of yours, if he suffers from extreme persecution, could be quite mercurial and his actions hard to predict. So please be careful, my dear."

"PLEASE SHUT THE door behind you," Branch Director Gaston said perfunctorily. This time they were alone.

Christine did as asked and took a seat in front of the branch director's desk, remaining quiet as Gaston finished up whatever she was jotting down.

The branch director closed the folder on her desk and gave Christine an appraising look. "What I am about to tell you is highly confidential and must not leave this office."

"Understood."

"How well do you know Paul Higgins? From his file I see that he joined your forensics team sixteen months ago."

"Yes, Paul is the most recent member of my unit. He has certainly made an excellent addition so far. His computer skills have proved second to none."

Gaston reopened the folder on her desk and turned a few pages. "Did you know when he was sixteen he successfully hacked into a local police station's database and gained critical information of ongoing criminal cases that were actively being investigated?"

Christine frowned. "No, I didn't. But then I wouldn't have since he came to us with preclearance from the home office in Washington. Surely they were aware of that beforehand."

Gaston nodded. "For your information, his father's a well-known trial lawyer in Milwaukee and had pulled some strings to get the matter scrubbed from his arrest record."

"May I ask then how you were able to find out about it?"

"First, what can you tell me about him? Has evidence ever been unaccounted for? Any occurrences brought to your attention that would raise an eyebrow? Downloads from databases you didn't request, for instance?"

Christine shifted uneasily in her chair. "No, none that I can think of offhand, none that have been brought to my attention."

Gaston tapped her polished fingernail on the desktop. "Look, I realize this isn't a comfortable conversation. I must inform you that we've confirmed there is an information leak originating from the Chicago office."

"We?" Christine reflected on what Roger Thorne had intimated about the planning process being used to ferret out an inside mole.

"The Canadian government is liaising with Homeland Security. Last week, listening devices installed on a house they're surveilling in Toronto revealed knowledge of our Statistical Unit's countermeasures, which you may know are quite elaborate, detailing sensitive logistics for this office referencing our branch's ongoing surveillance activities."

Christine shook her head. "Paul may be a relatively recent hire, but he is highly experienced and repeatedly demonstrates a degree of conscientiousness that has earned him respect among his colleagues, including myself. And while I had no idea of his juvenile misadventures in computing, I can think of no reason to suspect him for doing anything but excellent work here. I seriously doubt that Paul knows anything about countermeasures or that he obtained Statistical's access codes. Why would he?"

"Whoever leaked Statistical's data would, of course, necessarily have to be very good at covering his or her tracks, electronically speaking. Paul's ability to do good work for you only underscores in my mind the importance of your taking extra precautions to ensure that his skills are focused on doing just that."

Christine nodded slowly, not liking the direction the conversation was taking. "What extra precautions would you suggest?"

"I've decided that your unit could use another forensic data expert, at least temporarily. In fact, Roger Thorne got home office approval for it. His name is Ed Meachum. He's actually been positioned nearby for a week or so, working with his team. We've decided closer monitoring is desirable at this juncture. You'll find Ed easy to work with. He's got nearly twenty years with the Bureau. I would like you to introduce him to your staff this afternoon. He'll work closely with Higgins."

A moment passed before Christine could respond. "May I ask whether any other units are being subjected to this degree of internal scrutiny?"

"The Statistical Unit's computers share linked databases with

Washington. Procedures do not permit memory sticks or other portable storage devices in or out of their partitioned offices, as you no doubt know. Your work in forensics, however, is not so well secured because of the nature of your work, which requires more of a free rein, shall I say. Higgins has therefore been given quite a bit of latitude. He's broken the law before, which, in my book, means he bears careful watching over."

"When he was sixteen . . ."

"By the way," Gaston switched gears, "what have you got to share on the murder investigations?"

"Yesterday I interviewed a woman who rented a room five years ago to a CSU student whose death remains unsolved. I believe there are similarities at work with these recent murders and that unsolved crime."

"Good, Christine. I want you to press forward on these cases as you normally would, being sure you check in with Ned as need be, especially before you venture onto the CSU campus again." She smiled curtly. "Meanwhile Mr. Meachum will work closely with Higgins and monitor your team's activities. You're not to concern yourself with his day-to-day responsibilities. Ned Miranda has been fully advised of the situation. And Christine?"

Christine raised her eyebrows. "Yes?"

"I'm not jumping to conclusions about anyone's guilt, and you shouldn't jump to conclusions about anyone's loyalty. Are we clear?"

Christine nodded. "Perfectly."

CHAPTER
NINETEEN

AT A QUARTER to nine on Thursday morning, Christine stood at the Hertz counter at Indianapolis International Airport with her credit card out. The flight from Chicago had taken less than an hour. A lighted floor-to-ceiling advertising display of smiling faces at a sunny destination semi-caught her imagination while she waited at the rental car kiosk, but only for a moment. She burned to get to her interview with Randall Creighton, who knew as much about Batrachotoxin and poison dart frogs as Shamus Ferguson. Maybe more. Whether Chrissie Blakemore had taken a school trip to Creighton's lab had more than once crossed her mind, too.

Christine parked her rental car in the spaces marked for visitor parking. Beside the pebbled walkway near the entrance of the blue-tinted all-glass building, *Macalister Laboratories* was stenciled in muted gray letters on a sign low to the ground and gave an unmistakable aura of secrecy more closely aligned with *Keep out!* than *Welcome*.

Inside, she approached a reception counter and displayed her credentials.

"He'll be right out to meet you, Special Agent," said the dark-skinned woman, who sat behind an impressive enclosure that could double as a barrier in the event of any trouble, Christine thought.

A trim, well-tanned man with brown hair and a spirited step passed his ID card through the electronic reader inside the secure area, releasing the electronic lock. The door automatically slid open.

"Special Agent Prusik, I presume." His smooth bronzed skin didn't bear the likeness of someone who spent inordinate hours slumped over a microscope, as her mushroom-faced team back in Chicago did.

"Dr. Creighton," she said with her best smile. The receptionist eyed them as they shook hands.

Randall Creighton was tall, more than six feet, and dressed in an open-collar polo shirt and a blue blazer that had a fancy crest stitched across its breast pocket. He wore casual khaki slacks and a pair of tassel loafers without socks. *Was his plan to chat her up for a few minutes before heading out to the golf course?* Christine wondered.

"Call me Randy. Everyone does."

"Kristi," he addressed the receptionist. "Special Agent Prusik and I will be down in Conference Room A. See that we're not disturbed."

Randy had a bit of a saunter to his step, rocking his head back and forth as he led the way. His hair in back was a bit longish, approaching mullet territory. The man seemed in his comfort zone. Business up front, party in the back, Christine thought with a glimmer of a smile.

Eisen had filled Christine in on her drive to Macalister's headquarters. Creighton held advanced degrees in both pharmacology and biochemistry. Batrachotoxin was a significant area of research at Macalister, and a specialty of Creighton's personally. She and Eisen agreed that it was indeed more than coincidental that Peter Franklin had worked at both Macalister and the Pembroke Research Center, and that Creighton and Ferguson both vied for the same NIH research grants. Their documented trouble harassing women was easily discovered by Higgins. Had they darker secrets? Engaged in Batrachotoxin experimentation on human subjects even?

They passed a large well-lit botanical room filled with unusual plants, some festooning down from ceiling racks. One almost tree-size shrub had yellow, tubular blossoms. It stopped her dead. "Excuse me, Dr. Creighton, what kind of plant is that?"

"Brugmansia, it's a member of the nightshade family, extremely toxic," Creighton said. "Its milky sap contains powerful alkaloids, a high concentration of Scopolamine. The extractions are being studied for certain smooth muscle disorders. But you wouldn't want to make the mistake of ingesting it."

It was the same plant sketched by Chrissie Blakemore. Scopolamine was also identified in the contents of Blakemore's stomach, according to her file. "Do you allow students to view your facility?"

"From time to time we've had interns and a few college majors thinking of making a career in pharmacological research," he said. "They're carefully escorted."

"Does the name Chrissie Blakemore ring a bell?"

Creighton thought for a moment and then shook his head. "Don't recognize the name. If she was an intern, you might check with our human resources department to see whether there's a file on her."

At the end of the hallway, Creighton slipped his ID card through a magnetic reader and held the door open for her. The spacious room had a long conference table with chairs around it. It looked more like a lounge, though, with several nice leather cushion chairs facing the large plate glass view of an ominous dark band of clouds on the horizon.

"Shall we sit by the window?" he said. "The view is quite nice."

"No, the table is better. I can spread my things on it." She detected a frisson of alarm flash across his face.

She laid her briefcase flat on the table. "I understand your father headed up a lab at DuPont's Jackson Laboratory in New Jersey when you were growing up? Before you moved here so he could teach high school chemistry at an all boys' academy?"

A crinkle rose across Randy's forehead, marring the tan. "Look, I don't know what this is all about. Should I be calling my lawyer?"

Christine eyed him carefully, unprepared for such immediate defensiveness on his part, but she played along to see where it may lead. "Why don't we sit down and talk, Dr. Creighton."

He remained standing, dancing his fingertips nervously on the tabletop. "Look, if someone's filed a complaint, I'd rather call my lawyer first if you don't mind."

"What complaint would that be?"

Randy started nodding rapidly. "The past, I get it. You know about my legal scrapes as far as the women go. Somehow you government people always do an end run around confidential settlements, don't you? So yes, I'm a bit concerned when the FBI starts calling. Why shouldn't I be?"

Guilt and fear seemed to be coming off the man in waves. He grabbed the back of a conference chair with both hands now, flexing its cushion pillow.

"Is that why your marriage ended?" Christine threw out a guess based on Eisen's quick overview of Randall S. Creighton III's profile and personal history.

He started toward the door, shaking his head. "Honestly, you people never cease to amaze."

"Look, Dr. Creighton," she called after him, "if it makes you feel any easier, whatever you share with me here, now, is strictly off the record." She clicked shut her ballpoint pen and tucked it back inside her suit jacket. "Unless, of course, you'd rather that a team of my field agents descend on your lab and see what we find."

He quickly took a seat across from Christine.

"Talk to me," she said.

"All I know is she got the ecstasy from some guy at the bar," he said, leaning over the table in an unappealing, beseeching pose. "I didn't give it to her. No way would I do a thing like that. She was upset afterward, I understand. But I did not drug the—her. I'm not about doing that to dates."

He spoke in an agitated gush. Such frank disclosures and humiliation were not an uncommon response to the badge and a guilty mind's threat of public exposure.

"Tell me something I don't already know, Dr. Creighton."

Creighton got up, resumed his pacing, staring at the floor. "Okay, let's face it. I'd had too much to drink. Is that a crime?"

He grinned at Christine as if she were just another good old boy with whom he was sharing a war story. Impressive, Christine thought. She'd never been fashioned into the role of a good old boy before.

"See, I met her in this bar and we just drove over the Illinois line to this loud country music place. People were dancing. It all seemed fine. We were really connecting, you know what I mean."

Christine caught Creighton casting a prurient glance at her breasts. Quickly he looked away. She hadn't expected this—the behavior of a run-of-the-mill perp—from the man who headed up one of the most powerful research laboratories in the country.

"You're a prominent research scientist, right?" she said. "I'm guessing this place brings in a fair amount of government money and from private investors, right?"

"Of course, of course. We depend on NIH like everyone else. Venture capital, too."

Creighton quickly took a seat again, twitching like a tweaker overdue for his fix, his knees bumping the underside of the table.

"Tell me about the frogs, Dr. Creighton."

Presto! The man stiffened, his eyes narrowed, trying to divine her true purpose here, realizing he'd said much too much already.

"What? What did you say?" he said, his face scrunching up.

"Did you know that Shamus Ferguson's research lab at CSU had a break-in? Are you aware of the deaths that are related? The murders, I should say?"

She sat straighter in her chair as Creighton slunk lower in his. "This is a major FBI investigation, Dr. Creighton. Tell me about the frogs."

"I don't know what that frustrated fuck of an academic may have told you. I never broke into his goddamn lab! It's a load of bullshit that Shamus loves slinging. Ask anyone who knows the paranoid prick."

Creighton tugged off his jacket. Sweat patches darkened the pits of his polo shirt. The man looked as if he'd already spent a long hot day on the golf course, retrieving hooked shots from deep in the woods.

"Well, he won't be slinging it for much longer," she said.

His eyes immediately locked on hers. "Beg your pardon?"

"I mean that Professor Ferguson could be in some pretty hot water, sir." Christine watched him closely. "You've certainly heard the news of the death of the female CSU student?"

Creighton squinted at her, his jaw sagging open.

Based on what Eisen and Higgins had uncovered, Creighton and Ferguson were at best frenemies; on the surface they put their best foot forward to keep the research grant money coming, but behind closed doors, they busied themselves backstabbing and nay-saying each other. And neither could keep their fingers out of the pudding, so to speak, serially molesting women for a living, or worse, although no formal complaints had ever stuck.

Two type-A slimy frog–loving sleazes who both happened to work with extracts of the most poisonous biological toxin on earth, and who shared a winner-take-all no-holds-barred approach to life.

Creighton studied her face, then, quieter, said, "That hasn't anything to do with me."

"No? Well then why don't we discuss someone you do know, Randy. Someone who dearly paid the price," she said softly, leaning forward against the table. "A lab technician who worked at Macalister two years ago before returning to the Pembroke Research Center as a technician, where he was found dead in his car under mysterious circumstances."

"I don't know what you're talking about." His leg began shaking under the table.

"Oh, I think you very well know who I'm speaking of," she said. "Two years ago he was a summer intern here? Before he went back to Benson and petitioned CSU for reconsideration on his application for the PhD program? Ring a bell now?"

"Christ." He shook his head, neck muscles drawn tight. "Peter Franklin's death has nothing to do with me or Macalister. Franklin did work here. As a summer intern, that's all. His death came on Ferguson's watch, not mine. I had nothing to do with it, whatever you say." Stripped of the jaunty confidence that he'd displayed leading the way to the conference room, Randy Creighton's face glistened with patches of sweat under the ceiling spotlights.

"What concerns me, Randy, is the close timing of the break-in at the Pembroke Research Center. It happened right after Peter Franklin resumed working there as a technician, right on the heels of his internship with you here at Macalister, where I understand poison frog skins are in short supply because of international treaties prohibiting their trade."

Christine reached out and touched Creighton's forearm. "Off the record, how was Peter Franklin involved? Was he side-dealing in endangered species skins worth ten times their weight in gold?"

Creighton's confident smirk returned. "Do you actually believe some international trade law such as CITES puts a dent in smuggling? There are thousands upon thousands of rare animal collectors in the U.S. alone. Why do you think that is, Special Agent? For your information, poison frog skins are there for the asking, day or night, twenty-four/seven."

"So you and Ferguson worked cover for each other, running a smuggling operation? You want me to come back here with forty agents and pull apart your secure lab? You want that?"

Creighton grimaced. "You don't believe me?" He got up and walked to the corner table and tapped the computer keyboard there. "Check for yourself." He leaned closer to the monitor's screen, his fingers rapidly keying in a website—as if he'd just ordered up a batch of new frog skins himself a few hours ago, she thought.

"It's uncontrollable," he said, still stooped over the computer screen. "And it's mobile. It's everywhere. You can't pin that one on me. Even you, Special Agent, can order up whatever poison you want, even in the skin trade." He chuckled at his own double entendre.

"Dr. Creighton, once again, are you telling me that Macalister Pharmaceuticals is engaged in unlawful trade?"

"You're not listening to me, Agent Prusik. Of course that's not what I'm saying. I'm saying that Peter Franklin or anyone else for that matter has easy access to the marketplace." Creighton walked back to the table and sat. "The internet doesn't respect the law. You should know that better than I. See for yourself on the website I just opened. It's a global business, Special Agent Prusik. Like I said, twenty-four/seven—if you want it, all you have to do is click on Search."

"Dr. Creighton, I appreciate the little show-and-tell, but this isn't getting us anywhere." She glanced at her watch.

Creighton bunched his lips, mulling things. "You know I spoke to your lab technician?"

"Agent Eisen?"

"One thing I didn't know when I spoke with him. The final results for the DNA testing took longer to achieve with such a small sample."

"Are you referring to the CSU victim's tissue? Naomi Winchester?"

"There was one difference in the chemistry that we isolated—but it's a big one. The isotope points to a different species entirely than the poison frog skins we use for research here. Maybe Ferguson's sourcing included it, maybe not. Again, I have no personal knowledge of his operation or where he gets his supply."

"What exactly are you saying, Dr. Creighton?"

"Not all species of Dendrobates, the poison frogs, carry the same levels or types of biological toxin in their system. The point is the steroidal compounds we extracted from your victim's tissue are not the same as those from the frog specimens we have stored here at Macalister."

"Which suggests to you that the source is definitely from elsewhere?"

"It doesn't suggest that. It's absolute proof of it."

She turned back a few pages to the beginning of her notes, reviewing them for a few seconds.

"I have one more question for you right now, Dr. Creighton. I understand you've had a string of difficulties with female complaints as you earlier alluded to. In particular—"

He interrupted her and leaned forward with his elbows against the table. "Come on, those were all silly dates, nothing more. If I were to go around killing young women, I wouldn't do it with something that leads straight back to me, now would I?" He grinned as if he'd just revealed an airtight alibi to her.

What woman would fall for such callous cockiness in a man, Christine wondered. For the moment, she'd hit a dead end with Creighton. She excused herself without shaking the man's hand and showed herself out of the conference room. She leaned against the outside door with her shoulder, releasing a noticeable suck from the building's negative air pressure, and headed to her car without looking back.

As she drove away from the visitor parking, she glimpsed

Randy's slim silhouette in the ground floor conference room; he was standing alone at the window watching her leave. Christine gunned the engine in disgust. All that money and power wielded in the hands of such a sniveling pervert—what a waste. The randy Randy's misogynistic display was beyond anything that Christine would have expected from the head of a world-class pharmaceutical research facility. Fueled by enough alcohol and cocaine, the man's prurience could easily border on dangerous, maybe even psychotic, she surmised. Still, the question remained: Did he have it in him to inject female companions to their death? She'd need to have Eisen and Higgins dig deeper. There were too many connections between Creighton and Ferguson and the Pembroke Research Center, not the least of which was the still puzzling death of Peter Franklin.

THE SMELLS OF tamales and beef tacos mingled in the air with the sharper tang of leather goods that hung from vendor stalls at the open-air marketplace in downtown Oaxaca.

Trip tried to make contact with his seller's point person the day before, but there had been a glitch of some sort, which had made Trip exceedingly anxious. He rose early on Thursday morning and tried again. This time, his broken Spanish gained him the information he had come for. In exchange for a twenty-peso note, a merchant with an agave stand handed him a crude hand-drawn map that showed directions to Raul's casa, marked by an X.

A half hour later, Raul introduced himself in front of a wooden gate on a dirt side street and they shook hands. The seller's jet-black hair, stocky build, and high cheekbones were characteristic of an Indigenous man, Trip thought.

The man quickly unlatched the gate behind him. Trip followed the man into a yard full of scrawny chickens that were scratching and pecking at the dirt. Behind several leafy palms there stood a one-story padlocked shed. Inside the small building, Trip's eyes immediately focused on banks of glowing tanks that were stacked high against two sides of the room. A mass of squirming froglets caught his attention. Raul smiled, slipping on rubber gloves.

Quickly they concluded their transaction. Trip handed the man a wad of folded bills, the final payment in cash as the man had requested, in exchange for the small woven reed basket with a simple loop and spline closure.

Raul cautioned him, "Mucho agua, y no sol." Then he zipped his fingers across tight lips, and said, "Callarse la boca!" Translated roughly, the warning was obvious enough: "Keep your mouth shut."

Trip nodded. Carefully he cracked open the lid to inspect his purchase. The tops of several wet leaves protruded from the basket.

"Muy sensitivo, muy," Raul cautioned.

Trip's eyes drifted back to the bank of terrarium tanks. He tapped Raul on his shoulder, holding another wad of peso notes in his hand.

"Mas ranas," Trip said, pointing toward the terrarium filled with younger specimens. The voyage had been more tiring than he anticipated, and the meeting glitch the previous day had spooked him. He didn't fancy returning to this dusty remote place any time soon.

Raul agreed and turned to his cupboard, pulling on a fresh pair of kitchen rubber gloves, and then got busy.

Trip slipped on the gold frog ring, intrigued to know the extent of its efficacy. He'd armed the ring's pin with multiple coats from the last remaining skin supplied to him by Peter Franklin, God rest his soul.

He triggered the ring's needle while the man hunched over the display tank. With a new sense of empowerment gained from experience, Trip knuckled the back of the man's neck, jabbing home the ring's poison-dipped needle.

It was remarkable how swiftly the healthy-looking man with strong white teeth flopped to the floor.

Trip slipped on a pair of his own surgical gloves and scooped up six of the young golden poison froglets at once, depositing them carefully in an empty plastic container from the shelf. He liked what he saw. The smaller horde was a convenient six-pack serving—easier for travel, too.

Raul was down to the last of his involuntary hissing noises. Trip was quite satisfied the poison had done its work, enough so that he was confident of the ring's lethal efficacy for one more job.

Back in the privacy of the un–air-conditioned hotel room that he'd paid for in advance, he snapped on his new heavy-duty latex gloves and cleared the table to act as a makeshift lab surgery. He readied the lid of the Swiss-made portable liquid nitrogen canister, which fit nicely inside the sleeve of a king-size Thermos bottle for concealment and safe transport.

Carefully he unlatched the reed basket's lid and swung it wide. Under several moist leaves a slim golden leg protruded in the flexed position. With the long-armed forceps he raised the leaves, bringing into full view the pair of surreal golden amphibians clinging to each other. The glistening flesh beneath their chins pulsed with each breath. Their dark eyes watched. Neither frog made an effort to move.

With the aid of his forceps he grasped one creature firmly by the back of its head and placed it on the plastic sheet covering the table. With a four-inch biopic needle he lanced the tiny brain capsule between its large black eyes, just as the scientist had described in one of the scientific journals he'd read, and waited for the wriggling to stop.

He repeated the procedure with the other frog. He quickly gutted their carcasses, retaining only their precious golden skins, glistening with the highly toxic secretions.

A small cloud of vapors escaped when he unscrewed the lid of the liquid nitrogen canister. Quickly he submerged both limp skins into the clear super-cooled bath, instantly freezing them and sealing in the full lethal effect of their toxic flesh.

Likewise he quick-froze the six smaller amphibians after repeating the same procedure. The seedy hotel room had served its purpose. It was time to leave for the central plaza, where the spring break tour group was all staying.

Before vacating the room, he rechecked the gold ring, levering up the needle through the cameo's caricature of a frog's head. The glistening residue of toxin reflected on the end of the needle under the table light. He'd coated it more than ten times back at his house in Benson, Indiana. After witnessing the man expire so rapidly on the shack floor he was confident that re-arming it with toxin from his new purchase wasn't necessary. Plenty of toxin remained on the ring. Plenty.

Trip packed up and left.

An hour after he'd vacated the makeshift surgery in the seedy hotel room, a maid was busily cleaning. She entered the bathroom and found the toilet clogged. She flushed it and the water overflowed the bowl, bringing with it entrails and blood, and sending the cleaning woman screaming from the room.

IT WAS PAST noon on Thursday when she downed a Subway turkey sandwich and a cola drink. Christine headed south to Crosshaven to discuss the latest developments in the cases with Joe, feeling like she couldn't get there soon enough.

Out her windshield, the expansive flat farmlands gave way to hills and forests. Clouds threatened rain. She started filling in the blanks, circling the possibilities: Ferguson first and foremost; Randy Creighton, number two. His protestations notwithstanding, Creighton's disclosures about the variance in the molecular structure of the frog poison taken from Naomi Winchester's tissue sample would need to be double-checked by Leeds Hughes, her team geneticist. If what Creighton said was true, it would mean the poison came from the Pembroke Research Center or, as Creighton had suggested, it may have been sourced from the internet. This would require more yeoman work from Higgins, assuming Gaston's mole hunter Meachum hadn't detained Higgins already.

Two hours later the sky lowered, wrenched of any blue. One large raindrop struck the windshield, followed by another. A minute later, she switched her wipers to the highest setting and slowed the car to thirty-five as the downpour grew into a hissing frenzy, coloring the glass silvery white. Christine could barely make out the green highway sign indicating her exit. "Welcome to Crosshaven," she murmured to herself, "home of Sheriff Joe McFaron and interminable rainfall."

She scanned the vehicles pulled up in front of Shermie Dutcher's Diner. The sheriff's truck was not among them. A few minutes later she parked at the sheriff's office next to a white Taurus sedan with a sheriff's star decal pasted to the back window that matched one on the rear license plate. Christine made a dash for the door with her briefcase held over her head, hopping over rain puddles.

"Can I help you, ma'am?" Mary Carter was seated at her desk outside Joe's office. The dispatcher was wearing a wireless head-set and obviously following another line of conversation. Carter rocked back in her desk chair, balancing on the tiptoes of her black, police-issue boots. At five foot one and wearing a set of unbreakable styrene field-tested eyeglasses and a police uniform, including a three-inch-wide leather belt replete with a gun hol-ster and accessory loops for a Maglite flashlight, mace canister, rechargeable Taser, and a cell phone clip, she was ready for what-ever problem might present itself.

The dispatcher gave those who'd never seen her in action laughable pause as a police officer. But when a demanding situ-ation reared its ugly head, no one could deny her effectiveness. Time and again, Joe'd said, Carter worked her short stature to full advantage, using the element of surprise against mean-eyed drunks who never saw the butt end of her police baton coming. Once they'd caved to their knees, she'd lead them groaning, like compliant puppy dogs, to a waiting cell to sleep it off. It was an art she'd perfected.

Christine placed her things on a bench and perused the wall of announcements and warnings: one concerned drunk driving and another listed the key signs of illegal drug use. A few particularly nasty traffic accident photos made her think that she could have ended up on the wall, too, had that coal truck clipped her car two weeks ago.

She wondered which was worse: an outright killer on the loose or passenger cars having to play Russian roulette with coal carriers free to do mayhem to anyone unfortunate enough to end up in the twisted metal consequences—like Jane Pirrung had.

The dispatcher finished her phone call. "So how you been, Special Agent?" Mary Carter said, removing the headgear and stretching her back. "Christine Pruvit, am I right?"

Christine laughed at the unintended double entendre. "Prusik, you're close. And you're Mary Carter."

The short dispatcher circled around her desk and they shook hands. Next to Carter, whose jet-black curls came up to Christine's shoulder at most, the special agent—all of five-four herself—felt glamorously tall.

"Does the sheriff know you're coming?"

She sensed the dispatcher's keen awareness of her boss's schedule and movements. "I thought I'd drop by on my way to Benson," Christine said. "Catch him along the way if he happened to be here."

Carter tugged loose a moisture pad from a dispenser on her desk and removed her eyeglasses, patting the bridge of her nose with the lemony-scented tissue.

"I'll raise him on the radio and see what's keeping him. Usually he's back here by now, for the afternoon cruller run. With all this rain we've been having, there could be an accident somewhere."

"Please don't bother, Mary. I don't mind waiting. I have some work to catch up on."

"Help yourself to the desk in the corner. Part-time deputies don't use it much. By the way, the wifi pass code for the office is

'McFaron.' Original, ain't it?" Mary retreated to her alcove and took another incoming call.

AT 11 A.M. on Thursday morning, the air was crisp in the near mile-high city of Oaxaca. A fifties-era passenger bus clattered to a halt outside La Hacienda Oaxaca, a nineteenth-century hotel with wrought iron gates and window bars. The CSU students boarded the bus bound for Monte Albán, a mountaintop ruin that was the crowning achievement of the Zapotec a thousand years ago. Although abandoned for many centuries, its stone court-yards, temples, and underground crypts had weathered the test of time well. The ruins were an hour's drive up dusty switchbacks.

Tracy Wilson and Clara Huston sat in the back of the bus. They'd become friends two years earlier when Tracy was a se-nior and Clara a sophomore at CSU, having met at their sorority house. Even though Tracy no longer lived at the sorority, since graduating from college, and now was a second-year CSU law student, she and Clara had remained close friends and decided to take the spring break trip to Oaxaca together, where they shared a hotel room.

For the first half hour the bus lumbered through lush tropical foliage. Then it began to ascend a series of switchbacks that made Clara dizzy. Pine trees flashed by her open window in a blur. The air grew cooler in the mountains.

Tracy looked at her friend, whose eyes were closed, her palms gripping her stomach. It was obvious she didn't feel well. "You okay?"

Without turning her head, Clara said, "I don't dare move."

"La Tourista?"

She nodded. "The bus fumes aren't helping."

Tracy lifted a water bottle from her backpack and took a sip. "Want some water? You might feel better."

Clara shook her head. The driver missed a gear, downshifting. The bus suddenly lurched on its spent shocks. Diesel exhaust and the seesawing motion over ruts in the dirt road sent Clara Huston's authentic Mexican breakfast of tamales and eggs into her throat. She quickly leaned her head out the open window and retched. Tracy gently rubbed her friend's sweaty back as involuntary dry heaves seized Clara.

When Clara finally sat back in her seat, her face glistened with beads of perspiration. Loose hairs stuck to the sides of her temples.

"Feeling better now?"

"A little, I guess."

"Look, shall I ask the bus driver to take you back to the hotel?"

"Don't bother. It'll just take twice as long to go back. I'll rest when we get there."

Tracy looked down the aisle. Shamus Ferguson was turned sideways in his seat at the front of the bus, eyeing them. Tracy hadn't sat next to Clara for the evening bus ride from the airport to their Oaxaca hotel two days before. She'd seen the hulking professor leaning forward in his seat directly behind Clara's seat then, and wondered what he was doing. It looked creepy to her.

"I don't mean to pry, but are you taking a course from Ferguson?"

Clara nodded. "I did, Bio 201 last semester. Why do you ask?"

"Don't look now," Tracy said, "but I think he's staring right at you."

Clara didn't answer. She turned her head toward the window.

Tracy whispered into her friend's ear. "I've heard that he hits on women all the time at the university."

"I don't know anything about that." Their eyes met and Clara bit her lip.

Tracy nudged her with an elbow. "Jesus, Clara, not you!"

"It's not what you think. He's incredibly sweet when you get to know him."

Tracy shrugged. "All I'm saying is the man's got a reputation. Don't say I didn't tell you."

Arriving at their destination, Clara staggered off the bus, feeling too woozy to explore the ruins. Her forehead was burning up now. She assured the faculty chaperones and Tracy that she'd be fine resting beside the visitor center. Tracy got a fresh water bottle for Clara and then wandered off with several others in the direction of a great open grassy plaza surrounded on all sides by a mosaic of stone temples and altars built on the highest point of land.

The sun felt good on Clara's face. She drank the water, but wouldn't dare open her boxed lunch. Clara spent the remainder of the early afternoon curled on the cut grass bordering a large ball court "built for a bloodthirsty age," as she'd overheard Professor Overton say to a few students. In the distance, the bleached limestone edifices kept hushed their secrets from her; if Clara had had the strength to peruse the etched murals, she would have seen just how bloody the olden times on this windswept mountaintop had been. The vanquished team on the ball court were beheaded, but the spoils of war weren't savored for long as the victors—at least in their human form—were also beheaded, their sacrifice done for honor as a tribute to the gods.

At 4 p.m., the blaring of the bus horn signaled to the students that it was time to head back to their hotel. The four hours had passed quickly. Once or twice tourists had inquired if she was all right or wanted something to drink, and she'd politely declined. Each time she was awakened, she instinctively checked the grassy plaza, hoping she might see Tracy walking toward her. But there was no sign of Tracy.

The bus horn sounded again and students began to appear, walking toward the visitor center. An older couple pulled into the parking area in a rented lime green VW bug, no doubt on their way to see the ruins. Students began clambering onto the bus. Clara's stomach still had a pestilent burn that made her wish she'd never come to Mexico at all. She stooped as she climbed aboard the bus and took her seat in the back, closing her eyes in exhaustion.

An hour later the tour bus came to a halt in front of the large fountain in Oaxaca's central plaza, opposite their hotel. Mild afternoon air greeted the students as they stepped off the bus and mingled near their hotel's wrought iron gates. The hour-long ride down the mountainside had left them all dusty and tired.

Several students were gathered around Professor Overton, who was explaining the significance of the temple friezes that savagely depicted men wielding swords and cutting off heads. It seemed too freaky for Clara Huston to comprehend, who still suffered a disorienting nausea now joined with a bit of a panic because she couldn't locate Tracy anywhere.

Clara rushed across the street into the path of a car that braked suddenly. The driver yelled in Spanish out the window, shaking his fist. Clara paid him no attention and re-crossed the street, uncertain of where to look next. She interrupted the language professor to inquire if she'd seen her roommate, fearing that

Tracy may have missed getting back on the bus returning from the ruin. Dr. Overton dispersed the students to help Clara search for the missing student and headed into the hotel lobby to check with the tour bus operator.

Clara spotted two other classmates walking toward an open-air marketplace and started to cross the street again when a fresh bout of queasiness stopped her cold. On the bus ride back she'd been too sick to think about Tracy or anyone else, chucking her cookies out the window twice. How she wished that she'd stayed home for spring break.

AT THE HOTEL saloon, the barkeep had just placed Ferguson's second drink on a cocktail napkin when a commotion in the hotel lobby turned his head. Overton was motioning him over. Standing next to her was a uniformed Mexican police officer. Ferguson's stomach twisted. He joined them in the lobby and was told that Tracy Wilson, a second-year law student, was unaccounted for. Her travel roommate, Clara Huston, had not seen her get back on the bus returning to the hotel. No one had, in fact.

Ferguson felt his anxiety skyrocket. Overton admitted she hadn't taken a head count. The police officer looked at Ferguson.

He shrugged. "I didn't count either."

The two agreed that the bus had waited a full twenty minutes past the stated departure time, ensuring that everyone would have plenty of time to reboard. They explained to the police officer that Clara Huston, the missing girl's roommate, had said nothing to either chaperone at the time they left Monte Albán because she was feeling sick.

The cop left them a form to complete and to be returned to the police station. Meanwhile, two officers would drive to the ruins, now officially closed for the day, and collect the missing young woman as described to them. Overton said she'd go upstairs to let Clara Huston know the police were going back to pick up Tracy, so the girl wouldn't worry herself.

Ferguson returned to the bar, agitated by all the fuss and the fact that two Mexican cops were on their way back to the ruins. His watch read 5:30. He flashed on the lovely Clara, with her pear-shaped bottom. He'd assiduously studied it while she shuffled through her daypack, looking for a headscarf, before they'd embarked on the long bus ride to Oaxaca. She'd caught him looking and grinned coquettishly, the little minx—all that preparatory flirting after class in his office last semester was paying off. She'd probably be waiting for him upstairs now, toweling off her hair after washing away the dust and heat and nausea of the day. It had been a bad afternoon for her—first the stomach problems, and now anxiety over Tracy. It would be at least two hours before the police returned. Plenty of time for him to comfort her, and for them to get better acquainted.

STILL PARKED NEXT to the visitor center more than a thousand feet higher than Oaxaca City was the lime green VW bug—the last car that remained in the Monte Albán ruins parking area. The elderly couple who'd rented the VW had spent the last hour wandering the grounds of the ruins, examining tomb carvings and the sarcophagi of long-dead kings. But now they were half-jogging across the vast grassy expanse toward the visitor center, pained looks on both their faces, their breathing labored in the thin air and their faces glistening with sweat.

"Bis, Greta, Bis!" the older man panted as they climbed the stairs of the visitor center. The couple burst into the one-room center, which was empty save one lone security guard. The German tourists pointed back in the direction they'd run, shouting in guttural voices, "Tot! Jemand tot ist!" The guard stared at them, perplexed. It wasn't until they finally consulted their Spanish travel dictionary and found the word they were looking for—*muerte*—that the guard picked up the phone and called the police.

"PLEASE COME IN, Ed." Patricia Gaston motioned Ed Meachum to the chair in front of her desk. It was Thursday evening, after hours. The hefty agent's dark suit looked a size too small; with the broad shoulders of a linebacker he looked ready to burst through its seams. His bulk combined with his set jaw and massive shaved crown basically communicated a Don't Fuck With Me attitude.

"I understand you've recovered some incriminating information from Paul Higgins's computer?"

"Actually, it was a zip drive we found in his overcoat pocket. It contained a stupefying amount of Chicago office data." He shook his head in disbelief. "The quisling had managed to access Bureau databases for New York City, Boston, and Philadelphia, even." Meachum kicked air from his nose—a snort, more a personal tic than an acknowledgment of success. "He's either cocky confident or just plain stupid. Confronted, he denied any knowledge of tampering with the home office's firewalls and stealing classified information that was way beyond his pay grade or job responsibilities."

"Why would he leave incriminating evidence in his overcoat pocket? Couldn't it have been planted there by someone else?"

Meachum shook his head. "No. The files on the zip drive were clearly his. We secured his laptop computer from his apartment pursuant to a Foreign Intelligence Surveillance Act FISA warrant issued by the Northern District of Illinois here in Cook County. We've caught your mole red-handed."

Gaston nodded. "So how can we be sure he hasn't already leaked this information then?"

"We're questioning him. Fortunately, the zip drive doesn't contain any specific undercover operatives' names or dates, but it does detail some fairly intricate engagements concerning the Bureau's inter-agency cooperation with our major urban field offices and Canadian authorities. He'll be flown out tonight to a safe house. Believe me, Higgins will tell us everything, if he knows what's good for him."

"But why would he do it? Do you have any theories?"

Meachum nodded. "We pulled a temporary file he hadn't managed to deep-six from his computer using the hidden surveillance from the PTQP online program, which I think answers the question." Meachum opened a folder and placed it before Gaston.

"These are charges? They're for thousands of dollars. What is it from?" she asked.

"It's from No Limit Poker, a website, ma'am. Mr. Higgins seems to have bit off more than he can chew. In fact, the guy's maxed out three credit cards and is into the online service for an extra forty thousand dollars, not including unpaid interest charges. And another thing, a guy on my team followed him last week to some kind of meeting, like Gamblers Anonymous." Meachum let loose another snort. "I'd say pretty serious."

"What about Chicago? You said he compromised our data and operational plans?"

Meachum nodded. "Your agency contacts with the Mounted

Police in Toronto. Higgins has been feeding sensitive material and correspondence directly to a mosque off Queen Anne Boulevard up there that's being watched around the clock. It has been for a number of months. The Imam, Mohammed Nazir, preaches violence—not a big surprise there." Meachum snorted again. "The R.C.M.P. has been tracking Nazir's movements pretty much since 9/11. Your guy couldn't have picked a hotter bed to jump into, except maybe Hell itself."

"He's *not* my guy. *Not* my hire, and never would have passed muster from information we've gathered on his past criminal activities. How do we know he's operating alone? Is there anything on the zip drive implicating others here in the Chicago office?" she asked. "And in that regard, I'm assuming that Agent Miranda has brought to your attention his discovering an unauthorized burner phone in the possession of Leeds Hughes, who has no clearance to carry an auxiliary phone for the performance of his job description."

"We checked him out. He's clean. Hughes used the prepaid burner exclusively to keep in touch with his sister's twelve-year-old son—a latchkey kid—who has a similar phone with Hughes's number. Apparently, his sister's divorced and Mr. Hughes tries to help her out with her children. Hughes realizes he should have gotten your permission. The man didn't want to drag his family's dirty laundry out in the open."

Gaston nodded. "So I take it you've found no other accomplices of Higgins, either inside or out of the agency?"

Meachum shook his head. "We've interviewed almost the entire Chicago staff—one-on-one—obtained from each of them signed confidentiality statements to not discuss, searched all offices, and profiled everyone's work history going back." An inside joke of a smile snuck across Meachum's face. "I will say that your forensic scientist, Christine Prusik, certainly has a colorful profile."

"Is there anything tying her to any of these leaks?" Gaston's insistent tapping of her fingernail underscored her question.

"None so far. Then again, I wouldn't have expected any, given the nature of her job, which is generally confined to examining forensic evidence from crimes occurring stateside."

"That's all well and good, Ed. But I wouldn't have taken her principal forensics IT expert for an agency mole either. We have to be thorough. Half measures will afford us nothing, not when it comes to national security, and not on my watch."

"I couldn't agree more. As a safety precaution, I would suggest that you call her back to the office for a debriefing by my people. It's reasonable, given that Higgins is one of her direct reports."

Gaston nodded. "Thank you, Ed. I'll be in touch soon."

Meachum stood and turned to leave. Before she could pick up the phone to call Miranda, it rang.

"Gaston here." A long moment passed before she spoke again. When she did, it was simply to say, "Holy shit."

CHAPTER
TWENTY

"IT'S THE GAS chromatography readings." Jacob Graham glanced around the sparsely filled diner on the outskirts of Benson. An elderly couple sat quietly a few tables over, slowly sipping their coffees. It was Friday, and 7 a.m. was a little early as she'd got in late to the inn, after spending most of the previous afternoon catching up with Joe on case developments. "They definitely match our skins, Special Agent Prusik," he said, fingering his scraggly beard.

"You're referring to the stolen frog skins of two years ago?" Christine had asked Leeds Hughes to share the results of the tissue sample taken from Naomi Winchester's neck with Graham, who agreed to compare it to the Pembroke Research Center's stock.

"Yes, it's the same stock." Graham was unconsciously shredding a paper napkin at the edge of the table. The flesh on the young man's freckled arms had an up-all-night sheen to it, as did his worried face.

"Meaning that Naomi Winchester's death was likely the result of poison taken from Pembroke's liquid nitrogen supply room—"

"It absolutely *was* from our stock. I have no doubt, Agent Prusik. As far as Peter Franklin's death," he added, "Millard is probably right about that, too."

"I'm listening."

Graham let out a pent-up breath. "Look, everyone knows that Peter wasn't approved for the doctoral program. He took it pretty hard, too. Like Millard said."

The waitress put down their coffees and left.

"You know already that Peter appealed the decision. He felt that interning at Macalister and then coming back to work as a technician at Pembroke would increase his chances for reconsideration. But Ferguson didn't trust him. But that's not the reason I called you last night." Graham again furtively scoped the restaurant. "I'm feeling pretty upset, Agent Prusik, with all eyes now on my professor."

It had been close to 1 a.m. when Ned Miranda's call with the news of Tracy Wilson's death had awakened her. Things were moving fast now. But could Ferguson be so out of control as to murder one of the students under his supervision on a school-sponsored trip?

"You're not surprised that there'd be questions, are you, Jacob? Ferguson was responsible for those students. And one of them is now dead under what looks to be suspicious circumstances."

"Okay, I'm not surprised." Leaning forward, he hastened to add, "Nothing's a given, money-wise. I may not have a job next week, tomorrow for that matter. I need that job to stay in the doctoral program myself."

"It was my understanding the Pembroke Research Center was well-funded from government grants?"

He nodded. "Yeah, it is. NIH made a substantial multiyear commitment. But that was before all this. Let's not kid each other. I'm sure that commitment will be reconsidered if this thing gets any worse." Graham took a quick sip of his coffee. "Nothing's sacrosanct, Agent Prusik. Government money always comes with strings attached."

Graham's point was well taken. Yet Christine picked up something more from the research assistant's paranoid behavior, which couldn't be explained away by grant adjustments and fear of losing his job. His florid complexion had the look of a man besieged. She'd seen him turn the same color after she'd asked whether he knew Cindy Lawson, Winchester's roommate.

"There's something else." Graham placed his laptop on the table and waited for its program to load.

He tapped a few keys and swiveled the computer to face her: a grid of digital photos appeared on the screen, each the size of a postage stamp.

"I downloaded these photos off Shamus's computer late yesterday afternoon. He must have uploaded them to his cloud account while he was in Mexico because they're mostly of ancient temple ruins."

Christine gave the young researcher a serious look. "Hasn't the Indiana State Police or state crime lab requested you to turn over his computer files yet, Jacob?"

He looked at her, puzzled. "No. No one has contacted me. Not even the school officials. That's why I phoned you right away."

"What made you think to check his personal computer?"

"I'm his research assistant. I always check it whenever he goes on field trips. He runs out of disk space on his camera all the time and uploads the pictures to his cloud account."

Graham hunched himself sideways to view the screen with her, and began toggling through the photo array. "It's the last several pictures in particular that explain why I phoned you. I wouldn't have given it much thought, but take a look . . ."

He swiveled the laptop toward Christine and punched the enlarge view key. Suddenly one postage stamp–size picture filled the entire computer screen.

"This is a wide-angle shot taken from a distant perspective. It shows the layout of the ruins, which I verified is the Monte Albán site from an internet check," Graham said.

Christine's eyes fell on a man in a white suit walking across what looked like a grassy plaza. The striding figure put the vastness of the ancient city's dimensions into impressive perspective.

Graham opened up the next digital picture to full screen. The man in white was perhaps twenty feet away now, striding straight toward the photographer, up the same stone steps from where the first picture was taken. He had shoulder-length bleach blond hair that fell below a panama hat.

"There's one more picture from his last download," Graham said, clicking open the file to enlarge the frame. He turned the screen to face her once more. It was another image of the same man in the white suit, only in this screen shot the man had turned to the side. The picture was of his profile from less than ten feet away.

"Do you recognize this man?" Christine said.

"No, but I think Ferguson did."

"Why do you say that?"

"Because he focused the camera right on the man in this last frame. He centered the camera on just him. In the other pictures, the man is not the focus."

Christine angled the laptop to cut the glare coming in from the restaurant window. She looked more closely at the picture displayed on the screen. Sunlight fell across the leading edge of the man's chin, illuminating the silver-white of a well-trimmed beard that clashed awfully with the man's bleach blond hair. As Jacob Graham said, the hilltop background of the ancient temple was blurred out of focus.

"Have you and Professor Ferguson discussed these pictures yet?"

He shook his head. "He's given me explicit instructions . . ." The research assistant hesitated. "We're not supposed to discuss what happened in Mexico while the investigation's actively pursued on campus."

"Ferguson didn't specifically advise you not to cooperate, did he?"

"Why do you think I phoned you?" he said. "I thought these pictures might be relevant."

Christine considered Graham's disclosures. Something was off. Was he terrified of Ferguson? Whatever it was, Graham wasn't sharing it.

"So you phoned me," she said. "And here I am. Not CSU's dean of students, or even the local sheriff's office? Tell me, Jacob, where did you go during spring break?"

Graham eyed her indignantly. "I stuck around here. I get more work done in peace and quiet." He scratched his beard. "Why, is that a problem?"

"I bet you do like it nice and quiet, when everybody else is gone," Christine said, assessing the man's reactions. In a quieter voice: "Nothing but you and the trees and a bunch of empty dorm rooms. Am I right, Jacob?"

"What is that supposed to mean? I thought you'd want to see these pictures." Crimson splotches erupted on his throat. "You handed me your business card."

Christine recalled his awkwardness the last time she'd

questioned him, his suddenly going quiet when she'd mentioned that someone had broken into Naomi Winchester's dorm room after the police had taped it off.

"So tell me, Mr. Graham, with the campus crawling with cops now, you wouldn't be trying to implicate your professor, suggesting from this scanty picture evidence that he hired a hit man to knock off Tracy Wilson, would you?"

"Did you even know that Tracy Wilson ran track?" Graham said defensively. "And Peter Franklin, he was a long-distance runner and in great shape, like Millard told you."

"What does Peter Franklin have to do with these pictures?"

"All I'm saying is Tracy Wilson was in excellent physical condition. She'd have to be. She wouldn't have succumbed from exertion climbing around temples like that." There was a defiant edge to Graham's voice.

"You're not telling me everything, Jacob," she said in a quieter voice. "If you want my help, you need to come clean."

He snatched up the laptop and stuffed it inside his backpack. He slapped the memory stick containing the pictures down on the tabletop. "You're the special agent. And now you know what I know. Figure it out for yourself." He shouldered his bag and loped out of the restaurant.

Christine watched him hop into a dusty small car and squeal the tires, leaving the parking lot. What did he mean by *you know what I know*?

She picked up the memory stick. She'd overnight it to Eisen to see if his facial recognition software could identify the man in the white suit against the growing list of suspects. Clearly, the man's gray beard and long bleach blond hair told her it was a rather obvious disguise. And just as clear was Graham's discomfort when she started to probe.

POISON GREW WILD in his own backyard. He'd learned from his grandmother that as many things could not be safely eaten as could. When Trip was a boy, she'd shown him a patch of sweet-smelling flowers called lily of the valley. She'd stooped and ripped off a leaf of the aromatic flower and mashed it against his lips, demanding him to open up. Her taunting manner told him not to. With a wizened half-smile, she'd nodded, flagging that leaf, saying that's all it would have taken to choke him to death unless his stomach was pumped quickly, and that he could never get to the hospital in time to pump it out. She'd grinned in her strange, almost gleeful way, saying that Karl would find him too late, "a curled-up-on-the-ground, blue-faced dead boy is what," as if she wished it were true.

Afterward, until the first hard frost, when the deadly patch of sweet-smelling plants wilted, he'd counted every plant—all thirty-six of them—before breakfast and dinner each and every day, making sure the count didn't come up short.

His grandmother took him on many forays into Mother Nature. He learned about the bright orange, slimy yellow, and ghostly pale mushrooms and toadstools that broke through the earth out of nowhere after days of soaking rains. He learned about deadly wildflowers and noxious weeds. And of course there was the tropical Brugmansia plant that lived right on the porch most of the year, until it got too cold and Trip had to lug it inside. Its umbrella-like golden blooms scented the air sweetly with their heady fragrance, but the milky sap in its leaves was irreversibly toxic if ingested. But his grandmother's garden and the forays into her woods only tapped the surface of nature's poison portfolio. Spiders and snakes and hornets, the list of the deadly creatures and plants went on and on, and Trip's fascination with the lights-out universe did, too.

Everything had fallen into place in the academic committee's consideration of Peter Franklin, who'd petitioned for a review of his application to the PhD program. Before the committee convened to vote, Trip had had an opportunity to speak with Alice Catrall; he'd noticed that she stiffened each time Franklin's name was mentioned during an initial committee discussion. Trip saw an opportunity. After some careful coaxing and reassurances that anything she said to him would be held in the strictest confidence, Catrall disclosed that Franklin had taken her course as an undergraduate and had perjured himself on a term paper assignment.

Just like that, the plum of all plums fell into his lap, his for the taking. In short order, Trip caught up with the hopeful petitioner and disclosed to him what he knew, at the same time assuring Franklin that it would not be brought to the committee's attention. In fact, he guaranteed his admission to the doctoral program in exchange for one small favor. Franklin had merely to steal three skins of *Phyllobates terribilis*, the Golden Poison Dart Frog, which were freeze-dried in canisters of liquid nitrogen in a locked storage room at the Pembroke Research Center.

It was a crime Trip had asked of the young man, a very serious one that likely would be a game changer for everyone concerned if Franklin happened to be caught in the act. But Trip had measured the risk and Franklin's desperation well, and it delighted his ears when the hopeful technician agreed to do it without hesitation. Trip could hardly wait. All went smooth as silk. Once the skins were safely in hand, so to speak, Trip instructed Franklin to leave his car door unlocked so he could place the acceptance packet containing the committee's letter of approval in the back seat of the young man's used SUV.

What fun it had been when the young man got into the driver's seat and turned to reach for the envelope behind him, and instead got the inaugural jab of the gold ring. Trip had arrived earlier and positioned himself low behind the driver's seat, quietly waiting. He was cramped, and the jab had landed off the mark in Franklin's forearm. And he'd had concerns about the lethal dosage; none of the treatises explained it in terms other than monkeys and capybaras darted by Indigenous peoples from the South American jungle, and experimental rats and mice in the lab. In a sense, Peter was like a large experimental lab rat himself.

His concerns had been for naught. Everything had turned out splendidly.

The poison delivery system Trip had inherited, his grandmother's massive gold ring, couldn't be more perfect. Squatting on the ring's faceplate, usually reserved for a cameo insignia, was a three-dimensional Mesoamerican caricature of a frog—a symbol of worship. No lowly frog prince, the ring was 24-karat yellow gold. How perfect was that? The ring had a nifty small lever along its side. When activated, a needle would spring upward, protruding from the frog's mouth. A trick ring his grandmother once said, after she pulled it on him—without the poison, of course—but she'd jabbed the back of his neck hard enough to leave a small bruise.

Trip had triple-coated the ring's hairspring-mounted needle with a small patch of skin from the defrosted Golden Poison

Dart Frog carcass. He'd worn two sets of protective gloves while rubbing the secretion from the frog skin across the protruding needle. Then, still wearing the gloves, he'd reset the hairspring trigger, sliding the small lever on the ring, which caused the glistening armed tip to drop inside the amphibian figure's mouth, in the set position.

After injecting Peter Franklin, Trip had a first-row seat to the most incredible chemical reaction that he'd ever witnessed. The whole chassis of the car jiggled as the young man's body shook in spasm like there was no tomorrow. And for Peter there wasn't even a tonight. During the worst of the violent spasms, it would have seemed to a passerby like nothing more than some serious hanky-panky going on, some shadowy hot car sex.

The end came with an elongated whistle of air bleeding from Franklin's chest. Rather anti-climactic. Trip would have stayed longer to be absolutely sure. Instead, he jabbed the lab tech's now rigidified body once more in the neck. But it accomplished nothing. The electric charge of the man's body was already spent.

FRIDAY AFTERNOON, FOLLOWING her meeting with Graham, Christine crossed the CSU campus and took the stairway to the second floor of Ellis House—graduate student housing. Tracy Wilson's room wasn't cordoned off yet. She hadn't seen Sheriff Boynton or any state police on campus either. However, her timing couldn't have been more perfect.

A middle-aged man with silver hair, dressed in a navy suit, stood looking pensively out of the window into an empty parking lot. A similarly aged woman, presumably his wife, was sitting on the edge of the dead student's bed, wearing a two-piece Armani coal-black suit and matching pumps. The woman looked up as Christine entered the room.

"My name is Christine Prusik, Special Agent of the FBI."

TRIP STARED OUT the living room picture window of the Victorian-style home that his grandmother's father had built on high ground overlooking the great river that the Iroquois Nation called the Ohio, meaning "beautiful river." Its broad waters, brown from the heavy spring rains and runoff from the large farming tracts and industrial effluvial wastes, coursed powerfully below the steep bluff where the house stood. An oak tree, roots and all, could ride the current faster than a person could jog along its banks.

Sunny Mexico had never been his first plan. But then he hadn't planned on the damn cat jumping from the top of the bookcase to the desk and in the process knocking over the liquid nitrogen canister. He'd just unscrewed its insulated lid and was snapping on the second set of rubber gloves when the cat had jumped. The chilly liquid gas had soaked through the carpeting. Afterward, the Persian rug crumbled like bits of charred bacon.

The shriveled remains of the last frog skin he'd gotten from Peter Franklin quickly disintegrated in the room-temperature air and was reduced to pile of goop on the rug. He'd saved the amphibian skin in the freezer but couldn't be sure of its lethality. It was unfortunate, too, that he couldn't call upon the dead Franklin to steal him some more. The whole thing was just plain aggravating. It wasn't part of the plan.

He'd had to formulate a new plan with a quick online search, and much to his delight he discovered a prime source—a merchant who dealt in Golden Poison Dart Frogs exclusively. The black market dealer's location was secret, as expected. All interested parties were directed to a go-between, someone who worked an agave stand at the Oaxaca, Mexico, marketplace. A devotee of Mesoamerican history and prehistory, Trip knew that the city of Oaxaca was a major stop on the trade route for sellers of Peruvian wool blankets, warm hats, and coats from Chile, plus pottery and other ceramic wares. And thanks be his lucky stars, there was a CSU-sponsored tour to visit an ancient mountaintop ruin near Oaxaca.

The pace of the journey itself had taken a toll on him. Things hadn't gone as planned at the mountaintop Monte Albán ruins either. He'd armed the ring and picked a perfect ambush spot. The FBI was getting too close with its inquiries. He couldn't take the chance that someone would start talking more freely. Namely that Shamus Ferguson could connect the dots if pressed. Would.

At the ruins, he'd waited patiently in the subterranean crypt room, hiding behind the sarcophagus of a long-dead king, where he'd gauged that his target would be heading. But surprise, surprise, it wasn't to be. Instead, a rather attractive young woman with long blonde hair pulled tidily back in a ponytail walked into the dim-lit chamber. She looked somewhat familiar, but then again young blondes with smooth tan flesh pretty much all looked alike and were a common enough sight among vacationing students on spring break. The woman had advanced closer, perusing the wall carvings. She hadn't noticed him standing absolutely still in one corner of the burial room until he'd cleared his throat and she'd looked up and said, "Oh, I'm sorry. I didn't know you were here." She'd smiled at him, squinting in the darkness for a clearer look. He'd given her a congenial smile, and at that the young woman had gone back to studying the enormous stone sarcophagus that took up most of the burial chamber space, leaving only a narrow passageway between it and the carved mural walls for tourists to walk its circumference.

She'd gotten a good look at his face from only a few feet away. Her unexpected arrival had got him off his plan. She might wonder why he was standing alone in the dark and say something to the other students. The crypt room's centuries-old stone-carved friezes of ghoulish figures in feathered headdresses, their raised swords hacking off heads and arms, had been his only witnesses as he'd flicked the small lever on the side of the gold frog ring, releasing the needle that jutted up with enough deadly Batracho-toxin to kill several dozen more. The young woman had stooped for a closer look, sending her short shorts farther up the backs of her thighs. It was then that he'd gently tapped the back of her neck and she'd gone down swifter than he could get out of the way, her leg spasms nearly tripping him. Her eyes had glazed over immediately, their last worldly view the inside of an ancient burial chamber.

He'd climbed the darkened mossy steps of the underground crypt. In the glaring sunlight, he'd seen a tourist couple in matching tan outfits and sunhats approaching from a distance. Quickly, he'd ducked around the back side of the temple entrance and then hurried across the ancient Mesoamerican ball court where the games played had been for keeps—both victor and vanquished lost their heads in the name of honor. How fitting.

He left the ruins; the matter that still needed to be attended to would have to come later. And later was now. All was well that ended well. He rested the new portable liquid canister on his grandmother's writing desk and unscrewed its lid. No cat worries this time. He'd spared the feline the luxury of eight more lives. He gloved up and switched on the circular viewing lamp with its central magnifying glass, and prepared the ring.

NEWS OF TRACY Wilson's death on the school-sponsored Mexico trip spread. DEATH IN AN AZTEC CRYPT and COED MURDERED AMONG MEXICO RUINS, and worst: MURDER OR SACRIFICE AT JUNGLE TEMPLE? Satellite trucks and TV camera crews descended on Benson, Indiana's wooded CSU campus, assembling like vultures to a kill. Tweets numbered in the thousands in less than twenty-four hours, and the same rushed headlines filled other online social media websites.

Late Saturday afternoon, the Wilsons' private jet touched down in Benson, Indiana, after a four-hour flight from Oaxaca. They'd been kind enough to bring Christine there and back while transporting their daughter's body back to their hometown in Muncie, Indiana. How quickly Margery Wilson had commandeered Christine, invoking the compelling pleas that only a distraught mother can. It hadn't taken Christine long to agree to accompany them. She was brought along as extra muscle to ensure that a casket rode home in the cargo locker of the private jet. The Wilsons weren't going home empty-handed.

Even so, Christine had had to lie, assuring the Wilsons of the Bureau's approval when she'd only phoned Sheriff McFaron to let him know she was accompanying the Wilson family to Mexico to examine their daughter's body. She hadn't called to consult with him. There wasn't time to explain under the circumstances. Besides, what could he say to make her change her mind when there was no choice but for her to go? Joe had kept it short and wished her a safe trip.

Everything will be fine, Christine kept telling herself, so long as no one in Oaxaca contacts the Chicago branch office of the FBI to double-check. And fortunately they hadn't or she'd likely have been seeing the inside of a Mexican jail cell.

Christine had followed Dr. Humberto Salazar, the Mexican ME, into the mortuary where he removed the coverlet from Tracy Wilson's dead body. She'd eyed the young victim's body and suddenly felt a pang in her gut. *Just make it through the gates*, she told herself. *Just make it through the gates*. Her eyes had raced along the black seams between the white floor tiles—seams that suddenly ran red. Quickly she flicked her eyes left-right, left-right in hopes of averting a full meltdown.

When she'd lifted Wilson's shoulder-length blonde hair, Christine immediately focused the headset magnifier on the back of the young victim's neck. Her eyes came to rest on the distinctive puncture mark that she'd seen twice before. Without a doubt, it was the same MO. The same killer.

Salazar excised the tissue sample with a 15c sharp-point narrow scalpel as she had requested and placed it inside a Ziploc bag, which he put on a dry-ice packet in a small Styrofoam chest. Following the examination of Wilson's body, Dr. Salazar had then said, "How do you say in America, bad things come in threes?" and shown Christine two other bodies.

The moment the Wilson's jet had landed in Benson and Christine turned her phone back on, it started vibrating. Ned Miranda was trying to reach her. She let it go to voicemail. She'd call him back later. She felt drained and needed to shower.

Inside the rental car, she felt a resurgent confidence; mostly it was the protective shield of Margery and Clive Wilson as her allies. Money and power spoke volumes, a language Patricia Gaston undoubtedly understood. Christine had promised Margery Wilson that she'd find their daughter's killer, and maybe, with the power of patronage, she'd be able to do just that.

Christine keyed in Eisen's number. The call was routed to his voicemail. She hit redial, itching for the results of the facial recognition software that she'd asked him to run on the photos Jacob Graham had retrieved from Ferguson's cloud account.

A knock at Christine's window startled her—Ned Miranda was peering down with an inscrutable look. Her heart sank. She hurriedly scanned the plane hangar looking for her Protective Shield. The Wilsons' jet was already taxiing onto the runway. She watched it rocket down the tarmac, then climb steeply, wheels up. *Bye bye, Margery Wilson*, she thought. And bye bye, Christine.

She stepped out of the car and prepared for the worst. "Hello, Ned, funny seeing you here."

"I know about your interviewing Randall Creighton at Macalister. Patricia got pretty upset. You sure must have rattled the guy." The words came out sounding strangely nonconfrontational. Christine stared up at the sky and caught a gleam of sunlight against silver, the protective shield fast slipping away.

"I suppose you know about my trip to Mexico then, accompanying the family of Tracy Wilson?"

Miranda rubbed his chin. "You want to go somewhere to grab some coffee?"

Christine stared at him, unable to make sense of his collegial tone and relaxed body language. Finally she said, "Don't tell me you're looking for a public atmosphere to make an official arrest? I'm a big girl, Ned. Let's get it over with, here and now."

"I know you think of me as little more than Patricia's lackey,

Christine. So yes, you can always call me as a witness, if it ever comes down to that," he said, meaning an administrative hearing following her dismissal.

"So what gives? Why are you here then?"

"If you asked the branch director, she'd say it was to bring you in. Did you know Higgins was removed?" Miranda had dark rings under his eyes and creases down the sides of his narrow cheeks that aged him beyond his twenty-eight years. He looked like a wreck.

"So I've heard," she said. "Am I to assume you're here then to escort me back to join him?"

Miranda unzipped his briefcase on the hood of Christine's rental car. He handed her an accordion file—brown twine spooled tightly around its flap closure.

"More job description worksheets to review on the plane ride back?" she said glibly.

"Brian and I have been working together pretty late these last couple of days, with Higgins's help, too," he said, "before he was detained."

"Is that right?" She fingered through a few of the documents in the rope file, which obviously weren't reorganization or planning documents.

"These are student and teacher telephone interviews from LTC in Starksboro, Illinois, and CSU, in Benson, Indiana," he said. "Eisen and Higgins had made most of the calls earlier, but I made a few." He yawned as if for added proof.

Christine looked puzzled at the large X-Y axis graph with names running along the top and left margins. Jet lag wasn't helping her decipher its meaning.

"Look, can we go somewhere to spread this out?" he said. "I rented a car, too. Frankly, I wasn't sure that I'd find you here at the airport."

"How about you follow me," she said, staring at Miranda like it was the first time they'd met, unable to get over his apparent transformation. "I know a good place where we shouldn't be disturbed. It's an inn not far from the CSU campus, in fact. I could more than use a few hours of sleep once we're done."

Fifteen minutes later they were parked at Le Maquis Auberge. She checked in to stay for the night. The inn had an empty function room for private parties that the manager consented to their using.

"We compared all professors that taught at both the LTC and CSU campuses against the names of female students who took courses from them in the last year." Miranda unfolded the large spreadsheet showing teachers' names down the left side margin and female student names across each column.

"As you can see," he continued, "there are a total of sixty-six professors who, in the last school year, taught at least one class at both campuses. We found that a professor usually carries the majority of his or her coursework at one school, usually only teaching one course during the school year at the other campus."

"I'm surprised it's this many," Christine said, "who teach at both university campuses in different states."

"I was too until we discovered that the schools have a scholastic sharing arrangement, by order of the Indiana and Illinois legislatures, under which students from both campuses are eligible to matriculate in courses at the adjacent state's campus on a cooperative basis and get full credit toward their degree. In essence, the alliance increases course offerings without adding to their individual budgets. It's a profitable arrangement for both universities."

"I've got to stop you there, Ned," she said. "I'm tired, I'm confused, and I'm not at all sure what it is that I'm supposed to be hearing. Just what the hell is going on exactly? I mean, you show up at the Benson County airport unannounced, saying Gaston is pissed that I interviewed Creighton and wants my head on a platter. Then you tell me that that's not even why you're really here? Now, all of a sudden you turn information analyst on me? What gives?"

He stared hard at her, his expression unreadable. "Nothing gives, Christine. I want to catch this killer as much as you do and I'm not . . . happy . . . with everything that's been going on in the Chicago office lately. Let's just leave it at that." He cleared his throat. "Now, from the size eleven shoe prints that you photographed and lifted off the first cave floor, the killer is obviously a man. That cuts the list of professors by nearly half, leaving thirty-four male professors who taught at least one course at the other school in the last year."

Christine shook her head to clear it. "Okay. Okay, let's leave it at that. So tell me again why you limited your investigation to only professors? Why not include graduate student teaching assistants who may work on both campuses?"

"That's a good question." Miranda nodded. "We narrowed our search eliminating grad students after Higgins discovered an internet search leading to an IP address for a website in Oaxaca, Mexico, that offers poison frogs for sale. That search originated from a CSU faculty lounge not open to grad students or teaching assistants. Unfortunately, the computer is for the general convenience of any professor visiting the lounge, so Paul—before he was apprehended—wasn't able to identify the particular person who generated the search request."

Christine felt her hopes rise. "Well, then," she said, "I'd have to agree with your assumption. From my examination of Tracy Wilson's body, she was definitely murdered by the same killer we're after."

Miranda hesitated upon hearing that. "Perhaps we were wrong to place so much credence on Higgins's discovery, especially in light of his arrest."

Christine shook her head. "I'm inclined to believe that Paul's lead is solid. As for his arrest, Ned, I've heard what Gaston had to say and I don't buy one word of it. Yes, yes, he may have blundered his way into a police station's records when he was sixteen. But Higgins has more than acquitted himself while under my watch." Miranda made no attempt to challenge her. Clearly they were both tired. "Please go on."

"We were able to narrow the list to eleven professors and teaching fellows with faculty privileges on both campuses. Eliminating female students required convincing both school records departments to release the names of women in the top ten percent of their class standing, based on the fact Winchester and McKinley were both high-caliber students. That reduced the list to seventeen women who may have been approached by a male professor trying to hit on them."

He put down his pencil and looked up at Christine. "I thought we might go over the remaining eleven professors and teaching fellows together."

"Okay," Christine said slowly. "But how long have you and my guys been working on this? Does Gaston know about this? If she expects you to escort me back, I bet she won't be too thrilled to find out about your involvement with this?"

Miranda shrugged. "Patricia told me I'd failed her for not keeping strict tabs on you. Why didn't you tell me that you were planning to interview Randall Creighton? Or return to Chicago as you assured me?" For a moment the old taskmaster Ned reared in disapproval, then quickly disappeared. "I'm pretty much screwed however you look at it."

"So you've found me, Ned, just like Patricia wanted you to do. No need to fall on your sword."

He smiled in surrender. "Shall we get on with this before you fall asleep on me?"

An hour later they concluded their discussion. She'd spotted several names that she recognized—Ferguson's, of course, and it didn't surprise her to learn that Jacob Graham had taught an advanced biochemistry seminar at LTC last term either.

"So what are you suggesting we do, Ned? Do you want to co-ordinate with me here in Benson, or . . ."

He shook his head. "I'd better head back. My mission's accomplished." He forced a smile that she often reserved for herself: sardonic.

"All right," Christine said, appreciative that he wasn't constraining her movements as he'd so often tried to before. There was no point in either of them reiterating the obvious. Patricia would fire him for insubordination.

Christine followed Ned out to his car. "If you speak to Brian, I'm still waiting for that facial recognition analysis of digital photos that I uploaded to him. And Ned—it's so strange for me to be saying this to you—whatever I can do to help, you know . . .

testifying at your hearing, or whatever. Assuming, of course, that I still have a job, too."

They both smiled, sadly.

TRIP WATCHED THEM from across the street, containing as best he could the flashes of rage that had been getting worse. Seeing her hug Mister Dark Suit, he could barely restrain himself. The ringing in his ears ratcheted up like a field of crickets in high summer. He gripped the truck's steering wheel so tightly his fingers ached.

Watching her at the airport coming on to this eager beaver agent whom she'd invited back to her room, perhaps for a drink of wine and a taste of something else. . . . And now, here they were, saying their goodbyes after their cheap rendezvous. She was the same as the rest and needed to learn her lesson the hard way.

The tall dark suit got into the small Chevy compact and circled out of the inn's driveway, heading toward the airport road, Trip figured. He kept his distance. Police were crawling all over campus. So were TV satellite trucks and news people. Extra precautions were necessary. But that didn't forgive her shoving it right in his face deliberately like that. It was not okay to fuck with him like that.

Trip tugged down the greasy baseball cap he'd found crammed behind the seat in the truck that he'd stolen an hour earlier from a gas station back lot. He wore a pair of stained work gloves and a torn lumber shirt that had been tucked behind the front seat, too, as a crude disguise just in case. He followed the dark suit's car, having difficulty controlling his impulses. One moment he was looking out the window at ordinary trees and grass and sky and the road zooming by, and the next, he was hanging on to the steering wheel with all he had, barely able to keep the truck on the road, his head doing all the talking.

Railroad crossing lights flashed up ahead. The zebra-striped gates dropped across the road with a loud clanging of bells. No traffic was stopped on the other side. He checked his rearview. No one was behind him either. Rage when honed to a fine edge had a demonstrative calming effect—like the eye of the storm suddenly passing over making everything look brighter, fresher, more alive, the air cleansed of fuss and stir.

Trip registered the low booming sound of several large locomotive diesels—a freight train was approaching the crossing. He could feel the vibration of the several-thousand-horsepower engines rumbling through his steering wheel. A few hundred feet down the tracks weedy trees shivered as the long liner passed by, chugging in his direction.

He eased the old truck behind the agent's car, revving the motor with his foot. The high, yellow-painted sides of the front two diesel engines appeared through the trees a few hundred yards in the distance, moving at a good clip. He eased the truck closer, gauging the speed of the advancing train, then slammed the gas pedal to the floor, hurtling the small Chevy through the gate into the path of the oncoming freight.

The engineer had no time to react. No time to brake. The locomotive struck the driver's side full force, instantly crushing the small car, jettisoning a spray of sparks as it plowed the twisted wreckage out of sight farther down the tracks. The crunching of metal against metal faded as more and more freight cars slid by, hardly slowing at all.

Trip retraced his route to the gas station and parked the truck where he'd found it, leaving the ignition key under the floor mat, also where he'd found it. He walked a short ways down a side street to where his blue Toyota Yaris was parked and stuffed the work shirt, gloves, and greasy hat into a black plastic garbage bag to later burn in a trash barrel behind the barn on his property.

His rage returned to a simmer, scarcely more than his elevated heartbeats, but still very much there. He knew what had to be done. She couldn't be trusted. She was a fornicating fraud just like all the others. He chuckled to himself. She'd be miffed when she learned there'd be no more hanky-panky with Mister Dark Suit.

He smiled at another thought. That she'd be free tonight.

CHAPTER
TWENTY-ONE

CHRISTINE TOOK A much-needed shower while the inn manager sent her pants suit out to a two-hour dry cleaner. The quick turnaround service cost her ten dollars extra. With the towel tucked around her, she dried her hair and punched on the TV remote.

A breaking news bulletin from Benson, Indiana, caught her attention. Images of smoldering wreckage at a railroad crossing filled the screen as an on-the-scene reporter informed viewers that a car had attempted to cross the railroad tracks in front of an oncoming freight train.

Christine grabbed her phone and hit Ned Miranda's speed dial number. She got his voicemail. She phoned Brian Eisen.

"Brian, look, there's a news report on the TV—"

"Ned was in the car, Christine. He's dead. We just received word from the Benson County sheriff's office a few moments ago. I was about to phone you. They managed to retrieve his ID. That's all I know so far."

She dropped onto the bed, her breath caught in her throat. Ned had been seated next to her downstairs scarcely an hour ago.

"Christine? Hello?"

"Ned was just here, Brian. As in only minutes ago. We were

going over your and Paul's chart work. I'm astounded . . . by everything . . . I . . . Jesus." She let out a long breath.

Could it be suicide—Ned's sudden change of heart to help with the investigation, not following through with Gaston's orders to bring her back? Christine dismissed the panicky thought as absurd. He'd acquitted himself too well to take his own life.

"I'm assuming Bureau agents are on their way here?"

"Patricia's convening a meeting in the conference room in fifteen minutes," Eisen said. "I'm in an awkward position, Christine. I don't think Ned shared any of the investigative efforts we jointly produced with the branch director. And now, with Paul dismissed . . . I'm not sure what to say."

"I appreciate your concern, Brian. Don't divulge anything specific yet. Not until I check a few things out first. Call me right after Gaston's meeting. And Brian, have you got those digital pictures from Ferguson's assistant cross-compared yet?"

"It's on my to-do list. Sorry. Without Paul, I've gotten behind on things."

"I need you to run facial recognition on those pictures. Things are moving fast."

"I have to ask you, Christine." Eisen hesitated. "Word's out that Ned was on his way down there to fire you. Is it true?"

"Let's just say Ned had a change of heart in more ways than one."

Christine briefly told him about her flight to Mexico to examine Tracy Wilson's body. "I've air-expressed to you three more human tissue samples for analysis. Have Hughes take them to the Chicago consulting lab that we've used before. We need results pronto."

"Three samples did you say?"

"Things didn't go as smoothly as the killer may have planned in Mexico. Have Hughes get going on it when the samples arrive."

"Meaning they are all definitely connected?" Eisen said.

"A maid cleaning a hotel room where the CSU student group stayed was found dead—the same MO. The Mexican police also found a shack on this dead Indigenous man's property from the stink of death. Apparently, he'd raised poison frogs. Unfortunately, they were too decomposed to identify."

"So the killer covered his tracks then?" Eisen said. "Offing the local internet dealer? I'm assuming that's what you're thinking."

"It does look that way, which is why I need those pictures matched ASAP, Brian."

"Before you go, Christine, it may not be crucial, but a police complaint was filed last week at the Benson County sheriff's office, by a Madeleine Rizzo. She's a nurse at Benson Memorial Hospital. She was on her way to work and accepted a ride from someone she'd recently met at a bar. She complained that the guy grabbed her arm pretty hard when she tried to use her cell phone, and then he threatened her. She managed to get out of the car. It was Jacob Graham."

"Graham, Ferguson's research assistant?"

"That's what I thought, too. I called Sheriff Boynton in Benson and verified that a complaint had been officially filed against one and the same Jacob Graham, but apparently Rizzo got cold feet and didn't want to press charges in spite of her bruises. She'd been pretty shook up, according to Boynton."

"Thank you, Brian."

"I'll call you later with the facial recognition results," he said. Their call ended. So the enigmatic Jacob Graham had reason to be red-faced after all. According to the spreadsheet Miranda showed her, Graham had taught a class at LTC last semester. Perhaps Graham had called her to the restaurant to throw her further off the trail, pegging it all on pictures allegedly downloaded off Professor Ferguson's cloud account.

Another update flashed across the TV screen. Christine upped the volume with the remote.

"The Sheriff's Department is treating the accident as suspicious. Evidently, the crossing gate operated correctly and was in the lowered position at the time the victim's car crashed through the barrier and was struck by the train."

The television camera panned back, bringing into focus several law enforcement agents wearing navy blue windbreakers with *STATE POLICE* printed in large white letters yoked across the back. She reflected on the situation. Miranda did seem despondent, tired, but not foolish enough to try to outrun a train. He'd had plenty of time to catch his flight back. The air was clear for a change; no weather obstruction could be blamed for contributing to the accident. The crazy idea that had snuck into her head upon first seeing the news could no longer be ignored or shoved down. Dr. Katz had warned of a paranoid personality's hair trigger. Which meant one thing: the killer had been watching them. She was being shadowed. He was watching her movements and he'd seen her with Ned. And next he would be coming for her.

SHAMUS FERGUSON REFILLED his glass with the dark amber liquor and dropped heavily into the recliner chair, spilling some down the front of his shirt that he hadn't changed since he, Overton, and the spring break students had flown back. University officials had requested he not attend the ad hoc press conference held in front of the dean of student affairs' office when formal news of Tracy Wilson's death was delivered by Vice President Phillips, who would not answer the media hounds' questions beyond what had already been reported.

How much longer would it be, he wondered, before the media trucks would discover his lakeside cottage? Graham understood the game plan and would deflect the media calls that surely were flooding the Pembroke Research Center with the standard refrain: No comment.

Ferguson drained the contents of the tumbler and placed it on the floor beside his chair. From the small table beside his chair he lifted the Walther P38 9MM pistol, the prized souvenir that his old man had brought back from the German front in 1944. Over the years he'd rarely taken it out even to look at, other than to clean and oil the barrel as his father had shown him once a year. Mostly it had lain in its muslin cloth on the upper shelf in his bedroom closet. When he was a boy, he and his father would target practice with it in the backyard. Its accuracy was unparalleled, his dad had told him—truer even than the fabled Luger.

Ferguson hefted the finely crafted handgun. Its cross-hatched pistol grips grabbed nicely against his fleshy palm. The blued steel finish of the barrel signified its serious wartime purpose. He shoved himself to a stand and did the rounds. He'd drawn all the shades and locked all doors. He staggered to the door that led to the back deck first. Cracking the shade, he glanced through the deck rails. The roofline of the Range Rover protruded, well out of sight from anyone who might glance down the drive.

He staggered back through the living room, snatched up the empty tumbler from the floor, and refilled it from the half-finished bottle on the kitchen countertop. The rum went down smoothly. He stood in the middle of the living room, listening intently to nothing more than the elevated thumping of his own heart. He'd drunk too much—par for the course after all that had gone wrong. The clear implications from the sensational news reports were not good, and then there were the insinuations— you couldn't stop those cable channel slime bags from digging around his past scrapes, trying him in the press, calling him out. Worst of all was how it would reverberate back to NIH. His grants would be challenged. His work would come to a halt. The Pembroke Research Center, his brainchild and creation, would cease to be—or at least cease to be his.

The distant drone of a powerboat somewhere out on the lake drew his attention. From the slow chuff of its motor, he figured some guy slow trawling, fishing for nothing but a little bit of peace, maybe with the proverbial six-pack stowed under the oar seat and one opened and filling his free hand, the breeze in his face. What Ferguson wouldn't give to be in that guy's shoes right now.

Ferguson returned to the kitchen counter, unscrewed the cap on a new fifth, and returned with it to the recliner. From there he could see the front door easily, and over his shoulder a patch of lake water shimmered below the deck slats. Having to hide out in his own house pissed him off. He took a swig of Bacardi, clutching the pistol in his right hand. He wouldn't go down without a fight. They didn't know who the fuck they were tangling with. He lifted the bottle back to his lips and sucked hard.

THE DINNER INVITATION came unexpectedly and she'd surprised herself by welcoming it. Christine needed a break from the afternoon's confounding and shocking tragedy. Corbin Malinowski had given her directions to his residence and told her to come whenever she was ready. Christine entered his street address on the rental car's dash-mounted GPS. It was approximately three miles from campus and it backed up against state forest land, displayed on the car's A/V screen as solid pale green. A nice quiet spot, she thought. Pristine and beautiful, no doubt.

Leaving the inn, it crossed her mind to give Joe a quick call to let him know that she'd be out. She let go of the thought, not wanting to have a full-blown discussion of the day's tragic turn of events, which she herself hadn't yet fully comprehended beyond her gut reaction.

She keyed in the phone number Corbin had said for her to use. "Hi. It's Christine. I'm on my way over now. Is there anything I can bring?"

"Come as you are," he said. "You needn't worry about bringing anything other than yourself, Christine. I hope you like Southeast Asian cuisine. I'm cooking a pot of tom yum soup."

"Mmm, I can't wait. Be there in ten or fifteen, Corbin."

She quickly checked for messages; no word back from Eisen yet on the facial recognition. Graham was definitely a person of interest. It had been bold of him to call a meeting with her, very bold. Christine chided herself for not using the Indiana State Police resources. They had facial recognition software. Joe would have gladly assisted if she'd only thought to ask him. The state police's technology might not be as up to date as the Bureau's advanced programs, but she *had* options. Well, too late now to fret over it.

She followed the GPS directions but still missed the turn and had to back up the car. Christine recognized a cluster of houses displayed on the dash A/V screen—the very same development where Chrissie Blakemore had boarded was only a mile or so farther. Several large forsythia bushes in full bloom blocked the head of the driveway of the professor's house. She parked her rental next to his blue Toyota.

Malinowski opened the front door of the two-story ranch and greeted her from the entryway with a friendly wave and hello.

"We could have met for dinner at the inn or a restaurant, you know," she said as she approached along the walkway. "You didn't have to go to all this trouble on my behalf, Corbin."

"Please, please, come in." He motioned her inside with a welcoming smile.

She stepped into the entry and leaned forward to politely kiss his cheek, but he turned and hurried off to the kitchen where water was at a furious boil. As he did, Christine noticed that his limp seemed more pronounced.

Christine followed him. "You seem to have hurt your leg again?"

"Oh, it's nothing. It comes and goes with the change in weather. I think the humidity makes it act up a little more."

Silverware and large soup bowls on plates were set on an antique table near a picture window. A string quartet was playing on a stereo, delivering the aural architecture of pure genius—its distinct cascade of notes identified it as the Toccata and Fugue in D Minor for Organ by Johann Sebastian Bach. Of course.

"That recording has wonderful clarity," she said. "I have the same one and often play it on drives to and from crime scenes. Believe it or not, it helps me to concentrate."

He nodded. "I can imagine how it would be a very relaxing way to break up your workday, Christine. I can't think of a better partner to a gory crime scene than Johann Sebastian Bach." He flashed a wide grin through the kitchen pass-through space to the dining area.

Christine gazed out the living room window at a small grassy clearing bordered by a large hemlock grove. A dirt road led through the trees to a field beyond, where the outline of a barn roof loomed through the branches.

"Do you live near a farm, Corbin?"

He glanced up from the stove and said, "Oh, yes. Years ago there was an old farmhouse here. Much of the acreage was reclaimed by the state as an added buffer for the state forest. My property deed happened to come with the old barn." Malinowski busied himself slicing a fresh baguette with a serrated knife.

A framed schematic above the couch caught Christine's eye. She examined it closer—hand drawn in India black ink using a narrow-gauge Rapidograph technical pen—which she also favored for taking forensics notes. A key diagram at the bottom right corner indicated one inch equaled 100 feet. Depth-from-surface markers ran along the left hand edge: negative 50 feet, negative 150, down to 500 feet below the surface. Smaller channels branched off the main cavern like a rabbit warren; all intricately rendered, even showing overhanging cave formations and ones that rose from the cave floor. Like the ones she'd seen up close. Based on the key, the displayed section of cave was nearly a mile in length. Across the top, it read Clear Creek Formation.

"That's quite an impressive drawing," she said, pointing to the wall-mounted frame. "I didn't know you were so interested in caving, Corbin." Christine kept her voice cheerful in spite of a sudden apprehension.

Malinowski nodded, carrying the cutting board of sliced bread to the table. "That was some time ago. Shamus Ferguson—I'm sorry to be mentioning his name under the tragic circumstances of that young law student's recent death—but anyway, he'd invited me to go along on one of his club's weekend outings. So, on a lark, I went." He pointed at the framed drawing with the bread knife. "He gave me that copy of the spelunking club's diagram of a cave system they were mapping out at the time."

The professor chuckled. "Just that one time was more than enough for me, though. Such dark places aren't to my liking." He shivered his shoulders half-heartedly.

"I see." The date of the drawing was clearly marked in the right lower corner: April 2014. Barely a year ago.

Malinowski carried a large covered porcelain bowl to the table, steam rising from under its lid.

"Dinner is served. You may wish to let it cool for a few minutes. While we wait, may I offer you a glass of wine?"

"I'd love a glass."

He poured two glasses of a Cabernet and handed her one.

"Look, Corbin, I'm very touched that you asked me here to dinner." She smiled and took a sip. "This is excellent."

"It's from Chile. A very good copy of the French original, I must say."

Christine nodded. "Tell me the truth—you weren't hunched over your desk for the whole spring break, I hope?"

He canted his head to one side, considering her question. "I must confess to you that I was not. Alas, I was interrupted by some most unfortunate news. I received a notice from a cemetery in Veracruz, Mexico, a week ago. Families who own graves or markers for burial urns were given thirty days' notice to recover their loved one's remains or the graves would be lost forever. The land was to be transferred to a real estate developer apparently."

Christine put down the wineglass. "Mexico, did you say?" She recalled that when he'd phoned her last, he'd distinctly said that he was at his desk in the law school, grading papers.

He scrutinized her face for a split second, then continued. "My wife, Vera, died there six years ago. We'd been on a cruise when she took quite ill, and she died on board the ship. When it docked in Veracruz, I buried her there. You see, as she was of Jewish faith, I had to inter her body within three days, without embalming. It was as she would have wanted." He raised his eyebrows, and then looked up at Christine. "So, as I'm sure you can appreciate, I hastily made arrangements to retrieve her remains. I had little choice in the matter"—he shrugged—"as I wasn't prepared to hire a lawyer and file an ex parte motion in a Mexican court."

"Well, that is certainly dismaying to hear, Corbin. What sad news." It struck her that he'd not mentioned ever having a wife before. But then, why would he? "So you went to Veracruz?"

"Yes, I traveled by ship overnight from Houston to Veracruz. You see, I can't fly." He pointed to his ears. "I suffer from tinnitus, a nasty ringing sensation that is intolerable with the air pressure changes when airplanes go up and down."

She nodded slowly. "That's quite a drive from here, isn't it, Houston?"

"Not too bad via the interstate highways, really." He opened the pot lid and busied himself stirring the contents with the ladle. "Well, we don't want our soup to get cold. Shall we?"

"If you don't mind, Corbin, I do have just a few more questions. Then I'll not bring the matter up again." This time her smile was difficult to hold. "Peter Franklin has come to my attention again."

Malinowski let go of the ladle in the soup. It clanged noisily on the bottom of the ceramic pot. "Peter Franklin?" His brow knit ever so slightly. "Oh yes, that poor lad who unhappily was denied entrance to the PhD program in Biology." Malinowski shook his finger. "You had me there for a moment."

Christine didn't think for a second that she had.

"His death occurred shortly after a laboratory break-in at the Pembroke Research Center, where Franklin had worked as a technician," Christine said. "I understand that some dangerous biological material was stolen."

"I think you've mentioned this twice before already," he said with a grave look on his face.

"Do you mind if I visit your bathroom?" she said, steering her face into a smile.

"Why, of course not," Malinowski said. "It's the second door on the right, just past the front door."

In her mind's eye she was gazing down at Miranda and Eisen's spreadsheet again, this time ticking down the row of professors' names to one in particular, then ticking across the top columns listing the students' names who'd taken their courses, stopping on Ellen McKinley's name. Corbin Malinowski had taught two courses: one on civil rights at CSU's law school, and the other, a prelaw survey course to LTC undergraduates in Starksboro, Illinois, under the joint universities' sharing program. Ellen McKinley was listed as a student on the prelaw class roster for the winter semester. And Naomi Winchester's name appeared on Corbin's fall-winter Advanced Civil Disobedience course, too. Tracy Wilson's name was absent from any of the course listings. Wilson didn't fit the profile. Her grades put her somewhere mid-range in class standing—she was an average student at best, which meant more than likely Wilson's unfortunate fate was likely a case of being at the wrong place at the wrong time.

In the bathroom, Christine turned the faucet lever to cover her voice, and punched Joe McFaron's speed dial number. It rang through to his voicemail. "Joe, it's Christine. I'm at Corbin Malinowski's house in Benson. I need you to come right away. Call Sheriff Boynton. Please hurry, Joe." She gave him Malinowski's street address, describing the blind driveway by the forsythia bushes.

She flushed the toilet. Glancing up, Christine's eyes locked on the spine of an old book crammed under some others on a small shelf above the toilet seat: *The Natural History of Poisonous Frogs*. Her uneasiness escalated sharply. Christine pulled it out and opened the cover. The personal inscription inside: "To Trip, Careful what you wish for! Granny M."

She returned to the dining table. "Who's Trip?"

Malinowski refilled his wineglass. "Why do you ask?"

"I noticed the poison frog book in your bathroom, with the inscription 'To Trip.' Naturally I'm curious."

"Yes, I've noticed that you are," Malinowski said levelly. "My given name is Corbin Frederick Malinowski, the Third, hence the nickname 'Trip' for triple, which, alas, stuck from an early age. The book was a birthday present from my grandmother when I was a boy. She raised me to appreciate such things, you see."

He looked down between his elbows, releasing a small private chuckle. "Let's just say Grand Mal, as I used to fondly call her to myself, had an eccentric sense of humor."

"I bet." Her heart rate ratcheted up. Christine flashed on Ellen McKinley's cold dead body under the fluorescent lighting on the examining table at the coroner's office. "Earlier you said Peter

Franklin was denied entrance to the PhD program. But it's my understanding your committee actually hadn't yet voted." The words caught in her throat.

Malinowski put down his spoon and straightened his placemat. "Peter Franklin, Peter Franklin, what is it with this incessant intrigue of yours with Peter Franklin?"

"Corbin, you know very well why I came here to Benson. And I have to say you have been most helpful in my inquiries," Christine said, trying to placate the man now glaring at her.

"Yes, I understood that much, but only concerning the Winchester girl." He grasped the edges of his placemat with both hands.

"That's true, of course. And I must say, aside from your willingness, it's been very difficult to get much cooperation from the others."

Christine backpedaled as best she could. The cords in his neck were visible, his eyes harder. The easygoing classical music lover with whom she'd exchanged friendly banter a few moments ago now looked impatient and disturbed, and much, much colder.

She needed to find a way to get to the car, where her gun was tucked in its holster under the front seat.

"Perhaps, if I show you what I mean, you'll understand. Let me go to the car and get my file." Christine stood and left the table. "Be back in a jiffy."

Outside, she sat on the front seat and tried to reach McFaron again. The ringtone went through to his voicemail.

Damn!

It all came clear to her in a flash. The complete absence of any molestation or defacement of the victims' bodies by the killer, either peri- or postmortem. It had struck Christine as odd that when she leaned to greet him at the door with a kiss on his cheek he'd turned abruptly and walked back to the kitchen straightaway. And in fact, she now realized that Malinowski hadn't so much as touched her hand when he'd given her her wine. There'd been no physical contact of any sort, not even a handshake when they met.

Sitting in the front seat of the car, it hit Christine like a tub of ice water: Winchester and McKinley were top students, type-As, who'd fallen for an attentive, intelligent older man who no doubt made them feel special. They were daddy's girls. No doubt they had craved an older man's affection all their lives. As she had. A dull ache grew in the pit of her stomach.

As Christine reached down and unbuckled her gun holster, she heard the car door open. Instantly, the blur of a descending arm was followed by a mind-numbing thud.

CHAPTER
TWENTY-TWO

"SHERIFF'S OFFICE, MAY I help you?" Mary Carter spoke into her wireless headpiece. It was first thing Sunday morning. Carter usually took weekends off, but with the murders unnerving the larger community, she and McFaron were staying on duty until the killer was apprehended.

"My name is Brian Eisen. I'm with the Chicago branch office of the FBI. I work with Special Agent Christine Prusik. I've been trying to get hold of her with some information that she requested. She isn't answering her phone. Is Sheriff McFaron there by any chance?"

"Brian Eisen, how are you doing? The sheriff tells me that you're quite the whiz kid," Carter said in an extra-friendly tone of voice. "Hold on a sec, Brian. I'll put you right through to him."

She hurried around her desk corral. McFaron was standing in his office doorway, watching her.

"It's Brian Eisen, sounds urgent."

"I'll take it in here." McFaron hadn't heard from Christine since she'd rather impulsively left for Mexico with the Wilson family on Saturday. He picked up the phone.

"Where is she?" McFaron said without identifying himself.

"I thought *you'd* know, Sheriff," Eisen said. "There's been a terrible accident."

"You referring to that train wreck down in Benson?" McFaron tensed.

"Yes. An FBI agent was killed—Christine's boss, in fact. Ned Miranda."

"Was she in the car?" He'd seen the images on TV, but hadn't heard a report identifying the victim yet. Try as he might, he couldn't banish the horrifying thought of Christine crushed beyond recognition. But if she'd been in the car, Eisen wouldn't be looking for her.

"No, she wasn't. We talked right after the accident. She was at the inn where she'd stayed before. She asked me to run this facial recognition software on several pictures that were taken on the recent CSU trip to Mexico."

Christine hadn't filled McFaron in on any of this yet. As much as it bothered him, there was no time to indulge his irritation now. "What can you tell me, Brian?"

"We applied our enhanced face recognition technology to the three photographs and were able to achieve near sixty-five percent congruence based on a composite of facial markers. Unfortunately, the man in the picture was wearing a hat that shielded a large part of his forehead and brow."

"Cut to the chase, will you?"

"The man in the white suit was obviously wearing a wig. One shot in particular showed the features of his jaw and right cheekbone. In combination with enlargements of the two other frames, as I said, we achieved a high congruence for at least the lower face. It's not dispositive, but still highly significant."

"Christ almighty, who's the white suit already!"

"Corbin Malinowski, a law professor at CSU. He should be brought in for formal questioning, sir," Eisen said.

"I'll call Sheriff Boynton straightaway. Thank you for your help, Brian."

A search warrant would take too long. He had to trust that Boynton would cooperate. He searched his pants pocket for his cell phone, then grabbed his tan jacket and searched its pockets too.

"Hey, Mary, have you seen my cell phone?"

The dispatcher walked over to the coffee counter. "Right here where you left it, on its charger, and it looks like you've got a message. The light's blinking," Carter said, handing McFaron the phone.

He listened to Christine's whispered voice message from the previous night, quickly jotting down Malinowski's home address. "Let Sheriff Boynton know I'm on my way to this address." He handed her the piece of paper. "And tell him to meet me there fast."

McFaron grabbed his trooper hat and keys and was out the door before Mary had time to say goodbye.

HIGH ABOVE, A splinter of sunlight outlined the silhouette of a figure. The sharp sound of metal clanking carried through the dome-like cavern with remarkable clarity. The man's shadow was illuminated against the cave wall and then was gone; he'd exited through a small cleft in the cave's ceiling. There was no doubt in her mind that the man was Corbin Malinowski.

Christine shivered uncontrollably. Her head throbbed. Her wrists were bound tightly behind her back, her ankles duct-taped together. She'd come to her senses sometime during the night, stuffed in the trunk of a compact car, her knees uncomfortably wedged against her chest for what seemed like hours. Her mouth was taped and she breathed with difficulty through her nose. Dawn came as a thin seam of sunlight through the trunk's lid. When Malinowski had finally popped open the trunk, the scent of pine and hemlock filled her nostrils. He'd secured a rope around her chest and dragged her, hog-tied like some animal carcass, down a steep trail, scraping and tearing her shirt and pants. Bruised and sore, she'd been shoved through a rock fissure, her full weight pressing down as she dangled in the darkness. He'd lowered her in jerky stops, leaving her terrified that he'd let go of the rope, sending her plunging into the chasm.

Perhaps fifty feet down, her knees landed hard against the rock floor, sending a shockwave through her body and causing her to fall forward on her head. She must have passed out, because she didn't remember being uncoupled from the climbing harness.

Now alone in the darkness and working from memory of the shapes illuminated by his headlamp, Christine squirmed toward a gigantic calcified formation and, by leaning hard against the smooth rock, managed to get herself to a stand. She worked her taped wrists over the stalagmite's tip, resting her body weight, loosening ever so slightly the duct tape binding her wrists. The downward pressure against her wrists cut off the circulation to her hands, but she had little choice. Facing the formation, she scraped her cheek back and forth, loosening one end of the tape covering her mouth until she was able to suck air in through her mouth. With her teeth she bit through the binding on her wrists, freeing her hands. She rubbed her sore wrists and gently fingered the lumps on her head. She now remembered being struck while sitting in her rental car. She'd reacted a second too slow.

She gazed upward at the sliver of daylight filtering through the rock cleft entrance, perhaps sixty feet directly above her. Escape by that route was out of the question without a rope.

Christine hugged her arms around her chest. Her violent shivering wouldn't stop. She knew that her body's core temperature would soon drop dangerously low and that hypothermia would set in if she didn't find a way out quickly.

The other victims, their profiles, it confused her—why was she still alive? The fact that Malinowski was climbing out of the cave meant she should already be dead.

She hugged the stalagmite, straining to see into the depths of the cavern. In every direction the unreadable darkness lay waiting for her to make one false move. She thought she could hear faint dripping sounds from one direction—an underground stream?—but without a headlamp, it would be madness to blindly walk toward the water sounds. She might just as easily take a lethal header over a sheer drop-off as find safe passage out. The infernal darkness was pressing in on her and making her feel as if she'd been buried alive in a massive tomb.

Maintain focus! she counseled herself. Christine checked herself for any broken bones. There were none. She remembered her G-Shock's multifunctions and pressed the *Light* button, relishing the faint glow that illuminated the face of the timepiece. As crazy as it seemed, being able to read 11:45 a.m. eased her mind. It was another act within her control.

She prayed someone would spot Malinowski's car or see him and grow suspicious. They had to. She'd left word on Joe's cell phone, too. Joe would come.

The sound of clanking redirected her attention to the dome of the cavern. Malinowski was returning, descending the rope rapidly hand over hand. She clicked off her watch's light function.

From his headlamp's blazing light she was able to gauge the jumble of surrounding rocks and formations that lay between her and the killer. Had Malinowski returned because others were coming, searching for her? On the run meant that he'd more likely make a mistake, giving her opportunity. It was something. It was hope.

She heard him land on the cave floor.

Ten feet to her left, the aquamarine glow of moving water suddenly was awash under Malinowski's headlamp—he was searching for her. Christine maneuvered herself over a shelf of rock as quietly as she could, keeping her body low. She heard him stumble and bang his helmet against a low-hanging stalactite. She dared not glance up as a dancing light beam whizzed back and forth overhead. He was searching the terrain, getting closer. There weren't enough places to safely hide.

"Christine, Christine," he called in a singsong voice. "You should be dead by all accounts. No more playing, please." His cheerful tone underscored how much of a game she was to this sick bastard, and the thought of his having fun with her cleared Christine's brain fast.

She wormed on her belly, circling counterclockwise, nearer to the lapping sounds of the water as Malinowski's headlamp zigzagged rapidly, its blue-white beam catching a myriad of motes in its brilliant light just inches above her head. Had he really expected to find her dead? The blaze of the strong beam swept 360 degrees again, lighting up the hollow, projecting spiky shadows of the crystalline formations across the muted cavern walls. He was checking every nook and cranny, hunting her down as methodically as he might some irksome vermin.

Her forearm suddenly blazed white under Malinowski's

headlamp, and then its harsh beam glared into her face, blinding her. She shielded her eyes with the back of her hand.

"My, my, isn't life full of surprises," he said. There was an irritable edge to his voice this time. It obviously annoyed him to find her very much alive.

Malinowski unzipped a pack. Her eyes adjusted. She watched him fit a large golden ring over his index finger. He fiddled with the impressive lump of shiny gold. Whatever miracle explained her reason for still breathing, Christine couldn't afford to dillydally. She tumbled off into the darkness.

"Not so quick, Special Agent." Malinowski regained his position, this time directly over her. His headlamp drew nearer, brighter. A shadow crossed in front of the light. Then came a slap to her forearm; Christine felt a small stinging jab. The headlamp blazed in her face. Malinowski remained absolutely still, as if he were a doctor and she, his patient. He hovered over her without a sound, waiting. He'd obviously injected Christine with the poison. She was not long for this world. She didn't exactly know what this kind of death looked like, but Malinowski definitely did. Everything that she knew about the potent toxin told her that she should be dead by now.

Her heartbeats maintained a steady, although stressed out, rate. Something different welled up inside her. Not numbness, not fear of death, nor death throes either—she was seething, and the anger helped focus her rage. She had to move fast.

Christine flipped onto her back and arched high onto her elbows. A surge of adrenaline helped her swift-kick her legs back overhead. With all her bodily strength, she slammed both feet into the pit of his stomach, punching the air out of Malinowski. He fell backward, splashing into the current. As she continued her backward somersault follow-through, Christine went tumbling into the chilly current, too.

She lost contact with the professor, huffing and splashing in the frigid, fast-moving channel. She gained control of her breaths and started to breaststroke. Malinowski surfaced ahead of her. His headlamp illuminated the narrowing passageway where the stream's main course disappeared through the subterranean rock. The rapidly lowering ceiling hardly gave her head clearance.

Christine took several deep breaths and submerged, keeping her arms forward to protect her head from being bashed against jutting rocks or her captor's flailing arms. She surfaced in total darkness, took a deep breath, and dove under again. Those many times she'd swum the pool lengths underwater were being put to the test. With her powerful kick she breaststroked underwater along the dark chilly course. With her eyes wide open, she strained to see signs of light. She surfaced again in total darkness, catching her breath. Sounds of falling water grew louder.

Without warning she tumbled into a deeper channel that sped her along. The pulling strength of her arms markedly slowed and her flutter kick felt wooden. Numbness was sapping her body. She stopped stroking her arms, fighting just to keep her head above water.

Christine could discern the shiny lap of the current against the cavern rock. Muted filaments of daylight increased. Suddenly just ahead was an outlet. She found herself midstream in slower-moving water surrounded by overarching branches and rocks along the channel's banks. The smells of the loamy forest floor filled her nostrils. She angled toward the bank, her hands so numb she could hardly do more than hook her arm over a fallen branch and tug herself closer. Her shoe struck the rocky bottom and she gained a toehold against a submerged rock. Her hands were useless, completely numbed by the cold. She shoved with her feet and knees against the rocky creek bottom and rolled on her side over and over until safely on the bank, her teeth chattering madly. Her mind reeled from the effort. *Ellen McKinley*, she thought. *This is how Ellen McKinley died.*

Hunching like a caterpillar, she crawled forward and covered herself in last year's fallen leaves for what little warmth she could, and to hide from Malinowski. As best she could, she clutched a narrow pointed rock between her numbed fingers, squeezing and scraping her palm against it to regain feeling. It was a meager defense, but one she desperately needed.

Suddenly came the sound of rapid splashing and rustling—someone was staggering through the water, kicking up leaf mold along the forest floor in a hurried panic.

Christine squirmed lower beneath the leaves, covering her face as best she could. She was too spent to outrun him now. But her fingers were working a little better. She grasped the crude rock weapon tighter as the sounds drew nearer. The bastard was tracking her, just as he had inside the cave. She'd go for his kneecap with the pointed end of the rock. Put him down on the ground for good, and then finish him off with an almighty thrust to the temple, calling upon her man-to-man combat training days as a rookie at the Bureau.

A few crumbly yellowed beech leaves covered her face. A shadow flickered briefly, and then came again. He couldn't be far now. He was gauging his approach, planning how he'd finish her off right there on the creek bank.

Christine counted to three and came up fast, the leaves tumbling off her face in a Rambo-esque surprise move, her arm raised high overhead, the rock gripped tightly in her fist. She blinked rapidly, unsure what she was seeing in the sudden brightness of the daylight.

Christine let the rock slip from her fingers and rolled onto her knees. Tears filled her eyes as she looked eye to eye at her savior, who tongue-washed her face with soft warm licks. The bloodhound wore an orange search-and-rescue vest and gave a reconnoitering howl before sitting faithfully beside Christine. She wrapped her trembling arms around its warm body, grateful and relieved for what the dog's presence necessarily meant. Someone was coming to her rescue.

A man in an orange reflective vest and matching ball cap came into view above the limestone rubble at the top of the creek bank. The dog whined in acknowledgment. Too chilled to stand, Christine waved her arm weakly.

Her rescuer's master worked his way down the steep embankment and kneeled beside Christine and the dog. "I see Methuselah got to you first. Special Agent Prusik, I believe?"

She nodded. "Yes. Thank God."

"Name's Clyde Hulbert." He removed his knapsack and pulled out an emergency foil blanket that he wrapped around her shoulders. "This should hold you till the paramedics come."

She mumbled thanks with lips that didn't work quite right yet.

Hulbert took out a Thermos of hot coffee and poured some into the lid. "Drink this down, ma'am. It'll warm you." He helped her up to a sitting position, cupping her shoulders.

She took several sips. The black liquid hurt her teeth but felt good. "Listen, Clyde, you didn't happen to notice another man wearing climbing gear and a helmet nearby?"

"Sure haven't, ma'am. Old Methuselah made a beeline for you

pretty quick, though." Hulbert patted the dog's flank. "He had the scent from a shirt of yours the sheriff recovered from your bag in the rental car."

"Beg your pardon?"

Sheriff McFaron's trooper hat bobbed through the trees as he half-ran down through the steep-sided forest toward them. Her eyes caught the dazzling gleam of sunlight off the five-pointed badge pinned to his sheriff's jacket.

Hulbert's smile creased his weathered face. "Yes, ma'am. Sheriff Joe there found one of your shirts in your work case. You're lucky too. Methuselah picked up your scent straight off from the roadside and started running down the trail like there was no tomorrow. I could barely keep the old boy in my sights."

The bloodhound leaned against his master's leg. Hulbert rubbed under the dog's muzzle.

"I'm thankful that he did," she said, leaning over and stroking the hound's back. "Yes, you did good work, boy."

Joe slid down the eroded creek bank, his arms outstretched for balance. He crouched down next to Christine and hugged her close. "It's a might early to go for a swim even for a special agent, don't you think?" he said, trying to conceal the immense relief in his voice in finding her alive. Sweat glistened on his brow.

"Methuselah and I are going to head back to the truck so we can let the EMTs know exactly where you are, ma'am." Hulbert leashed his dog and they started off. "They should be here soon," he called over his shoulder. Methuselah gave a short bark.

"You were right, Joe."

"Malinowski?" he said. "There's a blue Toyota Yaris registered to him up by the roadside." He placed his trooper hat on the ground and wiped his forearm across his brow.

She told him how she'd tackled Malinowski into the stream inside the cave. "He may not have made it out. I lost touch with him."

"I'll put out an APB till we know that for sure, or find his dead body." He made a move to get up and she held him by the shoulder.

Christine rested her head against McFaron's chest. She'd survived. At least she'd managed that. But she'd unwittingly been taken in by the false kindnesses of a man who deeply hated women. What did that say about her? She'd bought into all his charms—his sincerity, gracious manner, appreciation of classical music, the whole act. Somehow he divined her vulnerability to an older man, or had sensed it from the start.

What struck her more was the fact that she was the only victim of Malinowski alive when she shouldn't be; her surviving made no sense. The first victim in Illinois had made it out of the cave, too, but only got as far as the muddy creek bank before succumbing. He'd pricked the armed ring against Christine's forearm when he returned to the cave, meaning it was armed with toxin, and meaning that she'd received a double dose.

Shaking her head, she sat up abruptly. Adrenaline coursed through her veins. "This is all wrong, Joe. I should be long ago dead."

McFaron rose to his knees, alarmed, staring at her. "What are you talking about, Christine?"

She examined her forearm and could see the faint outline of a skin prick and the ring image. She turned her back toward McFaron and wrenched up the back of her hair, wincing where Malinowski had struck her on the head. "Do you see any sign of a bruise, a distinct mark on the back of my neck?"

McFaron peered closer, examining her skin. "Yes, there is a small impression of some kind. I can see it."

"We need to excise that tissue, put it on ice, and overnight it to Eisen." The words spilled rapidly from her lips. "Before it dissipates, the tissue sample needs to be taken. You have to cut out the tissue, Joe. Here, too, on my arm." She raised the underside of her forearm, scraped from striking against rocks. "Right here, can't you see it?" She poked the flesh by a reddened spot. "Get Hulbert's medical kit from the emergency bag."

"Now hold on. Can you hear yourself talk? Don't you think you've been through enough for one day?" McFaron held her firmly by the shoulders. "You're not making sense. Your lips are blue. Your body temperature is borderline on the low side at best. I'm sure as hell not going to permit a paramedic to carve out the back of your neck and arm right here in the woods."

"I'm serious, Joe." Christine trembled. "Before anything else happens." Terror gripped her like it had in the cave, amping up her heart rate. A stand of trees across the creek bank panned silently forward, pressing in on her. Her sight was failing. Christine buried her face in the sheriff's chest. Her fingers started vibrating. Her breathing grew shallower with the growing realization that she must be dying.

"What's going on?" she heard Joe say in a strangely distant voice.

She clung to him and tried to force out an intelligent thought. "There's no known antidote, for God's sake!"

McFaron reached into Clyde Hulbert's rescue sack and emptied out the lunch bag. "Here, try breathing into this." He handed her the paper bag. "You're hyperventilating, that's all."

Christine took a few breaths from the bag and then grabbed

the cellophane-wrapped sandwich instead. She was starved. It was egg salad on white bread and it went down fast.

McFaron thought he heard the paramedics approaching. He yelled in their direction. "Over here! Down by the creek!"

He rubbed Christine's shoulders and massaged her back. "We need to get you out of those wet clothes and get your blood moving."

She removed her blouse and he helped her on with his jacket. Maybe the conditions had been different this time to explain her being alive? Had immersion in the water something to do with it? But it hadn't saved Ellen McKinley, who'd swum free.

"The paramedics will take you to the hospital and have you thoroughly checked out," McFaron said. "Until then, take it easy. I'm here with you. Nothing bad is going to happen."

Her heart rate slowed. She was warming up a little. Joe's words made sense. She curled herself into him, craving the warmth from his body.

"About Agent Miranda," McFaron said softly, leaning his lips against her forehead. "You knew that he was killed by a moving freight train?"

"I saw the television news report," she said, "and called Brian." *And then I went to have dinner with the murderer without the slightest reservation*, she thought.

"The crossing gate was snapped off. Skid marks on the pavement proved that his car was deliberately shoved into the path of the moving freight," McFaron said. "It's eerily similar to the accident involving Jane Pirrung a week before at the intersection out on the state highway."

Involuntary shivers continued to shake Christine. "It may feel better if I stand and walk some," she said, "to ward off the chill."

"Are you sure? The paramedics should be down shortly."

"Here, give me a hand up," she said. Her feet were numb inside her soaked oxfords. She held on to his shoulder and tapped the side of her head to rid her ear canal of water. Shafts of sunlight filtered through the trees. The sun was still high. It was after noon and she was walking out of the woods under her own steam.

Christine wrapped her arm around the sheriff's upper back and together they started up the embankment to the forest trail. EMT sirens wailed in the distance; they were just arriving at the trailhead. Hulbert was smoking a cigarette near his truck. The bloodhound wagged its tail, seeing them approach. McFaron handed Hulbert his rescue pack.

"Thank you," Christine said to them both. "It's good to be counted among the living today." Then she reached down and patted the blessed hound once more.

CHAPTER
TWENTY-THREE

LATE SUNDAY AFTERNOON she was admitted for observation at the Indianapolis Medical Center. Tissue samples were taken from her neck and forearm. For two days, her blood was analyzed, blood gases studied, and histological and pharmacological studies were conducted. Christine underwent a PET scan to rule out a subdermal pocket of toxin should it have lodged in one of her vertebrae or in the intervertebral disc space and not been absorbed. The doctors scanned her cranium, performed nerve conduction and heart rhythm tests. In all, two internists, a cardiologist, a rheumatologist, one of the state's best neurologists, and a histologist who specialized in tropical diseases examined her thoroughly.

Christine briefed them on Batrachotoxin and its role in the deaths of Naomi Winchester, Ellen McKinley, Tracy Wilson, the Oaxaca maid, and Raul, the Indigenous frog dealer. And very likely, Peter Franklin, too. The puncture marks on Christine indeed indicated an injection of some sort, but there was no other incriminating evidence to go with it. The marks were similar to ones she described on the other victims—except for the obvious fact she was alive and they weren't.

All test results came back negative for the presence of a foreign substance. In fact, they could find nothing really wrong with her that ice, rest, and a few over-the-counter pain pills wouldn't take care of. The doctors discharged her on Wednesday morning.

ONE WEEK LATER, Christine sat in the passenger seat of Sheriff McFaron's Explorer. They were driving on a secondary road in the southernmost reaches of Indiana that followed the broad banks of the Ohio River coursing far below them. McFaron eased the truck's brakes, unfamiliar with the twisting road.

"You want to hear something funny?" McFaron glanced at Christine from behind the wheel. "Except for service in the U.S. Army, I've lived my whole life here in Indiana. But would you believe I've never been down around these river towns before."

She caught glimpses of the great Ohio shimmering through breaks in the trees. "Thanks for volunteering to come with me, Joe," she said. "I could have come by myself or with another Bureau agent."

She didn't really mean what she said. She wanted to finish things up as a team with him by her side.

McFaron shook his head. "Not on my watch you're going in alone. Put that thought right out of your mind, Special Agent. Not after . . ."

She smiled at him. "Really, I'm glad you could come."

As at peace as she felt in Joe's company, a nagging thought was bothering her. If she could see Joe so clearly for the honest, decent man that he truly was, how could her sensibilities have so failed her with Corbin Malinowski? Her lapse of judgment was particularly confounding after Miranda had just shown her the spreadsheet that included his name and the other victims' names. Malinowski's timing had been impeccable, asking her to dinner before she'd put the pieces together—and just after he'd dispatched Ned; she had no doubt that he had.

Malinowski had masterfully manipulated her to his advantage. She tried not to let this realization eat at her. Her mother had been right all along: for too many years Christine had craved the attentions of a father figure that didn't exist. A father who rewarded, who praised, who held her close to his heart—not the emotionally aloof taskmaster who had her painfully gasping for breath at the end of every strenuous workout.

She steadied her gaze on Joe, a man who maintained an even keel and hadn't abandoned her in her worst moments, or when she impulsively forged ahead without including him in her thinking. There wasn't a deceitful bone in his body. She got what she saw in Joe. Other than his occasional brooding when things weren't right to his way of thinking. She could live with that. But mostly, she could rely on him.

Corbin Malinowski's blue Toyota had been flat-bedded to the state crime lab in Indianapolis where a forensics team was dusting it for prints and examining it to recover hair and fiber evidence in the state crime lab. State police divers had entered the cave from which Christine escaped and found no trace of Malinowski, other than one hundred fifty feet of 9mm Perlon climber's rope fixed to the cave entrance. They'd searched for a full mile downstream and combed the woods on either side without any luck. The police surmised that his body may have gotten wedged under a rock or caught on an underwater snag. It happened all too regularly to cavers during flash floods; often their bodies were never recovered. The thought made Christine shiver.

"Cold?" McFaron asked. "I've got a blanket in the back."

Christine smiled. "I'm fine, Joe." She was surprised to realize that she meant it.

McFaron's cell phone beeped on its dash mounting. The Bluetooth connection sparked to life through the truck's speaker system. It was a state police dispatcher who reported that an hour earlier Professor Shamus Ferguson's body had been found by his assistant, Jacob Graham. Ferguson hadn't returned any of Graham's calls, which caused the research assistant to drive out to the professor's lakeside cottage, where he'd found Ferguson's body slumped in an easy chair, an empty liquor bottle lying on the floor by the dead professor's side. Apparently Ferguson had been drinking heavily and may have suffered a heart attack, the dispatcher said. No foul play was suspected. The sheriff acknowledged the information and ended the call.

He and Christine glanced at each other.

"No foul play, my ass," she murmured. Although there was no proof connecting the man to any of the murders, something must have gotten under his skin bad enough to cause him to drown himself in a bottle.

"You're thinking toxicology may show something, I take it?" McFaron said.

"Not particularly, but it's more than just a little too coincidental that Shamus Ferguson of all people happens to conveniently turn up accidentally dead right now. That's all."

"It's not very convenient for him," McFaron said.

"Look, maybe we should turn back, Joe." Christine gazed out the passenger window, frustrated. "This is beginning to feel like a wild goose chase."

"We've come this far. Let's be quick about it. Don't worry. Ferguson will still be on ice when we get back."

The road twisted back on itself passing through a dense forest stand, following another river bend. She checked the GPS on the dash. Elegy was five miles ahead. Brian Eisen had discovered Malinowski's grandmother's death certificate and then located the old family residence outside Elegy, a hamlet along the banks of the Ohio River not far from the bridge that Christine had crossed to reach Louisville in order to visit her mother.

Eisen verified that the Elegy property had in fact been inherited by Corbin Malinowski from his grandmother. Christine had obtained a search warrant through a Circuit Court judge with the cooperation of the Scott County Sheriff's Department.

"The turnoff should be any moment, it's on the right. The house overlooks the river, as I understand," McFaron said.

Christine kept her eye out. Loamy smells of heavily silted river water flushed into her passenger-side window. The road climbed higher again. The GPS signaled that the turn was one hundred feet ahead. McFaron let his foot off the gas, then braked.

Trees bordered the old gravel driveway. Weeds grew high between the tire tracks where the sheriff turned in.

"The house must be in quite a ways," McFaron observed.

The air was cooler passing under a row of cedar boughs. Beyond the grove and perched high on a knoll was a massive Victorian three-story house with a limestone façade. A large wraparound porch overlooked what must be a majestic stretch of the river, Christine figured.

"People knew how to live in a grand style a hundred years ago," she said.

McFaron pulled up beside the porch and got out. Broken asphalt evidenced that the driveway once had been paved. Some shuttered garage bays stood to the left and were served by a connecting breezeway to the stately mansion.

"It doesn't look like anyone's been here for some time," he said. "The grass hasn't been cut; weeds are growing tall along the driveway."

Christine stepped out of the passenger door and trampled through some weeds getting to the porch steps. She opened her forensics case on the porch swing that hung by four rusted chains, and handed Joe a pair of latex gloves, then snapped on her own pair.

The front door was locked. McFaron had come prepared. He wedged the tongue of the short-handle crowbar into the door-jamb next to the lock mechanism and leaned his weight against the jamb, popping the door open without damaging it much.

"Look, we've got a lot of house to cover in a couple of hours," Christine said, focusing on the task. "Why don't you start upstairs while I search the main floor, okay?"

"Sounds like a good plan to me," he said, threading the safety chain back over its track inside the front door. She looked at him. "Consider it precautionary. I wouldn't want the errant raccoon to come wandering in on you."

The house felt unoccupied, the air fusty. Christine reconnoitered the downstairs, getting the lay of the land. The kitchen was old-fashioned, spare and cleanly kept. It had high ceilings and an ancient-looking white porcelain gas stove. No foodstuffs lay out on the counters, nor were there any dishes left out or signs of recent cooking. The fridge was of a more recent vintage, a Kenmore. Inside, its soft blue light illuminated bare shelves. The juice was still on, meaning Malinowski may have been using the place, at least intermittently. The sink was bone dry.

Through a swing door, Christine faced a long dining table.

Past an archway, Christine entered a sitting room of cushioned furnishings that wore no dustcovers. Malinowski hadn't moth-balled the place yet. A gold-and-green paisley fabric couch faced a large picture window. One arm was faded from sunlight. Perhaps he visited on the occasional weekend to check on things, or to get away to plot his next move?

A hand-knotted carpet runner with a repeating geometric pat-tern of mountains and forest led through a narrower doorway to an impressive library; bookshelves filled with old leather-bound volumes lined its walls. She perused the titles of an assortment of well-known novels and biographies, her eye catching on De-foe, Twain, Dickens, Flaubert, Joyce, Melville, Hawthorne, Dos-toyevsky, and Sartre. Nothing very recent, except for a number of treatises on biology and evolution; one had a publication date of 2012. Malinowski was definitely using the library.

Christine's eyes rose up the bookcase shelves and then froze. Perched on top of the last shelf was a creature so grotesque it took her breath away. Some kind of freak of nature, its menacing snout and squatted pose gave the impression that it might leap at any moment. It was cat-size but had the distinct appearance of a giant frog or toad. She'd never seen such a large amphibian before and wondered if it was even real.

Sunshine banked through a leaded glass window inset with family crest colors in blues and reds, coloring the surface of a writing desk fitted with vertical slits for storing envelopes, stamps, and pens and things. She sat at the writing desk, and her eye caught on a smaller bookshelf beside a cast-iron standup radiator. A row of black-spined journal volumes were neatly ar-ranged by Roman numerals I through X, with identifiers written in neat white ink along the spines.

She pulled out the first volume. Its lined pages were meticulously filled and dated, handwritten in a small manuscript print in black India ink by a Rapidograph pen. Dated entries in the first volume began with September 13, 1980. She scanned several pages—mostly sounding like a litany of crimes perpetrated against the author—Malinowski, she presumed—that Dr. Katz would no doubt subscribe as evidence of the beginning stages of a paranoid mind.

Christine withdrew the last volume from the shelf, marked with a Roman numeral X, and leafed through the journal, stopping at the last entry. It was dated October 13, 1984—the date of Malinowski's grandmother's death, she'd learned from Eisen. She calculated that at the time, Malinowski would have been seventeen.

Under the October 13 entry was a recipe of some sort:

"Prepare for Grand Mal the following: 1. Cut and dry eight leaves and stems of Brugmansia. 2. Boil for ten minutes. 3. Separately boil Darjeeling tea. 4. Combine the liquids. 5. Add four, not her usual two, teaspoons honey. 6. Freshen teapot with three added Brugmansia leaves for extra measure. 7. Wait five minutes to steep. 8. Serve on tray with her plate of favorite Pecan Sandies.

Grand Mal—she'd heard Malinowski refer to his grandmother by that name at his house for dinner. The reference was his sick idea of humor, Christine thought.

A floorboard creaked. She looked up.

"Joe?"

Christine kept silent, listening to the throb of her own pulse in both ears, hearing nothing else. A ray of sunlight came to rest on a metal cylinder sitting on the floor beside the desk. Its lid gleamed brighter for a moment, then dimmed under a passing cloud. It was a quart-size Thermos. An odd placement for it, she thought. She lifted the Thermos. Its weight surprised her; it appeared to be full. She placed it on the writing desk and unscrewed its steel lid. An inner stainless canister nested inside, like a Russian doll.

She removed the inner canister and carefully placed it beside the outer Thermos. It was a narrow portable unit, easy for traveling. A plaque on its side read *Danger! Liquid Nitrogen Can Instantly Freeze Live Tissue!* The contents of the smaller canister, presumably poison frog skins, must be stored inside at minus 321 degrees Fahrenheit, which Eisen had told her was the boiling point of liquid nitrogen at sea level. Liquid nitrogen was excellent for storing biological tissue for long periods of time.

Christine heard another bump—wood scraping wood. A tongue of cool air creased across her brow, bringing with it a subtle piney scent. She didn't call Joe's name this time. Not moving a muscle, not giving her position away, her mind quickly factoring that another door somewhere near this end of the house, or a window sash, had just been opened, letting in the outside air.

Instinctively, she reached down and unsnapped her ankle holster. She withdrew the Glock 26 concealed carry handgun and slowly rotated off the chair seat, maintaining a low crouch stance, a practiced training position, only this time it wasn't a scheduled checkup at the firing range. Her ears strained in the silence for another confirming indication of movement, the smallest vibration, to feed her more precise coordinates of the exact direction of the possible threat.

She shifted her weight evenly over the balls of her feet, scanning the perimeter of the library, twisting left then right, without taking a step that might give her own position away. She discerned the muffled thump and shuffle of Joe's weight shifting overhead, checking through the upstairs rooms.

The air stopped moving and the fusty odors of the old library books returned, meaning that whoever had opened the window and let in the small current had shut it without so much as a sound.

A barely audible shuffling noise turned her 180 degrees, in the direction of the kitchen. A drawer jerked open where it had caught, causing a slap of utensils against the old wood. Christine advanced cautiously toward the living room doorway, keeping her weight evenly distributed and her gun arm outstretched.

The muscles between her shoulders bunched with tension. It was one thing to aim a pistol, chest high, at empty space in a room, quite another to fix the crosshairs on a human being should one appear. Although she was an excellent shot, armed combat was not her forte.

She rolled her shoulders one way and then the other to loosen the knotted muscles. She canted her head to one side at the faint sound of footsteps over a rug. Behind her, a casement in the library shelving yawned open halfway, unexpectedly revealing a secret door faced with several shelves of books. Floors in old houses frequently settled off camber, she thought. Nothing in life stayed true forever.

Feeling a perceptible tremble in her gun hand, Christine steadied it by wrapping her left hand tightly around the grip.

"Joe, is that you?" She knew damn well it wasn't Joe—the sound had definitely come from the main floor and was too sneaky quiet to be the sheriff. She'd called out his name because she needed to hear her own voice to help gather her wits.

Christine turned and drew a bead with her gun, aiming the

pistol chest high at the center of the dark space beyond the half-cracked casement door in the library.

The interminable silence ramped up Christine's heart rate. It was a waiting game to see who would jump first. Whoever it was, was fishing, too, hoping that she'd take the bait and walk straight through the cracked doorway, into that dark hall and into a trap.

Think again, Buster.

Christine dried her left palm against her suit jacket, then resumed gripping the gun with both hands, steadying her aim at the center of the bookcase doorway, stepping sideways to the middle of the library floor, straining to see into the void behind the false bookcase.

Heat gathered at her throat. She unbuttoned the top button of her blouse and wiped the back of her sleeve across her brow, then quickly resumed her double-grip, training the gun into the darkened hall, her elbows locked out straight. It was time to end the waiting game.

"This is Special Agent Christine Prusik of the FBI. I'm armed and will shoot. Put down your weapon and show yourself now." She held the gun rock steady. "Show yourself right now with your arms raised!"

Christine enunciated the words loudly, hoping that Joe would overhear, concentrating on any sound or movement. But there was none.

She pulled out a book from a nearby shelf and tossed it into the dark passageway. No response; whoever was there wasn't biting. She backed toward the living room, and then into the dining room, which was a better vantage point and where there was better light by the picture windows.

Still facing the casement door, she backed through the living room archway. At the rush of footsteps behind her, Christine swerved, caught the flash of an upturned blade, and squeezed the trigger—the loud report and muzzle flash of her gun and the suddenness of his attack caught her off-guard. She fired low and stumbled against the dining table, knocking over one of the candelabra.

Heavier footsteps—Joe's—descended the main stairway in a rapid-fire cadence. "Stop or I'll shoot!" she heard McFaron yell as the front door slapped open.

Christine maintained her crouched stance, aiming the gun at the front hall foyer, working her way through the dining room. The open front door's small window curtain shivered in a breeze.

"You okay?" In Joe's right hand, now at his side, was his police-issue .45 caliber automatic. From his awkward stance it looked to her as if he'd never drawn the weapon in the heat of a moment before.

Christine nodded. "Whoever that was, sure isn't."

"Did you get a look at his face?"

She shook her head. "No. His arm was raised. The front of his coat covered his face. It happened so quickly."

Christine motioned for Joe to head out the door. She followed right after him, checking over her shoulder just in case.

They worked around to the side of the porch toward the garage area, single file, Joe in the lead. The muffled sound of a car motor erupted from one of the shut garage bays. They dropped off the porch landing and cautiously approached, guns drawn, walking side by side now as the engine inside the garage revved louder, booming off the interior walls.

The far garage bay door burst off its hinges. A dark compact with tinted windows careened wildly down the rutted drive under full acceleration, bouncing from side to side, spraying gravel and clods of dirt as it disappeared past the row of cedars farther down.

The Explorer's tires were flat, front and back, a repeat of the stunt done to the state police vans at the Naomi Winchester crime scene. The assailant must have bled out the air while they were inside searching the house. From his truck, McFaron radioed the Scott County sheriff for backup.

"It was a VW GTI hatchback," McFaron said, "like the one Pikey Arthur described seeing the day Naomi Winchester went missing."

They retraced their steps to the porch and went back inside.

"Why'd you shoot?" McFaron said, still looking dazed.

She pointed to the kitchen knife that lay on the dining room rug. "Bag that for prints, Joe."

"He won't get far," McFaron said. "The road follows the river either way. There's no way out. It's checkmate time, whoever the creep is."

"You're forgetting something, aren't you?" she said. "He's carrying one of my 9mm lead slugs in his gut."

HE'D SWUM CLEAR of the cave, drifted downstream in his insulated climbing suit, and avoided the search party. Before anyone had thought to stake out his place, he'd found his way through the woods safely back home and started the GTI hidden under a tarp in the barn. Two hours' drive time had taken him to Grand Mal's river bluff homestead. He'd hoped that Christine would figure it out and come after him—dare to stick her nose in his business one last time.

What puzzled him most was how she'd managed to rise from the dead. He'd freshly armed the frog ring with more than enough poison—watched the globs of Batrachotoxin-rich frog secretion harden on the ring's needle delivery system. He'd so looked forward to her final death throes, yet somehow the bitch had wriggled free and escaped.

Trip panted from behind the steering wheel, blood seeping from his side. He applied pressure with his palm, wondering whether somewhere in the world they made a drug that could throw the switch in his head to Off. Was there a transfusion for people like him? He tugged at the roll of duct tape and bit off a long segment, then another, and wrapped them over the hole in his side—kidney high—to stem the seepage.

He'd nearly closed the loop on her this time, despite her bringing the ding-dong sheriff along, as if that would make a difference. Even wounded he was still smarter. He was one step ahead, always. The FBI bitch had finally found out about his grandmother's place and his well-kept journals only because he'd wanted her to.

At the gas station ahead of the bridge that crossed the Ohio River to downtown Louisville, his next ride was there waiting for him idling beside the pump, its unsuspecting owner inside paying for gas or maybe using the restroom. He pulled the black GTI around the back next to a dumpster and several stained oil barrels, wincing as he removed his blood-stained shirt and tossed it into the dumpster. The duct tape was doing its job—no wonder the astronauts took it with them into space. He zipped up his windbreaker and wiped the blood off the VW door handle so not to draw unnecessary attention.

He was ready. Even after losing a pint of blood he could beat them at their own game. He got into the unoccupied car by the pump and drove off.

AFTER MCFARON HAD called the local sheriff's department and the state police, he checked the garage and storage outbuilding, where he found an old bicycle pump to reinflate the Explorer's tires.

Christine returned to the library, where she tested the hinge of the small casement door that was cleverly concealed in the bookcase and then ducked her head into the dark unadorned space behind it. Her eyes adjusted to the low light coming from a small inset window framed above a tight winding staircase.

The air was musty and noticeably warmer by the time she reached the cramped second-floor landing. A well-worn carpet—a repeating design of peafowl and fruit trees surrounded by interlacing vines and symbols that only an expert in local Persian culture might discern—extended the length of the mansion's hallway. All the doors off the hall were closed. Presumably these were bedrooms.

She continued up the tight, spiraling stairs to the third floor, wiping her beading brow with the back of her suit jacket. The air was noticeably stuffier. A much smaller hallway was contoured by the slope of the roofline. The room at the end drew her attention—or rather a wooden chair positioned in the middle of it had, where you wouldn't expect it to be. Christine unsnapped her gun holster as she moved slowly down the hallway.

She entered the small corner bedroom. Out the backyard window there was a magnificent view of a mile or more of the Ohio River. The other window overlooked the broken asphalt driveway and garage bays. With protective gloves on, Christine lifted the window sash and spoke McFaron's name down toward the open garage bay. She waited, but the sheriff didn't appear. He must be searching the outbuilding.

Christine flipped the light switch by the bedroom door a few times. The ceiling bulb was out, which explained why the chair was in the middle of the room. It hadn't yet been changed. Their arrival had interrupted him. Maybe took him by surprise? She doubted it had, given the killer's wily craftiness. She searched the cabinet drawers, which contained an old pair of khaki pants and a few button-down shirts. A display shelf was filled with old earthenware pieces and oddities. She lifted a clay figurine—six inches tall with bulbous eyes, its tongue extending from wide-set lips. The terracotta colors were muted grays and burnt orange, very old, perhaps a Mesoamerican deity of some kind, she wondered. She repositioned it back in its exact place outlined by a thin film of dust.

The bed covers looked hurriedly pulled up to the pillows, again suggesting that they may have surprised him. Or perhaps he'd just been resting, waiting for the sound of the car engine announcing their arrival. She sat at the foot of the bed and pulled up one end of the comforter. In the shadow of the mattress something rested on the wood floor, a darker wedge. Christine got down on her knees and picked up a black journal book that was exactly like the others she'd seen on the small shelf beside the library writing desk. Along its spine in white ink was printed the Roman numeral XI—the eleventh volume. In sequence.

Christine opened the journal. Its fresh new binding crinkled as she did. She quickly flipped through the crisp empty pages then went back to the first page; it was stuck to the second. Carefully she separated the pages with the thinner blade of her Swiss pocket knife. The words had the effect of primer powder.

Christine flew down the narrow stairway as fast as she dared, clutching the journal in one hand. She raced through the living and dining rooms and kitchen, out the front door onto the porch. "Joe!" she screamed as she leapt from the wraparound porch into the weeds. She swung open the Explorer's driver's-side door and banged on the horn until McFaron emerged from a garage bay at a run.

"I just filled the tires with air. What's going on?"

"How far are we from the bridge to Louisville?"

"Close," he said. "Maybe fifteen, twenty minutes. Why, what's the problem?"

"We've got to go now. Fast! It's my mother."

HE PASSED BY the front entry to the Randolph Arms Assisted Living Center and parked the red Taurus that he'd stolen by the gas pump—trusting people leaving their keys in the ignition was mystifyingly convenient. He was feeling light-headed now, but no worse than he'd felt twenty minutes ago at the gas station. The duct tape was holding up well. He skirted the large retirement home through its well-kept grounds, not wanting to draw the staff's attention to his worsening state. The large building with its many jutting wings was pleasingly rendered with flourishing touches around the window ledges and roofline, born of an age where they spared no expense in its construction—a remarkable makeover of some white elephant sanatorium from the '20s, he imagined, or a former retreat for tuberculosis victims.

He'd already ascertained the old woman's room assignment when he'd sent her the package—his special little tidbit of coming attractions. How he'd wished to have been a fly on the wall, especially when Christine identified the contents—which she surely had—and ruminated on its meaning.

Trip's breathing grew noticeably sluggish and shallower as

he struggled across the large rear lawn where some high-backed benches surrounded a viewing garden. He took a seat on the bench farthest from the rear sunroom where he could see some residents gathered, perhaps for a midday coffee and pastries. He flipped open the cell phone and punched the main number, leaning back his head, opening his airway as fully as possible.

In his best, professorial voice he spoke into the phone: "Yes, is this the front desk? Good, good. I have a small favor to ask. It's a very special favor for a dear old friend. I've a surprise present for her actually. The Randolph Arms has such a lovely garden in the back . . ." He kept his voice steady in spite of the increasing wavering of his heartbeats and worsening light-headedness. The bullet was doing its damage, but he still had plenty of strength left for this one last task.

The desk nurse took the bait. In fact, she'd sounded eager to be of assistance. Plan A was now in play. All he had to do was wait— but not for too long. His advantage was growing shorter with each passing minute. He glanced at his watch. If Yortza Prusik didn't make an appearance in the next two minutes, he'd have no choice but to barge past the feeble-minded residents and continue through the back patio doors straight to the mother's room. Plan B would be uglier. Riskier. Not his true style. But he hadn't figured on being shot either. An injured animal was always more dangerous, Grand Mal had once said to him.

A CROSS-WISE VIEW of the bridge loomed high overhead. They passed under its massive bridgeworks; the road leading to the interstate that crossed the river onto the Louisville side was maddeningly still three miles farther ahead. Christine knew that gut shot would slow him down, but was there time enough?

McFaron kept hard on the gas, the flashing red symbol on the dashboard indicating the strobe lights in his grille plate were pulsing. They'd alerted the Louisville police but lost cell service while trying to reach the Randolph Arms' front desk. She chided herself for not leaving her gun with her mother after all, given the slack security she'd already observed at the retirement home, regardless of the Randolph Arms' likely rules forbidding firearms.

McFaron accelerated up the entry ramp onto the interstate. The bridge was dead ahead. Christine kept punching redial. She double-checked her gun.

"Don't take this wrong," he said, keeping his eyes steady ahead as he performed a high-speed maneuver through traffic, "but the Louisville police sent a car over, Christine. They're on the scene by now. Their jurisdiction, their responsibility."

"It's my mother you're talking about, Joe. This prick mailed her a poison frog skin. So don't tell me whose responsibility this is."

"I'm with you. I get it. But you've shot him already. Remember that. He's not going to be functioning very well—"

"Cut the crap, Joe. I injured him at best. My mother is seventy-five and frail . . ." She couldn't finish the sentence, shuddering at the thought of how Malinowski might steal a worker's coat and smoothly pass himself off as a member of the staff, enter Yortza's room, saying he was a kindred spirit to her daughter, Christine, a fellow lover of Bach, all the while moving to within striking range. Would her mother see through his act as ably as she could see through Christine's?

What would've normally been fifteen torturous minutes was compressed into seven with the benefit of McFaron's flashing lights and speed. He jerked to a halt behind a Louisville police cruiser parked under the Randolph Arms' protective awning.

Inside, Christine flashed her badge credentials at the duty nurse without slowing down, hustling down the wing to her mother's room.

Yortza Prusik's room was empty. Christine went to the window. Three cops were standing beside a garden bench.

Christine fled out of Yortza's door into the hallway. She grabbed her mother's arm, nearly toppling the older woman to the floor. Her mother's hair was slick wet. She was wearing a terrycloth bathrobe.

"You're all right?" Christine said, as much a question as a statement of fact.

"Of course, I am. I always feel fine after my afternoon session in the pool. What is it, Christine?" The fracture line down Yortza's forehead creased ever so slightly. The older woman actually did look refreshed.

"Have you received a visitor, Mother?"

"Well, you of course!" Yortza chuckled. "Three times already this month, imagine that."

"Mother, I'll be right back." Christine hurried toward the sunroom. More residents had gathered, looking out the back patio to where the local police were standing.

Christine neared the officers and displayed her badge, her eyes on the person who held their attention. He was very pale, his face covered in the sheen of perspiration of the mortally wounded. Malinowski leaned heavily on the bench arm, panting, his wrists handcuffed in front of his waist.

"Is this the man you alerted us to, ma'am?" the local officer in charge asked after introducing himself. Christine confirmed that he was. The officer said an ambulance was on the way.

Seeing her, Malinowski managed a small smile in spite of his graven state. "Christine, too bad . . . I wanted so much . . . to surprise you . . ."

She ducked her head so only he would hear. "You're slipping, Corbin. Sending my mother the package, leaving the journal under your bed, you made it too easy."

He grinned. "Reach into my . . . coat pocket. The ring . . . is . . . for . . . you."

Briefly, his eyes widened as he let go of an exhalation.

The complete dilation of Malinowski's pupils told Christine that when the ambulance finally arrived, the trip back to the hospital would be a slower ride without benefit of a warning siren.

When Christine returned to her mother's room, McFaron was seated in a chair opposite Yortza, whose expression of complete approval Christine could clearly see.

McFaron looked up. "Everything okay out there?"

She nodded. "He's DOA."

"Christine, what have I told you about hanging around such dangerous customers?" Yortza shook her forefinger. "Your nice sheriff here, I can tell even he doesn't approve of it. Am I right, Sheriff?"

McFaron held up his palms, quickly standing. "Far be it from me to tangle with personal matters, ma'am. I will say, however, that your daughter is fiercely protective of those she loves."

Yortza eyed him with the same scrutiny that she would apply to her daughter, her forefinger still raised, but now pointing at McFaron. "Is that so? Well, then it's high time you do something about it, young man. Stop stalling around. Didn't your mother ever tell you that work isn't everything?"

Yortza glanced over at Christine. "My daughter thinks life is all about shooting and killing, while I sit here a living relic without a grandchild or any hopes of having one in sight."

"Mother . . ."

"I'm certainly relieved to find you well, Mrs. Prusik," McFaron said, filling in the awkward moment of silence. He looked at Christine. "I think we best leave soon. I'll give you a moment alone with your mother." He tipped his hat and left the room.

"What a nice man he is."

"Please don't start in. I know how good a man Sheriff McFaron is." Christine fished from her jacket pocket the plastic evidence bag that housed the silken box containing Malinowski's lethal weapon. She held the harmless-looking evidence bag in front of her mother's face. "This was going to be your present, Mother. This customer, as you say, killed five people—who knows, maybe more. He came here expressly to kill you."

"And what if he did?" Yortza said. "Would it really change anything? I'm an old woman with too little to look forward to."

It was a no-win situation. Christine leaned over her mother and hugged her close, feeling tears—or was it laughter?—beginning to well up inside. "I hear you. I'll make more of an effort."

Yortza smiled. "It's about time that you did." She held her daughter's arm and gazed at Christine. "Maybe next time you'll surprise me with something besides bringing killers to my doorstep?"

CHAPTER
TWENTY-FOUR

"EISEN GOT BACK the results on the steel liquid nitrogen canister at Malinowski's house in Elegy," Christine said, looking up from McFaron's kitchen table, which she'd taken over with her papers, laptop, and forensics case.

"Enough poison to go around, I would imagine," McFaron said, pouring himself another cup of coffee.

"Dead wrong, cowboy." She smiled at him. "And yes, please. I could use another caffeine hit, too." He refilled her mug.

She and Joe had shared a relaxing week together, aside from a few phone calls from Roger Thorne, who'd accepted an interim appointment as branch director of the Chicago Bureau office. It was ironic. In a million years, Christine would never have guessed that she'd be glad to be reporting to Thorne again.

The news satellite trucks and camera crews on the CSU campus had mostly moved on once the shocking disclosures about Professor Corbin Malinowski had been recycled ad nauseam, including his dramatic attempt on the life of an elderly woman at a retirement home, the mother of the FBI agent in charge of the investigation.

Before Christine could catch a flight back to Chicago, Patricia Gaston had smartly segued out of Bureau service into the private sector. She was now working for a large consulting firm based in

Washington, the seat of power and swag, which had always been her ultimate goal. It came with higher pay, better office perches, and greater views of stone memorials.

"Beg pardon?" Joe massaged the tops of her shoulders. "Eisen said what?"

"The frog skins in Malinowski's Thermos weren't the least bit deadly. Eisen had the material tested at Macalister, and for good measure at the University of Chicago lab, too. They weren't from Macalister's or Pembroke's frog skin stock. They were genuine Dendrobatidae skins all right, but they contained not one iota of lethal neuro- or cardio-toxin. It seems that the poison frogs Malinowski brought back with him from Mexico had lost their punch. Or rather," she added, "never had it in the first place."

McFaron looked at her puzzled. "That can't be right, can it?"

"Apparently, poison frogs raised in captivity don't produce the nasty stuff that kills you. Domesticated frogs lose their toxicity when fed on a diet of bland food. Developing deadly skin depends on a diet rich in native arthropods and ants found only in the equatorial rainforest of South America, not from canned fish food and crickets."

"Well, aren't you the lucky one then," McFaron said, wreathing his arms around her from behind.

"Eisen found the website on Malinowski's computer advertising wild-caught Golden Poison Frogs from a place out of Oaxaca, Mexico," Christine said. "Undoubtedly we'll be able to link that to the business of the dead Indigenous man in the hut with all the rotting frogs. Another very real possibility, which I confirmed reading one of Professor Ferguson's articles on poison frogs, is that Malinowski mistakenly purchased from the Mexican vendor one of many harmless wild-caught frog species, which can mimic the golden frog's coloration."

"Is that so?"

"Ironically, Malinowski must have brought with him to Mexico the last remaining poison frog skin that he'd had Peter Franklin steal for him from the Pembroke Center," she said, "which explains the three deaths in Oaxaca."

"Thank God for people selling homegrown harmless frogs over the internet," Joe said, kissing the top of her head. "I guess you could say one man's meat isn't necessarily another man's poison, after all."

McFaron looked pleased with his use of the adage.

"It's why I'm still here talking with you, Joe," she said softly, leaning back and kissing him on the lips.

"The license plate on Malinowski's Volkswagen GTI was his dead wife Vera's expired plate that he'd held on to," she said. "It was discovered abandoned behind a gas station near the bridge to Louisville, where he'd stolen another car."

McFaron shrugged. "Lucky for him the bastard wasn't stopped for a traffic violation."

"By the way," Christine said, "I spoke again to our in-house Bureau shrink, Dr. Katz, regarding the two traffic-related deaths."

"Agent Miranda's and the Pirrung girl in the coal truck accident on the highway?" McFaron said.

"Malinowski's preferred MO was poison, to be sure," Christine said. "Some sufferers of a persecution complex can experience sudden escalating bouts of paranoia, which can cause them to react explosively, uncontrollably sometimes. He must have encountered Pirrung at the local climbing store the night she died, and she probably said something that triggered his rage." She shook her head. "And then Malinowski later killed the clerk, who would have been a witness. Just my guess, but who knows."

"So you think Malinowski shoved her car from behind with his bumper into the coal truck right afterward?" Joe said.

"Seems likely to me. And Ned . . ." Christine was suddenly overwhelmed with sadness.

"Ned," Joe echoed. "I'm so sorry, Christine." He pulled her close.

"You know the best thing about you, Joe?" she said, after a comfortable silence, her head resting against his chest. "I make snap judgments of others all the time, take criticism poorly; I'm impatient with my staff, and I don't take orders well from anyone."

"Don't think too highly of yourself, do you?"

"And in case you haven't noticed, I'm not always right, either."

McFaron smiled. "Well, some of your quick decisions may cause you more suffering than anyone, but in the end, your determination sure gets you where you want to go. Congratulate yourself, Christine. It all worked out."

"Seriously, Joe. As much as we may disagree about a case, or how to best proceed"—she trained her gaze at his eyes—"you're always there for me. I *know* that."

"I'm with you, Christine. I always have been."

She kissed him.

His broad smile revealed a dimple on each cheek. "Well, I'm glad we got that settled," he said. He kissed her again, holding her close. "And I'll say this. You're pretty savvy in both departments—as a scientist . . . and in my arms, too."

"Why thank you, Sheriff." She lay back in McFaron's arms and they nestled.

CHRISTINE WAS WEARING one of the sheriff's bathrobes the next morning—her own clothes were in the dryer—when her cell phone rang. It was Roger Thorne, who advised her that he'd just emailed a confidential memo with an attachment to her encrypted account. He underscored that it was not for distribution. And then he dropped the bombshell.

Christine hung up and stared at McFaron, frowning.

"What's with the serious face?" he asked, buckling his belt, planning to head to his office to check on things.

"I just learned that Ned Miranda had been providing a radical Islamic group based in Toronto with classified Bureau documents. He'd planted incriminating evidence on Paul Higgins's computer."

"Jesus . . ."

"Evidently, they recovered a second cell phone, an unauthorized burner, from Miranda's overcoat pocket at the scene of the train accident. It confirmed that a number of calls had been placed between him and this Toronto cell." She glanced up at McFaron, profoundly unsettled by the news. Why would Miranda do such a thing? And why had he been so helpful right before his death? "That's not for circulation beyond this room, Joe."

"Understood."

"And there's more, I think." She opened her laptop at the kitchen table, typed in her name and password, and quickly read through the cover memo. She clicked on the attachment Thorne had sent. It was forty-seven pages long, a series of daily log reports. Each handwritten entry was initialed at the bottom with either an R.B. or M.H. Christine scrolled down through more log reports, the earliest of which was dated April 20, 2008—six years ago.

"Ever hear the name Harriet Landrieu before?"

McFaron shook his head. "What have you got there?"

"Apparently, she registered quite a few complaints against Corbin Malinowski over the past six years."

"Registered with whom?"

"With R.B., which I assume means Sheriff Rodney Boynton, and to whomever has the initials M.H."

"That'd be Martha Hendrickson," McFaron said, "Boynton's long-time dispatcher. She retired not too long ago. Rodney hasn't found a replacement yet." McFaron stepped around the table and leaned in for a closer view of the screen shot. He recognized Boynton's handwriting.

"–fifth call since April 20.

"–complainant Harriet Landrieu is the sister to Vera Malinowski, who reportedly died while aboard a cruise ship.

"–married to Corbin Malinowski III, CSU law professor."

At the bottom of the form, under *Action taken*, it said:

"–unsubstantiated claim. Matter closed. R.B."

"Well, I'll be . . ." McFaron said, reading over her shoulder.

Christine scrolled down through several more logged phone calls, stopping on another report initialed by M.H. at the bottom. The report was styled in the same bulleted phrases, like Sheriff Boynton's were, and indicated that the caller was distraught, spoke viciously of the accused, blaming Malinowski for her sister's death again and again.

Christine closed the lid on the laptop and turned to face Joe. "The night I went to his house for dinner, Malinowski had mentioned going to Veracruz by ship during the CSU spring break. To fetch his wife's remains, he said. Something about his receiving a notice from the Mexican authorities that the gravesite where he'd had her buried was being reclaimed for development purposes and that he had thirty days to retrieve her remains or forever lose them."

"Don't tell me you fell for that story?"

"By then, I'd pretty much put two and two together and asked him where the bathroom was located. That's when I tried to phone you, Joe." Christine shrugged. "The rest is history."

"I can't say I blame either Rodney or Martha," he said. "The fact of the matter is there was nothing for them really to follow up on. Right?"

She eyed him. "Well, I would have done something. You would have checked it out personally, too. You would have at least reported it to the Indiana State Police or, perhaps, even the FBI, if your resources were insufficient to follow up on the matter."

"Look, twenty-twenty hindsight is a wonderful thing, Christine. Let's be fair. The sister had no actual proof. Complaints from distraught family members after an unexpected death are common enough. If anything, animosity between unhappy relatives is what we're most likely to hear as law enforcement officers. Do you honestly believe under the circumstance due diligence would have required a full-on investigation?"

"Yes, Joe, I do," she said. "And obviously," she spoke more slowly now, "Rodney Boynton did, too."

"If you're so sure about that, why not give Rodney a call then? Ask him yourself. Whatever else you may think of him, the man's honest. He's got integrity. He sure helped me out on a number of matters when I first became sheriff."

"I can't. He was found dead this morning at his home."

"*What?*"

"A neighbor heard what he thought was a gunshot coming

from Boynton's house. He went over and knocked on the door, but got no answer. So he phoned Mrs. Hendrickson, whom the neighbor had seen on a number of occasions delivering files to Boynton's house.

"Hendrickson used a spare key that she had to Boynton's house and let herself in. Discovered his body slumped over his desk. He'd shot himself with his service pistol right through the mouth. Harriet Landrieu's file lay open on his desk."

McFaron took a seat slowly. "So why am I hearing this first-hand from you and not the state police?"

"Because Martha Hendrickson evidently had the foresight to call my Chicago office first, given the national news media's overexposure of everything that transpired in Benson and on the CSU campus. Roger Thorne has shared this information with me alone, out of respect for Sheriff Boynton. And respect for you." She flipped a finger back and forth between herself and Joe. "You won't be getting a call about it from the state police or hearing about it on the news."

"I didn't exactly see eye to eye with the man all the time, but he was a fine law enforcement officer. I knew him for a lot of years. He helped me. I . . . I just would never have expected this."

Christine sat across from him and took his hands. Joe had lost too many important people in his life—his father, his mother, then the grandfather who had raised him after their deaths. And now Rodney. "It's awful, Joe. I'm so sorry."

"I am too."

It was Christine's turn to pull Joe close, and she did. "You've always been there for me, Joe. And I am here for you."

ACKNOWLEDGMENTS

Were it not for my brilliant daughter, Marguerite, proclaiming her love for me and my first book, *Stone Maidens*, in a short video she posted on TikTok, this sequel may not have seen the light of day.

To my wonderful agent, Elisabeth Weed of the Book Group, who penciled through early drafts of this sequel (as she also had with *Stone Maidens*) and made many good comments and suggestions: I am blessed for her intelligence, sharp eye, and abiding support.

To Nan Gatewood Satter, who worked assiduously, wrenching the manuscript clean of extraneous material and my countless awkward attempts at romantic entanglements: I cannot give enough praise.

To Corey Hunter, who further rinsed the manuscript of unnecessary and wordy passages and scenes that took away from the pacing: for her hawk's eye attention to detail I am most grateful.

Thank you, HarperCollins, for your rousing enthusiasm and support for this sequel and its strong-willed protagonist, Christine Prusik! Special thanks to Emily Krump, Tessa James, Diahann Sturge, Jessica Rozler, Liate Stehlik, Kelly Rudolph, and Jennifer Hart. Under a tight timeline, without the HarperCollins team's essential guidance and easy-to-work-with cheerfulness, I doubt this project could have taken to the air, much less soared as high as it has!

To all my loyal BookTok community who read my first book, *Stone Maidens*, and who believed in me and my writing: I am deeply grateful. But for you there would be no sequel to read!

To both my talented sons, Nathaniel and Evan, and artist daughter-in-law, Jessie, and two grandchildren: I am blessed with their love and support.

To my wife, Cameron, whom I love dearly: were it not for her unwavering support during those many hours I spent tapping in the attic on my keyboard, Christine Prusik would not have walked among the dead again to solve another case.

ONE PLACE. MANY STORIES

Bold, innovative and
empowering publishing.

FOLLOW US ON:

@HQStories